Courage Rising

April - August 1871

Book # 16 in The Bregdan Chronicles
Sequel to Shining Through Dark Clouds

D1607948

Ginny Dye

Courage Rising

April - August 1871

Copyright © 2019 by Ginny Dye

Published by Bregdan Publishing
Bellingham, WA 98229

www.BregdanChronicles.net

www.GinnyDye.com

www.BregdanPublishing.com

ISBN# 9781086203707

Printed in the United States of America

For Stephanie Sutton

Thank you for being my Editor Extraordinaire! We have been on this adventure for 16 books. You have improved my writing... kept up with my crazy schedule... helped me keep track of all the characters and locations - making sure I don't turn blue eyes into brown or randomly change someone's name! I couldn't do this without you, and I have no intention of ever trying!

A Note from the Author

My great hope is that *Courage Shining* will both entertain, challenge you, and give you courage to face all the seasons of your life. I hope you will learn as much as I did during the months of research it took to write this book. Once again, I couldn't make it through an entire year, because there was just too much happening. As I move forward in the series, it seems there is so much going on in so many arenas, and I simply don't want to gloss over them. As a reader, you deserve to know all the things that created the world you live in now.

When I ended the Civil War in The Last, Long Night, I knew virtually nothing about Reconstruction. I have been shocked and mesmerized by all I have learned – not just about the North and the South – but now about the West.

I grew up in the South and lived for eleven years in Richmond, VA. I spent countless hours exploring the plantations that still line the banks of the James River and became fascinated by the history.

But you know, it's not the events that fascinate me so much – it's the people. That's all history is, you know. History is the story of people's lives. History reflects the consequences of their choices and actions – both good and bad. History is what has given you the world you live in today – both good and bad.

This truth is why I named this series The Bregdan Chronicles. Bregdan is a Gaelic term for weaving: Braiding. Every life that has been lived until today is a part of the woven braid of life. It takes every person's story to create history. Your life will help determine the course of history. You may think you don't have much of an impact. You do. Every action you take will reflect in someone else's life. Someone else's decisions. Someone else's future. Both good and bad. That is the ***Bregdan Principle***...

Every life that has been lived until today is a part of the woven braid of life.
It takes every person's story to create history.
Your life will help determine the course of history.
You may think you don't have much of an impact.
You do.
Every action you take will reflect in someone else's life.
Someone else's decisions.
Someone else's future.
Both good and bad.

My great hope as you read this book, and all that will follow, is that you will acknowledge the power you have, every day, to change the world around you by your decisions and actions. Then I will know the research and writing were all worthwhile.

Oh, and I hope you enjoy every moment of it and learn to love the characters as much as I do!

I'm constantly asked how many books will be in this series. I guess that depends on how long I live! My intention is to release two books a year – continuing to weave the lives of my characters into the times they lived. I hate to end a good book as much as anyone – always feeling so sad that I must leave the characters. You shouldn't have to be sad for a long time!

You are now reading the 16th book - # 17 will be released in Winter 2019. If you like what you read, you'll want to make sure you're on my mailing list at www.BregdanChronicles.net. I'll let you know each time a new one comes out so that you can take advantage of all my fun launch events, and you can enjoy my BLOG in between books!

Many more are coming!

Sincerely,
Ginny Dye

Chapter One
Late April 1871

Carrie Wallington took a deep breath of the fragrant spring air as she stepped out the front door of her father's house on Church Hill. Richmond, Virginia was at its best during the month of April. She leaned over the porch railing to inhale the sweet aroma of the milky-white magnolia blooms tucked in among dark green leaves. The towering tree produced an aroma so strong that it had wafted in through her bedroom window the night before.

"Did you eat something, Miss Carrie?"

Carrie turned around with a smile as May, the housekeeper and cook, appeared at the screen door behind her. "I don't have time this morning. I'll get something after I see my first patients."

May bustled out onto the porch, carrying a basket emitting steam. "You seemed to got enough time to smell them flowers," she scolded as she thrust the basket into Carrie's hands. "Just 'cause you're some fancy doctor don't mean you don't gots to eat. I made you two ham biscuits. You eat them," she said firmly, her black eyes flashing beneath her silvery hair.

Carrie knew better than to argue when May's face was set into stubborn lines. She truly wasn't hungry, but she couldn't deny that she probably would be before lunch. The biscuits would be available when she needed them. "Thank you."

"And I don't mean for you to stick them in your office until you think you oughta eat them," May added. "You got time to smell flowers, then you got time to eat." She waved her ample arm at the porch swing. "You sit down and eat them biscuits."

"I really don't have time," Carrie protested, thinking of all she had to do. It was her first day back at the Bregdan Medical Clinic after spending two weeks treating patients at her plantation practice.

"Nonsense," May said briskly. She strode over and blocked the stairs leading down to the walkway bordered by daffodils and glorious pink and white azaleas. "Now, unless you're planning on knocking over an old, black woman, I suggest you sit down and eat."

Carrie stared at her with astonishment.

"If I were you, I would just go ahead and eat them."

Carrie looked up as Elizabeth Gilbert sailed through the door, her lovely face wreathed with a smile, and then she nodded toward May. "Does she force you to eat, too?" She was torn between amusement and exasperation.

"Every morning," Elizabeth said cheerfully. "You may be able to charm your way around almost everyone else with your dark, wavy hair and green eyes, but May is immune to them." She grinned at the housekeeper. "Isn't that right, May?"

May grinned back at her. "You're right smart for an Italian, Miss Elizabeth. Miss Carrie over there ain't learned who runs things around here yet."

Elizabeth sighed. "For someone as smart as she is, I'm surprised Carrie's so slow to pick up on the simple things of life."

"Now, just wait a minute," Carrie sputtered as she tried to control her laughter. When the mirth bubbled out anyway, she sank onto the porch swing and opened the basket. "Fine," she conceded. "I'll eat the biscuits."

"I never had a doubt," May said serenely as she relinquished her post, opened the door and looked back. "Miss Elizabeth, there be more in there for you. Once you two lady doctors have eaten, you'll have the strength to face whatever you got to face today."

Carrie smiled and unwrapped a biscuit from its brightly colored napkin. Her first bite of the flaky biscuit, paired with a thick slice of Virginia ham, almost made her swoon. It also made her realize how hungry she actually was.

"Do you really still attempt to leave the house in the morning without eating?" Elizabeth asked. "I gave up after a couple of weeks." She took a bite of her biscuit and closed her eyes with pleasure.

Carrie shrugged. "What can I say? I'm hardheaded."

At that moment, May came back out carrying two hot cups of coffee and placed them on the table by the swing. She smiled at the sight of Carrie chewing her biscuit and disappeared back inside. Carrie reached for the drink and held it in her hands for a moment before taking a sip.

"I spent a lot of the ride in from the plantation yesterday thinking about what needed to be done at the clinic today."

It was Elizabeth's turn to shrug. "The clinic isn't going anywhere. We don't open for an hour," she reminded her calmly.

Carrie eyed Elizabeth as she took another bite, chewed and then swallowed. "Since when has my fiery Italian friend become so complacent?"

"Not complacent," Elizabeth corrected. "I'm feeling *confident* about what we're creating."

Carrie and Anthony had arrived too late the previous evening for the two women to have a chance for a real conversation. They'd eaten the supper May had prepared for them and then tumbled into bed.

"It's really going that well?" Carrie knew things had improved since their early days in January when they'd had no patients, but the expression on her friend and colleague's face said good things had happened in the two weeks she'd been on Cromwell Plantation.

"It's going that well," Elizabeth confirmed, her eyes shining with satisfaction. "Our last seminar had fifty women."

"*Fifty?*" Carrie stared at her with astonishment. "The most we've ever had was twenty-five!"

"Those twenty-five each brought a new person with them," Elizabeth replied. "At this rate, we're going to have to find another building for the seminars. Our room was bursting at the seams."

"How many are becoming patients?" Carrie was still trying to wrap her mind around the idea of fifty women attending their seminar. When Janie had first come up with the idea, they'd had no concept of how much it would turn their practice around.

"Fifteen of the twenty-five new attendees made appointments before they left."

Carrie gaped at her. "How are you and Janie handling the patient load?"

"We're managing," Elizabeth said lightly, but her eyes revealed how tired she was. "I'm glad you're here, though."

Carrie frowned. "We've got to find someone else for the practice. Now that Florence has gotten married and decided to stay in Paris, we need another doctor to join us." Carrie wouldn't give up her clinic on the plantation, but she didn't want her two friends to work themselves to into exhaustion either. Her thoughts flew across the ocean. "Has another letter come from Florence?"

"Not yet," Elizabeth answered. "She must be so wildly happy with her doctor husband that she doesn't have time for us."

Carrie knew that wasn't true. "I hope things are better in France. Just because the war is over and Paris is no longer under siege, that doesn't mean things aren't still hard." She knew that all too well. The South was still struggling to come back from the recent Civil War.

"You're right," Elizabeth agreed quickly. "I didn't really mean that. I watch the mail every day, but nothing has come so far. Florence promised she would write, so I know she will. As long as the steamer carrying the mail doesn't sink, we'll get a letter."

Carrie changed the subject. "Is it odd having Janie and Matthew gone?" During the two weeks she'd been on the plantation, Janie and Matthew had moved into the new home they'd purchased just a few blocks away.

"Odd, and unbelievably quiet. I'd gotten quite used to Robert and Annabelle making so much noise while they played."

Carrie knew she mostly meant Robert. Little Annabelle, at just seven months old, was certainly not playing yet. An easy baby, she hardly seemed to cry. She glanced toward the house. "How is May handling them being gone?"

Elizabeth chuckled. "May, Micah and Spencer are walking around like there was a funeral. Spencer spent an awful lot of time acting like a pony for Robert. The three of them loved having the children here."

Carrie knew that was true. May and Micah had been her father's servants since the end of the war, when he'd given them their freedom. They'd been technically free since the Emancipation Proclamation, but had chosen to stay at her father's house until the war ended, accepting his offer of employment. Spencer, Carrie's longtime friend and driver, had fallen in love with May, married her, and now shared her apartment in the house.

"Those three doted on those children," Carrie agreed. "I would have brought Frances and Minnie with me, but I didn't want them to miss school." She hated being away from her daughters.   There were times she wondered if trying to work at both clinics was worth the separation. Pushing the thought away, she took another bite of her biscuit.

"You girls gotta quit talkin' and get to eatin'!"

Carrie laughed as May's voice drifted to them from inside the house. She loved the home her father had purchased during the war. The three-story brick structure had served as a boarding house for many government workers during the war. It had become her haven when forced to escape the plantation, and was now the Richmond residence for many of the people who had entered their lives. Her father and Abby lived on the plantation full-time now, but the house was seldom empty.

"Where is Anthony this morning?"

"My wonderful husband was up before the first birds started singing to the dawn. He wanted to be down at River City Carriages before the first drivers arrived. He loved being on the plantation the last couple of weeks, but he knows the paperwork is piling up. He's expecting a lot of deliveries of grain and hay this week, as well."

"The business is doing well, isn't it?" Elizabeth asked.

"Extremcly well," Carrie said proudly. "Anthony had Marcus and Willard hire ten more drivers. He's bought more carriages and horses that will arrive next week. The number of visitors to the city is growing at a rapid rate, and they all need a carriage ride."

"Having the drivers act as tour guides through the city was a stroke of brilliance," Elizabeth said admiringly. "There are other carriage companies in Richmond, but none of them comes close to doing the amount of business that River City Carriages does."

Carrie nodded. "I love being married to a genius." Her smile softened when she thought of her handsome husband. "He's worked hard to make it a success. I'm quite proud of him."

"Eat!" May's voice was more insistent.

Carrie laughed and then pushed the final bite of biscuit into her mouth. "We're finished, May," she called.

"And we ate all of it," Elizabeth added loudly. "You don't have to come out to check."

Carrie's eyes widened. "Has she really come out to check?" she whispered.

"Oh yes," Elizabeth assured her. "She takes her job of feeding the women doctors of Richmond quite seriously."

Carrie and Elizabeth walked briskly toward the clinic. Spencer hadn't been pleased when they had turned down his offer of a ride, but they'd assured him that beautiful mornings were meant for walking. Unconvinced, he had warned them to be careful, and then had watched them until they'd turned the corner.

Carrie pushed down her feeling of discomfort. Spencer's job as her driver had included keeping her safe. It was his job to worry about her safety. There'd been no trouble at Bregdan Medical Clinic, despite the growing number of women and black patients coming to them for treatment.

Carrie gazed around with delight at the profusion of blooms. The purple lilacs were bursting from every bush, sending out a heady perfume that made her want to bury her face in them. Tulips swayed in the slight breeze, while Bluebells nestled under the sweeping branches of weeping Cherry trees. "It's so beautiful!"

"It's not the plantation," Elizabeth replied, "but on mornings like this, I can forget the crowded streets and sooty air. At least we're high enough up here on Church Hill to escape the worst of it." She wrinkled her nose with distaste.

"It's bad," Carrie agreed. "I don't mind coming for stints at the clinic, but I wouldn't want to live here full time." She eyed her friend. "How are you really handling being in Richmond?"

Elizabeth started to shrug, and then met her eyes. "It's hard at times," she admitted honestly. "I don't miss the frigid cold Boston winters, but with Janie and Matthew gone, it's been a little lonely." Her normally fiery eyes were soft with vulnerability.

"I'm sorry," Carrie answered, reaching over to squeeze her hand. She wasn't surprised her friend was lonely, but didn't know what to do about it. Richmonders were suspicious of Elizabeth because she was from Boston, she was Italian, and she was a doctor. Her patients adored her, but she'd had no real opportunity to create friendships. Carrie hoped that would change with time.

Elizabeth shook her head. "I'll be fine," she said firmly. "I'm just feeling a little sorry for myself today. I knew what I was getting myself into when I agreed to come to Richmond to start the clinic with you and Janie."

Carrie knew that wasn't true but remained silent. In reality, Elizabeth had no way of comprehending what life would be like in the South when she'd decided to join them. Her life in the North had not prepared her Southern attitudes and practices. Carrie had spent almost her entire life in the South but it was still difficult to navigate Southern culture. She was thrilled Matthew and Janie finally had a home for their growing family, but she knew their departure from her father's house had left a gaping hole for everyone.

Moments later, as if conjured by her thoughts, Janie appeared around the corner.

"Carrie!"

Carrie rushed forward to hug her friend. "Hello Janie!" It had only been two weeks since they'd last seen each other, but she'd missed her. "How is your new home? I can't wait to see it."

"It's wonderful, but I suspect Matthew is already regretting his decision to buy it," she said soberly.

"Why?" Carrie asked with alarm.

"Because he has to survive off my cooking again," Janie revealed, her light blue eyes gleaming with laughter. "I've become a better cook, but he's been horribly spoiled by May."

"He'll survive," Carrie replied lightly. "He didn't starve when y'all were in Philadelphia."

"He also didn't get chicken and dumplings," Janie said sadly.

"Oh, quit pretending it's him," Elizabeth answered. "You know you miss May's cooking as much as he does. Admit it."

"Easily," Janie said with a laugh. "I miss her cooking as much as I miss *not* having to cook. Coming home after a long day at the clinic doesn't make me eager to fix a meal." She shook her head. "I'm not complaining, however. I love every aspect of my life. I love being a doctor. I love being a wife, and I love being a mother."

"You'll love it even more when Matthew hires someone to help with the cooking and cleaning," Elizabeth observed astutely.

"Completely true," Janie said cheerfully as they approached the clinic. "At the rate our practice is growing, I shouldn't have to wait too long." Suddenly her smile faded, replaced by a frown of concern. "The front door to the clinic is open."

Carrie's stomach tightened with apprehension. She knew without asking that neither of her friends had carelessly left it open. She stopped abruptly at the beginning of the walkway to the clinic.

"Carrie?" Janie's voice quivered with nervousness.

"We don't know if someone is still in there," Carrie said quietly. Her mind raced as she tried to determine the best course of action. When she was younger, she would have raced into the building without considering the consequences. Countless experiences over the past years had infused her with more wisdom.

"There are three of us," Elizabeth said indignantly. "If someone is in there, we can handle it."

Carrie smiled slightly. "Did you bring a gun with you this morning?"

"No, but..."

"Do you have a weapon that will help you if there's someone waiting inside with a knife?"

"Well, no..." Elizabeth sputtered, and then stared at her with wide eyes. "Do you really believe that's possible?"

"Anything is possible," Janie muttered, her eyes latched on the open door.

"It could just be a patient," Elizabeth said, her tone indicating she knew that wasn't very likely.

"A patient that broke through our lock to get inside?" Carrie stared at the clinic, her eyes searching the windows to detect movement. There was none. A quick glance at her pocket watch told her the clinic was due to open in ten minutes. She didn't want to put any of their patients into a dangerous situation.

"What do we do?" Elizabeth asked uncertainly. "I feel rather silly standing out here just staring at the clinic."

Carrie agreed with her, but she wasn't going to venture into a dangerous situation. Her first thought had been to walk to River City Carriages to get Anthony and some of the drivers, but she didn't want arriving patients to assume the open door meant they should come inside. She wished they'd taken Spencer up on his offer of a ride.

"Good morning, ladies!"

Carrie felt a rush of relief and spun around when she heard the deep voice sound behind them. "Good morning, Officer Oxford." The tall, square-shouldered policeman standing behind her had a broad smile on his face. Suspicious of them at first, they had worn him down with their kindness and daily offerings of coffee and cookies that May insisted on sending.

Officer Oxford's eyes narrowed as he took in their faces. "Everything alright, Dr. Wallington?"

"We're not sure," Carrie answered. "The door was locked last night." She nodded her head toward the clinic. "Now it's open. We don't know how that happened."

Officer Oxford scowled. "Can't mean anything good." He pulled his gun from his holster and motioned for them to stand behind the tree stationed in front of the clinic. "I'm going in to see if anyone is there. Y'all stay out here where it's safe until I tell you to come in."

Carrie nodded, more than happy to comply with his orders. She joined Janie and Elizabeth behind the shelter of the towering oak. Peering around the trunk, she kept her eyes trained on Officer Oxford, praying he wouldn't be harmed.

"It could just be someone who broke in to get medicines," Janie offered.

Carrie met Janie's eyes but remained silent. Her gut told her it was something else. An increasing number of women and black patients was a wonderful thing, but it was highly likely that someone had finally decided to take action against what they perceived as a threat to the accepted standard of medical practice in the South.

"What do you think it is?" Elizabeth asked tensely, her eyes on the clinic as they watched Officer Oxford push open the door and step through.

A muffled expletive from the unseen officer floated back to them.

"More than someone stealing medicine," Carrie replied. Her stomach roiled with nervousness, sorrow and anger. She had no idea what they would find when they entered the clinic, but she knew it would be bad.

Officer Oxford appeared at the door. "I reckon you ladies can come in." His eyes were dark with anger. "You're not going to like what you find, however."

Carrie exchanged a look with Janie and Elizabeth, and then linked arms with them. "We'll deal with whatever it is," she said firmly.

Anthony looked up as Marcus and Willard entered his office. "Please close the door behind you."

The two men exchanged mystified glances as Marcus pulled the door closed and then settled into a chair. His tall, muscular frame swallowed it as it creaked in protest.

Willard claimed the other seat. His fair skin, topped by light brown hair, made Marcus' skin even blacker in comparison.

Anthony eyed Willard closely. His eyes still carried a haunted look from the loss of his wife, Grace, during the Spotswood Fire three and a half months earlier, but the look of total despair seemed to have eased some.

Marcus and his wife Hannah had Willard over for supper almost every night. The same black community that had long shunned the mixed-race couple had now gathered around the grieving husband to offer support.

"What's wrong?" Marcus asked bluntly. "It's written all over your face."

Anthony held up an envelope in response. "This was shoved under my office door when I got here this morning." He opened it, pulled out a sheet of paper, and began to read.

You got to stop your wife and those other women doctors. If you don't, River City Carriages will pay the price.

He lowered the page and waited.

"That's all it says?" Willard demanded.

"That's all it says."

Marcus sat quietly for a moment before he spoke. "What do you reckon it means?"

Anthony shrugged, not certain how concerned he should be. "It means there are people who don't want a medical clinic run by women in Richmond."

"So, they're going to attack the stables?" Marcus asked angrily.

Anthony shrugged again. "I don't know if it's an empty threat, or if there's a plan." He wasn't naïve enough to discount it, but he also didn't want to give it more credence than it was due. "We've received threats before," he reminded his managers. "There are a lot of people unhappy with us because we have both black and white employees, and because we have so many black drivers." He lifted his hands. "Nothing has happened."

"Yet." Willard's voice was quiet, but intense. "Has anything happened at the clinic?"

"Not that I know of," Anthony replied. "Carrie and I just returned to town last night."

An authoritative knock at the door interrupted him. "Come in," he called. He tensed when the door opened to reveal a short, thin policeman. "Hello, officer. What can I do for you?"

"Are you Anthony Wallington?"

"I am." Anthony knew that whatever he was about to hear wasn't going to be good. Had something happened to Carrie? He rose from his seat and stepped from behind the desk. "What's going on?"

"I'm Officer Garraty. Officer Oxford sent me to get you. There was a break-in at the Bregdan Medical Clinic."

"My wife?" Anthony asked sharply, keenly aware of the gleeful look lurking in the policeman's eyes. "Is Dr. Wallington alright? And the others? Dr. Justin and Dr. Guilford?"

"The women are fine," Officer Garraty assured him; his expression revealing he wished he couldn't report that. "The clinic doesn't look so good, however." The gleeful look returned.

Anthony stuffed down his impulse to punch the officer. Officer Garrity had blatantly refrained from referring to the women as doctors and was obviously thrilled something had happened to the clinic. Experience had taught him that just because a man was a police officer, it was no indication that Richmond residents would be treated fairly or equally.

He bit back his questions. He would know soon enough. He turned to Marcus and Willard. "Take care of things here. I'll be back as soon as I can."

"You don't want us to come?" Willard asked.

Anthony shook his head and handed Willard the threatening note he'd received. "Stay here," he said crisply. "I'll let you know how things are as soon as I can." He knew both of them would be concerned about the women, but he needed them here until he could assess the situation. They would understand his concern that something might happen at the stables.

Carrie bit back her cry of dismay when they entered the clinic. Janie and Elizabeth both gasped and then fell silent as they gazed around in horror, their hands covering their mouths.

Their beautiful clinic had been completely destroyed. Huge gaping holes in the plaster walls revealed broken wood lath beneath. Shards of plaster littered the floors. Every oil lantern had been ripped from the walls and smashed onto the wood floors, which had also been battered and cut. Kerosene created a filmy lather on the remaining plaster before it reappeared as pools on the floor. Every piece of furniture had been broken apart. Books and pamphlets had been ripped and shredded into such tiny pieces that it was obvious the vandals had been there for a long time, wreaking their havoc methodically.

"The medicines?" Janie asked in a shocked, hoarse voice.

Carrie knew what she would find before she slowly opened the door to the dispensary. The same level of destruction met her eyes. The cabinets holding their medicines had been ripped from the walls. Empty, smashed bottles littered the floor. She swallowed hard to keep the bile from rising in her throat.

Each of their offices had been decimated. Their medical books had been torn and cut. All their medical records had been pulled out of drawers and ripped apart and then piled in the middle of the rooms and soaked with kerosene.

"At least they didn't set it on fire," Janie said weakly.

Carrie and Elizabeth locked eyes. Both knew the kerosene-soaked piles of paper were a warning. If they started the clinic back up, it would be burned to the ground.

"What happened here?"

Carrie turned around as a shocked female voice rang through the building. She managed to keep her voice steady as she spoke. "Hello Darlene."

The middle-aged red-haired woman who had been at their first seminar advanced slowly through the building, her eyes burning with both shock and anger. "Who did this?"

"We don't know," Elizabeth answered, her voice cracking with pain.

"Someone who isn't happy about a woman-run medical clinic in Richmond," Janie added. Her blue eyes glimmered with weariness and pain.

Darlene continued to stare in anger at the destruction surrounding her. "Those stupid men," she said between clenched teeth.

Carrie stared at her. "Do you know who did this?"

"I can't say for sure, but I have some guesses," Darlene said crisply. She nudged a piece of broken glass out of the way using the toe of her boot. "Me and some more of your patients were stopped a few blocks away when we came out of the last seminar by a group of men. They warned us that we needed to stay away from this place or..."

"Or what?" Carrie demanded as Darlene's voice trailed away.

"Or they would make sure we didn't have a place to go to," Darlene finished weakly. She met Carrie's eyes squarely. "We didn't think they really meant it, Dr. Wallington. I'm sorry we didn't say anything."

Carrie shook her head. "You couldn't have stopped them, Darlene. You're not to blame."

Officer Oxford stepped forward. "Can you identify those men, ma'am?" he asked sternly.

Darlene hesitated, a look of fear darkening her eyes, but then her gaze swept the clinic. She straightened her shoulders and lifted her head. "I can," she said clearly. "I don't know their names and I've never seen them before, but if I see them again, I would recognize them."

At that moment, three other women entered the clinic with cries of horror.

"What happened here?" Ruth, another of their first patients, looked like she would be ill as her eyes swept the destruction.

Darlene spun around. "Those stupid men who threatened the clinic did what they said they would, Ruth," she said angrily. "We didn't report it, so now we have to make it right."

Ruth stared around wildly, obviously struggling to absorb what she was seeing.

Carrie understood the terror that filled Ruth's eyes. "Darlene, there is nothing any of you must do to make it right," she said gently, as she fought to control her own emotions. Regardless of what had happened, she didn't want to put any of their patients at risk.

"Nonsense!" Darlene barked. "You three doctors have changed the life of every woman who has entered this clinic. We had male doctors who had no idea how to help us, and not much concern over whether they could or not. Now we have doctors who care about us and know how to treat what ails us. This is our clinic every bit as much as it is yours." She gazed around at the destruction with fire in her eyes. "Ruth, you go tell as many of their patients as you can." She nodded her head at the other two women. "I know you two are here for the first time as patients, but you've been to a seminar. We've got to help set things right here. We're going to help them clean this place up so they can go back to being doctors!"

Carrie watched Ruth straighten her shoulders and nod her head.

Darlene waved her arm to shoo Ruth out the door, and then turned to the other two women. "Let's get to work." She turned back to Carrie. "Where do you want us to put all this stuff?"

Carrie exchanged a look with her partners. None of them had recovered from the shock of their discovery, and she knew from the look in their eyes that they were still filled with fear, but Darlene was determined to begin cleaning up. Forcing herself to think clearly, Carrie realized that no matter what their final decision was, they would, at the very least, have to repair the destruction of their leased building. "We'll pull it out back," she finally replied. "Once it's all out, we'll carry it away in wagons."

They would decide what to do about the clinic later.

Chapter Two

"Carrie."

Carrie turned from where she stood in her office doorway and flew into Anthony's arms. She buried her head in his chest, grateful for his solid strength. She managed to hold back the tears, but she couldn't stop her body from trembling.

Anthony pulled her tightly against him, remaining silent as he gently stroked her hair.

Carrie was grateful for his silence, knowing he was giving her time to pull herself together. When the trembling had stopped, and her breathing had returned to normal, she leaned far enough back to look up into his face. "How did you know?"

"Officer Oxford sent another officer to notify me. I came immediately."

"Thank you."

Anthony's face tensed with anger as he looked around. "They've completely destroyed the clinic."

"Not completely," Carrie replied, digging deep to find any remaining strength. "The building is still standing... and we still have our patients."

Anthony looked skeptical. "If any of them have the courage to walk back through the doors."

Darlene appeared around the corner at that moment. "If any of us have the *courage*?" She eyed Anthony. "Who are you?"

Carrie smiled at the righteous indignation on Darlene's face. "This is my husband, Anthony Wallington. Anthony, this is Darlene Witherspoon. She's leading a group of our patients in helping us clean up."

Anthony smiled warmly. "Thank you, Mrs. Witherspoon. I stand corrected. I should have known the patients of this clinic would have as much courage as their doctors."

Darlene's face softened. "These three doctors have changed a lot of lives here in Richmond, Mr. Wallington. Your wife led the first seminar I came to. I was terrified to come, but I did it anyway. Dr. Wallington told us that our being here took a lot of courage. She told us that all women have the *ability* to be brave, but too many choose to live with fear. She congratulated us for making a different choice." Her voice faltered. "I'll admit that when I saw what happened here, I wanted to run away, but then I thought about what she said that first day. I knew I needed to make another choice." Having said what she needed to, she turned away and moved back into the room she had appeared from.

Moments later, ten more women walked in the door behind Ruth. Their eyes were a mixture of horror and apprehension as they gazed around at the ruin, but all their lips were set with determination.

"We're here to help," one of the women called out. "We won't let them destroy our clinic."

Janie hurried forward; her hair hidden by a brightly colored handkerchief one of the other women had provided. "Thank you," she said fervently. "We can't tell you how much this means to us."

"And we can't tell you how much the three of you mean to us," another woman answered. "Tell us what to do."

Carrie watched the flurry of activity for a moment before returning to her office. She knew there was nothing left of the homeopathic remedies that had filled her cabinets. She was also aware all the herbal remedies they had created at the plantation had been destroyed, but her heart couldn't quite accept it yet.

"It's all gone?" Anthony asked quietly.

"Everything," Carrie confirmed, hoping the single word would drive home the reality.

"What will you do?"

"I don't know," she said slowly. She wanted to insist that she would order more homeopathic remedies immediately, but the image of all the papers, books and pamphlets soaked with kerosene oil had terrified her. She shook her head in a vain attempt to dispel the image. "I just want to get everything cleaned up," she said finally.

"I was going to get some of the men who have finished their driving shift to help, but it looks like your patients have got this under control."

"You're right about that, Mr. Wallington," Darlene sang out from the other room where she had obviously been listening. "It was men who did this, but women are going to fix it."

Darlene's defiant voice made Carrie smile. It also sparked an ember of courage. She remembered the terrified looks on the faces of every woman who had appeared at the first seminar. They had overcome their fear to do what was best for them and their family. Surely, she could do the same.

Moments later, she heard the sound of running feet outside. The ember that had started to glow, sputtered and died as fear swallowed it. Stiffening, she waited to see if the men who had destroyed the clinic had returned to do more. Her mind raced as she tried to figure out how to protect the women who were there to help. Officer Oxford and Anthony wouldn't be enough to stop a large group of angry vigilantes.

"Miss Carrie!"

Carrie's eyes widened as a young girl from the Black Quarters burst through the door. "Carmella? Honey, what are you doing here?" She hurried forward and put an arm around the girl's thin shoulders. It was impossible to miss the terror in her eyes.

Carmella's eyes teared up as she leaned against Carrie, but then she straightened with a look of determination. "They done got my mama and my Auntie Ann! You got to help!"

Anthony knelt in front of the little girl and took her hands. "What do you mean, Carmella? Who got them?"

Carmella stiffened and pulled back, obviously frightened by the strange man talking to her.

Carrie knelt next to Anthony. "This is my husband, Carmella. You can trust him, honey. Tell us what happened."

Carmella relaxed slightly but kept her eyes on Carrie as she talked. "Mama and Auntie Ann was coming here to see you this morning, Miss Carrie. Mama's gonna have another baby. She weren't feelin' so good this morning, so she talked Auntie Ann into bringing her here. Mama said you would take real good care of her." Her earnest voice faltered as tears clogged her eyes and throat. "The men got them, though. Mama made me run away when she saw them coming. Told me to come here." Her words came in bursts now as the sobs stole her breath. "I looked back... just one time... they were beatin' them... my mama... and Auntie Ann." She threw herself into Carrie's arms. "Why did they do that?"

There was no answer to the question that would make sense to the little girl, because there wasn't an answer that made any sense at all. Carrie hugged Carmella close and looked at Anthony.

"I'm going now," he said quietly. "Where should I bring them?"

Carrie bit her lip. There was nothing at Bregdan Medical Clinic to bring them to. She was also sickeningly certain they'd been attacked because they were coming here in the first place. Her first instinct was to take them back to the Black Quarters, but she didn't know how badly they were injured, and whether it would be safe to move them.

Janie appeared at her side. "Go," she urged. "Take your medical bag. We'll take care of things here."

Matthew appeared at the clinic door just then, his face etched with concern.

"Matthew!" Janie rushed into his arms and then looked up at him quizzically. "What are you doing here?"

"Anthony sent a driver to tell me what happened." His blue eyes, usually bright with good humor beneath his red hair, were grim as he gazed around at the destruction.

Elizabeth appeared with her medical bag. "I'm coming with you, Carrie. It might take two of us to treat the women. Officer Oxford has promised to stay to watch over things."

Darlene appeared in the doorway to Elizabeth's office. "You two go help those women. We'll take care of things here."

Carrie managed a weak smile of gratitude, reached for the medical bag she had placed in her destroyed office, and turned to take Carmella's hand. "Can you take me to where your mama and Auntie Ann are?" She hated to expose the little girl to what might have happened to the women, but it was the only way to locate them.

"Yessum," Carmella said seriously. "We was almost here. It ain't far." She turned and dashed out the door, her black braids slapping against her back.

Carrie, Anthony and Elizabeth ran down the walkway after the little girl.

A crowd had gathered outside the clinic – a cluster of people talking anxiously. Carrie saw the questions on their faces as they ran past, but there was no time to do anything more than nod in their direction. She knew the group included people who believed that whatever had happened; the clinic had gotten what it deserved. She also spotted several patients who were too afraid to walk inside and show their association with the clinic. She couldn't blame them, but it made the ache in her heart even more unbearable. They'd opened the clinic to help people, but perhaps they'd been wrong to believe Richmond would eventually accept them.

All thoughts fled her mind as they turned a corner and saw two huddled shapes on the sidewalk ahead.

"Mama!" Carmella screamed. "Auntie Ann!"

Carrie tensed, grabbed Anthony's arm, and then nodded toward the little girl.

Anthony understood instantly. He sprinted ahead, caught Carmella's hand, and pulled her to a stop. "Honey, let's let Miss Carrie and Dr. Gilbert take care of your mama and Auntie Ann."

Carmella, tears streaming down her face, looked at him with fear and confusion.

Carrie stopped just long enough to tilt the little girl's face up so their eyes would meet. "Carmella, will you help me by staying here with Mr. Anthony? I promise you that we'll take real good care of your mama and Auntie Ann." She prayed the women were still alive.

Carmella bit back her sobs and bravely nodded her head. "Alright, Miss Carrie."

Carrie hugged her tightly and then ran after Elizabeth who was already kneeling beside the two women. She knew by the look on her partner's face that it was bad.

Carrie reached the women and dropped her medical bag as she knelt. "Are they alive?" she asked quietly.

"Yes," Elizabeth whispered, her eyes narrowed with anger and worry. "It's bad, though."

Carrie wanted to weep as she took in the two women's beaten and swollen faces. Carmella's mama had a badly broken arm and blood flowed freely from cuts on her face and lips. Both eyes were battered and beginning to swell. Only time would tell what the beating had done to the baby she carried in her swollen womb. It would be impossible to tell until they could get her somewhere she could examine her more thoroughly. "Harriet," she said softly. "Can you hear me? It's Carrie."

A soft moan was her only answer, but it caused a flurry of hope. At least she could hear her. She turned to inspect Ann next. The tall, skinny woman seemed to have taken the worst of the beating. Both arms appeared to be broken, her nose was at an odd angle, and blood gushed from gaping wounds.

Anger filled Carrie. Neither of these two women had done anything more than attempt to seek medical care. Whatever had brought them to the clinic was now the least of their concerns. She forgot her fear as she poured her focus into helping them.

"Do you think we can move them?" Elizabeth asked.

"We have to," Carrie answered. "There's no way we can treat them without taking them somewhere." She looked around, hoping to see someone who could help. Tight knots of people had formed on the porches and sidewalk, but every expression was closed and defensive. They were obviously offended that there were two bleeding black women on their street.

Carrie wanted to scream at the ignorance and hatred surrounding her, but now was not the time. Forcing herself to ignore the people watching them, she leaned closer to Ann. "Ann, it's Carrie. Can you hear me?"

"Yes..." Ann's voice was thin and tortured. She tried to open her eyes, but they were swollen to narrow slits. "Carmella?" she whispered.

"Carmella is fine," Carrie assured her. "She came to get us at the clinic."

Ann sighed her relief and then slumped into unconsciousness.

Carrie knew it was for the best. However they were going to move them, it was sure to be painful. She cast around in her mind for a solution. Moments later, she heard the sound of a wagon approaching.

"It's Marcus!" Elizabeth exclaimed.

Marcus pulled the wagon to a stop in the street. He answered the question in their eyes. "Mrs. Witherspoon ran over to the stables and told us you would need help."

Carrie and Elizabeth's eyes locked. "Darlene!" they said in unison, both grateful for her quick thinking.

"We didn't have real blankets," Marcus said, "but we piled up as many horse blankets as we could find."

Carrie wasn't concerned about cleanliness right at that moment. Anything that would soften the ride for the women's broken bodies would be appreciated. "Thank you, Marcus."

She strode over to where Anthony sat on the sidewalk with Carmella in his lap. "Honey, do you know how to get back to your house?"

The little girl nodded quickly, but then stopped, a look of uncertainty in her eyes. "I'm not right sure, Miss Carrie," she said softly.

"Don't worry," Carrie said warmly. "The streets around here are very confusing." Her mind raced as she tried to determine where to treat the women. She could certainly take them to her father's house, but she didn't want them to have to endure that long a ride.

"I know where they live, but my house is closer," Marcus said. "We'll take them there. It's not far and Hannah will want to help. Harriet and Ann are members of our church. I already sent a man to the Quarters so there will be beds for them by the time we arrive."

Carrie knew he was also saying it would be best if the two women weren't taken to a house in the white part of Richmond. As much as she hated to accept it, she knew he was right. They had no way of knowing just how violent the men who had done this would become, or just how far they would go to attack anything to do with the clinic. She resisted the urge to look over her shoulder to see if a group of armed vigilantes were approaching them.

Gritting her teeth, she nodded. "Thank you."

Anthony and Marcus carefully lifted Harriet into the back of the wagon. She moaned once and then went slack. Ann's unconscious body was laid next to her.

Carrie prayed they would remain unconscious until they could get them into a bed.

She and Elizabeth climbed up into the wagon beside them, as Anthony joined Marcus on the driver's seat, holding Carmella's tiny body closely. Carmella, convinced Anthony was safe, clung to him like he was her only lifeline. She turned around often to stare down at her mama and auntie with frightened eyes, but didn't utter a word.

Peter Wilcher swung down from the last train car, glad to have finally arrived in Richmond. Usually, the long trip from New York City didn't bother him, but the crowded conditions had made it almost unbearable. The newspaper he wrote for, the *New York Tribune*, usually made sure he traveled in one of the business class sections, but the last-minute trip had deemed that impossible. He dropped his bag, stretched, and then looked around; hopeful he would find a River City Carriage. No one was expecting him, but he knew he would be welcome at Thomas' house on Church Hill. His stomach growled as he thought of May's cooking.

"Need a ride, Mister?"

Peter smiled when he saw the logo for River City Carriages painted on the side of the conveyance pulled up along the Broad Street Station. "I do."

The short, stocky driver leapt down from the carriage seat and grabbed his bag. "Where to?"

Peter gave him the address. "It's up on Church Hill."

The driver cocked his head as he absorbed the information. "Is that the house where Mr. Anthony lives?"

"It is," Peter agreed. "I'm a friend of the family."

The driver's face split with a grin. "It's a pleasure to be able to take you, sir. My name is Ricky."

"I'm Peter Wilcher. I was hoping to find a River City Carriage."

"We're everywhere," Ricky assured him proudly. "I got hired a few weeks back because the company is growing so quickly. I ain't never had a job that paid so well, and they treat us good, too."

Peter nodded. "I'm glad to hear it. Congratulations on your new job." He settled back against the seat and relaxed. "I'm eager to see Anthony and Dr. Wallington." He tensed when Ricky frowned. "Is there a problem?"

Ricky hesitated. "There was talk at the stables this morning," he said slowly, obviously not sure he should be revealing information. "Mr. Anthony got called away because of a problem at the clinic. Not too long after that, Marcus left with a wagon to help with two women who were hurt real bad."

Peter's whole body went rigid. "Who was hurt?" he snapped. "Was it Dr. Wallington? Dr. Justin?" Images of Carrie and Janie filled his mind. He knew they had another partner, but he'd never met her.

Ricky shrugged. "I don't know, Mr. Wilcher," he said apologetically. "That's all I heard before I had to start my shift."

Peter's thoughts raced. "Please take me to the clinic, Ricky. As quickly as possible."

"Yes'sir," Ricky responded. "The streets are crowded today, but I'll get you there as quick as I can." He picked up the reins and clucked for the horse to move forward.

Peter, despite his worry over his friends, was pleased at the condition of the horse. Too many New York City carriage horses were thin and poorly cared for. River City Carriage horses were sleek, shiny and well-fed. He knew they were also rotated half-way through the day so that none of them were overworked. He appreciated that Anthony was proving you could have a profitable business and still take care of your most valuable commodities – your horses and your drivers.

Unable to relax now, he leaned forward and willed the traffic to move faster.

Carrie was happy to see a group of men clustered outside Marcus and Hannah's modest clapboard house on the outskirts of the Black Quarters. As they drew closer, she could see the anger imprinted on each face. She didn't blame them for being angry and frustrated. Harriet and Ann had done nothing but venture into the white part of Richmond for medical care. They were being returned broken and bloody.

"Handle them very gently," Carrie urged as they drew up to the house.

Hannah appeared on the porch, her lovely face set in stern lines, and her eyes filled with sadness. "Bring them inside," she called. "Beds are ready for them."

The two women remained unconscious while the men gently carried them in.

Carrie and Elizabeth exchanged a grim look. Neither were certain the women would regain consciousness.

"Is my mama and auntie gonna be alright?" Carmella asked from the security of Anthony's arms.

"We're going to do our very best," Carrie replied, not willing to make a promise she wasn't sure she could keep.

"And my little sister or brother?" Carmella demanded.

Elizabeth squeezed her hand and parroted Carrie's words. "We're going to do our very best, Carmella."

"Carmella!"

Anthony turned as a strong voice rang out in the morning air.

Carrie was relieved to see Sampson, Carmella's father, running down the road. She had met the family several years earlier when the Black Militia had formed to provide protection for the Black Quarters. Sampson was a fine man who was committed to his family. Carmella needed her father.

"Daddy!" Carmella cried, her bravery fading now that her father had arrived. Great tears rolled from her eyes. "Daddy! They hurt Mama and Auntie Ann!"

Sampson pulled Carmella into his arms as soon as he reached the wagon. "I got you, little one. I got you." He met Carrie's eyes over his little girl's head. "What happened?" he mouthed.

Carrie looked to Anthony for help.

"I'll explain," Anthony said. "Carrie and Dr. Gilbert are going inside to treat your wife and sister."

Carrie hurried up the sidewalk with Elizabeth. She knew Sampson would be inside needing answers soon. She hoped to be able to assure him the women would live.

Peter climbed from the carriage, stunned to see a force of women walking in and out of the clinic, carrying what looked to be like broken furniture and piles of papers. "What's going on here?" he asked the woman closest to him.

"Who are you?" the red-haired woman demanded. "Did your friends send you to see what they had done so they can gloat?"

Peter stared at her, his heart pounding at the look of desperate pain and anger in her eyes. "What's happened?" he demanded. "Where is Carrie? And Janie?"

"Peter!"

Peter spun around when he heard a familiar voice call his name. "Janie!" He hurried toward the door where she was standing, her rigid body silhouetted by the sun that was now almost directly above them. "What's going on?"

Janie's posture crumpled as she stepped aside. "We had visitors last night."

Peter moved inside and then jolted to a standstill as he stared around in disbelief. "What the...?"

Matthew appeared from the back of the building. "Peter! What are you doing here?"

"I'm here on business," Peter said quickly. "My driver told me there might be a problem at the clinic, so I came to check things out." He continued to gaze around, his eyes refusing to process what he was seeing.

"It looks way better than it did," Matthew said grimly. "Evidently, there are people who are quite unhappy with Janie, Carrie and Elizabeth daring to run a clinic in Richmond."

Peter stepped through some of the rubble and peered into the rooms. "Everything has been destroyed?"

"Everything," Janie said hollowly.

Peter's mind heard the words but couldn't make sense of them. Why would people destroy a clinic that was helping others? He knew the answer even before he asked it, but the senselessness of it made him both furious and heartsick. "Carrie? Is she alright?"

"Yes," Matthew assured him. "She's with Elizabeth right now. They're treating two black women who were attacked close by."

Peter stared at him again. "What? Why?"

"They were two of their patients," Matthew continued. "They were attacked a block or so from here."

"Why?" Peter asked again. He was struggling to comprehend what he was seeing and hearing.

"We suspect because they were coming to the clinic for treatment," Janie answered, her eyes smudged with fatigue.

Peter looked at her more closely, recognizing the stark fear blended in with the fatigue. "How are they?"

Janie shrugged. "We don't know. We received word that Carrie and Elizabeth had them taken to Marcus and Hannah's house. They're treating them now."

"Elizabeth? Is that your other partner?"

Janie nodded absently. "Do you want to help?" Her voice sounded almost wooden.

Only then did Peter become aware of all the activity surrounding them. A group of women, their heads covered by handkerchiefs and bonnets, were scooping up and carrying armfuls of the debris still scattered through the clinic.

Matthew answered his unspoken question. "Nothing can be saved. We're carrying it out back. Anthony is sending some of his men with wagons to haul it all away."

"Count me in," Peter answered. More questions could wait until later. He had dealt with enough tragedy in his reporting career to recognize the dazed shock on Janie's face.

Chapter Three

It was late afternoon before Elizabeth stepped back from Ann. Her head was pounding, and her back was as tight as a fiddle bow, but she felt the flush of satisfaction that always came with saving a life. Ann was going to have a long road back to a full recovery, but both broken arms were set, her cracked ribs were wrapped, and her cuts had been treated or stitched. It had taken over one hundred stitches to close all the wounds before she'd slathered Carrie's herbal healing salve on them. She was grateful all of them carried a large amount of medical supplies in their bags. Ann had regained consciousness at one point, had murmured some words to Sampson, and then had fallen into a deep sleep. Seeing her brother had helped her. Rest was what she needed more than anything.

Elizabeth's feeling of satisfaction dissolved when she looked across the tiny room where Carrie sat with Harriet. Harriet's body would recover, but the severe beating had caused her to go into labor. Only six months along, it had been far too early to deliver a child. Her tiny son had lived just a few minutes before dying in her arms, while Sampson watched helplessly. Carrie had held the weeping woman in her arms for a long time before Harriet had lapsed into unconsciousness again. Working quickly, Carrie had set her broken arm and treated all her wounds. For the last hour she had simply sat with her patient, holding her hand.

Elizabeth watched her friend. She knew the little boy's death was a harsh reminder to Carrie of her own daughter's stillbirth. Carrie, more than anyone, would understand Harriet's pain.

Elizabeth's mind turned to the situation at hand. The bottle of healing salve Carrie had brought from the plantation the night before was the only one available. Their generous supply at the clinic had all been destroyed. Carrie would be forced to return to the plantation and bring back whatever her clinic there could spare. She knew there were children and women working hard to collect plants, and Polly was using every spare minute to make more remedies to meet the demand for both clinics, but losing their large supply was going to be a hardship." Elizabeth sucked in her breath as she acknowledged the truth. It would be a hardship only *if* they opened the clinic again.

She tightened her lips and looked out the window at the cluster of people milling around the yard. They had already received the news about the baby's death and were now waiting for word on Ann. Gathering the remnants of her weary resolve, Elizabeth opened the door and stepped outside the bedroom.

Hannah met her in the small living area. "How are they?"

Elizabeth met her eyes evenly. "Harriet is sleeping. Carrie is sitting with her. Ann will be alright, but it's going to take her a long time to heal."

"She's going to stay here," Hannah said firmly. "Her husband died last year. Sampson said he would take care of her, but he's going to have his hands full taking care of Harriet and Carmella."

Elizabeth listened, noticing Hannah said nothing about the loss of Sampson and Harriet's son. The black community had learned, long ago, how to stoically go on in the face of crushing loss. "I know you'll take good care of her." Hannah had been through her own losses and pain. Ann would be in good hands. "We'll check in on her every day for the next week. Infection is the greatest danger, but we'll change the dressing each day until we're sure the wounds are healing."

Hannah nodded. "Is Ann awake?"

"No. They're both sleeping," Elizabeth replied. "It's the best thing for them right now. Sampson can take Harriet home in the morning if she feels up to it, but I want her to stay here for tonight."

Hannah nodded again and turned away. "I'll let everyone know."

Elizabeth sagged with relief as she watched her walk out to her tiny yard. She'd been willing to break the news to everyone, but she was honest enough to acknowledge she'd dreaded it.

"You look tired."

Elizabeth managed a trembling smile when Anthony rose from a chair in the corner of the room. She should have known he wouldn't leave until she and Carrie were ready to go. "I'll survive. I'm in much better shape than Harriet and Ann." Her fatigue was replaced by a burning anger at what had been done to them. "Do you think they'll find who did this?"

Anthony shrugged. "I'm certain there are a lot of people who know, but..."

"But no one is going to step forward and tell," Elizabeth finished for him, her anger blazing hotter.

"Probably not," he admitted heavily. "I don't know what it's going to take to make racial issues better in Richmond. There are moments," he said reluctantly, "when I'm not sure it's possible."

Elizabeth stared at him, wishing with all her heart that she didn't agree with him. Boston wasn't perfect, by any means, but the hatred, animosity and fear vibrating in the air of the South was worse than she imagined possible.

Anthony shook his head, as if he wanted to banish his thoughts. "I assume Carrie is going to be here for a while?"

Elizabeth was happy for a change of subject. "Yes. She's sitting with Harriet while she sleeps. Carrie is holding her hand."

"She doesn't want her to be alone when she wakes up without her baby," Anthony murmured. His eyes shone with understanding. "Come on. I'll take you back to the clinic and come back here to wait for Carrie."

Elizabeth didn't argue. The idea of returning to the clinic - the opening shot in a horrible day - wasn't appealing, but the idea of going home to face the questions May, Micah and Spencer would fire at her wasn't appealing either. Besides, Janie would want to know what was going on. Stifling a yawn, she followed Anthony out the door.

Once outside, she was surprised to discover a delightfully warm afternoon, redolent with the aroma of flowers blooming through the Black Quarters. The people might struggle with poverty, but they were committed to their gardens, both flower and vegetable. It somehow seemed wrong for there to be such beauty surrounding her when there was such loss and pain inside the house behind her, but she welcomed the caressing breeze on her face as the people parted to make room for them.

"Thank you, Doc Gilbert."

"We're obliged, Doc Gilbert."

"Thank you for saving our Harriet and Ann."

Elizabeth smiled warmly, but remained silent. The events of the day were finally catching up with her. All she wanted was to go home, curl up in bed, and sleep. Surely, when she awoke, the horrors of the day wouldn't seem quite so horrible. Climbing onto the wagon seat beside Anthony, she sagged against the hard seat, vaguely aware of the unforgiving wood pressing into her back.

"Would you rather me take you home?" Anthony asked.

Elizabeth longed to say yes, but shook her head instead. "No, thank you. I need to go back to the clinic."

"Matthew came by here a little while ago. The women have gotten it all cleaned up."

Elizabeth considered his statement. There wouldn't be anything left to do. "Is Janie still there?"

"Yes," Anthony replied. "I gave Matthew the news about Harriet and Ann, but he said she'd already decided to wait there until you and Carrie got back."

Elizabeth felt a flash of alarm. "Was she there by herself when Matthew came here?" Visions of a horde of men returning to finish what they had started the night before filled her mind.

"No," Anthony said quickly. "Peter was there."

Elizabeth cocked her head. "Peter?"

"He's a good friend of ours. A journalist from New York City. He's in town for business. He was told by one of my drivers that there had been trouble at the clinic. He came to see if he could help."

Elizabeth tried to make her tired brain remember if she had heard of him before. "Is he the one who was with Willard when Grace died in the fire on Christmas Eve?"

"Yes."

Elizabeth pushed aside memories of that night. Arriving in Richmond the first week of January, she had only heard the stories; but the visions of the fire had haunted hcr dreams for many nights. "I'm glad Janie had someone with her." Her heart beat faster at the thought of being in the clinic by herself. "I don't know that I'll ever feel comfortable in the clinic alone again," she admitted, hating the fear she heard in her voice.

"I hope you won't," Anthony said firmly. "I can promise you I'll make sure that Carrie never is."

Elizabeth managed a small smile as she thought of her independent, strong-willed friend. "I'm sure she'll love that."

"She was smart enough to not go into the clinic by herself this morning," Anthony reminded her. "I'm confident she'll know being alone at the clinic isn't a good idea."

Elizabeth frowned, not able to keep herself from returning to their earlier conversation. "Do you believe it will always be like this? That we'll always have to be afraid of the clinic being destroyed? Just because we're women?" Her head began to pound. "Or wondering if someone is going to attack us like they did Harriet and Ann?"

The angry look on Anthony's face was the only answer she needed. She put a hand on his arm, suddenly not willing to have him put his anger into words. "Please don't answer that." There was no need for him to tell her what she already suspected.

Anthony turned to gaze searchingly into her face. He reached out to squeeze her hand, nodded, and remained silent.

"Elizabeth!"

Janie hurried down the walkway, her hands outstretched.

Elizabeth felt tears prick her eyes. "Janie," she murmured, welcoming the warm hug from her friend.

"Carrie?" Janie asked when she finally pulled away.

"She's staying with Harriet."

Janie needed no more explanation. "She's the best one to be there when Harriet wakes up."

Elizabeth knew they both understood there was nothing Carrie could say to alleviate Harriet's pain. Knowing Carrie understood would be enough.

A motion behind Janie made Elizabeth look up.

Janie followed her gaze. "Peter, come meet Elizabeth."

Elizabeth stared up at the tall, handsome man striding down the walkway with a concerned expression on his face.

"Elizabeth, this is Peter Wilcher. He's a good friend of Matthews from long ago. He's since become a good friend to all of us. Peter has been helping since he arrived several hours ago," Janie continued. "He even won Darlene over."

Elizabeth smiled, aware that her heart was beating faster. She was suddenly aware of how she must look. She was exhausted, her hair was a mess, and her dress was splattered with Ann's blood. She fought to keep her voice natural. "You passed quite a test, Peter. Darlene refused earlier to have any men help with the cleanup."

"She told me," Peter said easily. "After Janie asked if I would help, Darlene told me in no uncertain terms that it was men who had created the destruction, but it would be women who cleaned it up."

"So, how *did* you convince her?" Elizabeth was intrigued with how the tall Yankee with the New York accent had charmed Darlene. Of course, it was probably his dark eyes that still flashed with amusement after what must have been an excruciatingly long day. It would be difficult for any woman to resist them.

"I told her I would clean the storage closet."

Elizabeth stared at him with disbelief. The men who had destroyed the clinic had added insult to injury by urinating all over the storage closet. No one in their right mind would have volunteered to clean it. She cocked her head as she examined him. He met her gaze unflinchingly. "That would have won *me* over," she finally replied.

Peter laughed. "I knew I had to offer something drastic before she threw me out."

Another question sprang to Elizabeth's mind. "How did you know what had happened to the storage closet?"

Peter had the grace to look embarrassed. "Matthew might have whispered it to me when I came in. Said I would need it as leverage to stay."

Elizabeth laughed as a grin replaced the embarrassment. Her fatigue was suddenly forgotten.

Elizabeth stepped out onto the porch and inhaled the aroma of the magnolia tree. Dim light from the oil lamps lining the street cast a soft glow to the night. Spencer and Anthony had just driven off to bring Carrie home. Matthew and Janie had opted to stay home with their children after their long day.

"It's a beautiful night."

Elizabeth looked up with a smile as Peter stepped out onto the porch. "It certainly is."

She'd been delighted when Peter had informed her that he stayed at Thomas' house when he was in town on business or pleasure. As suspected, dinner had been a barrage of questions from May, Micah and Spencer. She didn't have the answer to most of them, but at least she'd been able to assure them that both Harriet and Ann would recover from their beating.

"You must be tired," Peter said. He settled down on the porch swing. "Care to join me?"

"Thank you," Elizabeth murmured politely, all too aware of her racing pulse. At the end of such a long, difficult day, she should have been completely exhausted. Instead, his appearance on the porch had energized her. She'd never had this reaction to a man. She had certainly had several men court her, but none of them had captured her attention more than her medical studies. She wasn't sure if she was amused or irritated by the fact that Peter seemed different.

"You're Italian," Peter observed. "The dark hair, olive complexion and dark eyes are a dead giveaway. And you're not from the South."

"Yes, to both things," Elizabeth agreed lightly. "I'm from Boston."

Peter raised a brow. "How are you enjoying your stay in the South?"

Elizabeth cocked her brow in response. "Perhaps today is not the best day to ask me that question?"

Peter laughed and changed the subject, quickly understanding she didn't want to talk about the events of the day anymore. "Is your family in Boston?"

"Yes. My father is a doctor. My mother keeps him sane and seems to raise more money for Women's Rights than any other woman in the city."

Peter smiled. "No wonder you're such good friends with Carrie and Janie."

"We share quite a bit in common," Elizabeth agreed. "When they decided to start the clinic here, and then invited me to join them, I agreed immediately." She saw him open his mouth to ask if she regretted her decision, but he closed it quickly. "My parents supported my decision. Even after what I almost did." She had no idea why she added the last comment, but there was something about Peter that made her determined to tell the truth.

Peter's brow went up again. "After what you almost did?"

"I ended my friendship with Carrie and Janie when they decided to embrace Homeopathy."

Peter cocked his head, but remained silent as he waited for her to finish the story.

"Traditional medicine was all I knew," Elizabeth continued, impressed that he hadn't immediately started to ply her with questions. "I believed the medical experts who told me Homeopathy was harmful and bad for the medical profession. I thought Carrie and Janie were betraying all they had learned. I saw how they were helping the people down in Moyamensing when the cholera epidemic came through Philadelphia, but I was too stubborn to reconsider my beliefs."

"You obviously came around," Peter said quietly.

Elizabeth felt a rush of gratitude that there was no judgement in his eyes. "I did," she agreed. "It wasn't just me that ended my friendship with Carrie and Janie, however. Florence did, as well..."

"The doctor who was caught up in the Paris Siege and ended up marrying a fellow American doctor," Peter asked. "I didn't know she was estranged from Carrie and Janie at one point."

"Yes, but there was also Alice."

Peter shook his head with confusion, but then his eyes cleared. "Wasn't she the one that was committed..." his voice trailed off as he tried to remember the details.

"By her stupid excuse of a husband? Committed to an insane asylum?" Elizabeth flushed with anger as she remembered. "Yes. I was so desperate to help Alice that I went to Carrie for help. I was sure Abby's connections in New York City would help us free her." She looked down for a moment, and then gazed back up into Peter's eyes. "In spite of how we turned from her and Janie, she graciously agreed to help. She was mortified and furious about what had happened to Alice. Without Carrie, Alice might still be locked up."

"That sounds like Carrie," Peter agreed. He looked at her more closely. "How do you feel about Homeopathy now?"

"Grateful that it exists," Elizabeth replied. "I'm also thankful for my training in more traditional medicine. I believe there's a place for both, though I easily admit I rely very heavily on Homeopathy and herbal medicines now. There are far too many quack remedies springing up on the market that do far more harm than good. The emphasis is on profit, rather than effectiveness. It's hard to hurt someone with lavender, comfrey and yarrow."

Peter nodded his agreement. "The three of you are doing wonderful things here in Richmond," he said warmly.

Elizabeth tensed when he tried to steer the conversation back to the clinic. She wasn't ready to think about it yet. "Tell me about you, Peter."

"Certainly. I'm a New Yorker, born and bred. My grandfather came over from Scotland before my father was born. He started out as your classic penniless immigrant, but he worked hard and built a successful business in New York City."

"Doing what?" Elizabeth loved to hear stories of success.

"He became a jeweler," Peter said proudly. "He started out just sweeping floors in a jewelry store, but he was determined to learn. He studied every book and article he could find, and asked thousands of questions." He smiled broadly. "The endless questions almost drove the owner crazy, but they also convinced him my grandfather was determined to succeed. He taught him everything he knew, and then willed the store to him when he passed away. My grandfather turned it into one of the most successful jewelry stores in Manhattan."

Elizabeth returned his smile. "And your father?"

"He followed in his father's footsteps. The two worked together for almost thirty years. Grandpa finally decided to retire a few years ago. If you want to call it that," he said fondly. "He still goes to the store almost every day, but he's passed off all the business issues to my father. The store has continued to thrive under my father's leadership. They're both happy, and Grandpa gets to spend a lot of time with his grandchildren now."

Elizabeth watched his face, impressed with the obvious love he had for his family. The comment about grandchildren gave her the open door she wanted. No one had indicated Peter was married, but no one had confirmed he wasn't, either. "Are any of the grandchildren yours?" she asked casually.

Pain flitted across Peter's face. "No. My wife and child both died several years ago from influenza while I was away covering a story."

"I'm so sorry," Elizabeth replied. She could only imagine how difficult it must have been to return home and discover his entire family was gone.

"Thank you," Peter said, shaking his head slightly. "I was blessed to have them in my life for as long as I did."

It was clear to Elizabeth that he didn't want to talk about his wife and child; any more than she wanted to talk about what had happened at the clinic. "Your grandfather and father didn't mind that you followed another path than the jewelry store?"

"No," he said quickly, flashing her a look of gratitude for understanding. "I think they both would have loved it, but they wanted me to do what I'm passionate about. Besides, I have two younger brothers who are filling in the gap. Someday, the store will become theirs. It works for all of us."

Elizabeth was intrigued by the man next to her that was so obviously intelligent and caring. It certainly didn't hurt that he was handsome. She wanted to know more about him. "Why journalism?"

"Because the truth has to be told," Peter said immediately. "I've seen far too many instances where journalism is used to promote someone's agenda. The news is supposed to report what has *happened*, not be fictionalized to support what someone *wants* to happen."

"You believe that's done?"

"More than anyone knows," Peter said grimly.

Elizabeth was confused. "Why would reporters make up news?"

Peter grimaced. "Money. Is there ever another reason? Reporters get paid to produce news. If they have a story that goes big, they'll be paid more. There are also reporters who receive payment for writing what a successful businessman or politician wants them to report." He paused for a long moment. "It's more than that, though. Reporters are humans. Humans with their own beliefs, agendas and prejudices. Too often, they use reporting the news to promote that. They take stories and twist them. They add facts that aren't really facts, or they ignore facts that don't promote what they want."

"They're using journalism as a weapon," Elizabeth said flatly. "I've read articles about how dangerous women doctors are. Articles that say we aren't trained as well as male doctors. Articles that say women aren't suited to be doctors." Her eyes flashed. "None of it's true, but when people read it in the newspaper, they believe it."

"You're right," Peter agreed. "There are reporters who use journalism as a weapon, without taking into consideration the long-term consequences."

"Or, perhaps they do, and they simply don't care."

Peter nodded his head to signal his agreement. "I wanted to be a voice of truth," he added.

"Does the *New York Tribune* try to get you to report news a certain way?"

"No," Peter said quickly. "They give me freedom to report the news the way I see it."

Elizabeth watched his face; not missing the flash in his eyes. "But they don't always *publish* the way you see it."

Peter gazed at her silently for a long minute. "You're very perceptive," he finally said, and then sighed. "It's true they don't always publish what I write. Is that because there are other more important things to publish, or because what I write doesn't support what they want to put out to the world?" He shook his head. "I'm not always sure. I suspect it's a mixture of both. I am grateful, however, that they publish *most* of what I write."

Elizabeth decided to change the subject. "How did you and Matthew meet? At a newspaper?"

Peter laughed. "No. We met during the war. We were both esteemed guests of Libby Prison."

Elizabeth stared at him. "You were a prisoner with Matthew here in Richmond?" She'd heard the stories, but hadn't heard Peter's name in connection to them.

"Yes. We also decided to *not* be prisoners together."

"You were part of the escape." Elizabeth thought about everything she had heard in regard to a group of men who broke out of Libby Prison after Matthew and some others dug a tunnel. "Did you help dig the tunnel?"

"I was and I did," Peter replied, a shadow crossing his eyes. "I was happy to relinquish my spot at the esteemed prison." He took a deep breath. "Since then, Matthew and I have worked together on many issues, but mostly he's just my good friend."

Elizabeth read the pain in his eyes. She fell silent, letting the night wrap its magic around them. Even though she could hear the train whistles and sounds from the factories floating up Church Hill, it was still beautiful.

"Do you miss Boston?" Peter asked.

"Every day," Elizabeth admitted. "The South is beautiful, but I miss the people in the North."

"Especially after a day like today," Peter said quietly, once again offering her an open door to talk.

Elizabeth drew a deep breath, finally able to entertain the subject. "Yes. Especially after a day like today. Carrie and Janie tried to warn me how different the South is, but I had no point of reference to understand. The North has its share of bigotry and prejudice, but it's nothing like down here. Southerners seem to hate everyone who isn't white, from the South, or willing to stay in the roles defined for them."

"That puts a lot of strikes against you," Peter commented.

Elizabeth laughed. "It does. An Italian, Yankee women daring to be a doctor most certainly does not make them happy."

"Neither do Southern women who dare to be doctors."

Elizabeth nodded thoughtfully. "In some ways, I think they hate Carrie and Janie more than they do me. They just chalk my stupidity up to being an Italian Yankee. They're more offended because Carrie and Janie are one of their own. Richmonders believe they should know better." She managed a smile.

"Your father has been quite successful," Peter commented.

"For an Italian?" Elizabeth asked. The question came out in a teasing tone of voice, but she could feel her insides tensing.

"For an Italian in a country that is so quick to believe erroneous stereotypes," Peter said evenly.

Elizabeth took a deep breath. "I'm sorry. It's a sore subject."

"It should be," Peter replied. "Despite the fact that our entire country is comprised of immigrants, too many Americans take pleasure in diminishing new groups of people who come here. I see it happen to the Irish. To Italians. To Jews." He shrugged. "Really, just about any group that doesn't fit the anglicized white version of the original settlers."

"Yet this country needs the labor of all those people they look down on," Elizabeth said angrily. She shook her head. "My father was like your grandfather. He was just a boy when he came here, completely penniless. My grandparents were poor farmers from the South of Italy. They died when he was just ten from influenza. He survived on the streets of New York by begging and working for almost nothing. He slept in any empty building he could find. Somehow, he got an education and became a doctor. He doesn't like to talk about it very much."

"Gilbert?"

Elizabeth nodded. "Our family name is Gilberto. He changed it to Gilbert before he went to medical school." She smiled. "I'm proud of being Italian."

"As you should be," Peter said, his eyes regarding her warmly.

Elizabeth's anger melted away.

Peter fell silent for another long moment. "Have you talked about what you're going to do with the clinic?"

Elizabeth tensed. "No." It was all she could bring herself to say as she fought the vision of the destroyed clinic. Just yesterday, they had laughed with, talked to, and treated over thirty patients. After they'd locked up, men had come in and destroyed everything they had worked so hard to build. The fear she had attempted to hold at bay most of the day came rushing back in.

Peter reached over and took one of her trembling hands in his own, grasping it firmly.

Elizabeth was surprised but didn't draw away. She didn't understand what she was feeling in regard to the handsome journalist, but after the long day, she relished the warm contact.

Chapter Four

Willard took deep breaths of the morning air as he strode up the hill toward River City Carriages. He wasn't due in to work for another two hours, but he had woken early. Going into work early was better than staying in a house that still echoed with Grace's presence. There were hours when he thought he could breathe normally again, but then a memory would crush down on him like an avalanche, stealing away the precious breath. At moments like that, all he could do was double-over from the grief and pray for it to pass quickly.

Being in the house was almost more agony than he could stand. Her smell. Her belongings. The memories that filled every corner. Every day, he thought about selling the house and moving away, but something inside told him leaving would not free him from the memories or the pain. Or the nightmares.

His dreams were still full of flames and screams. He suspected the sound of Grace burning to death would never truly leave him. He shuddered as he reached the barn, amazed that the memory of the dream could make him smell actual smoke.

A stronger smell of smoke wafted to him on the breeze. His eyes narrowed as he stared into the early dawn. A puff of smoke appeared in front of him as a faint orange glow split the darkness.

Willard froze for a moment and then sprinted to the stables. As he rounded the corner closest to the road, he saw the silhouettes of four men walking briskly down the alley that ran behind the long wooden structure. "Stop!"

He heard one of the men curse as the four of them spun in his direction. A second later, they whirled back around and burst into a run.

Willard gritted his teeth as he spotted the growing flames from a pile of lumber at the base of the stables. He wanted to chase the men, but he had no idea what he would actually do if he caught them. He was heavily outnumbered.

The shrill whinny of a horse on the other side of the burning wood brought him back to reality. The only important thing was to put out the fire. He had to save the stable and horses.

Stripping off his jacket, Willard ran forward. He kicked at the wood with his booted feet, sending the burning pieces into the dirt alley. The strong smell of kerosene revealed what had ignited them, and what was making them burn so quickly. One by one, he beat the flames out with his jacket. Once he had the flames extinguished, he ran into the barn for a bucket of water. It took several trips before every piece of wood was saturated to his satisfaction.

While he worked, he kept his eye on the alley. Would the men suspect he was alone? What if they regrouped and came back to finish what they'd started? Once he was confident any remaining sparks wouldn't ignite a fresh flame, he dashed into the barn, quickly unlocked the door to Anthony's office, reached into the desk drawer for the revolver that was kept there, and then ran back out to the alley.

Willard knew this was the work of whomever had left the note the day before. Evidently, destroying the clinic hadn't been enough. They were intent on destroying River City Carriages, as well.

Looking around carefully, he chose a hidden niche on the other side of the alley that would allow him to keep an eye out for anyone approaching from either direction. Sinking down on the ground, he waited... and watched.

Anthony was tense as he walked to the stables. He was starting his day early so he could be back at the house in time for breakfast. He presumed there was going to be an important conversation between Carrie, Janie and Elizabeth. He didn't want to miss it, yet he felt the urge to check on things at River City Carriages.

He had left Carrie sleeping peacefully, but a restless night meant she was going to be tired. Her mutterings as she tossed and turned told him she was agonizing over what had happened at the clinic. Loathe to wake her after she had finally fallen into a deep sleep, he had written a note, kissed her softly on the forehead and slipped out the door quietly.

Not wanting to be caught unaware by a surprise attack, he kept his eyes moving and looked behind him often so that no one would be able to slip up on him. His mind was focused on the letter he had received the day before. No one knew about it except himself, Willard and Marcus. There had been no need to add any more worry after the attack on the clinic, and on Harriet and Ann.

He patted his waistband to assure himself his pistol was snugged securely in his pants. He seldom carried his weapon, but now was not a time to be caught unarmed.

Anthony reached the stable without any trouble. He breathed a sigh of relief as he stepped forward to walk through the door.

"Anthony!"

Anthony stiffened as Willard's voice rang through the still air. It was early enough that other business owners were still a few hours away from arriving for work. "Willard?"

Willard appeared from behind the barn, the stable's revolver in his hand. His face and shirt were smudged with soot and his hands were black.

"What happened?" Anthony asked sharply.

"Someone tried to burn down the stables," Willard said angrily, and then explained what had happened.

"You're alright?" Anthony asked, his eyes searching the surrounding area for signs of more trouble.

"I'm fine," Willard said impatiently. "I wish I could have caught those cowards."

"I'm glad you didn't," Anthony said quietly. "Four against one are not good odds. Even cowards can be dangerous when they're backed into a corner." He reached out to grasp Willard's shoulder. "Thank you for saving the stables."

Willard shrugged, but met his eyes squarely. "You're welcome. The stables are important to a lot of people. To a lot of families."

Anthony's stomach clinched at the thought of what could have happened. The stables were full of horses that would have died horrific deaths if Willard had not put out the fire. Destroying the clinic was one thing – burning close to one hundred horses to death was another. His throat burned with anger. "What were you doing here so early?"

"I couldn't sleep," Willard responded. "I figured I might as well come into work early."

Anthony knew what he wasn't saying – that he wasn't able to face being alone in the house without Grace. Fire had taken his wife. Fire had almost taken his livelihood as well.

His anger burned hotter. Images of the destroyed clinic filled his mind, and then were replaced by images of what could have happened. With no one out and about so early in the morning, the fire would have been out of control before anyone sounded the alarm. By the time the fire engines could have arrived, the horses would have been dead, and everything else smoldering. His heart pounded as he realized what could have happened.

"All this just because Carrie, Janie and Elizabeth want to help the people of Richmond?" Willard asked with disbelief. "What's wrong with people?"

"I wish I could tell you," Anthony said heavily, thinking of his conversation with Elizabeth the day before. He forced his mind to think clearly. Letting anger muddle his thoughts wouldn't help anyone. "The important thing right now is to figure out how to keep it from happening again."

"The Black Militia," Willard said instantly. "Many of them are our drivers. They'll come down here to protect the stables."

Anthony shook his head. "You're right, but I fear their presence would just add fuel to the flames. The destruction of the clinic was an attack on the women, but the attack on the stables was about more than that. The Bregdan Medical Clinic may have prompted the note we received yesterday, but attacking Harriet and Ann showed it's equally a racial thing. We've all assumed they were attacked because they were on the way to the clinic, but how would anyone have known that?" He had lain awake for hours thinking about it. "If there is going to be a new series of attacks on Richmond blacks, then surrounding the stable with black men may create even more negative consequences."

"What are we going to do?" Willard ground out, his jaw clenched with fury.

Unfortunately, Anthony didn't have an answer. "We're going to call all the drivers in when they arrive for their shift in a little while and tell them what happened. We'll come up with an answer together." He pulled his pocket watch out and glanced at the time. There wasn't much chance he would be back to the house for breakfast, but it couldn't be helped.

Carrie was on the front porch, relaxing in the swing, when Matthew and Janie arrived with Robert and Annabelle. "Good morning," she called as they started up the walkway, relieved to hear her voice sound mostly normal after a night of little sleep.

"Good morning," Janie called back.

Carrie looked at her friend closely, recognizing the same bleary eyes she'd seen staring back at her from the mirror earlier. "You didn't sleep any better than I did."

"I suppose I didn't," Janie said wearily. "I hope May has some strong coffee."

"Just happen to have some right here," May said cheerfully as she pushed through the screen door holding a tray with three coffee cups.

Janie stared at her. "How did you know to bring three cups?"

"Ain't nothing magical about that," Micah said as he followed close behind her. "You lived here long enough to know that May sees every person walking down this street. Did you think you were going to sneak up on her?" He rolled his eyes. "Now, you bring those children to me."

"Micah!" Robert squealed as he launched himself into Micah's outstretched arms.

"That's right, little man," Micah said, his face glowing with happiness. "You come on inside. I gots a new game for us to play with."

"Yea!" Robert shouted. Without a backward glance, he turned and ran into the house.

May watched them go and then turned back to Matthew. "Now, I'll give you this tray of coffee if you give me my little girl."

Annabelle was staring at May with a wide grin, holding out her arms to be scooped up. Matthew handed her over willingly. "I'm not sure if the best part of coming here is the food or the childcare."

May snorted and pulled Annabelle close, grinning when the little girl laughed with delight. "I'll get the rest of breakfast ready as soon as I've had me a little Annabelle time," she announced. Moments later the screen door slapped shut.

Carrie's smile wasn't forced this time. "You just made Micah and May very happy."

"As well as Robert and Annabelle," Matthew confirmed. "Robert asks about them all the time. Sometimes I think we should move back in."

"That's the first good idea that head of yours is had for a while!"

Matthew laughed as May's voice floated to them from the house.

Carrie reached for the closest cup of steaming coffee and inhaled the aroma. She took a sip and closed her eyes. "I just might live," she moaned.

Janie followed suit, taking several sips before she opened her eyes. "The jury is still out on that one," she said wearily.

Matthew watched her sympathetically. "It took her a long time to drift into real sleep. Minutes later, Annabelle woke up demanding to be fed. I can help with a lot of things, but I'm rather limited in that area," he said with a grin.

"I couldn't go back to sleep after that," Janie admitted. "I..." Her voice trailed off.

Carrie knew what Janie was going to say, even though she stopped herself. "You couldn't go back to sleep because you didn't want to have any more dreams."

Janie met her eyes and nodded. "You too?"

"And me three." Elizabeth walked through the door; a cup of coffee clutched in her hands. Her normally cheerful face was lined with fatigue. "Where is Anthony?"

Carrie glanced down the road. "He went to the stables. He left a note saying he would be back for breakfast." She pushed down the feeling of uneasiness, hoping it was residue from the day before.

Anthony looked at the fifty men standing in the stable breezeway. When the barn had been built, he had positioned it so it would catch the breeze coming up from the river. There were large openings at both the front and back of the stalls. They stayed open throughout the day, with the back wooden windows closed only at night. Richmond summers and winters could be brutal, but he made sure the horses were as comfortable as possible. The blankets that covered the horses during the frigid months had been put away for the summer.

The men looking back at him, almost equal numbers of blacks and whites, had all proven themselves to be good and loyal workers.

"What's going on, Mr. Anthony?"

Anthony knew they were wondering why he had called them together instead of dispatching them to the streets. He smiled at the man who had asked. "It's Ricky, right?"

"Yessir, Mr. Anthony."

"You're new, aren't you?"

"Yessir. I started right before you left for the plantation two weeks ago."

Anthony nodded. "Well, someone tried to destroy your job last night," he said grimly.

Ricky's eyes widened at the exact moment forty-nine other pairs of eyes widened.

Striving to keep his voice even, Anthony told them what happened that morning. When he had filled them in on all the details he knew, he finished with, "If Willard hadn't come in to work early, River City Carriages would have been destroyed," he said grimly.

"Why?" An angry voice rang through the thick tension.

Anthony looked at Clayton, one of his first drivers. He had decided to tell them the whole truth. Keeping things from them wouldn't allow them to help create an answer.

Willard and Marcus watched from their position just outside the stable door. They'd wanted to be part of the meeting but were also watching for trouble.

Anthony reached into his pocket and pulled out the letter.

You got to stop your wife and those other women doctors. If you don't, River City Carriages will pay the price.

He lowered the letter and waited for the questions.

After a long moment of stunned quiet, Clayton was the first to speak. "I heard about the attack on the clinic yesterday. Is it as bad as I heard?"

"Yes." Anthony saw no reason to elaborate. He knew how the grapevine worked in the Black Quarters. He was sure the story had been complete.

"Is that why Harriet and Ann were beaten?" Clayton asked, his voice hard with anger.

"We don't know for sure," Anthony replied. "We assumed so, at first, but we're not sure the attackers had any way of knowing they were coming to the clinic to see the doctors."

A long silence followed this statement. He could see the men trying to analyze what his words meant.

"So... you be wondering if some whites just feel like beating up black people?"

Anthony locked eyes with Hector. The beefy black driver had worked for him at Cromwell Factory before it was burned to the ground. He knew the man to be both intelligent and thoughtful. "Yes."

Hector tightened his lips. "My first thought might not be so good then. I figured we could handle it by have the Black Militia watch over the stables. If you're thinking what you're thinking though, then it could just stir things up worse. Having the Black Militia watch over the Black Quarters is one thing." He paused. "Having them come into the white part of town could make it get more ugly." His eyes flashed with frustration.

"That's what I'm afraid of," Anthony agreed, grateful Hector realized the same thing. Hearing it from one of their own would make it easier for the other black drivers to accept.

"Then it's up to us."

Anthony looked over as Walter spoke. In his mid-thirties, Walter was medium height, but was strong and sinewy. Blue eyes gazed at him from beneath shaggy brown hair. A Confederate veteran, it had taken him time to adjust to working with blacks when he had been hired six months earlier, but once he had realized they were all just men trying to survive, his attitude changed. He and Hector were close friends.

"I can't ask that of anyone," Anthony protested. "I called you together because Marcus, Willard and I don't know the answer to our problem. Since this business exists because of your hard work, and because you benefit from the profits, we believed you should be a part of figuring out what to do."

"Ain't nothing confusing about the answer, Mr. Anthony," Walter said firmly. "If those fellas had burned down the stables, none of us would have a job. We wouldn't be able to support our families. I don't reckon it matters *why* they're intent on burning it down. It only matters that we don't let it happen."

Anthony agreed with him, but he knew it would be putting a lot on the men who would be driving during the day and protecting the stable at night.

Walter read his mind. "We've heard the stories about what it's like out on Cromwell Plantation. Those fellas work the fields all day and then take turns keeping guard at night. They're protecting what's theirs, and they're protecting their families." He rose and looked at the other white men gathered around. "It's up to us to make sure we protect what's ours. We got a bunch of stupid men who want to destroy our livelihood. It doesn't matter whether they're black or white. We can stop them. Are you with me?"

"Yes!"

Anthony watched every man in the breezeway. Without exception, they nodded their heads and spoke in unison.

Clayton stood next. "If we can't send the Black Militia down or show up ourselves to make sure nothing else happens, we can at least make sure it's the black drivers who take the early shift. That way, all the guards can get some sleep before they have to work the rest of the day and night."

"Thank you," Anthony said hoarsely, grateful emotion clogging his throat.

Walter shook his head. "Ain't nothing to thank us for, Mr. Anthony. Without you, we wouldn't have a job. And if we did, it wouldn't pay much. You've given us a job and you pay us real well. Besides that, you treat us right. We ain't gonna let someone take that away from us."

Anthony watched, the lump in his throat growing bigger, as every man in the breezeway rose to their feet – both black and white – their faces set with determination. He locked eyes with Willard and Marcus, knowing they were thinking the same thing.

Marcus spoke for all of them. "You give us hope," he said firmly. "The whole country seems to be going crazy right now. At least here, at River City Carriages, we're showing what can happen if we all just choose to work together."

Ricky cleared his throat. "I'll admit that when I started here a few weeks ago, I didn't know what it would be like. I ain't never worked with white men before. The only white folks I really knew were the ones who owned me before the war, and the overseer that beat me when he felt like it." His voice was more matter-of-fact than bitter. "I needed a job, and I knew you treated people right, Mr. Anthony, so I decided to take the job." His gaze swept the breezeway. "I've done learned a lot. All of us ain't nothing more than men trying to take care of ourselves and provide for our families. The color of our skin don't really matter. I ain't been treated with nothing but respect by everyone here. Just seems to make sense because if we all work to make River City Carriages the best it can be, it helps us all. I don't see nothing black or white about that."

Anthony smiled. "Thank you, Ricky. You've described the work environment we're striving to create." He paused for a moment and then answered the question he knew was in everyone's mind. "I don't know how long it's going to be necessary to protect the stables."

"Don't matter," Clayton said easily. "I done heard the men out at Cromwell been doing it for a few years now. All of us be making more money than we ever dreamed of making. If the time comes when it seems a good idea for the black drivers to act as guards, we'll step up. You can count on us to do whatever it takes."

Every head nodded their agreement. "Whatever it takes," they echoed.

May appeared at the porch door. "I done held breakfast as long as I can for Mr. Anthony. If y'all want food while it's hot, you're gonna have to come eat it now."

Carrie stood. "Of course. We'll come eat now. Anthony wouldn't want the meal you cooked to be ruined."

May fixed her with a knowing eye. "You worried about that man of yours?"

Carrie started to shake her head but knew no one watching her would be convinced. "After yesterday, I suppose I'm worried about everything." She looked down the road again, hoping to see Anthony's tall, slender shape moving toward her. Once again, the road was devoid of life.

"Do you want to all walk over to River City Carriages?" Peter asked quietly. "Eating a hot meal isn't as important as making sure Anthony is alright."

Carrie hesitated, not wanting to give into the fears that had kept her awake most of the night. She had no way of knowing what might be going on at River City Carriages, as any growing business could create demands that had nothing to do with danger. If something more had happened at the clinic, she didn't really want to know about it right then. *Something more* could only mean they'd burnt it to the ground. Eating breakfast wouldn't change the outcome of that. "No," she finally said. "Let's eat. I'm sure Anthony will be here soon."

The smell of bacon assaulted them as they walked in the door.

"There is no better smell in the world," Elizabeth moaned. "One of my most favorite memories from childhood is walking along the beaches near Boston when my family went for the summer months. Early in the morning, the smell of frying bacon seemed to almost envelop me. There was nothing better than walking next to the ocean, swallowed by the smell of bacon."

Peter laughed. "Are you going to swoon now? I don't believe I've ever heard such devotion to bacon."

Elizabeth glared at him. "I pity your lack of passion, Mr. New Yorker. Obviously, you've never had the privilege of my experience."

Peter laughed harder. "Guilty as charged." His expression changed. "Will you share it with me someday?"

Elizabeth flushed as she considered the question. "Only if you accept it with the serious consideration it is due," she replied. "I will not have an antagonist accompany me on a beach walk."

"I promise to accept it with completely serious consideration," Peter said solemnly, his lips twitching. "If I have the same religious experience you've had, I will even write an article about it."

Elizabeth nodded her head. "I will consider sharing it with you some day," she said primly.

Carrie swallowed her laughter and exchanged a look with Janie. Janie grinned, confirming she agreed with what Carrie saw happening between Peter and Elizabeth.

"If y'all have finished prattling on about bacon, it's ready for you to eat!"

May's indignant voice made them all laugh and hurry into the house.

Peter rubbed his hands together with a smile as they approached the table. "May, you never cease to thrill me with your cooking. I love Richmond for many reasons, but your cooking is at the top of my list."

May ducked her head, but not before Carrie saw the pleased smile on her lips.

The table was almost groaning beneath platters of fluffy pancakes, bottles of delicious maple syrup that Elizabeth's parents had sent them from a trip to Vermont, plates of crisp bacon, and fresh pots of coffee.

"There's only ten of us," Carrie protested. "That's enough food for half of Richmond!"

May shrugged. "When Mr. Anthony gets here, he'll eat enough for a bunch of normal people. Besides, you never know when company might come."

Carrie narrowed her eyes, alerted by something in May's voice. "Are we expecting company, May?"

"Now did I say that?" May demanded. "No." She waved her arm. "Sit down at the table and eat before that meal be plum cold!"

Carrie sat but didn't stop watching the housekeeper. "Don't think I don't realize you didn't answer my question, May."

May snorted and turned away. "I got me some bread rising in the kitchen. The rest of y'all might be able to sit around like lazy folks, but I got work to do."

Laughter followed her as she disappeared through the swinging door.

"Make sure you come out and eat with us when you've checked on the bread," Carrie called just before the door swung shut. "And send Micah and Spencer."

Carrie was finishing her pancakes when she heard the screen door open and close. Her fork froze on its way to her mouth as she waited to see who had arrived.

"Is there any food left, or did you vultures eat it all?" Anthony's cheerful voice rang through the house.

Carrie sagged with relief, but then tensed again when she saw her husband's face as he rounded the corner into the dining room. His voice was cheerful, but his eyes told a different story.

Everyone at the table saw the same thing.

"What happened?" Matthew asked. "We left you some food. You can sit down and eat, but only if you tell us what's wrong."

Anthony stopped in his tracks with a frown. "I'm not sure if it's a good thing or a bad thing that all of you know me so well."

"It's a good thing," Carrie said gently. She reached up and took her husband's hand, studying his troubled green eyes. "Sit down and eat something. Then you can talk to us."

Anthony sat, stared at the food, and then looked up. "I'm afraid I have no appetite."

Carrie's heart sank. "Tell us."

Anthony took a deep breath and then looked around the table. "Someone tried to burn down River City Carriages this morning."

Carrie gasped and covered her mouth with her hand. Stunned expressions and exclamations of dismay erupted from every mouth.

May slammed through the kitchen door, Micah and Spencer on her heels. "What you talking about, Mr. Anthony?"

Anthony told the story in a grim, tight voice, not leaving out any details. "If Willard hadn't been there, everything would have been destroyed."

"All the horses?" Carrie cried. "They would have burned all the *horses*?" Horror was etched on her face. "Why?"

Anthony took another deep breath. "I hoped you would never need to know."

Carrie looked at him wildly. "Know what? What else is there?" Her heart was pounding so hard she wasn't sure she could continue to breathe. The clinic. And now the stables. "Know what?" she repeated, louder this time.

Anthony grimaced and pulled out the note. He read it aloud for the third time in twenty-four hours.

You got to stop your wife and those other women doctors. If you don't, River City Carriages will pay the price.

Carrie's breath left her in a shuddering gush. "Because of us?" she managed to whisper.

"They were going to destroy the stable and all the beautiful horses?" Elizabeth cried. "Why?"

Janie sat silently, tears running down her cheeks. Suddenly, she began to shake all over. "They win," she said hollowly. "They win."

Matthew leaned over and wrapped his arms around Janie's slender body, his face etched with concern.

"Mama?" Robert had just walked into the room. His blue eyes were wide with fear and uncertainty. "Mama? What's wrong?" He ran forward and wrapped his arms around her legs.

Janie straightened. While the trembling didn't stop, she was somehow able to keep her voice steady. "I'm alright, Robert. I just got some bad news." She looked over his head. "Will you take him out to play, Micah?"

Micah nodded instantly and walked forward to scoop Robert up in his arms. "I have a surprise out back for you, Robert. Do you want to come see?"

Robert looked doubtful as he reached out a hand to his mother. "Mama?"

Janie smiled. "I'm alright, honey. I think you should go see what kind of surprise Micah has for you. I bet it's a good one."

Carrie knew she was watching the strength of a mother's love.

Robert still looked doubtful, but he stared up into the old man's face. "Is it a good surprise, Micah?"

Micah shrugged. "You remember Calico Girl?"

"The kitty?"

"Yep," Micah said solemnly. He lowered his voice as he leaned down closer to the little boy. "Calico Girl might just have had some kittens out back in the barn."

Robert's eyes widened. "Kittens?" he breathed. "Really?" He started to nod his head, but then looked back at Janie.

"Go with him," Janie urged. "It will make me very happy to think of you out there with the kittens."

Robert still stared at her for a long moment, and then looked up at Micah with a serious expression. "What about Annabelle?"

"Miss Annabelle is coming with us, too," Micah replied. "She's finishing up some milk in the kitchen. We're going to get her on the way outside."

Robert finally nodded. "I want to see the kittens."

As soon as Micah disappeared through the door, Janie laid her head down on the table and burst into sobs. "I... can't... do... this," she said in between gasps.

Carrie felt the tears rolling down her face. She did nothing to stop them. She'd faced opposition before, but nothing that had prepared her for the last twenty-four hours. Was it really just the morning before when she had walked toward the clinic with such excitement and anticipation? It seemed like a lifetime ago.

All she felt now was fear and dread.

Chapter Five

Elizabeth pushed back from the table and stood. Her slender figure was rigid with defiance as her dark eyes flashed. "We are not going to let them win," she declared.

Janie continued to sob, not giving any evidence that she'd heard.

Carrie stared at Elizabeth with dazed eyes. She was silent, but slowly began to shake her head. "I'm afraid," she finally whispered. "The clinic... Harriet and Ann... and now River City Carriages and all the horses..." Her voice trailed off on a note of despair.

"They weren't hurt," Elizabeth said, fighting to hold on to the spark of hope she felt. It was hard in the face of Janie and Carrie's obvious devastation. "Willard stopped it," she reminded her.

"This time," Carrie said in a broken voice. "*This time.* They'll come back." Her voice was audible. "They'll keep coming back to the clinic to destroy it if we try to rebuild. They'll keep coming back to River City Carriages." Her voice rose. "They'll hurt our patients. They'll kill the beautiful horses. They won't give up until we quit." She shook her head harder, the movement becoming frantic as her dark curls exploded from her bun. "We started the clinic to help people. If we don't quit now, we'll be *hurting* people."

"I will not go back to that clinic!" Janie cried, lifting her head long enough to stare around. "I *will not*. They win," she finished with a tortured whisper.

Elizabeth stared at her friends. She completely understood their fear. She wanted to do nothing more than jump on a train and return to Boston. Her father had offered her a place in his thriving practice. Leaving here was the smart thing to do. Why was she resisting?

May stalked over, sat down in a chair next to Janie, and then slammed her hand down on the table. Dishes and glasses rattled violently as the sound exploded through the room.

Janie straightened with a shocked look on her face. "What...?"

Carrie's head quit shaking as she stared at May with disbelief. "Why...?"

"All you girls listen to me. Right now," May said sternly. "And you listen up real good." Her voice rang through the suddenly still air.

Elizabeth sat down and watched the housekeeper carefully. She had no idea what she was going to say, but she had a feeling it was going to be good. She hoped so, because she could feel her own terror swelling as she watched her friends fall apart.

"Now," May continued in a softer voice. "I get why you girls be afraid, but there ain't no way you're gonna let those ignorant men win."

"They've already won," Janie said in the same hollow voice. "I won't ever go back to the clinic."

"Nonsense," May snapped. "Are you gonna turn away from all those patients who helped you clean up that god awful mess?"

Carrie sighed. "If we have them come back, we're just putting them in danger. What if those men return when the clinic is full of patients?"

May snorted. "Those cowards ain't got the courage to do that."

"Perhaps," Carrie replied in a listless voice. "But I don't have the courage to find out."

Elizabeth had never heard her friend sound so defeated. She fought to think of something to say that would eliminate the dead look in Carrie's eyes.

"Miss Carrie, you got more courage then all them men together," May retorted. "I see you live it every day."

Carrie shook her head. "Sometimes the smart thing to do is walk away, May. I could never live with myself if something happened to a patient or to the horses. Buildings can be rebuilt, but lives can't be restored when they're gone."

"What would Miss Abby say to you?" May demanded.

Carrie shrugged. "What does it matter?" she asked in a wooden tone.

Elizabeth watched the helpless look that filled Anthony and Matthew's faces. She was certain they'd never seen their wives like this. "What *would* Abby say, May?"

"Miss Abby and I had some real long talks 'bout her life in Philadelphia. About that time she had to take over her husband's factories when he died. There be times she was so scared she couldn't make herself get out of bed. She told me she just curled up in a fetal position and waited to die. She was right convinced it would be better than facin' whatever she had to face that day."

Carrie's eyes widened. "I knew it was hard, but she never told me all that."

"There be things you tell a friend, that you ain't gonna tell a daughter," May replied. "She told me she was scared almost every moment." She paused dramatically, waiting for both Carrie and Janie to look at her. When she had their attention, she continued. "I asked her how she kept going – being that she was so afraid." She paused again, her face a mixture of sternness and compassion. "Miss Abby told me scared is what you're feeling. Brave is what you're *doing.*"

Her words reverberated through the room, filling every corner. "I'm going to say that again, girls. Scared is what you're *feeling.* Brave is what you're *doing.*" She added emphasis to her last word.

"I know what you're trying to do," Janie whispered. "I battled through so many fears during the war. I battled through more when I went to medical school. We all overcame fears when we decided to start the clinic because we knew it would be hard..." Her voice faltered. "But now... others are paying the price for our bravery in opening the clinic. What's the point of being brave if it hurts the very people you're trying to help?" Her body started to tremble again.

Matthew took her hand and squeezed it tightly.

May was undaunted. "I reckon you be right that there's a chance somebody gonna get hurt if you open that clinic back up. There's also a chance it *won't* happen. What *will* happen if you quit, is that an awful lot of people gonna be hurt because you won't be there to help 'em."

Elizabeth felt a swell of bravery as she listened to May, but she knew her friends were still mired in memories and fear.

May saw it, too. "Girls, Miss Abby went through a whole lot of hard times. So did I. Back when I was a slave, I had three babies ripped away from me. Near broke my heart every time. I didn't want to have no more babies. That didn't matter nothing to the man who owned me. He figured I belonged to him in every way. He just kept on comin' to me. I was pregnant with my fourth baby when he sold me. I reckon his wife figured out what was going on. She didn't want me around anymore."

"What happened to your fourth child?" Elizabeth asked softly, horrified by what she was hearing.

"I had a miscarriage. Right before I was sold off on that auction block. I wanted to die more than anythin', but I couldn't figure out how to kill myself." She took a deep breath. "Miss Carrie, it was your daddy who bought me."

Carrie's head jerked up. "May..." she whispered. "I'm so sorry."

May shrugged. "I reckon it saved my life," she said matter-of-factly. "If I'd stayed there on that plantation, I know I would have killed myself. Ain't nobody can keep livin' that way. I ended up with a good life here."

Elizabeth stared at her. "How did you stand it? How did you keep going?"

May smiled slightly. "I was sold away from my own mama when I was twelve. I was scared something terrible to leave her." Her eyes took on a faraway look before she shook her head and continued. "That last night before the wagon came to send me to the auction block, my mama told me something I ain't never forgot."

"What was it?" Carrie whispered.

"My mama told me courage ain't having the strength to keep goin' – courage is keeping on goin' when you ain't got the strength." May cleared her throat. "I don't blame none of you girls for feelin' the way you do. I had to fight some of my own fears last night. Y'all did the right thing when you started that clinic. It's gonna to take a lot of courage to keep goin'. I happen to believe all three of you are brave enough to do it."

Spencer stepped forward to put his arm around May. "My wife is telling you the truth," he said firmly. "I seen you women do things no other women would ever dream of doing. I understand why you're afraid, but bowing down to fear never changed nothing." He looked at Carrie. "There were some times during the war when I was so scared of getting' in the wagon seat to drive you somewhere." He shook his head. "I could hardly bring myself to do it."

"How *did* you do it?" Carrie asked softly.

"I talked to Pastor Anthony about it. I asked him if a person could still be brave if they were tremblin' in their boots." Simon smiled as he remembered. "Pastor told me that it was the *only* time they could be brave. He told me that doing somethin' you wasn't afraid of wasn't being brave – it was just doing somethin' you wanted to do. Doing it while you were tremblin' in your boots... now that took a lot of courage."

Carrie smiled. "Pastor Anthony was a wise man."

May cocked her head. "Pastor Anthony was Jeremy's daddy, right?"

Carrie nodded. "Yes, he adopted him after my grandfather raped Old Sarah."

Elizabeth gaped at them. "This is a story I haven't heard."

Carrie managed another smile. "You've met Rose."

Elizabeth nodded, uncertain what Rose had to do with the story. "Of course."

"Jeremy is her twin," Carrie continued. "They were separated right after they were born because Jeremy was born white. My grandfather didn't want proof of the fact that he'd raped Sarah, so he sold Jeremy. He was lucky enough to be adopted by Pastor Marcus Anthony. Pastor Anthony was a great man." Her eyes softened. "He died before the war ended, but not before I found out the truth about who Jeremy really was."

Elizabeth's head whirled. "So, Rose is actually your aunt? And Jeremy is your *uncle*?" Her mind continued to race. "And your father is Rose and Jeremy's half-brother?"

Carrie nodded. "I know it's confusing, but it's true. We've all become family." She frowned again. "Jeremy left Richmond because he knew it wouldn't be safe to raise his own twins here. He and Marietta made a difficult choice because they wanted to protect their family. They knew when it was the right time to walk away."

Elizabeth knew where Carrie was headed.

"That's true," May said. "I hate that they left. I miss them and those babies somethin' fierce, but they made the decision that was right for them." She continued, not giving any of them time to respond. "The question you girls got to answer is why y'all decided to start the clinic down here in the first place." She paused for a long moment. *"Why?"* She gazed around the table. "Y'all can't make no decision about what comes next until you answer that question first."

"I decided to join the clinic because I believed we could make a difference," Elizabeth said firmly. The fear that had started to well in her had been tamped down by the stories she'd heard. Her voice grew firmer. "I admit that scared is what I'm feeling." She lifted her head. "But I want brave to be what I'm *doing*." She took a deep breath. "Carrie. Janie. I don't believe we're done here yet."

A pregnant silence fell over the table. The sound of children playing in the streets filtered in through the open window. A slight breeze caused the lace curtains to dance and sway, carrying in the aroma of the magnolia tree and lilac bushes.

Carrie was the first to speak, but it was a single word. "Anthony?"

Anthony took her hand. "I'll support whatever you decide, Carrie. You have a great practice out on Cromwell Plantation. If you decide you're done here, and that you only want to work on the plantation, I'll understand. However," he added in a strong voice, "don't make the decision based on what happened at River City Carriages. Just like the plantation must be guarded every single day, so must River City Carriages now. Whether the danger is due to the medical clinic or to our having black and white drivers, the men stepped up to protect their livelihood."

"They're going to guard it at night?" Carrie asked.

"They are. It was their idea," Anthony added. "It's why I was late to breakfast. I told them what happened. They came up with their own solution."

Carrie nodded thoughtfully.

"Ain't no reason some men can't protect the clinic, Miss Carrie," Spencer said. "Cowards operate when they believe no one can see them. You post a couple men inside the clinic every night to keep an eye on things. I don't believe you'll have more trouble."

Carrie's eyes narrowed. "What if someone tries to burn it down from outside?" Her voice trembled. "I can't bear to think of our guards burning to death."

"You have one outside and one inside," Spencer replied, his voice steady and reasonable.

"It could be done," Elizabeth answered. She knew Carrie was thinking about Minnie's family who had died just six months ago from a fire, and Grace who had died on Christmas Eve when the Spotswood Hotel had gone up in flames. The threat of the horses burning had been more than Carrie could handle. "We can take every precaution. Once word gets out that we've posted guards, I believe the trouble will stop."

"Or, they'll send enough people to overpower them," Carrie said, her eyes still shimmering with fear. She stared at Elizabeth. "Why aren't *you* afraid?"

"Oh, I'm afraid." Elizabeth said instantly. "I keep thinking, though, about something my father told me when I decided to go to medical school. He encouraged me to become a doctor, but he also knew how hard it was going to be since I'm a woman." She smiled slightly. "He told me I was going to be afraid a lot. He also told me to not be afraid of my fears, because they weren't there to scare me. They were there to let me know something is worth it." Her fear retreated another step as she repeated the words her father had spoken. She could see his passionate dark eyes, so like her own, and hear his passionate voice as she remembered. She thought about all the times he must have been terrified when he'd been an orphan on the streets of New York City.

Elizabeth took a deep breath. "It was true during medical school. I believe those words hold even more truth now. We started the clinic because we want to help people and make a difference. I'm can't think of anything more worthy than that."

"I don't think I can do it," Janie said haltingly, her eyes still glittering with pain.

Elizabeth gazed at her, and then reached over to take her icy hand. "Perhaps you can't," she said softly. "I understand." At some point while she'd been speaking, she had seen things more clearly. Repeating her father's words had given her a new perspective. The only person she could choose courage for was herself.

She took Carrie's hand next. "I understand if you decide to go back to the plantation and work there instead, Carrie." Elizabeth took a deep breath. "The three of us started the clinic together. That doesn't mean we all have to continue running it. I'm going back to the clinic tomorrow. It's what I came to Richmond to do. I don't believe I'm done yet. It will take me time to get it running again, but I'll do what it takes."

Carrie gaped at her. "You're staying? Even if we don't return to the clinic? You're not going back to Boston?"

"I'm staying," Elizabeth confirmed, surprised by the depth of her certainty. "The people of Richmond are just going to have to figure out how to deal with this Italian Yankee woman doctor treating patients."

"What if no one returns to the clinic?" Janie pressed. "What if they're all too afraid?"

Elizabeth shrugged. She took it as a good sign that Janie was asking questions. "Then I'll hold new seminars and I'll find new patients." She leaned down to look into Janie's weary eyes. "I came to Richmond because you and Carrie asked me to. I'm staying because I believe what we're doing is worth the risks."

Janie stared at her for a long moment, but then looked away. "I can't," she whispered. She peered into Matthew's face. "I'm sorry. I just can't."

"You have nothing to be sorry for," Matthew said firmly. He looked at Anthony and Carrie. "I'm taking my family out to the plantation. It will do us good to be out of the city for a while."

"I agree," Anthony replied. He raised a brow at Carrie. "Shall we all go together?"

Elizabeth was surprised when Carrie slowly shook her head.

"I'm staying here," Carrie said slowly, her voice revealing just how uncertain she was about her decision.

Elizabeth held her breath, afraid anything she might say would change Carrie's mind.

"Why?" Janie demanded. "You're as afraid as I am." Her voice was almost accusatory.

"We started the clinic because we believed it was important." Carrie tightened her lips and turned to look out the window for a long moment before turning back. "It's more than that, though. I chose to start the clinic with you because I believed it was needed. That it was what I was meant to do." Her voice faltered. "I'm terrified, but it's not like I haven't been terrified before, Janie. It's something I have to do."

Tears sprang to Janie's eyes. "Do you hate me? Do you think I'm weak?" The tears rolled down her cheeks. "Don't answer that. I already know I'm weak." She stared at Carrie and Elizabeth. "I'm sorry..."

"No," Carrie said firmly. "You have nothing to be sorry for. Neither of us hate you, and neither of us think you're weak. More than anyone, I know what you've overcome to become a doctor. More than anyone, I know the horrors of the war that we faced together. You're a strong, amazing woman, Janie Justin."

"I'm not right now," Janie said in a broken voice. "I'm so scared. I try to imagine walking back into the clinic..." She began to tremble again. "I can't do it." She shook her head violently. "I just can't do it."

Carrie threw her arms around her friend. "Go out to the plantation. Let Annie and Rose take care of you. Go for rides. Go for long walks. The future isn't important right now. Whatever happens, happens. You'll know what you're meant to do when you're ready to know it." She whispered in her ear. "I'll support you no matter what it is."

Elizabeth stepped forward and grabbed Janie's hand. "Carrie is right, Janie. The future isn't what's important right now." She smiled tenderly. "Will you eat some of Annie's rhubarb crumble for me? I know the gardens must be lush with it right now."

May snorted. "What's wrong with *my* rhubarb crumble?" she asked indignantly.

"Nothing," Elizabeth replied quickly, her eyes beginning to twinkle. "At least, I don't suppose there's anything wrong with it. How would I know? You've never made me one."

May opened her mouth to retort but closed it quickly. "I suppose I ain't," she grudgingly conceded. "I reckon I'll take care of that tonight." She cast a look at Spencer.

"Yes, dear," Spencer replied to her unspoken question. "I'll bring you in a whole mess of rhubarb." He winked at Elizabeth. "Thank you for shaming her into making it. I been wanting it ever since I saw it poppin' up in the garden."

"Well, why didn't you say so?" May demanded.

Spencer kissed the top of her head. "Because you already treat me better than any man deserves to be treated. I didn't want to give you even one more thing to do." Humming, he disappeared through the kitchen door.

Moments later, they all heard the backdoor swing shut. The faint sound of Robert's laughter and Annabelle's squeals of delight floated in before the closing door stopped it.

Matthew stood. "We should go, Janie. If we pack up quickly, we can leave today and make it to the plantation by dark."

Janie hesitated.   She looked uncertainly from Elizabeth to Carrie, her eyes searching their faces. Then she turned to Matthew and nodded. "I'm ready," she whispered.

Carrie watched through the window as Matthew, Janie and the children walked back down the road. Carrie frowned, troubled by the defeated slump of Janie's shoulders.

"She needs time, Miss Carrie," May said.

"I know," Carrie agreed. "The plantation is the best place for her."

"It's the best place for all of us," Elizabeth said. "There's no place I would rather be right now."

Carrie gazed at her. "Are you afraid if you go out to the plantation that you won't come back?"

Elizabeth considered the question. "I don't know," she finally admitted. "Are you afraid of that?"

"A little," Carrie admitted. "Perhaps a lot," she acknowledged with a tight smile. "I remember the first time I fell off a horse. I couldn't have been more than six. I'm not sure if I was more surprised or hurt, but I sat on the ground and cried. Miles knew I wasn't injured so he told me I had to get back up on the horse." She shook her head as she remembered. "I told him I didn't want to. I was afraid. He knelt next to me and told me the longer I waited to get back on, the more afraid I would be. He said the only thing a true horsewoman could do when they fell off a horse was to get back on." She smiled. "I wanted to be a horsewoman more than anything."

"Even at six years old?" Elizabeth asked with amusement.

"Oh, yes," Carrie assured her. "I wanted to be a horsewoman more than anything. Well, that and a doctor..."

"At *six*?" Elizabeth sounded disbelieving.

"Well, I didn't know the term *doctor*, but I knew I wanted to help make people feel better. I used to help my mother treat the slaves. It was never anything major, but I was fascinated."

Elizabeth nodded. "You got back on the horse?"

"I got back on," Carrie agreed. "It's a lesson I never forgot. I'm terrified to go back to the clinic tomorrow. I'm terrified of what might happen to River City Carriages. But..."

"But what?" Elizabeth pressed when she didn't immediately finish her statement.

"I'm more terrified of *not* returning to the clinic," Carrie finished as her thoughts reached their conclusion. Speaking the words made her realize how true they were. "I have to find a way to *do brave* even though I'm afraid."

Micah stepped back into the dining room as she was speaking. He nodded his head with approval. "My daddy called it courage rising."

Carrie looked up at him. "Courage rising? What does that mean?"

Micah sat down in the chair across from her and leaned forward on his lanky arms. His narrow face was more intense than she'd ever seen it. "My daddy was a fine man. That don't mean he weren't treated real bad when he was a slave. I saw him beaten more than once. Sometimes the man who owned us would be real kind. It almost seemed like he liked us. Then," he snapped his fingers for emphasis, "he would change just like that." He shook his head. "We never knew what to expect so we were scared all the time – even when he acted nice."

Carrie listened closely, aching as she saw the resigned pain in Micah's eyes. She knew there were many things you learned to live with; things that you never truly got over.

"My daddy knew I was scared all the time. One day he sat me down and told me that was part of our owner's plan. He wanted us to be afraid. My daddy told me he was gonna keep choosing to *not* be afraid just because our owner wanted him to be. He looked me dead in the eye and told me that he would make his courage rise every time someone tried to intimidate and scare him." Micah got a faraway look that said he was reliving his memories. Silence filled the dining room until he continued. "For years after, until I was sold away, every time someone tried to scare us, Daddy and I would look at each other and whisper *'Courage Rising'*." He looked up at Carrie. "Those two words done gotten me through a lot of scary times."

"Courage rising," Carrie and Elizabeth said in unison, then reached across the table to clasp hands.

Carrie turned to Anthony. "You're alright with my decision?"

"I'm proud of you," Anthony said firmly. "As long as you let me find the men who will guard the clinic. I want to be sure they can be trusted."

"Thank you," Carrie said lovingly. "Of course I'll let you."

"There is one other thing," Anthony said hesitantly.

Carrie raised a brow and waited.

"I think all of us should go to the plantation for a few days, at least. I know you both have to get back on the horse, Carrie, but the last day has been extremely traumatic. Being home on the plantation will give you some perspective and provide a break." He looked across the table. "You too, Elizabeth."

Anthony turned back to Carrie. "I know you're going to get back on the horse. You're not a child who needs to be convinced. You're a strong woman who is choosing to rise above her fears."

Carrie chuckled. "Courage rising," she sang out. Just saying the words helped.

"Courage rising," Micah agreed.

"I have a feeling we'll be saying that a lot in the future," Elizabeth said thoughtfully, and then turned to Carrie. "I think Anthony is right. We're going to come back and open the clinic. That doesn't mean we can't take a few days at the plantation. Besides, we need to bring back a new supply of medicines."

Carrie frowned as she considered her options. "I'm not certain of your assessment, Anthony. It took every bit of my courage this morning to not run back to the plantation, and never return. Besides, I have a supply of medicines in the basement here. I always keep it stocked in case of emergency."

May shook her head. "We got stuff down there, for sure, but ain't nothing like what you had at the clinic. Are you sure there be enough?"

Carrie forced herself to be honest. "No, but it will be enough for the patients who need us most." She looked at Elizabeth. "I think you should go out to the plantation. You told Janie there was no place you would rather be right now. I'll send you with a list. You and Polly can put together everything we need. I'll reopen the clinic while you're gone. I'll be going home in two weeks anyway. I can get things started back up here while you take a break."

"You're going to run the clinic on your own?" Elizabeth asked.

Carrie raised a brow. "Isn't that exactly what you were going to do?" Not waiting for an answer she already knew, she turned to Anthony. "I appreciate you wanting me to go home, but I really do feel I should stay here. Besides, I know you don't want to leave River City Carriages right now. If you went out to the plantation, you would be worrying constantly. After everything that's happened, I would rather be here with you."

Anthony stared at her for a several moments before he relented with a sigh. "You're correct on all counts. Will you at least wait until I can find adequate security for you?"

"That's a deal," Carrie agreed immediately. "It's going to take me a day or so to get new furniture anyway. We can walk over to the clinic later. I'll leave a note on the front door to let our patients know we'll be open soon."

"And to give notice to whoever did this that we're not running away," Elizabeth retorted.

Carrie turned to Peter. He had sat silently through the entire conversation, but she hadn't missed the admiring shine in his eyes every time he looked at Elizabeth. "Since we're not leaving, how about if you take Elizabeth out to the plantation?"

"What?" Elizabeth exclaimed. "Peter is in Richmond to work. If I hurry, I'm sure I can catch a ride with Matthew and Janie."

"Who will most certainly not be ready to share a four-hour carriage ride with a friend she believes she is disappointing," Carrie replied calmly. She turned to Peter. "Can you do it?"

"Not really," he admitted. He looked at Elizabeth with a smile. "But I'm going to. There is nothing I would like more than to go out to the plantation with you, Elizabeth. Will it be alright with you?"

Elizabeth stared at him, and then slowly nodded. "Yes," she answered with a warm smile.

Peter grinned in return. "It would be helpful if we could leave tomorrow morning. There are a few things I need to do."

"That works best for me, too," Elizabeth replied. "Now that I've shamed May into making her rhubarb crumble, I would hate to miss it. Can we leave early tomorrow morning, though? Now that we've decided to go, I'm eager to get there."

"As early as you like," Peter promised.

Carrie refrained from cheering, but she managed a sly wink at Anthony.

Chapter Six

Later that afternoon, Carrie meandered into the kitchen, drawn by the delicious smells. "Is that what I think it is?" she asked hopefully.

May chuckled. "That rhubarb crumble Miss Elizabeth asked for? Yep. I'm about to pull it out of the oven."

"Too bad it's still hours before supper," Carrie said pitifully.

May rolled her eyes. "There ain't nothing pathetic about you, Miss Carrie. Why don't you just come out and ask for some before supper?"

"May I have some now?" Carrie asked bluntly. She rubbed her stomach and blinked her eyes. "I think I might be starving."

"That would be your own fault," May said tartly. "If you'd done more than push around those pancakes and bacon this morning, you wouldn't be hungry."

Carrie frowned, all playfulness disappearing. "I couldn't eat." Her stomach rolled again as she thought about what had almost happened to the horses.

"I know, honey," May said sympathetically. "You know I'm real proud of you, don't you?"

"Thank you, May." Carrie said with surprise. She knew their housekeeper loved her, but she didn't often communicate her feelings. May focused on fussing at them and preparing amazing meals. "I appreciate that.

But, really, I should be thanking you. All three of us were about to go into full-blown panic. You're slamming your hand on the table allowed me to regain control."

May ducked her head. "You weren't upset?"

"No," Carrie said firmly. "I about jumped out of my skin but we all needed it. I've thought about what you said, ever since. The story you told about Abby really struck home. I know it was hard for her to take over her first husband's businesses, but I didn't realize how bad it got sometimes. I hope her words never leave me. *Scared is what you're feeling. Brave is what you're doing.*"

"You learn how to be brave every day you're living, Miss Carrie."

"I suppose you do," Carrie agreed. She watched as May pulled a deep pan of rhubarb crumble from the stove. The red juice, bubbling from beneath the oat crumble, made her mouth water as the fragrant aroma erupted in the kitchen. She moaned in anticipation.

"You can't eat it straight out of the oven," May scolded. She looked out the window and smiled with satisfaction. "Besides, you got someone to meet. You go on and get Miss Elizabeth. I saw her go up to her room a little while ago. She ain't gonna want to miss this either."

"Miss what?" Carrie's eyes followed May's. She saw Spencer strolling up the road with a woman beside him, but they were too far away for her to identify who it was. "Are they coming here?"

"Kinda hard for you to meet someone if they ain't coming here," May retorted. "Now, go on up and get

Miss Elizabeth. I'll dish up some of this crumble for everyone." She waved her hand toward the kitchen door. "Go."

Carrie went, her curiosity aroused. She knew it wouldn't be satisfied until she returned with Elizabeth. She climbed the stairs quickly and rapped on her friend's door.

"Come in," Elizabeth called.

"I'll come in, but I want you to come out," Carrie announced as she pushed the door open. "Spencer has brought someone to the house that he and May want us to meet."

Elizabeth frowned. "I'm not sure I feel like being social."

"Me either," Carrie agreed, "but this is one of those times when I don't believe our opinion is being asked. Besides," she added, knowing Elizabeth wouldn't be able to refuse, "May just pulled the rhubarb crumble out of the oven. She said she would dish some up when we got downstairs."

Elizabeth rose to her feet. "You should have started with that." She tucked her hand through Carrie's arm. "And, you should work on not being so obvious."

Carrie chuckled. There was no sense pretending she didn't know what Elizabeth was talking about. "I don't see the point in being coy. Besides, all I'm doing is providing an opportunity for you and Peter to get to know each other better. A four-hour carriage ride seems perfect."

Elizabeth narrowed her eyes, but then grinned. "Is he really as wonderful as he seems?"

"Every bit as wonderful as he seems," Carrie assured her. "It broke all our hearts when his wife and child died. He's poured his whole life into reporting since then. It's time for him to share his life with someone equally wonderful."

"Whoa!" Elizabeth exclaimed. "Don't you think you're making some big assumptions?" Her expression was alarmed.

Carrie shrugged. "Perhaps, but I've known Peter for many years. This is the first time I've seen his eyes alive in a very long time – at least about something more than a story he was reporting. I don't know what he's here to work on, but the fact that he's willing to walk away from it to go to the plantation with you tells me a lot." "Besides that," she added cheerfully, "I see the look on your face when he's around."

Elizabeth couldn't stop herself from blushing. "His eyes are alive?"

"Very alive," Carrie assured her. "I'm going to want every detail when you return from the plantation."

Spencer, May and Micah were seated at the dining room table when Carrie and Elizabeth came downstairs. Seated with them was a black woman Carrie had never seen.

Spencer rose to make the introductions. "I would like both of you to meet Dr. Rebecca Lee Crumpler."

Carrie jolted with surprise. "Dr. Crumpler? *The* Dr. Crumpler?"

Spencer looked disappointed. "You know her?"

"No, but I've always wanted to meet her," Carrie answered. "What a wonderful surprise!"

Spencer continued his introductions. "Rebecca, this is Dr. Carrie Wallington. And Dr. Elizabeth Gilbert."

Dr. Crumpler rose gracefully. Tall, with an erect posture, her hair was peppered with gray, but her light brown skin was remarkably unlined for someone who appeared to be at least forty. "It's a pleasure to meet you both," she said. "Spencer and May have told me many things about you." Her face softened with compassion. "He also told me on the way over what happened yesterday at your clinic. I'm not surprised, but I'm terribly sorry."

Elizabeth settled into a chair at the table. "I'm afraid I'm at a disadvantage. I appear to be the only one present who doesn't know who you are."

Carrie reached over to touch Dr. Crumpler's hand. "May I do the honors, please? And then you fill in the gaps?"

Dr. Crumpler nodded, a smile of amusement on her face.

Carrie turned to Elizabeth. "I learned about Dr. Crumpler during my last term. She's the first black woman to become a physician in the United States. She graduated from the New England Female Medical College in 1864. It was even more rare for any woman to be accepted into medical schools a decade ago, but it was unheard of for black women. Dr. Crumpler, however, was so talented as a nurse that her supervising doctor recommended her to medical school. When they accepted her in 1860, she was the first black woman to be accepted, and then to graduate. She practices medicine in Boston, treating mostly women and children." Her voice was full of awe as she looked at their guest.

"In Boston?" Elizabeth asked.

"No," Dr. Crumpler answered. "Dr. Wallington got the first part correct, though. And, I know you're from Boston, Dr. Gilbert. I love it there."

Carrie cocked her head. "Where do you practice?"

"I'm just finishing up my work here in Richmond."

Carrie gaped at her. "Excuse me? Here in *Richmond?*" She shook her head. "How could I not have known this?"

"If the stories I hear are correct," Dr. Crumpler said gently, "you've been finishing your own degree, getting certified in surgery, opening a clinic out on your family's plantation, and then starting the Bregdan Medical Clinic. Not to mention the work you've done for the residents of the Black Quarters. You've been a busy woman."

When Carrie shot a look at Spencer, he just shrugged. "What can I say, Miss Carrie? I'm proud of you and everythin' you been doing. I knew you would be eager to meet Rebecca here. She's not just a doctor. She's also part of our church."

"What have you been doing in Richmond?" Elizabeth asked eagerly.

"I've been working at the Freedmen's Bureau," Dr. Crumpler responded. "When I first started my practice in Boston, I primarily worked with poor black women and their children. There was certainly no one else treating them," she said indignantly. "When the war ended, and all the slaves were set free, I decided to come to Richmond with the Freedmen's Bureau to work with the women and children here. The white doctors won't have anything to do with them, so the Bureau was their only hope for care." She paused. "Until the two of you opened the Bregdan Medical Clinic, that is."

"Actually," Carrie replied, "there are three of us. At least until today." She'd seen the look on Janie's face when she walked out of the house. Her friend had gone through many hard times, but she'd never seen that blank, fearful expression before. She was uncomfortably certain that Janie would never return to the clinic.

"What happened today?" Dr. Crumpler probed gently.

Carrie looked at Spencer. "You didn't tell her?"

"I told her about the attack, but I didn't figure it was my place to say anything else," Spencer responded. "Since we was coming here, I figured you could tell her yourselves."

Carrie sighed. "I don't know how much Spencer told you," she began. "The clinic was completely demolished two nights ago. Everything was broken up, all the medicines were destroyed..." She swallowed hard. "They tore the walls and flooring up, and they ripped all our records, doused them with kerosene, and left them on the floor for us to find."

"To let you know what will happen if you try to start it again," Dr. Crumpler said angrily.

"Yes," Carrie replied with a nod. "As horrible as that was, the worse part was they attacked two women coming to the clinic from the Black Quarters. One was our patient. The other was her husband's sister, who was bringing her to the clinic. They were both beaten badly."

"Harriet and Ann are members of my church. I heard they had been hurt, but I don't know anything else. Will they be alright?" Dr. Crumpler asked sharply.

"I believe they'll recover fully," Carrie said, but her throat tightened. "Harriet was almost six months along in a pregnancy. The beating caused her to give birth. Her son lived only a few minutes."

Dr. Crumpler sighed, an expression of heavy sorrow crossing her face.

Carrie continued. "Dr. Janie Justin was terribly traumatized by what happened at the clinic..."

"Combined with what happened this morning," Elizabeth added.

"This morning?" Dr. Crumpler leaned forward to look at them more closely.

Carrie held back tears that threatened to erupt. Struggling to keep her voice normal, she explained. "My husband owns River City Carriages. Some men tried to burn it down this morning. He'd been warned yesterday that if we didn't stop running the clinic, his business would pay the price."

"One of the stable managers came to work early and stopped any damage," Elizabeth added. "But if he hadn't gotten there..."

A tight silence filled the room as everyone envisioned the repercussions if the fire had not been doused.

Dr. Crumpler finally nodded, her eyes full of sympathetic understanding. "Dr. Justin is too afraid to continue."

"At least for now," Carrie replied. "She and I worked together at Chimborazo Hospital during the war, and then attended medical school together. She's married and the mother of two young children. She's reached her limit."

"Understandable," Dr. Crumpler murmured. "We all have our breaking point."

"What has been your experience here in Richmond, Dr. Crumpler?" Elizabeth asked.

Dr. Crumpler hesitated, and then met their eyes squarely. "One I hope to never repeat," she said honestly. "From the time I arrived in your city, I've been treated with intense racism by everyone. Both the administration of the Freedmen's Bureau, and also the other physicians. The combination of my being both black and female was more than they could swallow. The men doctors all snubbed me, and druggists didn't want to fulfill my prescriptions..." Her face grew taut with memory as she spoke. "The majority of pharmacists wouldn't acknowledge the prescriptions I wrote. Then, there were those folks that wisecracked that the M.D. behind my name stood for nothing more than *Mule Driver*."

"I'm so sorry!" Carrie cried.

Dr. Crumpler shrugged. "It's not like I haven't been dealing with it from the moment I decided to become a doctor, but it does become wearisome. My patients made it all worthwhile, but I believe the Freedmen's Bureau won't be open much longer. I'm eager to go back to Boston and practice there." Sadness filled her eyes. "I hate to leave the people of Richmond but, like Dr. Justin, I believe I've had my fill."

"I thought the Freedmen's Bureau was doing good work," Carrie said, struck by the intensity of her expression.

"They are," Dr. Crumpler agreed. "And they have. They've been limited by what they can accomplish, however. The original idea was a good one. The Bureau was supposed to help millions of former black slaves and poor whites after the war. We've done a great deal in providing food, housing and medical aid. We've opened thousands of schools across the South and we've provided legal assistance, but there's an extreme shortage of funds and personnel. We have the politics of race and Reconstruction to thank for that."

Carrie didn't miss the bitterness behind the matter-of-fact words.

Dr. Crumpler interpreted her expression. "I sound more bitter than I actually am," she said frankly. "I realize everybody is groping in the dark. Congress. The Army. The Freedmen's Bureau. The country has no idea what to do with four million freed slaves. There's been no bureaucracy in place in America to administer a large welfare employment and land reform program. It hasn't been done as well as it should have been, but there are certainly people who care greatly. With such a huge undertaking, differing opinions about how it should be run are to be expected."

She paused and took a sip of the hot tea May had placed in front of her. "There are certainly Freedmen's Bureau agents who are corrupt or incompetent, but there are also many hardworking and brave people who have made huge contributions."

"Like you," Micah said.

Dr. Crumpler smiled her thanks. "I hope so. Over the last six years, we've fed millions of people, built hospitals and provided medical care, and built thousands of schools."

"The Bureau has also negotiated labor contracts of ex-slaves and settled labor disputes," Elizabeth added.

Dr. Crumpler eyed Elizabeth. "You sound knowledgeable."

"My cousin is a Freedmen's Bureau agent in Georgia."

Carrie stared at her. "I didn't know that."

"Gerald is twelve years older than I am. We're not close. Because of the age difference, I never knew him well, but he was very active in the Abolitionist Movement with the rest of my family. When the war ended, he was eager to help the emancipated slaves. My parents give me updates on what he's doing," Elizabeth explained. "He's written that he's helped former slaves legalize marriages and locate lost relatives. I know he's also assisted numerous black veterans. I'm proud of what he's doing."

"It's wonderful that your cousin has helped so many, but the fact remains that the South doesn't want us here," Dr. Crumpler said quietly. "They don't want us interfering with what they see as the *Black Problem*. They want us gone so they can deal with blacks the way they want to."

Carrie tensed, knowing what might happen without Congressional oversight. "Do believe the Bureau will disappear?"

"Yes. There is already tremendous pressure from Southern Democrats to dismantle the Bureau. As each Southern state ratifies the Fourteenth Amendment and re-enters Congress, they regain power." Dr. Crumpler sighed. "I'm worried what will happen when the Freedmen's Bureau closes. We've done a lot of good, but we've failed to provide long-term protection for blacks, and there is certainly no real measure of racial equality."

Carrie knew she was right. "After so many years of working down here, it must be discouraging to know that."

"It is," Dr. Crumpler agreed. She eyed Carrie closely. "Dr. Justin is giving up. What about you two?"

"I certainly considered it," Carrie answered honestly. "Just this morning, I was ready to walk away from the Bregdan Medical Clinic. As you mentioned earlier, I also have a practice on the plantation. I was going to return home and just work out there."

"And now?"

"And now, I realize that it's okay if I feel afraid – as long as I *do brave.*" She looked across the table. "May reminded me of that," she said affectionately, and then looked across the table. "Dr. Gilbert had already decided to stay. She was going to run the clinic single-handedly if she had to. Unfortunately, there will be times when she has to do just that. I divide my time between my plantation practice and here."

Elizabeth shrugged modestly. "At least I'll have you half the time, Carrie."

Dr. Crumpler watched them closely. "What are you going to do about your black patients? Once the Bureau closes, they're going to be more desperate than ever."

"You're right," Elizabeth agreed. "I don't believe it's safe for them to come to the Clinic anymore, but I don't have the time to run more than one clinic. With Carrie here only half-time, I just can't handle more." Her eyes looked tortured. "I hate to have to acknowledge that, but it's true."

Dr. Crumpler nodded. "I believe you're right. But first, could we forego our doctor titles and just go by our names. I would like for you to call me Rebecca."

Carrie smiled. "I would like that. Please call me Carrie. I don't really care much about titles."

"And I'm Elizabeth."

Rebecca smiled. "Now, what if I could help?"

"You would stay to work here?" Carrie asked with delight.

Rebecca dashed her hopes quickly. "No. I've already committed to a new practice in Boston." She smiled slightly. "I also admit I've had quite enough of Southern hospitality," she said wryly.

Carrie and Elizabeth chuckled and nodded their heads, but Carrie could tell Elizabeth was as curious as she was to know how Dr. Crumpler thought she could help.

"I have a young lady I've mentored for the past five years. Her name is Dr. Lucinda Marlboro. She's just recently graduated and is looking for a place to practice.

She's a former slave who has worked hard to attend medical school. I believe the people in the Black Quarters would love her and respond well to her." She gazed at Carrie and Elizabeth. "I know the people in the Quarters can't pay much, so I was hoping..."

"That we could pay her as an extension of Bregdan Medical Clinic," Carrie said. She looked at Elizabeth, hoping her expression revealed that she thought it was a good idea.

Elizabeth nodded slowly. "The people in the Quarters can pay her something, at least. We can supplement her income while she's growing her practice, assist her whenever possible, and welcome her as a colleague and friend." She smiled brilliantly. "I think it's a wonderful idea. It's not safe for our black patients to come to the clinic. At least not right now. We'll do everything we can to help them in the Quarters until we can do more. Having another doctor would insure they would receive care and not have to be in danger."

"We would love to talk to Dr. Marlboro. If you'll give me her address, I'll write her immediately and then arrange for a visit if she's interested," Carrie said. "Thank you for recommending her." She hesitated, wondering if she should say what she was thinking.

"Please speak freely, Carrie," Rebecca urged. "I can assure you Lucinda will be interested."

"I suppose I'm surprised you want Dr. Marlboro to come to Richmond," Carrie said honestly. "You've had a very difficult experience. I can't see things have changed enough to make Dr. Marlboro's experience any less difficult."

"You're quite right. I tried to talk Lucinda out of it, but she's convinced this is the only place she wants to be. I learned a long time ago that we all have to follow our hearts and have our own life experiences. Lucinda's time here may be as difficult as mine. It may also be less difficult..." She hesitated before she continued. "Or more difficult. When the Freedmen's Bureau actually closes, I believe life will become more dangerous for most black people in the South." She sighed. "I've told Lucinda that she has a place with me in Boston any time she wants it."

Carrie nodded. "I understand believing you're meant to do something, no matter the cost. I'm glad she's coming. We'll take good care of her. Thank you for helping facilitate this."

"Thank *you* for being open to the idea," Rebecca replied, her eyes shining with delight. She turned to May, Micah and Spencer. "I'm so grateful you invited me over. I'm eager to return to Boston, but I know my departure is going to leave a big hole in the Black Quarters. It makes me feel better to know Lucinda will be here to care for people, and it certainly makes me feel better to know she'll have all of you."

She turned to Elizabeth next. "But what about you, Elizabeth? Do you really believe you can run the clinic on your own when Carrie isn't here? What about your safety?"

Elizabeth looked uncomfortable but shrugged. "We're hiring guards to keep an eye on things."

"That will help," Rebecca replied, "but I have six years of experiencing the animosity of people here toward women doctors. It wasn't just that I was black.

If I had been a white doctor, I fear my experience would not have been greatly different."

"Yet you survived for six years," Elizabeth said lightly. "I will do the same."

Rebecca smiled, but her expression remained intense. "Will it be alright if I make inquiries about another woman doctor who might want a practice in the South?"

"Certainly," Elizabeth said quickly. "I also have hopes Janie will conquer her fears and decide to return to the clinic." She looked at Carrie. "I know that might not happen, but I'm going to hold on to hope."

"I am too," Carrie assured her. "Still, I would welcome talking with someone new. I hate the idea of you handling our patient load on your own."

Elizabeth looked at her closely, seeing past her casual expression. "What aren't you telling me?"

Carrie hesitated, but knew Elizabeth would most appreciate the truth. "Janie talked in the past about working with me on the plantation, but she believed she would be most valuable here in the city."

"She's right," Elizabeth retorted.

"Yes," Carrie agreed. "That doesn't mean she'll be able to do it, though. She and Matthew love the plantation. They love the life out there – for themselves and for their children. If she can't overcome her fears, she may decide practicing medicine with me on Cromwell is her best solution."

"Do you have room for her?" Rebecca asked.

"Yes. My practice is growing out there. I would welcome another doctor, but I know how much Janie is needed here. She's been passionate about helping the women of Richmond – until the attack yesterday."

Elizabeth sighed. "I'm still not going to give up hope, but I'll speak with a new doctor. If they're interested, we can arrange a visit during one of your scheduled times here."

"Do you have a surgeon when Carrie isn't here?" Rebecca asked.

"No," Carrie answered. "We had a fourth partner in the beginning. Before we opened the clinic, Florence's father took her to Paris as a graduation gift. They were caught up in the Franco-Prussian War and were trapped in Paris during the Siege. While she was there, she got involved with the American Hospital, fell in love with one of the doctors, and married. She decided to stay there and open a practice with her husband."

Rebecca chuckled. "That's quite a story."

"It is," Carrie agreed. "We're thrilled for her, but we're also without a surgeon when I'm not here." She smiled. "Do you have one of those up your sleeve, as well?"

"I just might. I'll make a few inquiries when I return home."

Carrie hesitated, but knew Rebecca would appreciate honesty, as well. "We tend to do things a little out of the norm at Bregdan Medical Clinic."

Rebecca raised a brow. "What do you mean?"

"The four of us met at the Woman's Medical College of Pennsylvania, but Janie and I left after our second year to pursue homeopathic medicine. She and I graduated from the Homeopathic Medical College of Pennsylvania." Carrie appreciated the gleam of approval in Rebecca's eyes. "We utilize the best parts of both worlds, but our medicines are primarily homeopathic or herbal."

"Who makes your herbal medicines?" Rebecca asked keenly.

"My assistant, Polly, is managing a large group of women and children who collect the plants. She works hard through the year to create them. I help when I can. We're teaching more women to create the mixtures and tinctures because we have such a huge demand."

Rebecca turned to Spencer and May. "You didn't tell me this part."

"We want to be clear from the beginning," Carrie said quickly. "We're proud of our medicine, and our results. We only want doctors who can respect and embrace both parts of medicine."

Rebecca smiled brightly. "I happen to agree with you completely. Though I was trained at the New England Female Medical College in more traditional medicine, there was a significant number of staff that valued homeopathy. I use it in my own practice, though I don't always reveal my methods." A sly smile spread over her face. "I can assure you Lucinda feels the same way. Her mama treated much of their plantation using plants in the woods while she was a slave."

Carrie was thrilled. "That's good to know."

Rebecca reached out to take Carrie's hand, and then Elizabeth's, linking the three women. "The two of you are doing fine work here in Richmond. I'm so grateful for a chance to meet you."

"The honor is mine," Carrie insisted.

"It's been a thrill," Elizabeth added. "If Dr. Marlboro chooses to work with us, I hope it means we will see you again."

"I'm sure you will, but this black woman is ready to be back in Boston," Rebecca said. "I won't return to the South often."

"Then we'll come see you and experience your work in Boston," Elizabeth assured her. "Lucinda will want to return home, and I've promised to take Carrie to Boston to visit."

"I'll look forward to it," Dr. Crumpler replied. She looked toward May. "Are you going to continue to just tempt us with the smell of that rhubarb crumble, or are you actually going to give us some?"

Elizabeth laughed. "A woman after my own heart."

"Coming right up," May said cheerfully.

A knock sounded at the door just as the kitchen door swung closed behind May.

A knock sounded at the door and Micah rose to answer it. He returned moments later with a thick envelope.

Carrie reached for it, and then turned to Elizabeth. "It's from Florence!"

Chapter 7

Carrie looked at the thick envelope longingly before she tucked it into her dress pocket. She wanted to know what Florence had to say, but it would be rude to read it while they had a guest.

Rebecca stood. "May, I think I'll come help you in the kitchen. I want to be as close to that rhubarb crumble as possible." She smiled at Carrie and Elizabeth. "I hope you don't mind if I leave you for a few minutes."

Carrie smiled her gratitude and motioned for Elizabeth to join her on the porch.

Once they'd settled on the swing, she pulled out the envelope and broke the seal eagerly.

Dear Carrie, Elizabeth and Janie,

I don't know when this letter will reach you, but it's long overdue. Most importantly, however, I'm not sure whether it will get to you at all if I don't send it today. I could tell you more, but I don't have the time.

Never did I dream, when I left America to go on a much-anticipated trip to Paris, that my life would so radically change. Knowing the three of you, you've already learned a lot about the war and the Paris Siege. It was a terrible, traumatic time, but I fear the city is about to experience one just as drastic.

Carrie locked eyes with Elizabeth. Peter hadn't said anything about new trouble in Paris. Of course, their own trouble had certainly not allowed him any time to tell them of world events.

"Keep reading," Elizabeth urged.

First, before I tell you of our new troubles, I must tell you I'm wildly happy with Silas Amberton. I don't know if you're aware that the Dr. Amberton we all studied under in Philadelphia, is his sister.

"His sister!" Elizabeth exclaimed. "I had Dr. Amberton for several courses. If her brother is anything like she is, Florence is a lucky woman."

"I had only one course with her, but I felt the same way. She is compassionate, as well as highly intelligent."

Carrie went back to reading.

I never imagined I would ever marry. Now, I can't imagine that I ever lived without Silas in my life. We opened our new clinic three weeks ago. I'm thrilled to be in practice with Silas, but I'm fearful of what we're about to be confronted with. When the Siege ended, I hoped we would never again have to treat people wounded in battle or protests.

France is a passionate and complicated country. Paris? Even more so. I know I can hardly do justice to the situation here in a hastily written letter, but I will do my best.

The city has experienced several uprisings in this century – led by radical, liberal Parisians. The city has a large population of working people who formed what is called the National Guard. They lost tens of thousands of their members during the Siege.

On top of that, since they are mostly working-class people, the Siege impacted them horribly. Most of the factories were closed down during the Siege because supplies couldn't be obtained. The suffering was terrible. There is so much I could tell you in regard to this, but I simply don't have the time. When we see each other again, I know we'll have many stories to share.

When the Armistice was negotiated at the end of January to end the Siege, we were all thrilled. An odd twist to the Armistice was that the French were forced to disarm their army, but the National Guard was allowed to keep their arms. It's important to note that the National Guard has about 300,000 men. They were allowed to keep their guns so they could maintain order in the city.

Carrie raised her brow. "Three hundred thousand men?" While she processed that number, she returned to reading.

It's also important to note that they have very little training and experience, not to mention virtually no discipline. The Guardsmen from the upper and middle-class tend to support the national government. The ones from the working-class neighborhoods are much more radical and politicized.

The National Guard led protests all during the Siege. I got caught up in one of them and ended up treating the wounded, while six people lay dead around me. I know you'll have many questions about that, but I can't explain more.

In mid-February, the new French Parliament elected Adolphe Thiers as Chief Executive of the French Third Republic.

Oh! You also need to know that at the end of the war, 400 obsolete muzzle loading cannons were left in the city. They may be obsolete, but they definitely work. The leadership of the National Guard decided to put the cannons in parks in the working-class neighborhoods. They wanted to keep them away from the regular army, but they also decided they could be used to defend Paris against any attack by the national government.

Thiers was very unhappy with this. Compromises were proposed but he's been intent on restoring order and national authority in Paris, so he wasn't interested in compromise. I suspect he may be regretting that decision right now.

Everything came to a head this morning when troops arrived to remove the cannons from the parks.

"When did Florence write this?" Elizabeth asked sharply.

Carrie flipped back to the first page. "March eighteenth."

Elizabeth's eyes burned with intensity. "Keep reading."

This morning, some of the soldiers from the French Army tried to reclaim 170 cannons that were in a neighborhood called Montmartre. It very quickly became ugly. A huge number of the National Guard gathered to stop them. The crowd kept growing, until they had surrounded the soldiers. One of the French Generals, General Lecomte, tried to withdraw, but they were too hemmed in. He ordered his soldiers to fire on the National Guard, but they refused. Many of them deserted and took their places with the Guardsmen!

General Lecomte and some of his officers were captured and taken to a National Guardsmen headquarters. They were pelted with rocks, struck, threatened and insulted by the crowd. I understand it was quite bad.

It got worse. By five o'clock this afternoon, they'd captured another prisoner – General Clement-Thomas. Evidently, he was especially hated because of the harsh discipline he imposed during the Siege. I don't know a lot about that.

What I do know is that a group of the National Guardsmen beat him and then shot him repeatedly. A few minutes later, they did the same to General Lecomte. They are both dead. I didn't know either of the men, and neither did Silas, but what happened to them was dreadful.

As of tonight, while I write this letter, the French Army has withdrawn. The new government, led by Thiers, is leaving as well – withdrawing to Versailles. For all intents and purposes, Paris is now under the control of the National Guard.

I fear what it will mean, but only time will tell. Silas assures me the French government won't allow them to remain in control, but the meaning of that scares me, as well. I know that only force will make the National Guard relinquish their control of Paris.

Once again, I am living in a city that will soon be at war. Only this time, it's with their fellow countrymen. Silas is sending this letter out tomorrow morning with a friend who is on the way to Le Havre to depart on a boat to England. From there, the letter will continue to your hands. I don't know what to expect from this latest development. If mail is stopped, I want to know you will at least receive this letter.

There are moments when I wish I had returned to America, but I want nothing more than to make a difference with Silas. Right now, that's here in Paris. I don't know what's coming, but we'll be here to care for people when it happens. Oh, there is so much I can tell you, but Silas just informed me that if I'm to get this onto the next boat to America, I must finish quickly.

I love you all so very much. I hope all is going well. I would love to receive a long letter from you.

"She hasn't received my letter?" Elizabeth exclaimed. "I mailed it almost two months ago."

"I'm sure she has it by now," Carrie assured her, staring at the papers in her hand. "As well as the one I wrote. It took us almost six weeks to get *this* letter." She sighed heavily. "Six weeks? What is going on in Paris? I hope she's safe." She stared east, wishing she could see across the ocean, all the way to Europe.

Elizabeth nodded somberly. "You know what it's like to live in a city at war. I hate that our dear Florence is having to experience it, as well. I pray she's safe," she said anxiously. "I'm glad she has Silas."

Carrie nodded and then looked down the road. "When will Peter be back? He might have more information."

"I don't know," Elizabeth replied. "I suspect he's taking care of some business. I heard him tell May he would be home in time for dinner." She glanced at the screen door. "You know, the only way to deal with such disturbing news is with rhubarb crumble."

Despite herself, Carrie laughed. "Rhubarb crumble? That's what you're thinking about?"

Elizabeth shrugged. "Talking about it worked to get some of that terrible distress from your eyes." She smiled. "I'm as worried as you are, but there's nothing we can do about any of it right now. We have a guest, and May has created a wonderful treat for us. I say we go inside and have some of it."

Carrie returned her smile. Elizabeth was right. They could do nothing about the situation in Paris right now. The delicious smells wafting out the door made her decision. She folded the letter and stuffed it into her pocket. "Let's go eat!"

One hour later, Peter strode into the house. "Am I smelling rhubarb crumble?" His wide grin faded when he saw the empty dish on the table. He leaned over and sniffed. "You ate it *all*?" he asked pitifully.

"Did you sound so pathetic when you were a child, too?" Elizabeth asked with a laugh.

"I have every right to sound pathetic," Peter said indignantly. "I've been looking forward to this all day."

"Perhaps," Elizabeth said dismissively, "but I was the one who got May to make it."

"Only because you shamed her into it."

"There could be truth to that," Elizabeth admitted. "In this situation, however, I believe the end justified the means." She smiled and batted her eyes. "I'm sorry you were too late to benefit."

"Oh, for land's sake," May exclaimed. "The two of you are talking pure nonsense. Mr. Peter, did you ever know me to make just one of *anything?*"

"There's another one?" Peter asked hopefully.

"There are *five* more," May responded. "Spencer brought me in more rhubarb than I ever seen in one pickin'."

"See, I told you the rhubarb needed to be cooked," Elizabeth said calmly. "It has me to thank that it's no longer languishing in your garden. It has the joy of fulfilling its purpose."

May rolled her eyes. "Does every Yankee talk such nonsense, or is it just the Italian ones?"

Rebecca laughed. "I suspect it's just the Boston Italians." She looked across the table. "You're laying it on a little thick, Elizabeth."

Elizabeth shrugged. "There's no sense having a talent that you don't use. Mine happens to be the use of words to achieve a goal."

"You mean you know how to say what you need to in order to get your way," Peter replied as he marched back in from the kitchen with a new dish of rhubarb crumble.

"Call it what you will," Elizabeth answered, her lips twitching. "As a reporter, I suspect you have no room to pass judgement. You know the power of words. Regardless, I enjoyed every bite of the rhubarb crumble, and I will enjoy even more of it." She smacked her lips dramatically.

"Not from this dish," Peter answered, holding it away from her reaching hand. "If it had been up to you, you would have denied me the sustenance I came to

Richmond for. I'm afraid that's something I may never be able to forgive you for." His eyes were dancing.

"Stop!" Carrie demanded, laughing at their sparring. "Y'all will have four hours in the carriage tomorrow to drive each other crazy with your words." Her laughter died away as thoughts of Florence crowded in. "Peter, I have something important to ask you."

"Not until he gives me that dish," May said firmly. "Mr. Peter, you are not going to sit in this fine dining room and eat out of a serving dish like a common man."

Peter sighed. "But I *am* a common man."

"Not in this house, you ain't," May replied with a snort. She snatched the dish from his hands. "I'll dish you up some."

"Will you dish me up a lot?" Peter asked. "You wouldn't deny a starving man, would you?"

"You better quit with your nonsense, or you won't get none at all," May said tartly. "I was the one who made that rhubarb crumble. I can also be the one to take it away!"

Peter nodded solemnly; his expression contrite. "Yes, ma'am. I trust you have my best interests at heart, May."

May shook her head and disappeared into the kitchen in search of a bowl. Her chuckle was silenced by the swinging door.

Carrie wanted to ask Peter a serious question, but she was thrilled to watch the exchanges between him and Elizabeth. She'd never seen Peter like this. His eyes were dancing with fun as his face creased with a big smile. More than ever, she was glad he was taking

Elizabeth to the plantation. They were clearly good for each other.

Peter turned to her. "What is this important question you have for me, Carrie?"

"Before I ask you, I'd like to introduce you to our esteemed guest. Peter Wilcher, this is Dr. Rebecca Lee Crumpler."

Peter's eyes widened. "The first black female physician. You graduated from the New England Female Medical College. It's a pleasure to meet you."

Rebecca smiled. "I'm honored that you know who I am."

"I wrote a series of articles several years ago about women in medicine. I figured since I was surrounded by female doctors that I should learn more about it." Peter paused. "I also wanted to do my part in helping change people's erroneous perceptions about women in medicine."

Rebecca narrowed her eyes as she appraised him. "Under the rhubarb crumb obsession there is a serious journalist? I'm surprised."

"So are my parents," Peter said with amusement. "I prefer to keep people off guard. I find I discover far more truth that way." He turned to Carrie. "Now, what's your question?"

"Do you know what's going on in Paris right now?" Carrie was aware of having a guest, but she also believed Rebecca, since she knew a little about Florence, would be interested in whatever he had to say.

The laughter died from Peter's eyes. "I don't know everything, but I get updates from my editor because he knows I'm interested. Why?"

"We received a letter from Florence today. It was mailed on March 19th." She watched Peter's face darken.

"The day after the National Guard killed the two French generals and took control of Paris."

"You know about it?" Carrie demanded. "Why didn't you tell us?"

"He's hardly had a chance!" Elizabeth jumped to his defense. "He's been helping us with the clinic ever since he stepped off the train yesterday."

"You're right, of course. I'm sorry, Peter," Carrie said apologetically.

Peter shook his head. "There's no need for an apology. I know you're concerned about Florence – which is why I get updates."

May walked in and placed a bowl of rhubarb crumble in front of him. She also laid down a silver platter with a teapot and several empty cups. "I can tell by the look on your face that Miss Carrie and Miss Elizabeth aren't going to like what you have to say. Take a few bites of that before you start."

Peter obeyed, closing his eyes in ecstasy while he slowly chewed, wiped his mouth, and then gazed at Carrie and Elizabeth. "Paris is a mess right now. It's been six weeks since the National Guard took over Paris. They started what they're calling the Commune. It's a Socialist form of government. The men running it refuse to acknowledge the French government. They're determined to separate Paris from the rest of the country, though their intention is to take over the entire country in time."

Carrie considered his response. Her primary concern was Florence and Silas' safety. "Is Paris in upheaval?"

"Only if you oppose them. Or if you're a Catholic priest."

"Excuse me?" Elizabeth asked. "What does that mean?"

"The Commune proposed many decrees when they took over the city," Peter explained. "They tend toward a progressive, secular and highly democratic social democracy. At least, that's how it's being described. Many of the proposed decrees are wonderful things for the working class of Paris, but they tend to view those that have money with a significant measure of disdain. They also declared a separation of church and state."

"What's terrible about that?" Carrie asked. "It's one of the founding principles of our own country."

"True," Peter conceded. "It's not like the separation of church and state here, however. The Commune has had a hostile relationship with the Catholic Church from the very beginning. Two weeks after the Commune was established, they voted a decree accusing the Catholic Church of complicity in the crimes of the monarchy. Their decree declared the separation of church and state, confiscated the state funds allotted to the Church, and seized the property of religious congregations. On top of that, they ordered that Catholic schools cease religious education and become secular."

"Oh my..." Carrie murmured. "I know Catholics here in America have a hard time, but it's not like that."

Peter nodded before he continued. "The latest report coming through shows that two hundred priests, nuns and monks have been arrested. Twenty-six churches have been closed to the public. The situation becomes more dangerous for Catholic clergy every day."

"That's terrible," Elizabeth cried. "Just because they're Catholic?"

"That," Peter confirmed. "But also because they've announced their support of the French Government. Anyone who doesn't support the Commune is in danger of retribution."

"How is that democratic?" Carrie asked.

"Evidently their idea of democracy only extends to the members of the National Guard, and the working-class people of Paris," Peter said sardonically.

"What's the French government going to do about it?" Carrie asked. Only six years had passed since America went to war when part of the country attempted to break away.

Peter read her expression accurately. "About what you would expect. The Armistice after the Franco-Prussian War further decimated the number of French troops that had already been severely weakened by the war. The prisoners of war were released, but they're still rebuilding. It's taken their new Chief Executive..."

"Adolphe Thiers," Elizabeth finished. "Florence mentioned him in her letter."

"Yes," Peter replied. "Adolphe Thiers. He's working hard to rebuild the French Army. My reports say that when he's confident it's strong enough, he'll take Paris back."

"And the people of Paris will pay the price," Carrie said sadly. "Including Florence." She appreciated that Peter remained silent, not bothering to refute her statement.

Elizabeth broke the intense silence. "Is anything happening now?"

Peter hesitated.

"We'd rather know the truth," Carrie reminded him.

"I know," Peter agreed. "On April second, the National Guard decided to launch an offensive against the French Army in Versailles, where Their has his government now. They sent five battalions across the Seine River, but were quickly repulsed by the Army. Five of the Guardsmen were captured." He hesitated again, but then continued. "Four of them were captured with their arms. All of them were shot and killed."

Carrie covered her mouth. "They executed them? Instead of taking them as prisoners of war?"

Peter nodded grimly. "Despite their failure, the National Guard decided to attack again the next day. They were convinced, in spite of what had happened the day before, that French Army soldiers would refuse to fire on the National Guard. They were counting on a repeat of the day the army came to retrieve he cannons." His lips twisted. "They prepared a massive offensive of twenty-seven thousand men who advanced in three columns. They were expected to converge in twenty-four hours at the gates of the Palace of Versailles."

"I'm guessing it didn't turn out that way," Elizabeth said.

"They advanced without cavalry to protect the flanks, without artillery, without stores of food and ammunition, and without ambulances. They were completely convinced of rapid success." Peter scowled. "They didn't get far. They passed by the line of forts outside the city, believing them to be occupied by the National Guard. They somehow missed the fact that the French Army had re-occupied the forts just a week earlier. The same Army that obviously had no qualms about firing on fellow Frenchmen. The columns of Guardsmen soon came under heavy artillery and rifle fire. It didn't take long for them to break rank and flee back to Paris." His eyes darkened. "Except for all the prisoners they took." His voice grew even grimmer. "Every one of them was shot and killed."

A heavy silence fell on the room.

"I hate war," Carrie whispered, her throat constricting even tighter at the idea of Florence caught in the thick of the fighting. She was quite certain that Florence and Silas had treated, and were continuing to treat, many of the wounded fighters.

"I do, too," Peter agreed. "It's all such a tragic waste of life."

"What's going to happen now?" Elizabeth asked with wide eyes.

"That was my last report," Peter replied. "I haven't been back to New York City to receive more information. I know I would have been informed if the Commune had fallen, so I can only assume plans are still being made for an attack on Paris." He spread his hands. "I wish I could tell you more."

Another somber silence fell on the room. Though France was an ocean away, a friend of theirs was caught up in the struggle. Their worry shrank the vastness of the ocean to a mere puddle. One of their own was in danger.

"What are you doing here, Mr. Peter?" May demanded. "Other than bringing us bad news and helping out the women with the clinic."

Carrie appreciated her attempt to change the subject.

Peter smiled. "Do I have to have a reason to visit my favorite cook in the country?"

"No. I know you do, though," May said keenly. "You always got a reason for being down here in Richmond. We ain't given you a single chance to tell us what it is. I reckon it ought to be your turn for a little while."

Peter looked longingly at his bowl of rhubarb crumble. "If I tell you, may I finish this in peace?"

Chuckles filled the room.

"May is right, Peter," Carrie said. "You always have a reason for being here. Usually, they aren't pleasant. What brings you here this time?"

"I'm writing a series of articles about the work of the Freedmen's Bureau." Peter focused on Dr. Crumpler. "I'm aware you've spent the last six years working with them, Dr. Crumpler."

"That's true," Rebecca agreed. She repeated much of what she had shared with all of them earlier, and then said, "I'm aware the Bureau struggles with a severe shortage of funds and personnel. I suspect it will soon close entirely."

Carrie waited until Rebecca was finished, and then asked the question burning in her mind. "What happened, Peter? Why did the funding disappear? Why aren't they finishing what they started?"

"All good questions," Peter replied. "If the Bureau had gone as planned, I believe we would be living in another type of country right now. A lot of people don't know that it was created as the Bureau of Refugees, Freedmen, and Abandoned Lands. In the beginning, it was meant to do far more than just aid the emancipated slaves. It was intended to handle what was expected to be another major problem created by the war – the disposition of property that was either abandoned during the war or confiscated from its owners at the end. It was also meant to handle property owned by the Confederate Government that was seized by the Union at the end of the war."

He paused for a drink of tea before he continued. "Those lands were essential to the original design of the bureau. Congress assumed the new agency wouldn't require federal funds because it could carry out its work through the sale or rental of hundreds of thousands of acres of abandoned and confiscated property. It was planned to be self-sustaining."

"President Johnson changed all that," Carrie said wryly.

Elizabeth looked confused. "I'm sorry. I know I should probably already be aware of what happened, but I'm not."

It was May who answered. "That President Johnson didn't much like the Freedmen's Bureau. Truth be told, he didn't like anything that would make life easier for all the slaves that got freed. He waited until Congress went on a break. It was right after President Lincoln was shot. He knew what was supposed to happen, but he just went ahead and pardoned all those leaders and slave owners. Then he gave them back their property. By the time he was done, there weren't much money to pay for the Freedmen's Bureau."

"That's right," Peter said. "The Bureau was renewed in 1866. Congress gave it a small appropriation, but not enough to run it the way it needed to be run. They renewed it one more time but gave it even less money. Last year, it was ordered to cease almost all operations. There are a few places where it still operates, like here in Richmond, but that won't last much longer." He looked at Dr. Crumpler. "I'm sorry."

Rebecca shrugged but her eyes glittered with sadness. "I've had my fill, Peter. I did my best, but now I'm going home to Boston where I belong." Her expression tightened. "Things are going to get bad down here, though. With no one to oversee what's happening to the freed slaves, I'm afraid many of them will lose what little freedom they gained since Emancipation. They will never have to be slaves again, but there's more than one kind of slavery," she said grimly. "Southerners are becoming creative about how to ensure they keep blacks in captivity and under their control."

Peter's expression revealed he felt the same way. "I wish I could refute your analysis, but I can't. I'm down here to interview some of the teachers, as well. Most of the funding from the Bureau went to education. Whatever its shortcomings, the Bureau has educated tens of thousands of black students who would never have been able to go to school." He looked at Carrie. "Not many students had the benefit of a school like the one Rose started on Cromwell Plantation. Without the Bureau, they would have had nothing."

Rebecca cocked her head. "There's a school on the plantation, Carrie? In addition to the medical clinic?"

"Yes. The school is taught by my best friend, Rose Samuels. She teaches both black and white students from the area." Carrie smiled. "She's an amazing teacher. She started teaching at a secret school on the plantation before the war started."

Rebecca stared at her in confusion. "Who was she teaching? Why did it have to be secret?"

Carrie's smile widened. "Rose used to belong to my father. We grew up together, but she was a slave. In time, I found out she was also my aunt."

Rebecca's eyes widened. "Your aunt?" she echoed.

Carrie laughed. "I'll tell you the whole story someday. It's really quite fascinating."

"Obviously," Rebecca responded. "I'm going to hold you to telling me the story."

Carrie nodded and turned back to Peter. She'd seen something in his eyes that puzzled her. "Do you believe the Bureau fell short in educating black children?"

Peter answered by pulling out a small notebook. He flipped to a dog-eared page. "In Virginia alone, the Bureau spent between one hundred ninety and two hundred twenty-five thousand dollars on education in the last five years. Even if you go with the higher number, the government allocated only nine cents a year for each of the five hundred and twelve freed slaves."

Carrie stared at him. "I didn't know that," she murmured. "I suppose I thought all children would have the same opportunity Rose has given our area children."

"Far from it," Peter said flatly. His expression grew more serious. "Now that Virginia has established a Board of Education, it's going to be impossible for Rose to continue to operate her school in the same way. She'll no longer be able to teach both black and white students. The Board of Education has mandated segregation for all schools." He took a deep breath. "Does she know?"

"She knows," Carrie answered. "She's hoping that our distance from Richmond will make it possible for her to continue school the way it is for a while longer."

"And when she's given notice?"

Carrie shrugged. "She'll deal with it then."

Chapter Eight

Carrie and Anthony walked arm-in-arm up the walkway to the Bregdan Medical Clinic. It had taken her three days of hard work to refurnish the clinic and get it ready for patients. While they weren't as well-stocked with remedies and treatments as they had been before the attack, she'd been pleasantly surprised by t how much had been stored in the basement of her father's house. They were prepared for the worst emergencies. It was going to take a tremendous amount of work to restock the emergency supply she was determined to have at the house, as well as restocking the clinic with all they would need, but she knew Elizabeth and Polly were working hard to do that.

Her thoughts flew to Janie as they approached the door. Carrie was sure her friend was struggling with guilt and feelings of failure, but she hoped being on the plantation was providing her relief from the trauma of the attacks.

"Are you expecting patients today?"

Anthony's question brought her back to the present as he reached for the door handle. Carrie tensed as the door began to open, not quite ready to answer the question. Though she had spent most of the last three days at the clinic, it hadn't been open for business. That would change in less than an hour.

The night guards Anthony had hired, Joshua and Leonard, had helped her with the furniture when it had arrived by wagon the morning before. While there were many people in town who looked at the clinic with disdain, the owner of the furniture store was the husband of one of her patients – a woman who would have lost her baby if Janie hadn't saved her. He'd contacted her the day after the attack to let her know he would work with her to replace everything quickly, at a significant discount. The wagon had rolled up the morning before at eight o'clock.

Arthur and Oscar, the day guards, arrived every morning by nine o'clock, staying until Joshua and Leonard returned at nine o'clock at night. Anthony had sent other workers to repair the structural damage of the building, but the guards had helped her with everything else. She'd appreciated their help, but mostly she'd appreciated the sense of safety they gave her. They had, quite simply, made it possible for her to be there.

Just as she had every day since the attack, Carrie held her breath when the door swung all the way open. She knew she would never forget the moment she'd seen the terrible destruction in the clinic. She wondered if she would ever quit expecting to see it again.

Chiding herself, but not able to resist the urge, she glanced over her shoulder to determine if anyone was lurking behind the bushes or the trees, or whether there was anyone on the road staring at her with hatred.

"Everything is fine," Anthony said reassuringly as he squeezed her hand. "The clinic is just like you left it last night."

Carrie forced herself to relax when she realized it was true. Only then did she answer his question about whether she was expecting patients. "Elizabeth and I did our best to remember all our patients, but I'm sure we missed some. We made a list before she left for the plantation. I had notes taken to everyone on the list, to let them know the clinic would re-open today, but they may well be too frightened to return. There are many women who couldn't be seen for their appointments while the clinic has been closed, but I don't know who they were, because the appointment book was destroyed." An image of the kerosene-soaked pile of papers flashed into her mind, but she forced it back. She couldn't quite control the tremor that rippled through her body.

Anthony turned her so he could look down into her face. "Are you sure you want to do this, Carrie?"

"No," Carrie answered honestly. "I know, however, that I *am* going to do this." She took a deep breath and forced herself to examine the clinic to make sure everything was ready. The waiting room had been outfitted with hunter green sofas and chairs. Vibrant pillows provided splashes of color. She'd ordered a coffee table and several end tables that held fresh flowers from May's garden. New oil lanterns adorned the rebuilt walls. A colorful rug covered the scarred wood, and new paintings hung on the walls. Someone who had never been here before would see nothing but a cozy, welcoming waiting room.

"It looks wonderful," Anthony said admiringly. "Your office?"

"My desk arrived yesterday, along with the chairs and the cabinets for medical records. I'm expecting my surgical table to be delivered today. Some of my equipment will take longer to arrive, but I have enough to do most procedures." In truth, she'd welcomed the frenetic activity of the last several days. It had helped tamp down the fear that threatened to rise and swallow her during moments when her guard was down.

"Good morning, Dr. Wallington."

A tall, burly man appeared from the back of the clinic.

Carrie smiled. "Good morning, Joshua. How was everything last night?" Her new guard was reserved, but his sharp eyes and ears didn't miss a thing.

"Quiet as a mouse," he said cheerfully. "Same for Leonard outside. I reckon the word has gotten out that we don't aim for anything to happen to Bregdan Medical Clinic." He patted the gun at his waistline. "The cowards who destroyed this place won't have the chance to do it again."

Carrie wished she could be so sure. She had a degree of confidence that the clinic was safe while the guards were there, but she was still scared of what might happen if they were overwhelmed by a large group of attackers. So far, all she had been doing was refurnishing the clinic. What might happen when the attackers realized she was defying their message and reopening? She forced back the tremor that she knew would alert Anthony to just how frightened she was.

Opening the clinic again on her own had been her decision. No one had made her do it. As May had told her many times in the last few days: *It's okay to feel afraid, Miss Carrie. You can feel afraid and still do brave.*

Micah sent her off every morning with a warm hug as he whispered, *"Courage rising, Miss Carrie"* in her ear.

There were moments when she felt brave and courageous, but far too many when she didn't. The sound of the door opening made her whirl around. She hated the knowledge that her heart had leapt into her throat.

"Good morning, Dr. Wallington!" Darlene burst in with a radiant smile, her red hair flashing in the sun that streamed through the open door. "I told everyone those idiot men wouldn't keep y'all from re-opening the clinic!"

Carrie stared open-mouthed as Darlene waltzed through the door, followed closely by the twenty other women who had helped clean the clinic the day of the attack. All of them looked cheerfully defiant, with broad smiles on their faces. They called out greetings as they crowded into the waiting room.

"Good morning," Carrie managed, grateful her voice wasn't shaking. She realized they had all come to offer her encouragement for the re-opening. Her heart swelled with gratitude.

Darlene looked around with a frown. "Where are Dr. Gilbert and Dr. Justin?"

"Dr. Gilbert has gone out to my clinic on the plantation to restock the medicines that were destroyed," Carrie replied. "She'll be back in a week."

Darlene held her gaze with a piercing look. "And Dr. Justin?"

Carrie smiled and told the story she and Elizabeth had agreed on. "Dr. Justin had a vacation scheduled for while I was in town. She and her family are on the plantation as well, getting a well-deserved rest." She carefully avoided mention of when Janie would return. Most of the women nodded their heads, but a few, including Darlene, were watching dubiously, as if they suspected she wasn't telling them the entire truth. Let them think what they wanted – she and Elizabeth had decided they would leave the door open for Janie to return. If that didn't happen, they would simply tell the truth then.

She gazed around at the women, grateful for their support. "Do all of you have appointments?"

"Not a single one of us, Dr. Wallington," Darlene replied. "We just figured that any new patients would feel better about things if they saw a waiting room full of women." She settled down into an empty chair. "We're going to sit right here for a while to let people know we're not afraid." She cut her eyes toward a window.

Carrie knew Darlene was sending a message to any attackers who may be watching that they had failed in their attempt to shut down the clinic. She felt her own courage rising as she looked into Darlene's eyes.

"Thank you," she said softly, her eyes sweeping the room to take them all in. "All of you are wonderful."

Ruth, one of their first seminar attendees, spoke for them. "The three of you have taught us that women have to take care of each other, Dr. Wallington. We're here for you, Dr. Gilbert and Dr. Justin." She looked at Anthony. "You can go on over to River City Carriages, Mr. Wallington. We'll take care of things here."

Carrie's throat tightened as Anthony smiled, exchanged a long look with her, and then departed. She wished Janie could be there to see what she'd had such a vital part in creating.

The sound of the door opening caused her to turn again.

A thin woman with an anxious, pinched face peered into the room, her eyes widening when she saw the large group of women. "Is this the Bregdan Medical Clinic?" she asked uncertainly.

"It is," Carrie assured her. "I'm Dr. Wallington. Do you have an appointment?"

"I do." The woman's answer was little more than a whisper.

"Please come in," Carrie said warmly. "I'm sorry, but can I get your name? We had a problem with our appointment book. Let me get you checked in and then I'll examine you." She'd decided that if patients asked about the attack, she would be forthright. If they didn't, she wasn't going to plant fear in them by bringing it up.

"Alright," the woman answered. "I'm Mrs. Josiah Buchanan."

Carrie smiled gently. "It's nice to meet you, Mrs. Buchanan. Do you have a first name?" She'd learned that far too many women identified themselves simply through their husband's name. The three partners had decided early on that they wanted to help each woman embrace their own identity – the one they had been born with.

The woman looked surprised to be asked, but then returned Carrie's smile with a weak one of her own. "Delilah," she said shyly.

"Welcome Delilah," Darlene called out. "You're in the perfect place for whatever ails you. Come on over and sit here with us while Dr. Wallington gets ready for you. Every one of us are patients here."

Delilah's eyes widened further, but she walked over and settled down next to Darlene.

Carrie watched for a moment as the women began to chat, and then slipped into her office to make sure she had everything ready for her first patient.

Bregdan Medical Clinic was back in business.

Carrie hurried to pack her last bag. She and Anthony weren't leaving for the plantation for two days, but she had important things to do before she left that didn't include packing. The sound of wagon wheels on the cobblestone road caused her to rush to the window. She smiled when she saw Peter and Elizabeth approaching the house. They must have left the plantation as soon as it was light enough to travel. Her smile widened when she realized they were driving the wagon, instead of the carriage they'd left in. She knew the back of the wagon would be full of carefully packed bottles of remedies, and countless tins of herbs. She had made do in the last week with what they'd had, but the clinic cabinets were woefully empty. Tomorrow they would be full.

"Welcome back to Richmond!" Carrie called as she stepped out onto the porch just as the wagon drew to a stop. Dark clouds on the horizon warned of an approaching storm. She hurried down to the road. "Let's drive on to the clinic and get all this unloaded before it rains."

Elizabeth glanced over her shoulder, her eyes widening when she saw the dark bank of clouds rolling in from the east. "It was clear just an hour ago," she gasped.

"Welcome to a Southern spring," Carrie replied with a laugh. "By the end of your first spring and summer, you'll be used to storms brewing out of a clear blue sky." A close look showed the relaxed expression of happiness in Elizabeth's eyes. "How was the plantation?" she asked casually.

"Wonderful," Elizabeth replied.

"Perfect," Peter said firmly. "I hated to leave."

Carrie smiled. Her plan had succeeded beautifully. If they didn't already know it, this was a couple falling in love. The faint sound of thunder rumbling in the distance propelled her into action. "Let's go!" she exclaimed. She climbed onto the driver's seat beside them and gripped the railing as Peter urged the two geldings forward.

Later that evening, Carrie found Elizabeth curled up on her window seat, inhaling the fresh scents that always followed a thunderstorm. Lanterns flickered in the breeze, the light causing the pattern on the light green wallpaper to appear to dance. White lace curtains and a white bedspread created a restful haven. "Too tired to talk?"

Elizabeth responded by patting the empty space on the window seat.

Carrie sat down, turned to face her friend, and leaned back against the wall. Settled in, she took a deep breath. The lilacs would soon be gone, but there were still enough to perfume the air. "Glorious," she murmured. Then she leaned forward and grasped Elizabeth's hand. "I want all the details."

Elizabeth cocked her head. "Details?" she asked innocently. "I thought we were going to discuss Dr. Marlboro's visit tomorrow."

"Hardly," Carrie scoffed. "I won't say a word about that until you've told me about your week with Peter."

"It was nice," Elizabeth said casually.

Carrie stared at her. "Really? You think you can get away with saying '*It was nice*'?" She shook her head. "I saw your face when you arrived. I've been watching the two of you together."

"It was *very* nice," Elizabeth said, barely emphasizing *very*.

Carrie knew how to play this game. She smiled and stood. "Good night."

Elizabeth narrowed her eyes. "You can't leave yet. We haven't talked about Dr. Marlboro."

Carrie shrugged. "She's coming tomorrow. I'm sure we'll all have a *nice* time." She turned to leave.

Elizabeth dissolved into laughter. "Stay. You win."

Carrie smirked and reclaimed her space on the window seat. "Was there ever any doubt?"

Elizabeth shook her head. "It's always at least worth a try."

Carrie grasped her hand again. "All the details," she demanded. "And, you can go ahead and thank me for sending you out to the plantation with Peter."

Elizabeth bowed her head. "Thank you from the bottom of my heart," she said dramatically. She looked up with shining eyes. "Peter is so wonderful. I never imagined I would meet someone like him. I feel like I've known him my entire life. He's so easy to talk to."

"Talk to or argue with?" Carrie teased.

Elizabeth raised a brow. "I'm Italian," she replied, as if that were the only answer needed. "Besides, he likes to argue and debate as much as I do. The funny thing is that there's almost no point. We seem to agree on just about everything."

"Doesn't that take the fun out of it for you?" Carrie asked with amusement.

Elizabeth laughed easily. "Actually, no. We both enjoy the sparring because we know our core values are the same. I'm sure we'll find things to truly argue about in the future, but for now it's enough to know we agree on the things we feel most passionate about."

Carrie raised a brow. "The future? That sounds promising."

Elizabeth flushed and smiled. "He has to return to New York City once he's finished his assignment here.

He was lucky that his editor agreed to him taking time off to go to the plantation, but he has another assignment waiting for him up North. He's going to be back in Richmond next month, though."

Carrie grinned. "He has another assignment here so soon? That's unusual."

Elizabeth matched her grin. "He proposed a story his editor couldn't refuse."

Carrie's eyes narrowed at the expression on Elizabeth's face. "What story might that be?"

"How three women started a medical clinic in the former capitol of the Confederacy." Elizabeth's eyes shone with delight.

Carrie own sense of delight faded almost as quickly as it appeared. Having a story written about them might provide protection because of the exposure – it might also make them more of a target. Her heart pounded as she considered the possible consequences.

Elizabeth grabbed both her hands. "I know what you're thinking, but Peter believes writing the story will make us so famous that no one would dare come after us. He won't do it, though, unless you agree."

Carrie took deep breaths to steady her heart. "Courage rising..." she whispered, more to herself than anyone else. She nodded slowly as the words caused her heart to resume its natural rhythm. "Alright. Let's do it." She took a deep breath and then changed the subject, not wanting to think further about what might come from a newspaper article about them. "How's Janie?"

The laughter died in Elizabeth's eyes. "Wounded." She opened her mouth as if she was going to elaborate, but shook her head and remained silent.

Carrie got more from the single word answer than a long-winded response. Without asking, she knew Janie had refused to talk about the attack, had refused to talk about returning, and had probably avoided Elizabeth so that she wouldn't be confronted with her fear. Frowning, she stared out the window. It was time for her to go home. Janie needed her.

Wordlessly, she handed over the letter she had in her dress pocket. "This is the letter from Dr. Marlboro."

Elizabeth reached for it eagerly.

Dear Dr. Wallington and Dr. Gilbert,

Thank you for your openness in exploring the possibility of me becoming part of your practice in Richmond. My mentor, Dr. Crumpler, has nothing but wonderful things to say about both of you. I have made plans to arrive in Richmond on May tenth. She tells me I'm welcome to stay at Mr. Thomas Cromwell's house while I'm there. I'm grateful for the hospitality. I look forward to meeting you both, and to discussing whether I will be a good fit for Richmond.

Sincerely,

Dr. Lucinda Marlboro

Elizabeth read it quickly and then looked up. "It will be wonderful to meet her."

Carrie nodded. "She's needed in the Black Quarters."

"Harriet and Ann?" Elizabeth asked. "How are they? We've talked about so much since I arrived, but you haven't mentioned them."

"They're both doing good," Carrie assured her. "Harriet is still dealing with the grief of losing her son, but she has a strong support system in her family, her church and the community. Her arm will remain in the cast for another few weeks, but she's managing." She smiled. "Ann is a force to be reckoned with. She's staying with Marcus and Hannah until her casts come off because she needs help, but don't try to tell her that. She's walking all over the Black Quarters, and is tutoring many of the children. She's not letting two arm casts slow her down. I check on them every few days, but they're doing well."

Elizabeth sighed with relief. "I'm so glad to hear it. I felt terrible about leaving you with everything."

"But not so terrible that you didn't have a magnificent time with Peter," Carrie teased.

Elizabeth opened her mouth to protest and then laughed. "That's true." Then her face sobered. "What you did here is amazing, Carrie. You went from being terrified, to single-handedly opening the clinic. Thank you."

Carrie turned to gaze out the window, letting the cool night air wash over her. "I'm still scared every single day. I have longer times now when I forget what happened, but then something will send it rushing back over me. There are still moments I feel I'll drown in the fear," she said honestly. "Until I think about what Abby said to May."

"Feel the fear, but *do* brave?" Elizabeth asked.

"Yes." Carrie turned to her friend. "I'm ready to go home. I'm doing brave, but I'll admit it's exhausting."

She frowned. "I hate that I'm leaving you here alone, however."

"What? You think I can't do what you just did?" Elizabeth demanded, her tone light enough to assure Carrie she wasn't offended.

"Oh, I know you can do it, but it's not exactly fun. When it was you and Janie working together, it was different. Now you'll be alone." Carrie gazed at her. "I'm going to worry about you."

"Just like I worried about you while I was out on the plantation. I'll admit I had a splendid time with Peter, but I still thought about you constantly." Her eyes blazed with intensity.

"I know you did," Carrie replied. "We'll get through this time. I'll be back in two weeks, and I know Rebecca is trying to find us another doctor. We'll also send a letter to Dr. Strikener at the Homeopathic Medical College. He might know of someone crazy enough to join us down here."

"I wrote Dr. Amberton, as well," Elizabeth revealed. "I mailed the letter when we got into Richmond today. Now that Florence is married to her brother, she may well be willing to send someone our direction. If we're really lucky, she will be a surgeon."

Carrie smiled. "The right person will come at the right time. Until then, we'll do the best we can."

Carrie and Elizabeth were waiting on the porch late the next morning when Dr. Lucinda Marlboro arrived.

They hurried down the sidewalk to greet her as the driver leapt from his seat and pulled her baggage from the back of the carriage.

"Welcome to Richmond, Dr. Marlboro," Elizabeth said.

"We're thrilled to have you here," Carrie added.

Dr. Marlboro smiled and stepped from the carriage. She was tall and elegant, her black hair smoothed back into a bun. Her skin glowed and her eyes were lively. "Hello. Thank you so much for having a carriage meet me at the station. I was quite surprised to hear my name called soon after I stepped onto the train platform." She gazed around as she talked. "It's so beautiful here. Spring is in full bloom in Boston, but it's certainly not this warm yet."

Carrie smiled. "Have you ever spent a summer in the South?"

"Many," Dr. Marlboro said dryly. "My summers were spent picking cotton in Mississippi. After spending the last eight years in Boston, however, I've almost been able to forget the terrible heat and humidity. Almost... Please tell me it doesn't get as hot in Virginia."

"It gets hot, but I assure you it doesn't match Mississippi heat," Carrie said quickly. "I had to promise Dr. Gilbert the same thing when we were trying to lure her to our practice here."

Dr. Marlboro turned to Elizabeth. "What has been your experience?"

Elizabeth shrugged. "I have no idea. I've loved my first spring, but this will be my first summer. I suspect it will be easier to endure a Southern summer than it is to endure a Boston winter."

Dr. Marlboro looked skeptical but nodded pleasantly. "Perhaps you're right. Boston winters can be brutal."

May stepped out onto the porch. "Supper is almost ready," she called. "You three might as well do your talking inside."

"We'll be right in," Carrie replied. She looked at the driver standing next to the carriage. "You're Quincy, aren't you?"

"Yes, ma'am." Quincy bobbed his head, his eyes shining with pleasure. "I'm surprised you remember. Your husband has a lot of drivers."

"It's important to me to know everyone," Carrie said warmly. "Without you, we wouldn't have a business. Thank you for bringing Dr. Marlboro. Would you be so kind as to put her baggage on the porch?"

"Of course," Quincy replied. It took him just a few moments to fulfill her request and return. "Is there anything else, ma'am?"

"No, thank you. I hope you have a pleasant rest of your day."

"The same to you, Dr. Wallington," Quincy replied earnestly. He picked up the reins and urged the horse forward.

Carrie walked into the house with Elizabeth and Dr. Marlboro. She could feel their guest eyeing her closely. She turned as they entered the foyer and met Dr. Marlboro's eyes. "What is it?"

Their guest looked embarrassed. "I'm sorry. I'm being rude."

Carrie smiled. "Not if you have a question for me. If we're going to determine whether you will be a good fit for our practice, we should begin with open honesty."

Dr. Marlboro smiled. "Dr. Crumpler told me I would like both of you. She was right."

Elizabeth shook her head. "Can we all just do away with the doctor titles? I appreciate the need for them in a professional setting, but when I'm home, I'm just Elizabeth."

"Agreed," Dr. Marlboro replied quickly. "I would appreciate it if you would call me Lucinda."

"I'm Carrie." Carrie turned back to their guest. "Now, why were you looking at me like that?"

Lucinda dropped her gaze for a moment and then looked back up. "I've seen very few people in the South treat blacks with respect. You seem genuine."

Carrie understood the puzzled question in Lucinda's eyes. "People are people, Lucinda. I believe everyone deserves to be treated with respect."

"You seem to not see the color of the skin," Lucinda said slowly. "Is that true?"

Carrie took her time answering. It was something she'd thought about a great deal. "I don't think it's possible for anyone to not see the color of skin," she finally said. "I believe the difference is that the color of someone's skin doesn't matter to me. I much prefer to find out who they are as people and learn what their character is. There are white people I don't particularly care for. There are also black people I don't particularly care for. Likewise, I have tremendous respect and liking for people of all races. It's more than that though," she continued, her thoughts congealing as she spoke.

"I believe it's *important* to see race, especially right now. When I see someone black, I instantly know at least some of the struggles and battles they're fighting. I can never fully understand, no matter how hard I try, though. A white person can't possibly know what it is to be black in this country. Being black in the South is even more daunting. I want to do everything I can to help whites understand, and I want to help every black person that I can overcome those challenges." She paused. "Including mulattoes."

Lucinda smiled. "It's obvious?"

Carrie returned her smile. "The blue eyes and light skin are a dead giveaway. At least to me."

"It doesn't bother you?"

Carrie chuckled. "My best friend, who is also my aunt, is dark-skinned. Rose was born when my grandfather raped one of our slaves. Her twin brother -my uncle - was born white. Jeremy has blond hair and blue eyes. He has twins of us own. One is very white, the other is obviously mulatto."

Lucinda's eyes brightened. "That's quite a story." She looked around. "Will I have a chance to meet them while I'm here?"

Carrie shook her head regretfully. "I'm afraid not. Rose and her family live on the plantation. Jeremy and his wife, Marietta, lived here in Richmond but were afraid to raise the twins in the South. They moved to Philadelphia shortly after they were born. Jeremy runs one of my family's factories there."

Lucinda looked uncomfortable. "Will I be in danger here?"

Carrie hesitated, but remembered her promise to communicate with open honesty. "I don't know, Lucinda. I would like to say you would be perfectly safe, but the truth is that while it's hard to be black in Richmond, it's even harder to be mulatto. Southern whites tend to take it as a personal offense that someone of their own produced a child that isn't fully white."

Lucinda cocked her head. "Do they have any idea how prevalent it was during the days of slavery? Just how many mulattoes are in this country?"

"They prefer to not be bothered with facts that don't fit their view of life," Carrie said flatly. "I want you to decide to stay here, but I want you to understand what you might face."

Lucinda nodded thoughtfully. "What was it like for Jeremy?"

"Jeremy is an unusual case," Carrie answered. "He was adopted by a white family when he was just a baby. He never knew he was half black until he was in his twenties. He easily passed as completely white."

"And after he discovered the truth?"

Carrie smiled. "He and Rose are very close. He refused to deny his heritage because he wanted to make things better for Rose and her family. He worked closely with many people in the Black Quarters to make improvements." She frowned. "As more Richmonders discovered he was actually mulatto, it became more difficult for him. I suspect he and Marietta would have stayed, however, if he hadn't had the twins to consider."

Lucinda turned to gaze at Elizabeth. "Do you have a hard time here?"

Elizabeth met her eyes. "Because I'm an Italian Yankee who obviously looks like one and definitely sounds like one?" She smiled and shrugged. "I've certainly had comments and looks that made me feel uncomfortable, but I also have friends here that make me feel safe." She paused. "I'm assuming Rebecca told you about the attack on the clinic?"

"She did."

"The truth of the matter is that all of us are at risk," Elizabeth said. "We're women who are daring to challenge Southern tradition by being doctors who treat other women. Whether we're white, Italian, black or mulatto, we always have to be careful." She eyed Lucinda. "I'm sure you're already aware of this. A black woman daring to be a doctor didn't get away without some tough experiences, even in Boston."

"That's true," Lucinda agreed.

Carrie watched their guest carefully, recognizing the pain of the memories that had caused Lucinda's eyes to darken. It was easy to imagine the bigotry their guest had endured to become a physician. "Why did you decide to come to the South, Lucinda?"

"Because I feel I owe it to my people. I know I'm half-white, but as far as the country is concerned, I'm black. Even in Boston, I'm viewed as a black woman." She paused briefly. "I know how hard it is for blacks to get medical treatment in the South. I want to help because I was so lucky. When I was set free from slavery, I went to New Orleans. I was eighteen. There was a mulatto woman there, Beth Trudeau, who saw something in me. I had learned how to read on the plantation where I was a slave..."

"How?" Carrie asked, intrigued by the story. "It was outlawed in the South."

"Our owner was a good man. He bought my mother when he saw her on the auction block with a child who was obviously half-white. I was two. I was the result of my mother being raped by one of her previous owner's sons. His family was horrified by what he'd done, but they didn't want to face the evidence on the rape on a daily basis, so they sold us." She smiled. "It was the best thing that could have happened to her. My mother remarried on the plantation when I was six. She had two more children. I considered him my true father. He was a fine man. I worked cotton in the fields when I was old enough, but our owner allowed us to have our nights free. My mother was a healer. She taught me about the medicinal qualities of plants and herbs. I was fascinated from the moment I realized how magical the plants could be."

Carrie smiled, recognizing the same fascination she had developed while helping her mother, and then later learning about the plants from Sarah.

"One of the other slaves knew how to read," Lucinda continued. "She decided to teach anyone who wanted to learn. I jumped at the chance when I was just seven. Once I learned how to make sense of the letters, I couldn't get my hands on enough books. My owner allowed me to take books from his library. He even bought some of the books I asked for."

"That's unusual," Carrie murmured, thinking of how Rose had risked a beating to take books from the

Cromwell library. Her father hadn't been cruel, but at that point in his life he had definitely believed slaves were incapable of learning.

"Yes," Lucinda agreed. "I think he privately hated slavery, but he believed it was the only way to run the cotton plantation he'd inherited from his father. We worked hard, but it wasn't that terrible of a life. We ate well, he clothed us, and I got to learn. Of course, I was thrilled when I heard about the Emancipation Proclamation. I'd had a lot of dreams that I never imagined could come true. Suddenly, I was free. I believe my owner was happy, too. He could set us all free and not be different from all the other plantation owners." She shook her head slightly. "When I told him I was leaving, he gave me a letter and enough money to get to New Orleans. It was the closest town of any size. The letter was to Beth Trudeau. She took me in and helped me go to school. I cleaned her house and cooked, but most of my time was spent studying. When I was ready, she paid for me to travel to Boston, and then covered the tuition for medical school."

"Extraordinary," Elizabeth murmured, and then raised a brow. "Why aren't you looking for a practice in New Orleans?"

Lucinda laughed. "If I am never that hot again, it will be too soon. When I left Mississippi and New Orleans, I vowed to never return. I love Beth, but she knows if she wants to see me, she must come to Boston."

"Has she?" Carrie asked, amazed by the story she was hearing.

"Every year since I left," Lucinda answered. "She's like a mother to me."

"Your own mother?" Elizabeth asked. "What happened to her?"

Lucinda's eyes darkened. "She chose to stay in the South with my father and my siblings. She loved the plantation where I grew up, so they decided to work there once they were free. She left the fields and took care of the house, though. Her life was much easier, and she was happy. I talked her into visiting one time, but she said humans weren't meant to be cold." She smiled slightly, but it faded quickly. "Mama was taken by cholera four years ago. My father died, as well." She shook her head as if to dispel the memories and looked at Carrie. "I've known who you were since right after they died," she revealed.

Carrie's eyes widened. "How?"

"My mother and father died in the cholera epidemic that took so many lives all over the country in 1867. I don't remember her name, but I met a student from the Women's Medical College at a conference in Boston, shortly after you dropped out to study Homeopathy. I had just started medical school. She told me of the success you had with the homeopathic remedies for hundreds of Irish and black cholera patients in Moyamensing. I was fascinated and wanted to go to the homeopathic college in Philadelphia, but I stayed in Boston to help care for my younger brother and sister after my parents died. Beth paid for their travel to join me after they passed away, and she has paid for their schooling. I couldn't move, but I made sure to learn everything I could about homeopathy. Rebecca has been an amazing mentor. She sent me as many resources as she could get her hands on, and directed me to faculty that was friendly toward homeopathy." Lucinda reached out to take Carrie's hand. "It's only because of you that my education was so well-rounded. I can't tell you what an honor it is to finally meet you."

Carrie blinked back tears. "Thank you for telling me that."

"Y'all ever gonna get done yapping?" May called. "You walk just about twenty more feet, and you can yap at the dining room table that has food on it."

The three women laughed as they hurried into the dining room.

Early the next morning, Carrie turned around in the wagon seat and waved good-bye to Elizabeth and Lucinda once more. The two women had gotten up early to see them off. The sun was just beginning to lighten the sky but was still far below the horizon.

"Lucinda is a wonderful woman," Anthony said.

"She is," Carrie agreed. "She's going to be perfect for the Black Quarters, and I'm glad she and Elizabeth will have each other for support."

"Did you ask her about living here at the house?"

"We did, but after visiting the Quarters yesterday afternoon, she decided to live there. She'll move down in two weeks. Marcus and Hannah are going to rent her their extra room once I take the casts off Ann's arms. Ann will move back in with Harriet's family, and Lucinda will take her place. Lucinda feels strongly that she'll have a better relationship with her patients if she lives there, but it's more than that."

"She knows it will be easier to reach them if there's an emergency," Anthony said knowingly. "With things the way they are right now, it could be dangerous for her to travel into the Quarters, and it could be dangerous for patients to attempt to reach her in an emergency."

"Correct," Carrie said heavily. "It's going to be hard for Lucinda no matter where she is, but having us to work with is going to make it easier." She shook her head and pushed away lingering thoughts. "Let's go home."

Chapter Nine

"Mama! Daddy!" Frances ran toward the carriage, her light brown braids bouncing off her back. "You're home!"

Minnie was right behind her, red braids glowing in the sun that had deepened her freckles. "Carrie! Anthony! It's about time you got home."

Carrie was thrilled to see her two daughters. Minnie, whom they adopted only six months earlier, was still uncomfortable using anything but their first names, but she was just glad her daughter was happy. After the devastation of losing her entire family in a Philadelphia boarding house fire, being on the plantation was healing her a little more each day.

Carrie jumped down from the wagon and pulled her daughters close, one in each arm as she hugged them. "I missed you both," she whispered, emotion clogging her throat. Leaving them was far harder than she imagined it would be when she'd agreed to split her time between the clinics. She knew they were loved and well-cared for on the plantation, but that didn't make her miss them any less. She held them at arm's length and inspected them. "You've grown since I last saw you."

Minnie giggled. "You say that every time you come home."

"That's because it's true every time I come home."

"She's right, you know." Anthony had pulled the carriage up to the barn and then rejoined them.

"Daddy!"

"Anthony!"

He laughed as he pulled his daughter's close. "I missed you."

Carrie met his eyes when he looked over the tops of their heads. She knew he was thinking the exact same thing she was. What she didn't know was what they were going to do about it. When they had decided on the plan that would have them splitting their time between Richmond and the plantation, they had assumed the girls would be with them in both places. It hadn't taken long to realize that moving the girls back and forth wasn't the best for them. They were happy in school and with their friends. Not to mention how completely at home they both felt on the plantation.

"Welcome home!"

Abby's voice pulled her thoughts back to the present. Smiling, Carrie ran up the stairs to envelope her mother in her arms. "I missed you."

Abby hugged her warmly, and then held her back so she could examine her. Her piercing gray eyes, full of both wisdom and compassion, always saw straight through to her soul. "I'm glad you're home. You need to be here."

Carrie nodded, tears pricking her eyes. "Yes," she whispered. She knew they would talk later. For now, it was enough simply to feel Abby's arms around her.

When Carrie stepped back, her father swept her into a strong embrace. She'd not heard him come up behind her. "Father!"

"I'm glad you're alright, Carrie. I was worried." Her father's vibrant blue eyes seemed to glow even brighter beneath his silver hair. Once blond, the war years had turned it gray far sooner than it should have.

"I know," Carrie replied. "I'm sorry. I had to stay, though."

"Of course you did," her father said quietly. "I've spent most of your life worrying about you. I don't suppose it will change now. Besides," he added gently, "I'm proud of what you did. Elizabeth explained what happened."

"Did everything go as you hoped?" Abby asked. "Is the clinic open again?"

"Yes. Thanks to you and May."

Abby raised a brow. "Come again?"

"The morning after the attack, I was so terrified I could hardly breathe. I was certain I couldn't ever be in the clinic again. I was ready to come home and just work on the plantation." Carrie smiled. "May listened to all she could, and then banged her hand down on the dining room table to break through our panic." A quick laugh escaped her lips. "She certainly got our attention. That's when she told me just how hard things had been for you in Philadelphia, when you were left alone to run the factories. I knew things had been difficult, but I didn't have a clear picture of how much you truly struggled." Her voice softened. "She told us what you told her. *It's alright to feel the fear, as long as you do brave.*" As always, saying the words made things clearer for Carrie. "I knew I had to stay in Richmond and *do brave.*"

Abby caught her tight in another hug. "I'm proud of you," she whispered.

Carrie finally pulled back, laughing as she watched Anthony cavort on the lawn with their daughters in a raucous game of tag. Moments later, John and Hope dashed from the house to run down to the grass and join in the game.

"The girls missed you."

"Not as much as I missed them," Carrie replied. "Did they cause any trouble?"

"Not a bit," Abby assured her. "Your father and I adore being with our grandchildren. We lavish them with love, but they still miss you."

Carrie sighed. "I know. I don't know what to do."

Abby gazed at her for a long moment and then smiled gently. "You and Anthony will make the right decision."

Carrie wasn't so certain, but she took comfort in Abby's confidence. She looked around. Rose wouldn't be home from school yet, and Moses would still be in the tobacco fields, but she was surprised Janie hadn't come out to greet her. "How is Janie?"

"I don't know," Abby said, her eyes darkening with concern. "We haven't seen her for a week."

Abby's words momentarily stunned Carrie into silence. "What do you mean? I thought she and Matthew were here. Where is she?"

"Harold is out of town working on a story for the *New York Times*, so Susan decided she'd stay here and let Matthew, Janie and the kids use their house. We haven't seen them since they left."

Carrie swallowed hard. Harold was Matthew's twin. It wasn't surprising that he and Susan would be generous enough to share their house while he was out of town, but Carrie knew it meant far more than that. Janie was withdrawing from everyone. "I've got to go see her," she whispered.

"She needs you," Abby agreed. Her eyes turned to the lawn where Anthony was being jumped on by shrieking children.

Carrie understood the unspoken message. "I'll go see her in the morning." Turning, she ran down the steps to join in the fun.

Carrie pulled Granite to a stop and dismounted. She had expected Robert to come barreling out the front door, but the house remained silent. She frowned as she examined the curtained windows. Harold and Susan had built an adorable home on the land her father had sold them at a wonderful price. Susan loved the plantation so much that Harold had surprised her with a smaller replica of the Cromwell plantation house. It glowed white in the early morning May sunshine – one story, with the white columns Susan loved held up the porch roof. Two rocking chairs, identical to the ones at the plantation porch, sat near the front door. Harold had even planted matching oak trees flanking the porch, so they would one day tower above the house.

Carrie walked up the steps, listening carefully for any noise. She heard nothing, but every instinct told her Janie was inside. Most likely, Matthew had taken the children for an outing to give his wife some time alone. She knocked firmly on the door.

The house remained silent.

"Janie!" Carrie called. "Please let me in. I want to talk."

Nothing.

Carrie hesitated and then grabbed the door handle, hopeful it wouldn't be locked. She breathed a sigh of relief when the door swung open. "Janie," she called again. "I'm coming in." She walked through the foyer, crossed the parlor, and opened the door to Harold and Susan's room.

Janie was on the bed, the covers held up to her neck. She remained silent as Carrie walked closer.

Carrie was horrified at how much weight her friend had lost, but it was the dead look in her eyes that tore at her heart. Why had she stayed in Richmond? She should have been here with her friend. No patient was worth more than the woman she had gone through so much with. "Janie," she whispered. She strode forward and gripped one of the hands holding the covers. It was ice cold.

"Hello," she said softly.

Janie gazed at her for a long moment and nodded slightly before looking away in shame.

Carrie was at a loss for what to say. How could she break through the shield Janie had put around herself? Slowly, memories of her own pain after Robert's murder filtered through her disbelief. The cause of the trauma was different, but the lost, dead look in Janie's eyes was the same as how she'd felt. Words, no matter how well-meaning, had meant nothing to her then.

Carrie silently climbed onto the bed next to her friend, wrapped an arm around her, and pulled her close. With her other hand, she stroked Janie's hair while she prayed for wisdom.

Janie's rigid body remained still and unpliable. She didn't pull away, but she held herself aloof and withdrawn.

Carrie continued to hold her close. The only thing she knew to do was simply be there with her. She watched out the window as birds flitted through the limbs of the young oak tree. Someday it would nest dozens of birds. Now, it was a fleeting haven for birds passing through.

Finally, after what seemed an eternity, Janie spoke. "I'm sorry," she whispered.

"There's nothing to be sorry for," Carrie replied. "What happened was terrible."

"You stayed," Janie said in a trembling voice.

"This isn't about comparisons," Carrie said firmly, but gently. "We all have our breaking points. Mine came when Robert was killed. I walked away from living for a long time. The pain was so great I could scarcely breathe at times. The people who cared about me did all the things I was incapable of doing."

Janie was silent for a long moment as she thought about what Carrie said. "That's different. You lost your husband. I just..."

"You just have given everything you have in your heart for a long time," Carrie finished for her. "You worked at the Moyamensing Clinic while you were in school. You've had two beautiful children. You finished your medical degree against all odds. You've launched a clinic that has reached dozens of women in a city that largely doesn't think we should be there. Seeing the violent destruction of what you worked so hard to create was your breaking point. It is completely understandable."

Carrie fell silent and waited. She was content to let it go on for as long as was needed. She had no expectation of how Janie would respond – or if she would respond at all. The only sound in the room was the ticking of the grandfather clock in the corner. Even the birds, as if they sensed the solemnity of the moment, had gone quiet.

"I can't go... back," Janie finally said with a trembling voice.

"Alright," Carrie said calmly. She had already suspected this was what would happen.

"You're not mad? Or disappointed?" Janie's voice was both disbelieving and hopeful.

"Not a bit," Carrie assured her. "I understand what you're feeling."

Another silence took over the room.

Carrie was the one who broke it this time. "May I ask if you still want to be a doctor? If you don't know the answer to the question, that's alright."

Janie waited so long to answer that Carrie suspected she wasn't going to.

"How can I?" Janie said in a quivering voice. "I can't go back."

Carrie was ready with the answer. "Stay here on the plantation with me. I need another doctor in my practice. We can still work together – we'll just do it in a different way."

Janie sucked in her breath. "Stay here on Cromwell?"

Carrie listened closely, certain she heard desperate hope in Janie's voice. "Yes."

Janie shook her head. "What about Elizabeth?" Her voice was thin and reedy, but at least she was talking.

"This isn't about Elizabeth," Carrie said firmly. "It's not about me, either. This is about what is best for you and your family."

"Matthew and the children would love to live here," Janie admitted, a little more hope shining through the deadness in her voice.

Carrie couldn't see her face, but she knew her friend's soft blue eyes were showing just a little more life. She truly did understand. Janie's tender heart had simply endured more than it could bear. Carrie wanted to give her hope, but she also wanted to be truthful. "You do realize there could be trouble out here, as well?"

"It's different here," Janie replied. "I feel safe on Cromwell Plantation."

Carrie did too. They'd experienced more than their share of attacks and violence, but cocooned by everyone's love, she still felt safe when she was here.

"Besides, there's always the tunnel."

Carrie laughed at the trace of humor in Janie's voice. She also recognized the truth of her comment. "Yes, there is always the tunnel." The hidden tunnel on the plantation had saved all of them more than once. No matter what happened, they would always have that safe haven.

Janie twisted so she could gaze up into Carrie's eyes. "You're truly not disappointed or mad?"

Carrie smiled. "Not a bit. I hate the attack on the clinic happened, but is it alright to say that I'm thrilled we'll be working out here together? That I'm thrilled you'll be here when I'm not? Polly is a wonderful assistant, but the clinic has grown enough that it needs two doctors. My patients are so grateful to receive treatment that they don't care one whit that I'm a woman. They also know that if anything happens to the clinic, no one will be able to receive care. There are a lot of people who watch over it."

"Yes," Janie said softly. "I've seen that. Carrie, if you're quite certain, then the answer is yes." She gazed out the window, her eyes showing more of the life Carrie loved. "What are we going to do about the house in Richmond? Where are we going to live? Harold and Susan will be back in a week. We can't stay here."

Carrie had thought through all that. "Stay out here for the extra week. Enjoy being with Matthew and the children. Eat a lot of food to gain back the weight you've lost. When Harold returns, you can come back to the main house just until something else can be done. Besides, you might decide you don't want to stay on the plantation long-term. You could decide to practice up North somewhere. Philadelphia. Boston. New York."

Janie shuddered. "I never want to live in a big city again, Carrie. I want to be here on the plantation. I want my children to grow up here, surrounded by people who love them. I want them to have the animals and be able to swim in the river." She paused. "Cromwell feels like home."

Carrie smiled happily. "Well then, welcome home, Dr. Justin."

Carrie was waiting for Rose when she stepped out of the schoolhouse. They'd seen each other the night before but had hardly been able to talk.

"Carrie!" Rose raised a brow. "What is Maple doing here?"

Carrie had ridden home from Janie's, gone by the stable to tack up Rose's mare, Maple, and then come to the school. "How about a ride to the river? Frances and Minnie are taking care of John and Hope."

"The children are already home?" she asked with surprise.

Carrie laughed. "Ned brought them home long ago. What were you doing in there? School was dismissed almost two hours ago. I've been here almost an hour. I wasn't sure you were ever going to come out, but I didn't want to interrupt what must have been important."

Rose sighed but didn't answer. "Can we talk about it while we ride?"

"Of course," Carrie said instantly, not missing the look of worry in her best friend's eyes. "Annie said she would keep dinner hot for us if we don't get back in time."

"That's nice of her," Rose said absently, her eyes taking on a faraway look.

"Rose..." Carrie felt a twinge of alarm.

"How's Janie?" Rose asked.

Clearly, Rose wasn't ready to talk about what was troubling her, but Carrie figured if she was willing to go for a ride, she wasn't fearing an attack on the plantation. Carrie would give her time to process whatever was going on.

"Better," she replied. She told Rose about their conversation and about Janie's decision to stay.

"She's staying here on the plantation?" Rose asked with delight. "That's wonderful news! I've been so worried about her. I know Matthew has been, as well."

"It's going to be great for everyone," Carrie agreed.

Rose frowned. "What about Elizabeth?"

"It will be a challenge, but we're looking for someone else to join the practice. Elizabeth knew there was a very likely chance that Janie wouldn't return. Besides, I'll be there half the month."

"For how long?" Rose asked quietly.

"How long for what?" Carrie asked. She knew what Rose was getting ready to ask, but she chose to stall the need for an immediate answer.

"How long are you going to be willing to go back and forth? When you decided to do this, you thought the girls would be with you when you were in Richmond. It hasn't turned out that way. You're there. Frances and Minnie are here." She stopped Maple and turned to meet Carrie's eyes. "Are you happy with that?"

That was a question Carrie could answer. "No."

"What are you going to do about it?"

"I don't know," Carrie admitted. "It's getting harder and harder to be apart from them. We opened the clinic in January. It's May. I've been away from them six weeks of that time. I know the girls are happy here, but I miss them terribly."

"They miss you, too," Rose answered, a serious look in her eyes.

Carrie tensed. "What aren't you telling me?" When Rose hesitated, she felt a jolt of alarm. "Rose? Tell me."

Rose sighed. "Minnie is back to having a hard time in school. She had started doing so much better, but now she seems so sad. I've asked her about it. She just tells me that she misses you and Anthony."

Carrie felt a surge of sadness as Rose's words sank into her mind and heart. "I thought I was doing the right thing letting the girls stay here."

"I believe you are," Rose answered.

"But you just said Minnie is having a hard time in school because she misses us."

"I did."

Carrie gritted her teeth. Whenever her friend acted like this, she was trying to get Carrie to see something on her own. This time, Carrie didn't have to try – she'd been seeing it for weeks. "I know what you're saying." A crush of confusion, frustration and guilt swirled through her.

"What am I saying?"

"You're saying I should stay here on the plantation. Not continue with the clinic."

"I'm not saying anything," Rose protested. "I'm just giving you information."

"Hogwash," Carrie said impatiently. "You're just like your mama – leading me right where she wanted me to go with her questions and observations."

"There might be truth to that," Rose admitted with a twinkle in her eyes.

"I'm confused," Carrie admitted. "I love the clinic here on the plantation, but one of the reasons I did the internship for my surgical certification was so that the clinic in Richmond would have that to offer. With Florence not returning..." She fought to make sense of her thoughts as she watched the flashes of red as cardinals darted from one tree to the next. "I feel guilty."

"About what?"

"Everything. I feel guilty about leaving the girls. I feel guilty about leaving Elizabeth. I feel guilty about not being there for Richmond patients when they need a surgeon." Carrie clinched her fists as all the feelings she'd been holding back threatened to overwhelm her. "I feel guilty about not being here for patients when I'm in Richmond."

"That's a powerful amount of guilt," Rose replied calmly. "You must feel like you're going to drown at times." Her dark eyes glowed with knowing.

Carrie just nodded. Rose already knew she felt all that. There was no need to voice the thoughts her best friend already knew and understood.

"What do you want?"

Carrie shrugged. "What does it matter?"

"It completely matters," Rose said bluntly. "As far as I can tell, no matter what you do, you're going to feel guilty about it. If you're going to feel guilty no matter what, what's the decision you would feel *best* about in the midst of your guilt?"

"I'm going to have to analyze that sentence to see if it even makes sense."

"You know exactly what I'm saying," Rose replied. "You're just avoiding answering it. What do *you* want?" She spoke deliberately, as if speaking to one of her students who was slow in understanding.

Carrie searched for a way out of the conversation. "I thought we were going to ride and talk about whatever is causing the worried look you had when you left the school."

Rose chuckled. "We might eventually get to that – if you stop avoiding what we're talking about right now."

Carrie laughed, but she knew Rose was right. No matter what she decided, she was going to feel guilty about it. The question she had to answer, was what decision would give her the *most* peace? "I had a long conversation with your mama one day, right before I turned eighteen. I wanted to leave the plantation more than anything, but I felt guilty for wanting it because I knew how horrified my mother would be. A good Southern girl always followed her mother's direction."

"What did she say?"

Carrie thought back to that day. She and Sarah had been sitting on chairs, watching the children play in the slave quarters clearing while their parents worked the tobacco fields. Sarah, dressed in white, as always, had looked at her with wise eyes and taken her hand. Carrie smiled as she remembered. "She told me that it was good guilt if it made me do what I needed to in order to be true to myself. She told me I owed it to myself to be myself." She felt the words resonate again. "Then she told me it was false guilt if I felt it just because I wasn't being what someone else thought I should be."

Rose smiled. "That sounds like Mama. How would you answer that now? What is it you need to do to truly be yourself?"

Carrie gazed at Rose. Backlit by the sun filtering through the trees, her slender, erect figure seemed to be surrounded by a halo of light that illuminated her beautiful face. "You look like an angel," she said suddenly.

Rose rolled her eyes. "I can assure you I'm not. You know that better than anyone. But I *am* persistent. What is it that *you* want, Carrie?"

Carrie hesitated, but then answered honestly. "I want to be on the plantation with my girls. With you and Moses, and the children. With Father and Abby. With Granite. With Susan and the horses. With my patients. With everyone." Saying the words out loud made her realize just how much she truly wanted to be here. She reached down and put a hand on Granite's shimmering neck before she looked up. "What do I do about the Bregdan Medical Clinic?"

"You help Elizabeth find another doctor. Or two. Surely, there must be other women physicians who are crazy enough to want to come down to the South," Rose replied.

Carrie knew Rose was right, and she was certain what she wanted, but it wasn't alleviating the guilt of making the decision she wanted to make. "I don't understand why I started the clinic, if I'm not meant to be part of it."

"You'll always be a part of it, to some degree, but your job was to plant the seed and cultivate it until it sprouted. Now it's someone else's job to water it, fertilize it, and nurture it." A flicker of pain flashed in Rose's eyes. "We're not always meant to see something all the way through, even if we want to."

Carrie watched her friend closely. "We're not just talking about me anymore, are we?"

It was Rose's turn to sigh. "No," she admitted.

"What happened?"

"First," Rose said, "what have you decided? We're not leaving this conversation unfinished."

Carrie knew only one decision was going to give her peace. "I'm staying on the plantation," she said firmly. "I'll help Elizabeth make the transition, but I'm not going to keep leaving Frances and Minnie."

"Being a parent changes things, doesn't it?" Rose asked softly.

"I had no idea just how much it would change things. It's not a sacrifice, though," Carrie said thoughtfully. "There's nothing I love more than being with Frances and Minnie. I know it's best for them to be here on the plantation, but I miss them every day I'm away from them."

"How will Anthony feel about this?"

Carrie's heart swelled as she thought of her husband. "He told me on the way back to the plantation that he would understand if I didn't want to keep traveling back and forth. It's not necessary for him to be in Richmond two weeks at a time. He can still go there when needed. I can take the girls into Richmond for fun trips, without them missing school."

"You didn't already jump on that opportunity?" Rose asked in disbelief. She shook her head and laughed. "Don't bother to answer that. I already know you feel guilty about making your decision." Her eyes sharpened. "How do you feel about staying? You believe you're making the right decision for the girls, but how does staying make *you* feel?"

Carrie pulled Sarah's words back into her mind as she pushed back the guilt that she knew wasn't hers to carry. "Fabulous," she said happily. "Absolutely fabulous!" She laughed and turned to Rose. "Your turn, my friend. What's going on at the school?"

"Let's just enjoy the fact that you're staying on the plantation," Rose answered.

"I intend to," Carrie retorted. "But not until you tell me what's created that look in your eyes. I would prefer you just tell me – not make me push you as hard as you pushed me."

"That hardly seems fair," Rose replied. "Pushing for answers is half the fun."

Carrie glared at her and remained silent.

"Fine." Rose's smile faded, replaced by worry and frustration. "I can't teach my white students anymore. I have to send them all away."

Chapter Ten

Carrie gaped at her. "What are you talking about?"

Rose struggled to calm her racing thoughts. Focusing on Carrie's problems for a while had been a welcome relief. As everything came flooding back in, it was suddenly more than she could handle. "I'll race you to the river," she called as she urged Maple into a canter.

Maple was a gentle, wonderful mare. Fast, she was not. Granite could win the race and not exert himself at all. This was a game they often played. Granite had always been the fastest, strongest horse on the plantation. Now that he was aging, Carrie was careful to not let him overexert himself. Racing Maple gave him the feeling of being victorious, but he never even broke a sweat.

Rose leaned over Maple's neck, letting the wind blow against her face, longing for it to blow away all her troubles. She knew they would be waiting for her on the banks of the James River, but she could pretend for a few minutes.

"See you there!" Carrie called as Granite easily passed them.

Rose watched the tall, gray Thoroughbred's strides eat the road stretched out ahead of them. Moments later, he and Carrie disappeared into the shadow of the trees, following the trail that led to the river.

Rose was content to let Maple follow at her pace. Her mare might not be fast, but her gaits were as smooth as glass. Riding her was a joy. She lifted her face to relish the feel of the sun and the beauty of the azure blue sky. A thin, white film of clouds scuttled in the breeze, but the horizon was clear. There would be no thunderstorm today.

She scanned the fields stretched out before her, wondering if she would see Moses in the distance. She knew her husband was checking on the new crop of tobacco that blanketed the plantation in a fresh coat of green. This crop, more than any since he had taken over running the plantation, was vitally important. The previous year's crop had been lost to a massive flood just one week before it would have been harvested. The sense of loss had been made easier by the realization that their son, John, hadn't been lost in the flood that had swept him away from the banks of the raging river. It was a miracle that had saved him. Rose hoped a similar miracle would create a successful harvest to make up for all they had lost.

Maple dipped into the woods, following the trail she knew so well, without Rose seeing Moses. She ducked low lying branches as they flew down the trail. Making sure a branch didn't knock her off Maple's back was enough to take her mind off her troubles.

Carrie was waiting when they broke out of the woods onto the riverbank.

Rose pulled Maple down to a walk, not wanting the mare to twist her leg on a rock or boulder. She rode next to Carrie and gazed out over the river. The bright blue water shimmered in the late afternoon sun. A soft breeze created a sheen of ripples over the water that stretched as far as the eye could see. Faint circles on the surface revealed there were fish just below, waiting for bugs to land so they could snap them up. Today, as always, the river filled her with peace. She took deep breaths of the late spring air.

"It's incredible out here," Carrie said softly.

Rose was in complete agreement. She loved every season on Cromwell Plantation, but spring was by far her favorite. The cold winter had been swallowed by warmth and color, but they weren't yet dealing with the heat, humidity and mosquitoes that were waiting just beyond the horizon. Summer would be there soon. "The water is almost warm enough for swimming," she murmured.

"Almost," Carrie replied. "Frances has told Minnie all about our swimming last summer. Minnie can hardly wait for it to be her turn." She smiled with anticipation, but then became serious. "Talk."

Rose wished she could just stare at the river in silence, but she knew if the roles were reversed that she would want Carrie to tell her what was going on. "A representative from the Board of Education came to the school today as I was sending the children home."

Carrie frowned. "I didn't think they would come out here so quickly."

"I didn't either," Rose said ruefully. "I'm quite sure someone from the KKK made sure they were aware of my school." She was thrilled the new Virginia constitution had mandated free public education for every child in the state just a year earlier, but she had hoped the black members of the General Assembly would keep the state from segregating black and white students. Their efforts had failed.

Thomas Bayne, a convention delegate who had escaped from slavery twenty years earlier had introduced an amendment that would have prohibited segregation in the schools. The proposed amendment of the state constitution had failed by a vote of fifty-six to fifteen. Despite that failure, there was still hope the General Assembly would prohibit segregation in the final bill and plan. That hadn't happened. Most of the black assemblymen objected to the denial of equal rights laid out by the Fourteenth Amendment, but their votes against the bill's passage had done no good.

The bill required racial segregation of Virginia schools.

"Peter told us this might happen," Carrie reminded her gently.

"Yes. We talked about it at length when he was here with Elizabeth." Rose shook her head. "Many good things are happening for students across the state. The new state superintendent, William Ruffner, has worked very hard to build the system's infrastructure. He's already created more than fifteen hundred free public schools and he's hired thousands of teachers. I hear that by August, there will be twenty-eight hundred schools, and at least three thousand teachers." Her face creased with anxiety. "The problem is huge, however. It will take far more schools and teachers to change things. Peter told me about the 1870 Census while he was here."

Carrie watched the emotions play across her friend's face. "We didn't talk about that while he was in Richmond."

Rose, still trying to avoid the conversation that had happened that afternoon, filled her in on what she'd learned. "The Census of 1870 revealed just how poorly educated most Virginians are. About forty-four percent of all people in the state older than ten can't read. One of every four white Virginians older than ten can't write." Her frown deepened. "Nine out of *every ten* black people can't write."

"Still?" Carrie was shocked. "I had no idea it was that high."

"Still," Rose said grimly. "The Freedmen's Bureau has done great things, but they haven't had long enough to meet the massive need. Only 11,000 freed slaves have gone to school – out of more than half a million. The vast majority haven't had any education at all above an elementary level."

"Which makes your school even more unusual," Carrie said proudly. "When students get done at your school, they can go on to college."

Rose swallowed hard. "Only the black students now." She looked at Carrie. "I have to send all the white students home."

"I don't understand," Carrie protested. "I thought that if it came to this, you would separate the classes and teach them at a different time."

Rose blinked back the tears pricking her eyelids. "I thought so, too. As it turns out, black teachers can't have white students."

Carrie's eyes widened. "They won't *allow* you to teach them?"

Rose nodded, still trying to absorb what she'd been told. The representative hadn't been rude. In fact, the man, Philip Lofton, had seemed almost apologetic. In the end, however, he had been quite firm. By Virginia law, she could not teach white students.

"You could teach them anyway," Carrie said angrily. "This is just wrong. I want Frances and Minnie to have you as a teacher. They adore you."

"Believe me, I've considered it. I spent the first hour, after he left, working on ways I could go around the Board of Education's mandate." Rose scowled. "If I got caught though, I would lose my teaching certification." She blinked rapidly. "I wouldn't be able to teach anyone, Carrie."

Carrie felt the pain of her admission. "I'm so sorry," she finally said. "How can the Board of Education think this will help students?"

"All they care about is that there's no mixing of the races," Rose said bitterly. After all they had gone through to create harmony among their students, she couldn't believe it was all going to be undone by state law. She was both infuriated and distraught.

"Does Alvin know?"

"No." Rose was dreading the conversation with her most supportive white parent. In the beginning, Alvin had been violently opposed to his children learning in a school with black children and a black teacher. His children, however, had thrived at Rose's school. Alvin's mind had opened, allowing him to become good friends with Jeb, the black employee of Cromwell Plantation that acted as a guard when school was in session. Alvin oversaw a group of white parents who protected the school anytime they suspected there was danger. "He's going to be upset. So will all the other parents."

"As they should be," Carrie retorted. "As *I* am. What's the good of the Fourteenth Amendment giving blacks equal rights, if they're not going to be given equal opportunity? And who thought separating them wouldn't also be a hardship on white students?"

"Good questions," Rose responded. "Right now, however, they're taking rights away from the white students as a byproduct of keeping blacks in their place." She heard the bitterness in her voice but made no attempt to control it. After all they had been through to create a school where every student thrived, it was unthinkable that a new law could strip it all away.

"What are your white students going to do? What about Frances and Minnie?"

Rose shrugged. "The representative said there are plans to start a school out in this area after the summer, but he couldn't tell me when or where. I'm not going to be able to answer anyone's questions right now." She gritted her teeth. "I have no idea when I'll be able to."

Carrie looked thoughtful. "Can white teachers have black students?"

"For now," Rose said. "I have no idea what it will be like in the future."

A long silence stretched out as both them considered how they would deal with the ramifications of the Board of Education's mandate.

"Is Phoebe still coming back?" Carrie asked? "Isn't she graduating from Oberlin this month?"

"Yes." Rose had already thought about what Carrie was thinking. Phoebe Waterston had accompanied her daughter Felicia home from school the year before. Phoebe had fallen in love with the school and the plantation and had asked if she could return to teach. "She's bringing Felicia home next week. I'm excited to have her teach with me, but she can't do more. I thought about having Phoebe teach the white students, but I was informed we couldn't have white students in the school at all."

Carrie's eyes widened, and then narrowed with outrage. "They're not allowed in the *building*? My daughters legally can't enter the schoolhouse?"

"Not as students," Rose whispered, her gut clenching as she said the words.

Then we do it another way," Carrie said angrily.

Rose loved it when Carrie got angry. She was usually easy-going, but injustice always raised her ire. "What do you have in mind?" She didn't want to get her hopes up. She had to find a way to tell her students that the government wasn't going to allow them to go to school together anymore. And she had to do it in such a way that wouldn't drive a wedge in the new relationships. If the South continued in this direction, anything that had been accomplished during Reconstruction was going to be wiped out by the prevailing attitudes in the South.

"We build another school," Carrie said matter-of-factly.

Rose blinked. "Another school?"

"Of course. There's plenty of land where your school is. Besides, the clinic is already attached to it." Carrie's eyes were shining as her idea took shape in her mind. "We'll expand the clinic and turn it into an additional school for the white students. Phoebe will teach them. She'll have you as her mentor, but you will each teach your own students."

Rose tried to envision what Carrie saw in her mind, tamping down the flutter of excitement her words had created. "What about your patients? Where will you treat them?"

Carrie lifted her shoulders carelessly. "We're outgrowing it, anyway. We'll build another one. It will be close, but it will be separate."

"But you could expand the existing clinic and not have to build another one," Rose replied, not at all sure why she was arguing.

Carrie raised a brow before she reached out and took her hand. "You know this is a brilliant idea. Why are you resisting it?"

It was a good question. Rose forced herself to face it honestly. What she saw made her cringe. "Because talking to that representative made me feel I'm somehow less of a teacher because I'm black," she said slowly. "He made me think I'm doing a disservice to my white students by not giving them a white teacher." Saying the words made her feel sick inside. The man had made her feel less of a person because of her color. There had certainly been plenty of times in her life when she'd been made to feel that way, but to have a representative from the Virginia Board of Education walk into her school and diminish her as a person had been a serious blow. She held a hand to her stomach as it tightened with both humiliation and anger.

"That man was an idiot," Carrie said flatly. "I'm sorry he made you feel that way, but he was absolutely wrong. *Every* student you have is lucky to have you as a teacher. I'll move the clinic in order to create another school, but only on one condition."

Rose felt hope as she gathered strength from Carrier's indignation and her determination to find a solution. "What?"

"That you continue to tutor Frances and Minnie at home. I'm sure Phoebe is a fine teacher, but I refuse to rob my girls of the best teacher they'll ever have just because there are idiots running the Board of Education." Carrie's eyes were flashing. "I dare any of them to come into my home and tell me what I can or can't do with my children's education."

Rose managed a genuine smile. "Thank you."

"Don't you dare thank me," Carrie said firmly. "You will *not* give that man the power to diminish you, Rose Samuels." Carrie held onto her hand, squeezing it more tightly. "Do you hear me?"

"Yes, ma'am," Rose said meekly, but this time her eyes were dancing as her thoughts became free to imagine the future. "We do everything differently here already. School shouldn't be an exception. We'll take care of everyone our way, but still within the bounds of the law."

"*Stupid* laws," Carrie reminded her.

"Yes," Rose agreed. "Stupid laws."

A long silence fell between the friends. The sun was sinking low on the horizon, casting a rosy glow across the sky. Tree swallows began to emerge, their iridescent greenish-blue heads catching the rays of the sun, while their white breasts and bellies glowed against the surface of the river as they dipped down to catch the early evening bugs. Fish broke the surface as they gobbled their share of the mosquitoes hovering above them.

Rose watched the birds, enjoying their colorful display. "I'm glad the swallows are back."

"Me too," Carrie said softly. "They winter farther South, but return here each May to nest in tree cavities and hollow stumps. They haven't been back for long."

Rose shook her head. "How do you know all this?"

Carrie chuckled. "Miles and my father used to bring me down to watch them when I was a child, and I've seen them every year, but it was your daughter that taught me about them. I brought Felicia down here one day last year. The swallows were out in mass. She was so intrigued that she went home and dug through the library until she found a book that gave her information." She watched silently for a few minutes. "Many of the swallows we're seeing now were born here last year. They've returned to nest and raise their own brood."

"Like we have," Rose said softly, watching the swallows dip and rise with what looked like no effort. She felt the sick feeling from the afternoon meeting ebb away. Her natural courage and spirit were returning. "Have you felt the water yet?"

Carrie turned, her expression saying she knew where her friend was going with her seemingly innocent question. "Not yet." She smiled. "Remember the rule, though. We can't test the water on the first swim of the year. We just have to deal with however cold it may be."

Rose grinned, slipped from Maple and then tied her loosely to a close branch.

Carrie slid off Granite, removed his saddle and bridle, and left him to watch. She already knew he wouldn't go anywhere. She patted him on the neck and then began to strip.

Rose looked around. "You're sure no one will see us?"

"What?" Carrie teased. "You're getting so old you can't risk going for a swim late in the afternoon?"

Rose stuck out her tongue and pulled at her clothing. Once she was down to her underclothes, she reached for Carrie's hand. "Let's do this!"

Shrieking with delight, the two friends ran across the shore and plunged into the placid river.

"It's freezing!" Rose cried when she came up gasping for breath.

"Nonsense!" Carrie retorted. "It's perfect." Laughing, she splashed water toward her friend.

Rose laughed and splashed back.

The battle was on.

Later, the two women lay on the bank, their clothes back on to protect them from the chilly spring air. They breathed in the heavenly aroma of the evening.

Carrie finally stood. "As much as I hate to end a perfect afternoon, we have to head back if we're going to beat the darkness."

It was Rose's turn to tease now. "What? You're getting too old to find your way down the trails at night?"

"Never," Carrie fired back as she quickly put Granite's saddle and bridle back on. "I happen to know, however, that we have two men waiting for us who will worry if we're not back before dark. I don't want to turn their hair grey any sooner than is necessary. Besides, there's rhubarb crumble waiting for us."

Rose tightened Maple's saddle girth and whipped her head around. "Annie made rhubarb crumble?"

"Yep. She found out May made some for us in Richmond, so of course she had to make some to prove hers is best."

"I'm happy to say hers is best," Rose responded. She laughed as she mounted Maple. "I think it's going to be fairly obvious what we've been doing. If my hair looks as wild as yours does, our swimming adventure won't remain a secret."

Carrie laughed. "You're right. I already know what I'll be doing tomorrow afternoon. Once Frances and Minnie know we've been swimming, they'll insist it's their turn."

"Let's make it a special afternoon," Rose suggested. "We'll bring Frances and Minnie, but we'll also bring Amber and Angel."

"What about Hope?" Carrie asked.

Rose hesitated. "She's only five."

Carrie cocked her head. "How old were you when Miles brought us down here?"

Rose shook her head. "I don't remember."

"I do. You were five. You had just come to live in the house with me. Miles knew how sad you were, so he brought us swimming. We both loved it." Carrie climbed into Granite's saddle. "Besides, the river is shallow and calm here. She'll be fine."

Rose knew she was hesitant because John had come so close to drowning in the river the summer before. She also knew better than to let her fear keep her children from experiencing all of life they could. "Swimming it is," she said firmly.

Minnie eyed the water with both anticipation and dread.

Frances took her hand. "You don't have to be afraid," she assured her. "I felt the same way when Mama brought me here last year."

"I've never been swimming," Minnie said nervously.

"There's nothing to it," Frances said confidently. "Mama and I will help you."

Carrie smiled as she listened to the girls. Her favorite memories of the summer before were of the times she and Frances had shared here at the river. The knowledge that she now had *two* daughters to create memories with almost took her breath away.

"Mama? Do I really get to go swimming?"

Rose lowered the heavy picnic hamper Annie had prepared for them to the ground beside the big log on the bank. "You do, Hope."

Hope's dark eyes were as large as saucers beneath her tightly braided hair. "And John doesn't?"

"Not this time," Rose answered. "This time it's just for the girls. Your brother will get to go soon, though."

Hope cocked her head and stared at the water. "And you think I'm big enough to do this?" Her voice sounded doubtful.

Rose knelt in front of her daughter. "I do," she assured her. "Don't you?" She met Carrie's eyes over her daughter's head.

Carrie suspected Rose was hoping for a reason to not take her daughter for a swim. She was being brave, but Carrie knew she would forever carry the image of John almost drowning in the same river she was about to take Hope swimming in. It didn't even begin to resemble the swollen, muddy mess that had rampaged past them during the flood, but it would always hold the memories.

Hope continued to stare at the glistening water.

Carrie walked over and took the little girl's hand. "Isn't the river beautiful?"

"Yes," Hope whispered.

"Are you afraid?" Carrie asked gently.

"Yes," Hope's answer was barely discernible.

Carrie crouched down to look into her frightened eyes. "Why?"

Hope hesitated, but then turned to stare at her. "John said the river would take me away from everyone." Her voice trembled. "Is that true?"

"No," Rose said firmly. She took a gentle hold of her daughter's shoulder and turned her to face the river. "It's not true. See how calm the water is? It's very safe. If it wasn't, I wouldn't take you swimming."

Hope considered her mama's answer before her face crumpled with confusion. "Why did John tell me that, then?"

Rose took a deep breath. "John almost had a bad thing happen in the river, honey. Your daddy saved him, but I'm sure he has bad memories. Most importantly, though, he loves you and doesn't want you to get hurt."

Hope continued to stare at the water, and then turned her gaze to watching longingly as Frances, Minnie, Amber and Angel pulled off their clothing, giggling as they piled them into heaps on the bank.

Carrie knew she wanted to join the big girls more than anything else. "You're going to be extra safe today, Hope."

Hope turned to stare at her hopefully. "I am? Why?"

"Because you've got *all* of us to keep you safe," Carrie said confidently. In truth, she was surprised Hope was reluctant. The little girl was usually always the first one to demand to try something new, and always the first one to do it. John's experience was obviously more traumatic for Hope than any of them had recognized.

"I'm going to be with you," Rose said soothingly.

"And I'll be right there," Carrie promised.

"So will I," Frances said as she walked over.

"Me too," Minnie said, pushing past her own fear to make Hope feel safe.

"And me!" Amber added.

"Which leaves me," Angel said brightly. "With all of us watching out for you, you'll be as safe as if you were in your own bed."

Hope gazed up at all of them and then slowly nodded. "Alright," she murmured. She began to unbutton her dress, her eyes locked on the water.

Carrie turned to Angel. "Do you know how to swim?"

Angel cocked her head, her narrow face intense. "I'm not sure I would say I know how to swim, but I feel right at home in the water." A flash of pain filled her eyes, but she blinked and forced a smile. "My daddy and I had to cross over a lot of streams and rivers when we walked from North Carolina to get here to the plantation. The first time I had to cross one, it was real scary. By the last one, I knew the water wouldn't hurt me."

Carrie's heart swelled with emotion. Angel had lost everyone in her family except her father, when the KKK had broken into their North Carolina cabin the year before. They'd killed her family and left her father for dead. Thinking their job was finished, they left, not realizing she was soundly sleeping in the back room.

Angel and her father had narrowly escaped when the vigilantes had ended their attack by setting the cabin on fire. Angel was slowly coming back to life. To see her trying to encourage Hope was a wonderful thing.

Hope stared up at Angel. "Will you hold my hand?" she asked softly. Hope loved everyone on the plantation, but she had taken a special liking to Angel.

"Of course," Angel said quickly. She glanced up at Rose, who looked both appreciative and apprehensive. "Your mama can take your other hand."

Hope reached out her other hand.

Rose breathed a sigh of relief and smiled brightly as she took her daughter's tiny hand.

Carrie turned to Minnie. "Are you ready?"

Minnie, her blue eyes large with anticipation, nodded bravely. "Yes."

"Let's all go in together," Amber said excitedly. "At the same time."

"That's a great idea," Carrie replied. She could hardly believe Amber was almost fifteen. She'd been only six when Robert had almost died during the second year of the war. Amber's family had taken him into their home and nursed him back to health – along the way, helping him to release all his prejudices. Her entire family had come to Cromwell Plantation when Robert had almost died again at the end of the war. Amber had somehow been able to break through his lethargy and depression to bring him back to life. Robert had repaid her by teaching her everything he knew about horses and giving Amber her beautiful mare, All My Heart. His final gift had been to give his life to save her - throwing his body over hers to shield her from a vigilante's bullet. The little girl had grown into a confident young woman that was one of the best horsewomen she had ever known.

Carrie pulled her thoughts back to the present. She grabbed Frances' and Minnie's hands as all of them lined up on the riverbank. "You all know the rules, don't you?" she called above the laughs and giggles.

"We have to go all the way in, no matter how cold it is," Frances answered.

"And we have to stay on this side of the log that's sitting on the sandbar," Angel added.

Carrie and Rose had drilled that rule into them. They knew the river was calm and shallow on the bank side of the log. On the other side, the river flowed faster. A good swimmer could handle it. None of the girls could.

"And do what Mama tells me to do," Hope said solemnly as she tightly gripped Angel and Rose's hands.

"Right," Carrie sang out. "On the count of three, we all run in together."

"One!" Rose yelled.

"Two!" Frances cried.

"Three!" Carrie called loudly as she began to run forward, Frances and Minnie at her side.

Moments later, squeals and shrieks erupted in the afternoon air.

Carrie was grateful that another day of warm temperatures seemed to have taken the frigid bite from the water. She realized it was probably the joy of all of them swimming together that made the water more comfortable, however. Whatever the reason, the water was delightful.

"I love this!" Minnie cried as she splashed in the river, the sun flashing off her red hair. "I really love it!"

Carrie reached down and gave her a quick hug. "I knew you would," she said softly. Her heart surged with joy as she saw the happy look on her daughter's face.

Minnie grinned up at her, "Just like I love you, Mama!"

Carrie froze for a moment, wanting to capture every facet of this magical moment in her mind. "I love you too, Minnie," she said fervently, unsure if Minnie realized what she had just said.

She had.

"It's really alright if I call you Mama?" Minnie said, her blue eyes suddenly large and vulnerable. "Do you think my mama in heaven feels bad?"

"I think she's happy," Carrie replied. She believed that was true. She hoped Dierdre was watching right at that moment. The woman who had been her cook in Philadelphia would be thrilled to know Minnie had a new home, with all the opportunities Dierdre had hoped for her children when she left Ireland to come to America.

"I'm happy too," Minnie announced, her eyes once more shining with fun.

Just then Hope bounced over to splash water into Minnie's face. "I got you!" she shouted. Her shrieks of alarm when she had run into the water had quickly turned into giggles and laughs of delight. "I got you!"

Minnie's face lit up with laughter as she splashed water back at Hope. "I got you too!"

The next hour passed in a haze of fun as they played and splashed in the water.

They would teach Minnie, Hope and Angel how to swim during the hot summer ahead, but for today, Carrie was happy just watching the girls fall in love with the river the same way she had.

Carrie and Rose spread out blankets, and then pulled out the containers of food Annie had packed in the picnic hamper.

"It's a good thing we didn't try to do this on horseback," Rose commented as she lifted out smaller baskets stuffed with fragrant fried chicken. "There's enough food here for an army."

Carrie nodded as she pulled out containers of potato salad, deviled eggs, and carrot strips. They had decided to bring everyone through the tunnel so they could stay past dark. Lanterns directly inside the tunnel door would illuminate their way back.

"Are there biscuits in there?" Amber asked as she walked over to peer into the basket.

"Have you ever known Annie to send a basket of food without biscuits?" Rose retorted. She grinned as she pulled out two bulging cloths full of fluffy biscuits. The aroma made her mouth water.

"What's for dessert?" Minnie asked. "I'm starving!"

Carrie was sure that was true. The sun had already sunk below the horizon, leaving golden streaks through the darkening blue sky.

"Can I start the fire?" Amber asked.

"I don't know," Rose answered. "Can you?"

Amber rolled her eyes. "We're on a picnic, Rose. Who cares how I talk?"

Rose's answer was a steady stare.

"Fine," Amber muttered good-naturedly. "*May* I start the fire?"

"I would love that," Rose responded with a smile. "Thank you."

Minnie leaned over close to Frances and whispered, "I'm glad you warned me about Rose before we got here."

Rose lifted a brow. "Frances warned you about me?"

Minnie lifted shocked eyes to Rose's face as she covered her mouth with her hand. "I didn't mean for you to hear me."

"But I did," Rose said, amusement dancing in her eyes. "What did Frances warn you about?"

Minnie looked at Frances, searching for a way out of her dilemma. "You're the one who said it. I reckon you should be the one to answer Rose."

"You *reckon*?" Rose asked.

Minnie's eyes flew back to Rose. "I'm... sorry," she stuttered. "I meant to say I *think* you should be the one to answer Rose." Her eyes searched out Carrie's face next, obviously hoping she would rescue her.

Carrie burst out laughing. "Frances told Minnie that every word that came out of her mouth would have to go through the *Rose Filter*. She told her that you would make them speak correctly all the time because you care about their future."

Rose nodded. "That's true, Minnie." Then she turned to Frances. "The *Rose Filter*? Thank you."

"For what?" Frances asked, her eyes searching Rose's face. "You're really not mad?"

Minnie spoke before Rose could answer the question. "Don't it get tiresome?"

Rose raised a brow.

"I mean, *doesn't* it get tiresome, always having to watch everything you say?"   Minnie spoke clearly, enunciating each word.

"It does," Rose admitted.

"Why do you worry about it so much, then?" Minnie asked.

The laughter died in Rose's eyes as she looked around at all of them. "Because I never want anyone to judge me and think I'm not intelligent because of the way I speak.   Too many people already believe I'm ignorant, or less than them, because I'm black. I don't want to support their belief by not speaking correctly." She took the time to gaze into each of the girl's eyes. "I never want anyone to judge you or think you're not as intelligent either.   All of you are smart, bright girls. I want everyone to see you that way. That's why every word you say has to go through the *Rose Filter*."

Silence fell over the group as her explanation sank in.

"That's a very good reason," Minnie finally said.

Rose chuckled "I'm so glad you think so." She waved her hand toward the blanket loaded with food. "Enough serious talk. I'm hungry. What about the rest of you?"

"I'm starving!" Minnie repeated as she jumped up. "I still don't know what we're having for dessert, though."

Amber leapt to her feet, as well. "I'll start the fire while you give everyone their food."

Carrie nodded her gratitude. "Thank you." Then she gazed down at Minnie. "Does pound cake with fresh strawberries sound good to you?"

"Yummy!" Minnie cried as she rubbed her stomach with anticipation.

Carrie sighed with happiness as she watched everyone's faces glowing in the firelight. The flames leapt upward as sparks danced into the dark sky that was jeweled with brilliant stars. There wasn't a crumb of food left.

The laughter and talk had died down, leaving only the sound of the water lapping against the shore as it rolled the small rocks up the bank and then back down. Moments later, the crickets and frogs added their song to the night.

She had made the right decision. Cromwell Plantation was her home. It was her girl's home. It was where she wanted to be more than anything. The guilt floated away as she looked over at Frances and Minnie. Both girls looked tired, but completely relaxed and happy as they leaned back against a log and stared up at the canopy of stars overhead.

<u>Chapter Eleven</u>
Sunday, May 21, 1871

Dr. Florence Amberton stood in the doorway to her new medical clinic, housed in a centuries old stone building, and peered down the street. She had arrived early to care for patients being housed in the clinic's back rooms because the hospitals were once again full of men wounded in the fighting. The sun had not yet risen above the buildings flanking the narrow cobblestoned roads, but there was enough light to see that the street was unusually empty. There were no shop patrons sweeping their front walks, no women hanging laundry, and no children venturing out to play in the early morning.

Florence gazed up at the rooms above the shops and businesses. She could almost feel the fear radiating from the windows, and she could sense eyes peering out from behind curtains pulled tight, as if they could somehow block out the danger. She shivered and pulled her head back inside the doorway, though her eyes kept sweeping the distance. She could sense something about to happen.

"What are you doing?"

Florence looked over her shoulder as her husband, Dr. Silas Amberton, strode through their waiting room to join her. She smiled at him, admiring his swarthy good looks, as she always did, but then frowned. "What's about to happen, Silas?" She made no attempt to control the frightened tremor in her voice. Anyone in their right mind would be terrified.

The last month had been full of fighting around Paris. Ousted by the Commune two months earlier, the French National Army was relentlessly moving forward to reclaim the city. All the forts defending Paris had fallen as the Army's relentless drive swept away everything the Commune and the National Guard put up as a defense. The Army was moving slowly and methodically, not rushing, but not slowing their pace either.

The evidence poured into the Amberton's clinic every day. They weren't designed to house patients, but they had ten cots filling their small back rooms. Just as had happened during the Siege, far too many of the men being treated in area hospitals were dying from substandard medical care. Their clinic had only lost one patient so far.

Silas put a hand on her shoulder but remained silent.

Florence tensed, feeling the stress radiating from his body. Forcing herself to take a deep, steadying breath, she turned to face him. "Tell me."

Silas gazed at her, a soft tenderness mixing with his stern expression. Somehow, the combination of the two was more unnerving than anything he could say. The raw emotion in his eyes caused her stomach to constrict with anxiety.

Silas stepped around her and pulled the door closed. He paused and then locked it securely.

Florence watched him with a sick sense of dread. "The French Army is in the city, aren't they?"

Silas met her eyes evenly. "Yes."

Florence sucked in her breath, resisting the urge to wrench the door open and look outside. "The Red Cross flag we have hanging over the door will keep us safe," she said slowly. "Won't it?" She knew her voice was shaky, but she still didn't care.

"I believe so," Silas replied.

Florence stared at him, seeing in his eyes what he didn't want to say. Under normal circumstances, the Red Cross flag would keep them safe. In a country embroiled in a civil war, protocol oftentimes didn't come into consideration. The number of National Guardsmen being executed for carrying arms or having gunpowder on their hands was steadily climbing. When Frenchmen were so easily killing other Frenchmen, the Army would probably not look favorably on a clinic housing wounded Guardsmen. "Do we know how far they've made it into the city?"

Silas shook his head. "No. One of the Guardsmen that we treated last week and released, came by here and stopped long enough to give me the news that the Army had breached the defenses."

Florence narrowed her blue eyes. "Was it Pierre?"

Silas sighed as he nodded.

Florence tightened her lips. "He lost a leg during the Siege but insisted on returning to the fight when the Commune took over, in spite of the fact that he's walking around on a wooden stump. He took a bullet two weeks ago that I removed from his arm. He's going back for more? How many more times is he going to make me perform surgery on him?" Anger and frustration surged through her. She had been so happy to save his life, even though he had lost his leg. It had been a wonderful day when she'd told him he could return to his wife and children. She shook her head with dismay.

"He believes he's making life better for his family," Silas responded.

Florence barely refrained from rolling her eyes. "We both know that's not what's happening. Remember what Minister Washburne said last night at dinner?" She no longer lived at the Minister's opulent residence, having moved into a sunny apartment with Silas after their wedding, but they were often guests. "He told us the Communards running the Commune are brigands, assassins and scoundrels." She repeated what he'd said verbatim, using his clipped northern accent. He hadn't revealed anything they didn't already know, but hearing the Minister say it had somehow made it more real. "They started out with some good policies, but they're proving themselves to be nothing but bullies. As far as I'm concerned, they're as bad as, or worse than, the government they're so disdainful of." Her voice dripped with scorn. The things she'd watched happen during the past two months had sickened and infuriated her.

Suddenly, tears threatened to engulf her. She swallowed hard, refusing to give into them.

Silas put his arms around her gently, pulling her into his broad chest. "I'm sorry all of this has been so hard."

Florence buried her head into his chest, grateful for the brief refuge. "It's hard for both of us." She blinked furiously, refusing to let the tears win. She didn't want her patients to see her with swollen, bloodshot eyes. "I thought all this would be over when the Siege ended. I had visions of us working to rebuild Paris into the city you fell in love with. I never dreamed we would be right back in the middle of a war – watching the French fight each other and then execute any men they catch." The ridiculous futility of it all made her want to scream.

"Can I ask a question?"

Florence pushed back and look up into Silas' face, surprised by the hint of sheepishness in his voice. "Of course. What is it?"

"I was embarrassed to admit at dinner last night that I don't know what a brigand is. I forgot to ask you about it on the way home."

Florence chuckled, her heart flooding with love for this strong man who could still be vulnerable. "A brigand is a member of a gang that ambushes and robs people."

Silas raised a brow. "How do you know that?"

"Simply because I'm not too proud to ask," Florence retorted with a smile. "When you left the dining room to talk to someone, I asked Minister Washburne what it meant." Her smile widened. "Thankfully, I don't have to deal with male ego like you do."

Silas smiled back at her. "My male ego is happy to be made fun of, as long as it makes the fear in your eyes disappear for a little while." He took her hand before she could respond. "Let's go check on our patients."

Florence was able to smile naturally when she checked on her first patient, a young man in his twenties with the narrow face and sunken eyes that testified to his hunger during the Siege. Food was more available in the city now, but the National Guardsmen serving in the forts outside the city were not privy to much of it. Jean Claude had arrived on May eighth, the day Fort Issy, under intense bombardment, had finally been abandoned by the National Guard. Knowing what would happen to Guardsmen who were captured, Jean Claude's friends had carried him into town on their backs because there were no wagons to transport him. There was no doubt they had saved his life.

The city had known then that it was just a matter of time before the Army entered Paris. Fort Issy was the last key strategic point around the city. Once it had fallen, bitter fighting had brought the French Army closer to the walls of the city they had been cast out from.

Florence tried to push all that out of her mind. "How are you this morning, Jean Claude?"

He stared up at her with burning eyes. "I don't feel good," he muttered in French.

Florence laid her hand on his forehead, thankful she was growing more fluent in her adopted language. *"Je suis vraiment desolee."* Then she repeated it in English. "I'm so sorry." Every one of her patients asked her to teach them English. She was happy to comply because she knew it helped keep their mind off their pain.

"Your fever is back," she murmured, concerned that his infection had gotten worse. She tightened her lips as she considered how to bring it under control. She unwrapped the bandage around his leg, holding back her wince as she examined the inflamed skin around the bullet wound. She'd succeeded in removing the bullet, she realized infection had set in and was already rampaging through his body.

"Am I going to die?" Jean Claude asked quietly. His voice was steady, but his eyes showed his fear.

"Not under my care," Florence said brightly, all too aware how many National Guardsmen were dying all over the city from infections and sepsis. She thought longingly of the American hospital she and Silas had served in during the Siege, with its open, airy tents. Here at the clinic, the windows were open to let in a draft, but the news from the morning mandated that the doors remain closed.

An idea sprang to her mind. "Nurse Campbell!"

Their normally cheerful nurse, her face lined with worry and fatigue, looked up from beside a patient's bed, light brown hair framing lovely amber eyes. She'd come from America; traveling from Baltimore to assist in the American Hospital. When Silas and Florence decided to start their own clinic, she had eagerly offered to join them. Florence wondered if she, too, regretted staying.

"Yes, Dr. Amberton?"

Florence's mind was spinning. "Will you please go to the market and get me as many onions as they have?"

Nurse Campbell cocked her head, as if she was certain she hadn't heard correctly. "Onions?"

Florence didn't have time to explain. "Yes, please. I need them quickly.   I'll finish changing Gustave's bandage."

"Yes, Dr. Amberton." Nurse Campbell reached for her bag, unlocked the door and stepped outside quickly.

Florence relocked the door and returned to Jean Claude's bedside. "You're going to be fine," she assured him. She handed him a glass of cool water. "I'll be back to take care of your leg soon."

Jean Claude stared at her with the same curious expression Nurse Campbell had given her.   "With onions?"

"With onions," Florence said calmly.   "I'll explain later."

She moved over to the patient Nurse Campbell had been working on.   "How are you this morning, Gustave?"

"Not wanting to be in this bed," Gustave growled, his face fierce looking below his shaggy black hair. The narrow bed had only intensified the impact of his tall, powerful body.

"The National Guard can do without you for a while," Florence said soothingly.   "There are two hundred thousand Guardsmen in the city. They'll take care of anything that might happen." She hoped her patients weren't aware that the French Army had already entered Paris.

"That's not true," Gustave protested. His English was impeccable because he'd spent many years in London at a boarding school.   "We heard Pierre talking to Dr. Amberton." He paused. "The *other* Dr. Amberton," he said with a slight smile, and then hurried on. "We know the Army is in the city. There aren't two hundred thousand Guardsmen," he said fiercely. "They made every able-bodied man in Paris become a member of the National Guard, but most of them don't have the courage to be a fighter." His eyes glowed with pride and passion.

Florence bit her tongue to keep from adding that the ones who didn't fight had the wisdom to know when something was futile, but she knew making that statement in a room full of convalescing soldiers would not be wise on *her* part. "I see," she replied, focusing on cleaning the wound so she could wrap it again. She was glad it showed no signs of infection, but he was still too ill to fight. She was glad for that, too. Perhaps Gustave would live through the civil war and go home to his wife and children.

Oblivious to her thoughts, Gustave continued. "The last I heard, there are only about twenty-five thousand Guardsmen who are fighting." His eyes glittered with fury. "I pity the cowards who don't care enough to fight for what they believe in," he said angrily. "Pity is the wrong word," he added. "I despise them!" The last words came out in a hiss.

Florence changed the subject. It wouldn't do for Gustave to rile up the anger of her patients. Her job was to heal them, not enrage them enough to make them go back into battle before they were ready. She knew these men, however wrongly, believed the Commune was committed to making life better for them. Years of unrest and dissatisfaction within the working class had finally boiled over into rebellion. She could understand that. What she couldn't understand was why they were willing to blindly follow the lead of men who were proving to be bullies.

The men who had started the Commune, and who were now running it, had skillfully stoked Parisian anger and discontent. While she agreed there were many things that needed to change, as far as she could tell, the leaders didn't have a clue how to actually make that happen.

Little more than a month earlier, the Commune leaders had begun to fight among themselves. They couldn't agree on whether they should focus on absolute priority to military defense, or to political and social freedoms and reform as they had promised. Ultimately, the majority promoted military defense. Despite protests from members, the Council of the Commune had voted for the creation of what they called the Committee of Public Safety.

Florence finished wrapping Gustave's leg, and then began to unwrap the bandage on his arm.

Her thoughts continued to flow. The Committee, in direct contradiction of its name, had been given extensive powers to hunt down and imprison enemies of the Commune. The arrests had begun immediately; based on suspicion of treason, intelligence with the enemy, or insults to the Commune.

Florence fought to keep her breathing even as she thought of the increasing number of prisoners. They had arrested generals and recent commanders of the National Guard who hadn't performed their duties in the way the Commune leaders wanted. Many high religious officials had been arrested, including the

Archbishop of Paris. Part of their strategy was to hold prisoners for personal reprisals, but every offered exchange had been turned down by Thiers. The new leader of the French government refused to negotiate.

The number of prisoners continued to rise.

Florence wondered how quickly the Commune leaders would turn against the loyal Guardsmen filling her clinic if they were suddenly unwilling to follow their lead and dared to voice their opposition.

A rap at the back door made Florence jump. Silas left the patient he was working on in the adjoining room and crossed to the door quickly. He opened it and slipped outside, silently mouthing, 'Please lock it,' before closing the door securely behind him.

Florence did as asked. Every instinct told her to not lock him out, but she was confident he was standing right outside the door, receiving whatever news was being delivered.

"Who is that?" Jean Claude asked, his face looking more feverish.

Florence hurried over to bathe his forehead with a cool washcloth, giving him more water to drink. She regretted sending Nurse Campbell to the market for onions. In her worry over Jean Claude's fever, she'd forgotten how dangerous it could be for anyone to be out on the streets. It was too late to do anything about it now, but she kept her eyes trained on the window, watching for Nurse Campbell's slender, petite figure.

"I don't know," Florence said calmly as she laid the cloth over his forehead. When it was hot, she removed it and rinsed it in cool water again. She hated that they'd run out of ice the day before. She had expected another delivery that morning, but she realized there wasn't going to be one. "Probably just a delivery man."

Jean Claude's expression said he didn't believe her, but he closed his eyes as the cool water offered a brief respite.

A rap at the front door caused Florence to spring forward. She glanced out the window and breathed a sigh of relief when she saw Nurse Campbell – though if it had been a soldier, she would have had no choice but to open the door anyway.

Nurse Campbell, her eyes wide with fright, slipped inside carrying a cloth bag bulging with onions.

"Are you alright?" Florence asked anxiously. "What happened?"

"Nothing," her nurse responded as she took deep breaths to calm herself. "Most people are hiding in their homes. The market owner was closing up shop when I got there, but he allowed me to run in and get the onions they had. He told me the French Army is in the city. Just as I was returning, I heard gunshots in the distance." Nurse Campbell's breathing became fast and shallow again. "A lot of gunfire," she muttered, her eyes fixed on the door as if she expected soldiers to pound on the door at any minute.

Florence reached for the onions, knowing there was nothing she could do about what was happening outside. She looked toward the back door but resisted the urge to go after Silas. She had to focus on their patients. "Sit down and have some water, Josephine. Thank you for making the trip to get the onions. I'm sorry I put you in danger. I wasn't thinking clearly."

"Nonsense," Nurse Campbell scoffed. Being back in the clinic was restoring some of her normal spirit. "Obviously you needed them." The curious look from earlier returned to her face. "What are you going to do with them?"

Florence smiled. "Come with me. I'll show you." She hurried into their tiny little kitchen area and began to peel an onion.

Nurse Campbell followed her lead, also copying her when she began to chop them into small pieces.

Once the onions were chopped, Florence put them all into a large bowl, added some honey from the jar she kept in the cabinet for tea, and then ground the mixture into a paste with a pestle.

"Are we having this for lunch?" Nurse Campbell asked with a twinkle in her eye.

Florence was grateful for anything that would keep their minds off the encroaching danger outside. "This will hopefully cure Jean Claude's infection and take away his fever."

"*Onions?*" This time the question came from Jean Claude. "Are you going to put them on me?"

"I am," Florence said cheerfully, thankful she had remembered the remedy that Carrie swore by for infection. She carried the bowl out to Jean Claude's bed and placed it on the small table wedged tightly between his cot and the next patient.

Frederic watched them with dull eyes. The middle-aged man with a thick red beard had almost died from pneumonia. She believed he would live, but she doubted he would ever be the vibrant man he had once been. There'd been too much damage to his lungs. She would have preferred to send him home, but he lived in a tiny hovel with no ventilation and no access to fresh air. He was too weak to care for himself, and his wife had died during the Siege from the same pneumonia that had almost taken him. He was staying at the clinic until he was stronger.

Florence folded back Jean Claude's bandage again, wiped it completely clean with warm water heated over the tiny wood stove in the kitchen, and then put a generous amount of the onion poultice on the wound, pressing it deep down into the remaining hole where the bullet had lodged, and the infection now festered. "I'm sorry. I know it hurts," Florence said softly.

Jean Claude shrugged, only his gritted teeth and narrowed eyes showing how painful it was. "I can take it," he ground out.

Florence worked quickly, wrapping the wound with a fresh bandage when she was done.

Jean Claude sagged back against his pillow, the relief evident on his face. "How often are you going to do that?"

"Every six hours, until the infection is gone." Florence wiped her hands on a fresh cloth. She would smell strongly of onion, but it was an aroma she didn't mind – especially if it would heal Jean Claude's wound.

"Do you think it will work?"

Florence nodded. "I'm confident it will." The truth was that she hoped she hadn't waited too long to utilize Carrie's remedy. "The onion actually absorbs the infection and fever from your body."

"Where did you learn how to do that?" Jean Claude asked.

"One of my closest friends in America is a doctor, too. Dr. Carrie Wallington. She learned this remedy when she was younger from..." Florence hesitated, not wanting to delve into the subject of American slavery. "A friend," she finished. "Dr. Wallington uses a myriad..." Florence stopped herself again. Jean Claude wouldn't know the word myriad. "She uses a lot of different plants to create things that will heal people."

Jean Claude nodded thoughtfully. "I know about that. My grandmother and mother used to make remedies from plants. I thought it was something just for women to know, so I never learned about it."

Florence smiled, ready to tell him about more herbal remedies, but the opening of the back door interrupted her. The grim look on Silas' face told her he'd received bad news. When he gestured toward the back room, she put the final pin into Jean Claude's bandage and prepared to follow him.

"Come on, Doc. You have to tell us what's going on." Gustave's voice rang clearly through the room.

"We can take it," Jean Claude said weakly. "Not knowing what's happening out there is harder than anything you can tell us."

Nods and grunts of agreement followed his statement.

Silas hesitated for a moment before joining Florence. "You're right," he replied, his voice strong enough for every patient to hear. "I'm sure all of you are aware the French Army has entered the city."

"How many?" Gustave demanded.

Silas met the soldier's demanding gaze. "All I know right now is that there are tens of thousands of them.

They came into the city about four o'clock this morning. They've occupied the Auteuil and Passy neighborhoods."

"More than twenty-five thousand?" Gustave asked.

Florence thought about his earlier statement that the National Guard had only about twenty-five thousand fighting men.

"I've been told there are over double that amount," Silas replied evenly.

A thick silence fell over the room.

Jean Claude was the one who finally broke it. "That's what the person who knocked on the door came to tell you?"

"Yes.

Florence saw the flash in Silas' eyes that revealed that wasn't all he had been told.

Gustave saw it too. "Tell us everything, Doc." His voice was both demanding and demoralized.

Silas sighed. "The leaders of the Commune are holding the trial for Gustave Cluseret, the former commander of the National Guard."

"It's wrong what they're doing to Commander Cluseret," Gustave cried. "They're accusing him of betraying the cause. He's never done anything but support it." He looked at Florence wildly. "He's a good man. He fought in *your* Civil War, Dr. Amberton."

Florence stared at him with surprise, glimpsing the same expression on Silas' face. "I didn't know that."

"Well, he did," Gustave assured her. "He was born in France and served in the military until he was thirty-eight. When your war started, he resigned his commission and went to fight."

"North or South?" Silas asked keenly.

"The North, of course!" Gustave responded.

Florence wouldn't have been surprised if Cluseret had fought for the South. They'd rebelled against the government, just as the Commune was doing now.

"He fought under General McClellan and General Fremont," Gustave boasted, "an eventually became a general himself. When the war ended he joined a band of adventurers and left for Ireland. That's when he joined the Fenian insurrection against England." His accent thickened as his fervor grew. "He managed to escape arrest when the Fenians collapsed, by he still had a death sentence hanging over his head. When he came back to France a few years ago, he heard about the Commune and decided to come help us regain our rights." Gustave's eyes glowed with passion. "Cluseret is an amazing man. These charges against him are bogus!"

Florence didn't know anything about Commander Cluseret, but it surely seemed he had committed his life to fighting and violence. Of course, the fact that the Commune had ousted him might mean that he actually cared about the rights of the working man. The looks of respect and adoration on every patient's face certainly indicated that.

"What about the trial?" Jean Claude asked, bringing everyone's thoughts back to the present.

"General Dombrowski, the current National Guard commander, sent a message to the Commune leaders that the army is inside the city. He asked for reinforcements and proposed an immediate counterattack," Silas told them.

"Good for him," Gustave growled.

"We're going to drive them back," another patient said firmly.

"They're not staying in our city!"

Florence was once again glad their patients were too sick to return to the battle that day. If they were capable, she knew everyone of them would have rushed from the clinic to fight for Paris.

"What did the leaders say?" Jean Claude asked with narrowed eyes.

Florence was impressed with his intuition and perception. He could tell, just as she could, that Silas still hadn't told them everything he'd learned.

"The leaders of the Commune aren't taking action," Silas said in a resigned voice. It was obvious he knew how the news would impact their patients.

"What do you mean?" Gustave sputtered.

Silas shrugged. "They received the message and went back to holding the trial. My source told me they weren't sending reinforcements or planning a counterattack. At least not right now. They're deliberating the fate of Cluseret."

Stunned silence met his announcement.

The only sound was the noise of gunfire in the distance. A sound that was growing louder the longer the silence stretched out.

Florence joined the patients in staring at her husband. What did their decision to not counterattack mean? What was going to happen to Paris if the French Army wasn't going to meet resistance? The gunfire indicated they were indeed meeting resistance, but she shivered at the idea of what it would mean for the smaller number of National Guard who were fighting to defend a city the Commune leaders seemed to have turned away from.

Chapter Twelve

Florence was rousted from a troubled sleep by the sound of clanging bells early the next morning. She bit back a groan as her sore muscles rebelled against a night on the wooden floor. Afraid to leave their patients because they didn't know if they would be able to return the next day, she and Silas had chosen to stay at the clinic with Nurse Campbell. Because all the cots were taken, their only choice had been to cover themselves with a blanket and make the floor their bed.

"What is that noise?" Nurse Campbell asked, pushing herself off the floor with a groan that revealed the floor had been no kinder to her muscles.

"Silas?" Florence asked wearily.

Silas stood and stretched, the lines on his face attesting to a long, uncomfortable night. "The bells usually ring as some kind of announcement." He walked over to the front of the clinic and looked out the window. "There are pieces of paper on the light poles. I'm going to get one."

Florence was frightened for him to go outside, but she knew all of them, including their patients, needed to know what the papers said. What if the French Army was demanding their surrender? What if someone was about to pound on the door and force them to give up their prisoners? She fought to push aside the frightening *ifs* as Silas slowly opened the door, peered out, and then ran to the closest light pole. He ripped off the sheet of paper attached to it and ran back inside.

"What does it say?" Gustave called. "I haven't slept all night. I could see people moving up and down the street through the window, but I didn't hear anything."

Silas held the paper up to the lantern as he turned up the light.

In the name of this glorious France, mother of all the popular revolutions, permanent home of the ideas of justice and solidarity which should be and will be the laws of the world, march at the enemy, and may your revolutionary energy show him that someone can sell Paris, but no one can give it up, or conquer it! The Commune counts on you, count on the Commune!

Florence stared at him. Did the Commune seriously believe that by calling regular French citizens to arms, they could win in battle against the French Army? The Army had proven in the last weeks how well-armed they were, and how determined they were to reclaim Paris.

"The National Guard will answer the call!" Gustave shouted.

Florence couldn't control her thoughts any longer. "They're calling French citizens to slaughter!" she protested. "No one is going to be able to stop the Army from taking the city."

Gustave scowled. "Is that what you want to happen, Doc?"

"Frankly, I don't care," Florence retorted. The long sleepless night had pushed her to the limits of her endurance. "I'm an American doctor who chose to help because I got caught in the Siege. My husband and I chose to stay because we want to help restore Paris to its former glory. As far as I can tell, all anyone wants to do is destroy everything around us – including the people."

Gustave stared at her with hard eyes before looking away. "We don't have a choice. Things can't keep going the way they've been going."

"You're probably right," Florence agreed, "but what the Commune is doing isn't working, either." She walked over and put a hand on Gustave's arm. "Are you really willing to watch thousands of Parisians die for a lost cause? Surely you realize they can't beat the French Army."

Jean Claude, his clear eyes revealing the onion poultice was working, shook his head. "What do you suggest? We just give up and bow down to the government that's been beating us down for years?" He spoke rapidly in French, his eyes burning with a passion that replaced the fever burning the day before.

Florence struggled to follow his words with her limited French skills.

"I know something about your own Civil War," Jean Claude continued. "The government beat down the South because they were stronger and better-equipped. They had more soldiers. But aren't the same problems still there? Aren't people still angry? Do you have a better America?"

Florence stared at him, not able to refute his argument. As a Northerner, she was glad the South had lost, but she was all too aware that the problems which had ignited the Civil War were far from being resolved.

"Will more people dying make France a better country?" Nurse Campbell asked in a soft voice as she stepped up beside Florence.

Florence shot her a look of gratitude.

"I don't know," Jean Claude responded. "But what if America hadn't had their Civil War? Would it be better if slavery was still allowed?"

"No," Florence admitted. She couldn't deny he was making valid points.

"We feel we're slaves in our country," Jean Claude said flatly. "We're tired of living in poverty while so many people enjoy great wealth because of what we do. We fight because we are tired of living this way!"

Silas stepped up next to her. "I understand. I was a doctor during the American Civil War. I understood *why* the war was happening, but it didn't change the result of hundreds of thousands of men dying. And more being wounded. It didn't change the fact that wives were left without husbands, and children without fathers. The war was fought. The South lost, but in reality," he said firmly, "the whole country lost. America is still reeling from the pain and devastation. Slavery has been abolished, but the beliefs that caused it have not changed for most people. It's still a mess."

"Is that why you left?" Gustave asked.

"I was so tired of the killing and the pain," Silas responded. "I wanted to escape my country and come somewhere beautiful." He paused and then shook his head sadly. "Paris was once beautiful. Your war with Germany, and now with each other, has destroyed almost all I loved about the city."

Jean Claude gazed at him. "I met a man once. An American. He'd been a soldier for the South. He was a farmer before the war started. He told me the North came through and destroyed all the things he loved about his home. He left because he nothing he loved survived the war."

Silas sighed. "It's true. The South was devastated in so many areas. I left because I wanted to get away from all of it."

Florence watched Silas' face as he spoke. She saw the pain shimmering in his eyes. She'd watched the joy ebb from his soul the longer the Commune, and all the fighting it had caused, existed. He'd run from the very thing he was once again living with every day. She knew he stayed because he felt responsible for his patients, but how long would that last? Would he ever be able to rediscover the joy of Paris? Would she ever see what he had seen when he first arrived?

She had only been in Paris for two weeks before the Siege had changed everything. She had been captivated by the beautiful city, but nothing remained. Gone were all the trees Silas had loved. She could almost imagine what Paris would look like in bloom, but it would be years before a tree would bloom again. The entire city had been denuded because of people's desperate need for firewood. The buildings looked unkempt and uncared for. The people still carried the gaunt, hollow-eyed look of near starvation. Ongoing war and the never-ending flow of funeral processions had stolen the joy from every person she saw.

A burst of gunfire caused her heart to quicken with fear. A moment later, the burst became a staccato of gunshots far too close for comfort. Tightening her lips, Florence knew the only thing that would allow her to survive this was to keep busy. She calmly began to unwrap Jean Claude's bandage. She'd changed the onion poultice twice. The clarity in his eyes made her eager to see the wound.

Nurse Campbell came over to peer down. "How does it look?"

Florence finished unwrapping it, and then stepped back with a smile. "See for yourself."

Jean Claude pushed himself up so he could peer down at his bullet wound. "The infection is gone." His voice was full of wonder. "Because of onions?"

Florence had hoped it would work but had appeared far more confident than she'd felt. "Because of onions," she said happily. "Dr. Wallington has assured me many times that God already created everything we need in nature to stay well and to heal. I do believe she's right." Florence was surprised when a wave of homesickness swept over her. She missed her family, but right then she felt an overwhelming sadness that she couldn't see Carrie, Janie and Elizabeth. She had so many questions that letters received months apart could never answer.

The gunfire faded away.

Florence, Silas and Nurse Campbell moved from patient to patient.

Florence had lost track of time as she tended patients and dealt with the fatigue caused by a night of sleeping on the hard floor. Her fear, dulled by her weariness, sprang back to life when the sound of explosions and gunfire in the distance began again.

"It's started," Jean Claude snapped. "Those are the sound of artillery mixed in with the gunfire."

Florence froze with the realization that an actual battle was taking place within hearing distance. If the volume was any indication, it was within *close* hearing distance. She exchanged a long look with Silas and then went back to work. What choice did they have?

A pounding at the back door made her stiffen with surprise. She barely managed to hold back a scream. Showing panic would certainly not help her patients.

Silas rushed to the door, peered out of the curtained window next to it, and then quickly threw it open and pulled someone in, closing the door behind him in a flash. "Pierre!"

Florence stared at the man with a sinking heart. Blood was pouring down his face and his eyes were wide with terror. She hurried forward, took Pierre's hand, and led him to the examining table. "What happened?" she asked as she gently parted the hair on his forehead. There was a gaping wound that would require stitches, but she'd seen far worse in the last months.

"I was running to get away," Pierre said in a barely coherent voice. "They were shooting at me. I probably would have been hit if I hadn't fallen into one of the barricades they're putting up all over the city. That's how I got this cut."

Florence peered into his eyes, seeing something she hadn't seen the other three times she'd treated him. She'd seen pain. She'd seen defiance. She'd seen anger. This was different. She gently lifted the man's chin so she could gaze into his eyes. The terror she had seen there when he rushed in through the door was still there, but the depth of it was startling. Pierre's normally dark eyes were black with agony and fear.

"Pierre, what happened?" Silas walked over and put a strong hand on the man's shoulder.

Pierre wrenched his eyes toward Silas, latching on to his face as if he could perhaps bring himself to tell a man what he'd experienced. "They... killed... them," he muttered, each word wrenched from his mouth as if he couldn't form them because of the horror each one elicited.

"In the battle?" Silas asked quietly, exchanging a look of concern with Florence. Pierre had already been in many battles. None had seemed to impact him like this. Perhaps he had finally reached his limit of blood and death.

"No..." Pierre shuddered. "Sixteen men... captured... on the Rue du Bac... they said a few things about their crimes... and then they..." His strangled voice fell silent.

Florence already knew what he was going to say, but it didn't lessen the horror. "The Army shot them all, didn't they?"

Pierre's eyes shot in her direction. He gulped, closed his eyes for a long moment and then nodded. "They just lined them up and shot them." His voice was tight with disbelief. "Some of the Guard told me it was happening, but I couldn't believe them." His eyes closed again. "I *wouldn't* believe them," he muttered.

Florence felt sick to her stomach. The executions had begun, just as Minister Washburne had predicted. Who knew where it would end?

The Army had only been in Paris for two days. It was clear they were intent on revenge.

"Is it only May 23rd?" Florence asked. "Has it really only been two days?" Every part of her ached from another night on the cold, hard floor. Even if they would have dared to leave the relative safety of the clinic, they were surer than ever that they would probably not get back to treat the men relying on them. Thankfully, they had laid in generous stores of food when the fighting had escalated around Paris. They'd learned the lessons of the Siege well. They had enough food for a month, but she was quite sure she wouldn't survive sleeping on the floor that long.

"Yes," Silas responded as he stifled a yawn. He took her face in his hands. "Florence, I'm sorry."

Florence blinked up at him, his six-foot frame only a couple of inches taller than hers. "For what?" Silas ran a hair through the strands of red hair that had escaped her braid during the night. She'd given up trying to control it in a bun.

"For talking you into staying," he said apologetically.

"You didn't talk me into it," Florence said steadily. "You asked me I wanted to stay, and I said yes."

"You wouldn't have stayed except for me," Silas argued.

"That's true," Florence said gently. "I chose to stay with the man I love." She reached up and touched his face. "I don't regret it."

Silas stared at her. "How is that possible?"

"Because there's nowhere else I would rather be than with you, my love. I'm not thrilled with being in Paris right now, but I would take it over being in the safety of America without you."

Silas searched her eyes. "You mean that?"

"With every fiber of my being." Florence knew it was true.

"Thank you," Silas said softly. "But, when all this is over..."

His words were cut off by a tentative knock on the back door. Florence tensed. She'd learned to dread that sound. It never brought anything but bad news. Considering the gunfire and artillery explosions had never ceased during the long night, she was sure they were about to receive a disastrous report.

"I'll get it," Silas said grimly, his eyes revealing he also expected bad news.

"Dr. Amberton!"

Florence looked up as Nurse Campbell headed toward her. It took only a brief look to see she was clearly upset. "What's wrong?" she asked sharply.

"They're gone!"

Florence didn't need to ask what she meant. She'd been surprised none of her patients had insisted on going back into battle before now. Evidently, they'd decided it would be easier to leave during the night, so she couldn't try to talk them out of it. "How many?" she asked quietly.

"Gustav. Gabriel. Arthur. Victor. Antoine." Nurse Campbell ticked off the names on her fingers. "They've gone to fight."

Florence knew there was nothing she could do about it. She'd hoped to keep the men in the clinic until they had completely healed, but she'd also known the news of the executions would either terrify them or ignite them into action. Obviously, five of the men had decided continuing the fight was more important than their lives. While she could appreciate the passion, she already knew the futility of it.

"Let's fix breakfast for everyone," Florence said quietly. "We'll continue to care for the ones we have." She thought of the empty beds. "And treat more if they come."

Visitors throughout the day brought news that the French Army was taking back major portions of the city, including the butte of Montmartre, the location where just two months earlier the Guardsmen had captured and executed two French generals.

When Silas stepped back into the clinic after the latest visitor, Florence knew he had received devastating news. She hesitated before she went to him, certain she would rather not hear whatever he had to say, but also certain she needed to know so she could be as prepared as possible for whatever might be coming.

Silas turned away from the window when he heard her approach. "The whole city has gone crazy," he said flatly. "I know things like this happened during our own war, but having it just blocks away makes it somehow more shocking."

Florence put a hand on his arm and waited.

"The army took Montmartre today."

Florence continued to wait. They'd already received that report. From the look in Silas' eyes, something else horrific must have happened.

"They captured forty-two Guardsmen and several women – I don't know how many."

Florence stiffened, resisting the urge to turn away so she didn't have to listen to what she knew was coming. After the plea for fighters had gone out the morning before, many of the responders had been women and children.

Silas' voice was wooden. "After they captured them, they took them to the same house where the Guardsmen executed the two generals in March..." He swallowed hard. "They... shot all of them."

Florence held a hand to her mouth, fighting to control the bile threatening to erupt.

Silas continued, his voice now emotionless. "The Army also seized the barricades around la Madeleine church. They didn't bother to take the three hundred prisoners anywhere. They just shot them there..." He swallowed again as he eyes took on a glazed look. "They're all dead."

"No!" Florence cried. The tears she had fought to control all day rolled down her cheeks in a hot stream. "No..." she whispered. When Silas held out his arms, she rushed into them, sobs wracking her body. The men who had left that morning, the ones they had fought so hard to save, had told Jean Claude they were going to fortify the barricades at the Madeleine church. Silas' news meant all of them had either been killed in the battle or executed. She fought the urge to scream as she buried her face in Silas' chest.

When she could breathe again, Florence gazed up at her husband. "This morning, right before Pierre came with news of the first executions you started to say something. You said, '*When this is all over...*' What were you going to say?" Suddenly, it was imperative that she know. Justifiable or not, she hoped it would give her something to hold on to until all the horrors ended.

Silas looked at her tenderly and opened his mouth.

"They're burning it!" A man ran past the clinic, shouting at the top of his lungs. "Ils brûlent la ville!"

Florence and Silas gasped simultaneously. "They're burning the city!" Florence cried as they ran to the window. They could see plumes of black smoke in the distance, but they had no idea what was burning, or who was burning it.

Another man ran by, his eyes wild with fear. "The National Guard has gone mad! They've vowed to burn the city before they will give it to the Government!"

Florence groaned and looked over her shoulder at the rows of cots with patients staring back at her.

Jean Claude swung his good leg out of the bed, slowly maneuvered the bandaged one, grabbed hold of his crutches, and hobbled to the window.

Florence didn't bother to tell him that walking might be bad for his leg. For all she knew they were all going to burn to death. There was no way they could evacuate their patients. Even if they could, there was no guarantee they wouldn't all be shot by the Army if they made the attempt.

"What are they burning?" Jean Claude asked.

Silas shrugged, his face a stone mask. "You know what we know," he said flatly. His eyes raked the horizon. More dark plumes of smoke snaked toward the sky.

Florence watched silently. She hated the helpless feeling that engulfed her, but she already knew what choice she and Silas would make. They'd made a vow to care for their patients. The two of them could conceivably slip through undetected and make it to Minister Washburne's house, but she already knew they wouldn't. She took deep breaths as she fought to steady her emotions.

"You can make it out of here," Jean Claude said. "You don't need to do more than you've done." He spoke in slow, halting English so she would be certain to understand him.

"Thank you," Florence said softly, his compassion somehow lessening her fear. "We're staying here with you. Whatever happens, we'll deal with it together."

All through the long afternoon, and into the night, the smoke intensified in the city. Streams of people, running from the fires, screamed and cried what they'd seen as they passed the clinic.

Units of the National Guard, utterly failing in their attempts to fight the Army, had decided to take revenge by burning public buildings that symbolized the government. Throughout the afternoon, they had taken cans of oil and set fires to buildings near the city center. Dozens of buildings were burning throughout Paris.

The last report they'd received had been the most terrible. The Tuileries Palace had been the home of most of the French monarchs from Henry IV to Napoleon III. During the time the Commune was in control, it had been defended by a garrison of three hundred National Guard. When it had become clear they were going to lose the battle, the commander of the garrison gave the order to burn the palace. The walls, floors, curtains and woodwork were soaked with oil and turpentine. Barrels of gunpowder were placed at the foot of the grand staircase and in the courtyard. Then the fires were set.

The entire palace, except for the southernmost part, had exploded into flames that engulfed everything inside. No one knew how long the fire would burn, but it was certain that the beautiful palace that was a sign of French opulence would be completely gutted.

Florence and Silas closed all the windows to offer what protection they could from the acrid smoke, wetted cloths to put over everyone's mouths, and settled in to wait. There was no way to know if the flames would blow out of control and engulf the entire city. At the moment, the night was still. While it caused the smoke to create deeper and thicker pockets as the buildings burned, at least there wasn't wind to blow the embers onto other buildings.

Florence stared numbly at the faint orange glow glimmering through the dark smoke. She was beyond tired. Beyond caring. Beyond being enraged. She had just enough energy to take one breath after another. She clung to Silas' hand, trying to absorb enough strength to take the next breath.

Five days later, the fighting, the executions and the burning were all over.

Hundreds of men and women had been executed. Thousands more had died. The majority of the dead were National Guard, but the Army had experienced its share of fatalities, as well. The Palace had burned for forty-eight hours. The Hotel de Ville had been torched. Dozens of government buildings and ministries had been destroyed, along with the personal homes of many people associated with the reign of Napoleon III.

The horrible destruction, on top of the hardships of the Siege, had laid waste to the Jewel of Europe.

Florence and Silas moved numbly down the road toward their apartment. They wanted nothing more than a bath and a change of clothes. Smoke still hung in the air as they passed gutted building after gutted building. They had released all their patients so they could go home and see if there was anything left of the world they had known. They'd saved their lives, but had no idea if any of them had a life to return to.

Florence tried to look away from the people they passed, not sure she could handle more devastation, but it was impossible to miss the looks of utter wretchedness. It was impossible to not hear the wails of women crying for their husbands, and the piteous cries of children calling for their fathers *and* their mothers. The agony and pain stole her breath for what seemed the millionth time in the last week.

"It's only been seven days," she muttered, more to herself than anyone.

Silas heard her. "It seems a lifetime," he growled, his eyes bleary and bloodshot.

Stubble made his swarthy features even darker, but he was still the most handsome man Florence had ever seen. She reached out and took his hand.

Silas gazed down at her. "When this is all over..."

Florence met his eyes steadily, prepared for whatever he would say. "Yes?"

"We're going home."

Florence cocked her head. "Home?"

"To America," Silas said hoarsely. "If you will join me, Dr. Amberton." His eyes hardened. "Paris will no longer hold anything but horrible memories for me. It was my refuge for years after our war. It will never again be that." His eyes softened as quickly as they had hardened. "You are my refuge now, Florence. Let's return to America and build our life there. If we're going to help rebuild a country, I would rather rebuild my own."

A bright smile came across Florence's face, allowing her to forget her intense weariness for a moment. "I would love to return to America with you, Dr. Amberton. My home is wherever you are." She turned and threw her arms around him. "We've done all we can for Paris, and we've lived through it. I'm ready to leave. Let's go home."

Silas smiled and leaned down to kiss her. "Where do you want to go when we get to America?"

Florence laughed. "I don't care. We'll figure that out later. Right now, it will be enough to be on a boat that is moving *away* from France."

Chapter Thirteen

Carrie stepped outside and took deep breaths of the fresh morning air.

"It's going to be a perfect day for the Spring Celebration!"

Carrie spun around when she heard Rose's voice behind her. "You're up early." She walked over and settled into one of the rocking chairs beside her friend before she took a sip of the steaming coffee Annie had handed her on the way out.

"I have a lot on my mind." Rose shook her head at Carrie's questioning look. "I'm not worried about the school. I'm just thinking about everything that needs to be done – especially since Phoebe arrives with Felicia tomorrow. I'm disappointed they aren't here for the Spring Celebration, but there's not much that can be done when a train breaks down."

Matthew had gone into Richmond on business two days earlier. He was supposed to return with Phoebe and Felicia but had instead come back with a telegram informing him they would be two days late. He'd also delivered news that Peter was coming to Richmond on the same day. Peter was going to drive everyone, including Elizabeth, out to the plantation.

"I think you should set all that aside for the Spring Celebration," Carrie responded, smiling as she looked out over the plantation.

Granite gleamed in the first rays of the sun rising over the trees, his gray coat looking like burnished silver. Mares, with their foals, dotted the pastures. As the stock size increased, the pasture available for the horses had expanded. It now stretched all the way to the tree line, bordered by fences that gleamed white against the verdant green grass and trees. Whinnies and nickers filled the air as the horses moved toward the barn, anticipating their morning feed.

Moses had decided a Spring Celebration was in order since the flood the previous September had wiped out their annual Harvest Celebration. There had been a spate of hot days, but this mid-June morning was picture perfect. A late afternoon storm the day before had cleared the air, washed away the humidity, and ushered in cooler temperatures.

Clanging pots and delicious aromas wafting from the kitchen confirmed that Annie was up early to resume cooking.

Carrie glanced toward the house and chuckled. "You would think Annie had to cook for all of the hundred people coming today. She hasn't been out of the kitchen for days."

Rose lifted her hands in a show of futility. "Moses and I have reminded her several times that every family coming is bringing food, but she just sets her lips and tells us that whatever they're bringing won't be as good as what she can cook."

Carrie laughed. "She's right, you know."

"Of course she is, but I don't want her killing herself in the kitchen."

"A body never died from hard work!" Annie retorted as opened the screen door and walked out onto the porch with a tray of ham biscuits and cinnamon rolls.

"Annie!" Carrie protested. "You don't have to bring us food. You have far too much to do. I was coming in to get something."

"Nonsense," Annie snorted. "In spite of what y'all be spouting off about out here, I reckon I can handle what goes on in my kitchen." She slapped the tray down on a table and stepped back with her fists planted on her hips. "Besides, I need you to tell me these cinnamon rolls are the best you ever tasted."

Carrie already knew that was true, but she obeyed the command, closing her eyes in ecstasy as she took a bite of the warm rolls. She groaned as the taste of cinnamon and brown sugar exploded in her mouth. "Delicious," she murmured. "They're the best I've ever tasted." She was glad May wasn't here. She dreaded the day she would ever have to choose between something Annie or May had cooked. The two women had only met each other once, but the ongoing competition between them was epic. There was an unspoken agreement that everyone would make sure the two women never shared a kitchen.

Annie eyed her. "Better than May's?" she demanded.

"Definitely," Carrie assured her. She took another bite to prove her point.

"Humpf! I already knew that." Annie's voice was full of satisfaction as she turned back toward the house. "I got work to do."

Carrie and Janie grinned at each other when the door closed behind her.

"Did you have your fingers crossed?" Rose whispered.

Carrie rolled her eyes. "I hate when Annie and May make me choose." She spoke in a whisper, her eye on the door to make sure Annie didn't surprise them again. "I learned a long time ago to just say whatever they want to hear. They're both extraordinary cooks. I figure heaven will forgive me a few lies to make them feel good."

Moses appeared from around the back of the house. His muscles gleamed with sweat, even in the early morning air. "Are you lying to my mama again?" he demanded, careful to keep his voice low. His eyes danced with amusement.

Carrie's response was to hand him the platter of cinnamon rolls. "Eat these and hush."

Moses grinned as he shoved one in his mouth. "No one is a better cook than my mama," he declared.

Carrie rolled her eyes again. He always assured May that *she* was the best cook he'd ever seen whenever he was in Richmond, and away from Annie's listening ears. "What are you doing back there?"

"Miles, John and I are building the bonfire for tonight."

Rose raised a brow. "You talked our son into getting up this early to build a bonfire?"

"I promised him a long ride around the plantation with all the other children tomorrow."

Rose raised the other brow. "You're going to take another day off from the fields?"

"Miles is going to take them all."

Carrie stared at him, hoping she hadn't heard him clearly. "By himself? *All* of them?"

"Do you think it's too much for him?" Moses asked.

Carrie had opened her mouth to answer before she saw the twinkle in his eyes. She burst out laughing. "You planned this all along, didn't you?"

Moses shook his head. "I have no idea what you mean," he said innocently.

"You know good and well that I'm not going to let Miles take all the children around the plantation by himself," Carrie replied. "You also know that no one knows every inch of the plantation the way I do." Her indignation was tempered by amusement of how skillfully Moses had manipulated her.

"Well, now that you mention it," Moses' deep voice filled the porch. "It might be a bit much for him," he agreed. He sat down in the rocker next to Rose and reached for another cinnamon roll. "Does that mean you'll go with them?"

Carrie laughed again as she nodded her head. "Yes. It sounds like fun."

Moses grinned. "Thank you. Actually, Miles was planning on doing it by himself. He might be just fine, but I know just my children are a handful. I couldn't imagine him having to control all of them." He paused for another bite. "It's going to take a lot of food for that many hungry children. I figured y'all could end up on the bank outside the tunnel. I'll carry the picnic hampers out there for Mama. They'll be inside the tunnel door."

"It sounds delightful," Carrie assured him. She knew they would be back before everyone else arrived from

Richmond. Suddenly, she hesitated. "Do you think Felicia will be disappointed? We can wait for two or three days so she can join us."

Rose shook her head. "She'll be fine. She and I will go riding at some point, but I think she'll appreciate some time to just settle in before anything is expected of her. She'll only be here a couple of weeks before she returns to Oberlin."

Carrie nodded. "Tomorrow it is."

The wagons started rolling onto the plantation about two o'clock. Laughing children piled out of the wagons, followed by their parents loaded down with picnic hampers and blankets. The children immediately ran out to the lawn where they began to play chase, darting through the trees into the woods and then back out again.

The men carried the picnic hampers to the tables built that morning. Sawing and pounding had filled the air as they erected enough to hold the mountains of food that were coming. They had been placed under the tall oak trees that offered protection from the bright sun. While it was cooler, it was still a warm day. The picnic hampers would stay packed until the evening meal. The Tournament wouldn't start for two hours. The children would have plenty of time to get tired out, while the adults would have the opportunity to talk and catch up.

Rose watched the activity with a big smile. It had hurt her heart to tell her white students she could no longer be their teacher. It hurt all the more to tell them good-bye on the last day of school a week earlier. She knew she would continue to see them, but the reality that she could no longer be their teacher was a bitter pill to swallow. It had been excruciating to attempt to answer all their questions, when it was still so hard for her to understand herself.

"It's wrong, you know. You should still be their teacher."

Rose turned when Alvin Williams appeared at her side. "I know," she agreed. "There's also nothing I can do about it." She had talked with Alvin and his wife, Amanda, at length after the School Board representative had visited. That was followed by several meetings with the other white parents who were disappointed Rose wouldn't be teaching their children anymore, while also being relieved that another school would be ready for them before school started up again.

"Violet cried her eyes out on the last day of school. She said she didn't want anyone to be her teacher but you."

Rose's heart swelled with love. Ten-year-old Violet, and her eleven-year-old brother, Silas, were two of her favorite students. "I'm going to miss teaching her," she said softly. "I'll still be able to see them out on the playground, though." The thought of the fence that would have to separate the two playgrounds made her teeth grit with anger.

Alvin didn't miss it. "You're as furious about this as I am, aren't you?"

Rose had put on a positive face for her students and parents, but Alvin was a friend. "Yes." She sighed. "I'm also heartbroken." She watched little Violet leave the game of chase and dash over to where Amber had set up a hopscotch area for the children. "I'll miss teaching Violet. She's incredibly bright and she gives the best hugs."

Alvin watched his daughter. Violet grabbed the hand of her best friend, a nine-year-old black girl named Kathy. The two girls, laughing and shrieking, lined up on the hopscotch boards. "Your school made me believe things were changing." He shook his head. "When I fought in the war, I believed all the blacks should stay slaves. I gave up an arm and half my leg because I thought the South should stay the way it was. It took you and your school to show me how wrong I was. It took Jeb to show me I could be friends with a black man." He gazed around at the throngs of people. "Look at that. Whites and blacks are talking to each other like color don't matter."

"It *doesn't* matter," Rose replied.

"You're right," Alvin agreed, "but they're going to *make* it matter." His eyes blazed. "I reckon those people who are running things don't want blacks and whites to be friendly with each other. They figure that will take away some of their power. God forbid they should lose some of their precious power," he said angrily. "Or their money. There's lots of plantation owners who are angry because they have to pay for their labor now. I've heard them talking. If they can beat down the freed slaves, then they believe they can pay them less money. One way to beat them down is to make sure they don't get everything the whites do."

Rose listened closely, amazed that this was the same man who had once refused to let his children come to her school.

"That's not all, though," Alvin continued. "If they keep everyone separate, they're gonna keep the whites believing they're better than blacks. I used to be just like that. I figure they're gonna keep stoking the hatred and prejudice. If they can keep us fighting each other, we're not gonna pay too much attention to the fact we're being used."

Abby had walked up while Alvin was talking. "You have a very astute insight, Alvin," she said admiringly.

Alvin turned toward Abby. "You're a businesswoman, Mrs. Cromwell. Do you think I'm right?"

"I do," Abby assured him. "It goes deeper than the racial issue, however. You're absolutely right about the desire to separate blacks and whites, but it's also being aimed at immigrants now. There are millions of immigrants pouring into America. They're coming from Ireland, England, Germany, Italy, Sweden, Norway and so many other countries. They believe they're coming to the land of opportunity, but in reality, they're being forced to work for a pittance in factories." Her grey eyes were full of disdain. "Their children work horrible hours for even less money than their parents because they have no other choice if their family is going to survive."

Rose knew this wasn't exactly Spring Celebration conversation, but celebrating a new season couldn't undo what was happening.

"I've heard that doesn't happen in Cromwell Factories," Alvin replied.

"It certainly doesn't," Abby said firmly. "We don't employ children and we pay a fair wage to the men and women who work for us. In addition, we decided a few days ag to open a school in the Moyamensing factory for our employees children."

Rose gasped. "I didn't know that! Abby, that's wonderful."

Abby smiled. "Thank you, but you can credit your brother. It was Jeremy's idea. We just agreed to allocate some of the profits to make it happen. I was waiting for the right moment to tell you, but the preparations for the Spring Celebration have kept us busy."

"It will change lives, Mrs. Cromwell," Alvin said warmly. "I been watching my children. The more they learn, the smarter they seem to be. It just makes them want to learn more. I don't have much of a chance to do anything with my life anymore, but it's different for them." He smiled. "My little Violet is already talking about going to college. Me and Amanda keep telling her and Silas that they can do anything they want."

The three of them fell silent, watching the children play. There was a group rolling hoops out in the large open area of the lawn. Jump ropes were whirling. Beanbags were being tossed at a board with holes in it, and there were still children playing chase.

A group of men were playing horseshoes to the side of the house. By the sound of the whoops and hollers, mixed in with clanging metal, they were having a wonderful time. Peter had brought several sets with him on his last trip to Richmond, along with a set of the rules that had been established in England in 1869. All the men had played horseshoes for years, but now they were intent on learning the rules so they could set up competitions.

Groups of women dotted the lawn, laughing and talking in tight clumps.

Alvin returned to the earlier conversation. "Mrs. Cromwell, why are they doing it?"

Abby knew precisely what he was talking about. "Because they can," she said sadly. "America has become fixated on business profits. Corporations are at the center of it."

Alvin cocked his head. "I don't reckon I know anything about corporations." He looked embarrassed.

"Most people don't," Abby assured him. "The sad thing is that they're impacting millions of lives."

"Can you tell me more about them?" Alvin asked. "I know this is supposed to be a celebration. I'll get around to the celebrating, but right now I'm trying to make sense out of this world."

Rose doubted anyone could make sense out of the world right now, but she understood Alvin's need to try, and she applauded his hunger for more information. He may not have ever had the chance for the education his children were receiving, but he had given them their appetite for knowledge. She also knew he was reading all the books his children brought home from school, and had asked her for more. Educated or not, he was highly intelligent.

"All of us are," Abby said gently. "This is a very complicated issue that I could talk about for hours, but I'll do my best to simplify it. Not because you wouldn't understand it," she said quickly, "but because I truly could talk for hours, and this isn't the time."

When she paused, Rose knew Abby was attempting to marshal her thoughts.

"One of the reasons for our Revolutionary War almost one hundred years ago was because English corporations dominated American trade. They used their power to claim most of the wealth in America. After a fighting a war to end English rule, our country's founders had a healthy fear of corporations. They worked hard to limit their power." Abby paused, realizing she hadn't answered Alvin's initial question. "You asked me what a corporation is. Most businesses in America are owned by individuals, or perhaps a partnership of two or more people. Like Cromwell Plantation. Thomas used to own it by himself. Now, he and Moses own it in a partnership. Our country and our economy were built on businesses like this. A corporation is very different. It's a company or a group of people who are allowed to act as a single entity – like being one person. The difference is that the corporation is separate and distinct from its owner."

"Why?" Alvin asked keenly.

Abby paused, her brow knit in thought. "Because a corporation is owned by their stockholders." She stopped again; obviously aware she was using terms Alvin wouldn't understand. "Stockholders are people who invest their money in a corporation. They do that so they can share in the profits of the company. The other reason people are willing to do that is because they don't have to be responsible for the corporation's debts or illegal activity."

Alvin mulled over her words and then shook his head. "Are you telling me they can put their money into something, but not be responsible for anything bad that the corporation does – even if they're the ones that do the bad thing?"

"Yes, that's exactly what I'm saying," Abby replied. "You put it better than I did."

"How is that fair? Why would the government allow that?" Alvin demanded.

"That's a great question," Abby responded. "It used to be very difficult to become a corporation. You could only apply to become one if you were in existence to benefit the public. You could only get one if you were doing something like constructing roads or canals."

"Or railroads," Rose added.

"Exactly," Abby agreed. "It was hard to become a corporation, and often harder to stay one because there were so many restrictions imposed by each state. They did that because no one wanted a repeat of what had happened when we were under English rule."

"Well, from what you're saying, it seems to be happening again," Alvin observed. "Why?"

"Greed," Abby said flatly. "Many states tried to fight it, but corporate money is powerful. One of the effects of the Civil War was that corporations became very wealthy because of all the spending that was done to support the war. Now they're using their money and influence to control Congress and state capitals. They're bribing everyone who will take their money. Just in the last six years, the lawmakers who were elected to represent and protect American citizens have made decisions that are very bad for the country. They decided corporate stockholders don't have to be responsible for illegal actions. They've changed state laws so that corporations can have their way. They've also extended the amount of time a corporation can exist so they can keep making money.

Alvin looked puzzled. "All of this sure sounds like it's bad, but I don't understand how it's impacting me." He glanced toward the cluster of people on the lawn. "Or any of them."

"Most people don't," Abby responded, glancing toward the house.

Rose suspected Abby was wondering if she was needed back at the house. "Just a few more minutes," she pleaded. She'd heard snippets of this before, but this was the first time she'd heard it laid out so clearly. She was fascinated, and quite sure she needed to understand what Abby was saying.

Abby smiled and nodded. "American corporations have taken over more and more control of labor. Working people no longer have the rights they used to. They've also taken over more control of our resources – taking far more than their share because the government wants to keep them happy. That wasn't enough, however. They're also taking control of America's political sovereignty. In short," she said angrily, "we're in danger of corporations running our country."

Rose tensed as she thought of the ramifications of what she was hearing. Corporations had the power to change everything about America.

Alvin had another question. "What is political sovereignty?"

"Another thing most people don't know," Abby replied. "Perhaps the easiest way to understand it is that political sovereignty is the power of the people. In our American democracy, it means we're supposed to be governed by the people who vote our lawmakers into office. The lawmakers are supposed to do what the people who put them in office want them to do."

"*Supposed* to?" Alvin asked. "I thought that's how it was working."

Abby's voice was grim when she answered. "With corporations bribing our government officials, the will of the people means less and less. The very thing we fought the Revolutionary War over is being allowed to thrive in our country once again."

"America used to be a country of farmers and independent business owners," Abby continued. "The industrial revolution is changing all that. It's brought some good change to America," she conceded, "but it's also forced millions to work in factories. Because they're no longer dependent on their own work, they're scared of becoming unemployed." Her eyes darkened. "Corporations have learned how to take advantage of that fear. Company towns, where the employee is dependent on their employer for everything, are becoming very common. If someone dares to complain, they're forced to leave their home, and their names get put on a blacklist so they can never get another job.

People are afraid to complain about being treated horribly, or about the fact they were laid off so the factories can hire their children for a fraction of what they were paying them. They're afraid that if they say anything, their children will be fired too. Without anyone in the family working, they'll starve and be homeless."

Rose felt her own anger rising. What she was hearing was nothing more than a new definition of slavery.

Abby's voice grew more passionate. "People are angry and frustrated. Who can blame them? The corporations and politicians are creating situations where whites believe blacks or immigrants are to blame for their problems. Blacks believe whites are to blame for *their* problems. Immigrants believe the freed slaves are to blame for the fact that they can't get jobs." She lifted her hands and rolled her eyes. "All their anger and frustration needs an outlet, so they're taking it out on the ones they believe are to blame." Her eyes blazed. "Except the corporations, and the politicians allowing them to take control, are the real ones to blame. They're stoking the discontent by paying so poorly and treating people so terribly. Their profits soar, while the people working to make the money are left to suffer."

Abby looked at Alvin. "You asked how this will impact you? You were impacted last year when the KKK attacked your house and your family because you let Violet and Silas attend a black school. Since whites are being taught to blame blacks for their problems, you're a threat to them because you don't believe that. You were impacted on Christmas Eve when you had to leave your home and your family to fight off an attack by the KKK on the plantation." She took a deep breath. "You're being impacted again because the government is putting segregation laws into the Virginia constitution that will make things harder for blacks, and stoke more prejudice and anger among whites. Not to mention that they've taken away your right to decide where your children go to school."

"What's going to happen?" Rose demanded. "This can't continue."

Abby frowned; her anger absorbed by a deep sadness in her eyes. "I'm afraid it will continue for the foreseeable future. The politicians are the only ones who can change things, but they have been bought. In the meanwhile, the corporations become more powerful. The American economy has become dependent on them, but..." her voice trailed off.

"But what?" Alvin asked, his eyes and voice both fearful and angry.

"I believe we're headed for another economic crash," Abby said wearily. "While so many people believe corporations are strengthening our economy, the truth is that they're weakening it. When the crash happens, people are going to blame President Grant and Congress, but the real reason is because of the rapid, unregulated growth of business. The corporations have bought so many politicians that the rules put in place to control them are disappearing."

Alvin stared at her. "How do you know all this?"

"Do you mean how can I know all this since I'm only a woman?" Abby's eyes were amused.

Alvin flushed, but shook his head. "No, Mrs. Cromwell. I don't mean that at all. After watching you, and Miss Rose, and Miss Carrie, I reckon I know that a woman can do anything she sets her mind to do. I'm just wondering how you learned all this."

Abby reached out a hand and touched his arm. "Thank you for that," she said softly.

"My wife knows all this because she's brilliant." Thomas' voice sounded just behind them.

Rose looked up, startled. She'd been so absorbed in the discussion that she hadn't seen him approach.

Thomas walked over and put an arm around Abby's waist. "I'm going to let you answer that question, my dear, but then you have people clamoring to see you."

Abby smiled up at him, and then looked back at Alvin. "When my first husband died, I was suddenly responsible for all his factories. When he was alive, we used to talk about how volatile the American economy was. He taught me how to pay attention to the signs that indicated things were about to get bad. He was able to ride out all the ups and downs of the economy, but only because he had the information to make wise decisions. He taught me what I needed to know. I've been watching the signs ever since."

A high-pitched squeal and an eruption of laughter from the children made Abby pause and smile before she continued. "I was still running the factories in Philadelphia until shortly after the war. When Thomas and I married, I hired managers for those factories and moved here." She smiled at Thomas and tucked a hand through his arm. "We operated another factory in Richmond until it was burned down. We still own the factories in Philadelphia. I saw what was happening with the corporations, so I've made sure to learn all I could. There are a lot of people who use the lack of knowledge as an excuse for what happens to them." Abby's eyes flashed with passion. "I believe we're all responsible for learning the things we need to know. I believe knowledge is the greatest power we have."

Rose couldn't have agreed more. The respect she had for Abby was already immense. It was even more so now.

"What's going to happen when things get bad?" Alvin asked anxiously.

Thomas held up his hand, a wide smile on his face to reduce the sting of what he was about to say. "I said I'd only let her answer one more question, Alvin. Don't worry, though. You can ask it again after the Spring Celebration. There's nothing my wife loves more than to share her vast amount of knowledge."

"Thomas!"

Thomas smiled broadly. "Can I help it if I'm proud of how brilliant you are? Part of that pride comes from the fact you're so willing to share what you know. You're a natural born teacher, my dear, but right now you're needed to be a natural born hostess."

Abby returned his smile. "Well, since you put it that way." She turned to Alvin. "It's been wonderful to talk to you. I look forward to continuing our conversation in the future."

"Thank you, Mrs. Cromwell," Alvin said earnestly. "I've learned a lot today."

"One other thing, Alvin," Thomas said.

"Yes, Mr. Cromwell?"

"I can hear that you really want to understand what's going on in our country. Abby is right about the power of knowledge. You've become a good friend to our family. Any time you want to borrow a book from my library, or read one of the nation's newspapers, you're welcome to."

Alvin's eyes widened. "Thank you, sir! You can be sure I'll take you up on that offer."

"Mrs. Samuels!" Violet ran up and jolted to a stop, ending their discussion.

Rose leaned down and smiled warmly. "Hello Violet."

"Mrs. Samuels, I won the hopscotch game. I beat *every*body!" Violet's eyes glowed with pride and pleasure.

"That's wonderful," Rose said enthusiastically. As much as she had benefitted from the intense discussion, she was ready to relax and have fun. She held out her hand. "Will you show me how you do it?"

"Oh yes!" Violet gushed, her face glowing with delight. "I'll be right pleased to show you!"

"Violet..." Rose began.

Violet gasped, thought quickly, and then grinned. "I meant to say I'll be *very* pleased to show you!"

Rose nodded her approval, biting back her smile as she thought of Frances warning Minnie about every word having to go through the *Rose Filter*. That was a label she was happy to have attached to her.

Carrie glanced toward the arena as her father climbed the steps of the platform. Battling feelings of sadness, she slipped into the coolness of the barn. Her sadness intensified when she saw Granite. His head was raised high and his ears pricked forward, as his intelligent eyes watched the activity in the arena. He whinnied as soon as he saw her, stomping his hoof for extra emphasis.

Carrie sighed and hurried over to him. "Not this year," she said, hoping her voice was steady.

Granite swung his massive head around so he could stare at her. It was easy to read his expression.

"Those days are over, boy" Carrie said as she stroked his velvety neck. It broke her heart that Granite could no longer compete in the Tournament. Her mind flew back eleven years. She could recall every moment of the day she had met Robert Borden. It was the day just before he and Granite had competed in the Tournament at Blackwell Plantation. Carrie had dreamed for many years of competing on her horse, but women weren't allowed to compete then. The next best thing was to let their tall, handsome guest prove what Granite could do.

Against everyone's expectations, Robert and Granite had won. The thrill was just as strong today as it had been eleven years ago. Carrie closed her eyes and leaned her head against her gelding. Memories of Robert, as well as the years she had shared with her beloved horse threatened to swamp her. She'd already lost Robert. The knowledge that Granite was getting older and needed to slow down almost took her breath away.

She'd known that fact for a while, but the sounds of the Tournament about to take place drove it home in a painful way she hadn't anticipated.

Granite whinnied again and butted her with his head.

"I'm sorry," she whispered. She wished she could take him and go for a long ride, just the two of them. She didn't want to watch the other riders and horses competing, but she knew it would be rude to leave. She was also quite certain that it would be easier for Granite to not watch something he could no longer do. She stroked his neck, lost in the memories.

The Tournament on Blackwell Plantation had been the last one before the war had disrupted their lives. When the war had ended, they decided to resume them on Cromwell Plantation as part of the Harvest Celebration. There was no question that any female who wanted to ride would be allowed. It had been a fierce competition between her and Amber ever since. Other people competed but knew in advance they had little chance of winning.

She watched through the door as Amber mounted Eclipse, the Cromwell Stable stud, and began to warm him up with easy laps around the arena. The towering bay Thoroughbred was a perfect specimen. He was lightning fast, and he produced beautiful foals that claimed top dollar on the market.

Amber was one of the few who could handle the massive stallion. In truth, there was little *handling* when it came to the two of them. Eclipse adored Amber and would do anything she asked, anticipating what she wanted even before she asked. She'd been so small when she started riding him, that no one had initially believed she could handle him. She quickly proved everyone wrong.

As Carrie watched, eight other riders entered the arena. There were some nice horses, but none of them could compare to Eclipse. She suspected some of them competed so they could say they'd been in the same arena with the legendary Eclipse.

The arena was quickly surrounded by the festival goers. Their laughs and calls of encouragement to the riders filled the air. It still thrilled Carrie to see an almost even mix of black and white faces in the crowd.

"Are you going out there?"

Carrie turned when she heard Anthony's voice. The compassionate look in his eyes brought her tears to the surface again. She swallowed hard. "I was going to...," she murmured. Then she shook her head. "I can't," she admitted, silently begging him to understand. "I'm going to stay in here with Granite."

Anthony's strong arms wrapped her in an embrace. "I thought you would."

Carrie didn't bother to ask him if he thought she was making a wrong choice. It didn't matter. It was the only choice she could live with.

Chapter Fourteen

"Ladies and gentlemen, it is now time for the charge of the knights." Thomas' gaze and powerful voice swept over the crowd before he turned his attention to the competitors. "Ladies and gentlemen, you are gathered here today to participate in the most chivalrous and gallant sport known. It has been called the sport of kings, and well it should. It has come down to us from the Crusades, being at that time a very hazardous undertaking. You probably know, but I intend to tell you once more..." He allowed his voice to trail off as laughter rippled through the crowd.

Carrie smiled with affection as she watched her father. His silver hair, erect posture, and carefully chosen suit made him quite elegant. He seemed to become more handsome with time. Every year he said the same thing when he mounted the platform. It was now part of the tradition everyone loved and expected, just as they had all the years they had attended the Blackwell Plantation competition. She never tired of it.

"As you probably know," he continued, "the knights of that day rode in full armor, charging down the lists at each other with the intent that the best man would knock his opponent from his horse. It was a rough and dangerous pastime. Many were seriously hurt. Some were killed. But we, in this day, have gotten soft and tender—as well as much smarter, I believe—and have eliminated the danger and roughness of the sport." Again, laughter riffled through the crowd, but no one spoke up to mar the seriousness of the charge.

All levity left Thomas' voice as he leaned forward to address the riders. "But with all that, it is still a challenging and fascinating sport. One that tests the horsemanship, dexterity, skill, quickness of eye, steadiness and control of the rider, and the speed, smoothness of gait and training of the horse. It is an honorable sport, and I do not need to mention that a knight taking any undue advantage of their opponents will be ruled out of the tournament."

Every rider nodded their head solemnly.

Having pressed his point home to the competitors, Thomas continued with the instructions.

Carrie knew the rules by heart, but still she listened attentively, watching the intensity on each rider's face. They may not believe they could beat Eclipse and Amber, but they would give it their all.

"The three ring hangers are spaced twenty yards apart. The start is twenty yards from the first ring—making the total length of the list sixty yards. Any rider taking more than seven seconds from the start to the last ring will be ruled out. Should anything untoward happen during the tilt that would prevent the rider from having a fair try at the rings, they will so indicate by lowering their lance and making no try at the rings. The judges will decide whether the rider is entitled to another tilt."

Carrie glanced over at the judging table. Abby, Janie and Moses smiled brightly as they waved their hands to the crowd.

Thomas nodded to the judges and then continued. "All rings must be taken off the lances by the judges. No others will be counted. The rings on the first tilt will be two inches in diameter; on the second tilt, one and a half; on the third tilt, one; on the fourth tilt, three quarters; and on the fifth and last tilt—if there are competitors left—one half inch."

Having dispensed with the rules, Thomas smiled and regarded the riders warmly. "Welcome to this year's Tournament. All of you are riding not only to win, but to gain the coveted honor of crowning the lady or gentleman of your choice, the King or Queen of Love and Beauty at the dance later tonight. The next four riders, in order of their success, will have the privilege of honoring the person of their choice as person-in-waiting for the chosen royalty. Only the members of the court will participate in the opening dance tonight." He smiled again, making eye contact with each competitor. "Good luck to you. May the best man or woman..." Thomas hesitated as he looked at John mounted on Cafi, "Or boy... win!" The tall chestnut gelding had given the seven-year-old a new lease on life after the flood had killed his beloved Rascal.

Another mighty blow on the horn announced the beginning of the competition. A rousing cheer rose from the crowd, along with a whoop from the riders as they galloped their horses in the direction of the starting line.

Carrie turned away and buried her face in Granite's neck. She could feel him quivering with anticipation. She wished she knew how to explain to him that he wasn't competing because she loved him too much to allow him to do anything that would shorten his time with her. If it had been a mere matter of him no longer being fast enough to win, she would have happily ridden him. Miles had told her, however, that Granite would pour his heart out to please her – at the risk of his own health. She would never let that happen.

The last few weeks with him had been exquisite. She rode him every morning before she went to the clinic to work, savoring every moment of the dawn. As soon as she'd been given permission to ride him alone as a girl, it had been their favorite time of the day. It still was.

Anthony joined her sometimes. Other times, she'd been able to convince Frances or Minnie to accompany her. She loved their company, but it was the mornings she went solo, alone with her beloved horse that meant the most to her. From everything she could tell, he was still strong and healthy. He was slowing down, but he certainly didn't seem ill. She didn't know how long she had left with him, but she intended to make the most of it.

As expected, Amber had won the Tournament. Much to almost everyone's surprise, her stiffest competition had come from John. Carrie and Rose were the only ones not surprised. They had witnessed the hours he and Cafi spent practicing in the arena, sometimes waiting until it was almost dark because he said capturing the rings when he couldn't see them very well would make him focus harder. Obviously, it was something he'd seen Amber do through the years. They'd been astonished that a seven-year-old would exhibit such perseverance. All the practice had paid off.

Amber and John were the only ones to capture all the rings, all the way to the final tilt, but Eclipse's speed had the final say. Cafi was no match for the powerful stallion that had won many races on the Chicago racetracks before retiring as a stud.

Thomas strode into the bright light emitted by the roaring bonfire in the middle of the clearing behind the house. Musicians, already tuned and ready to go, gave him accompaniment as he raised his hand to get everyone's attention. "It's time for the Queen of the Dance to select her King," he called loudly. He looked toward the house. "Will the Queen please proceed?"

The crowd fell silent as the back door opened. Amber, looking elegant in a soft yellow gown, swept down the steps, her head held regally.

Carrie gazed at her with admiration. Gone was the awkward, uncertain girl who had won the Tournament several years earlier. In her place, was a beautiful young lady who shone with confidence and happiness.

"She's exquisite," Anthony murmured.

"Rose and Janie did her hair after supper," Carrie told him. "She's wearing a dress I wore for one of the Blackwell Balls years ago. I had no idea why I kept some of those things, but now I'm glad I did. We're the same size now. She had so much fun selecting what she would wear."

Anthony smiled. "So, the girl who used to only care about horses is becoming a young lady."

"She is," Carrie agreed, wishing with all her heart that Robert could see her now.

Amber walked to stand next to Thomas, bestowing a smile on everyone when she had taken her spot.

"Good evening, Queen Amber," Thomas said seriously, his voice loud enough for everyone to hear.

"Good evening," Amber replied.

"Congratulations once again on your victory today. Are you prepared to select your King?"

Carrie knew her father was as curious as the rest of them to see who Amber would select. As far as they knew, her only interest was in horses. She'd already asked Rose if Amber seemed to have her eye on anyone at school, but she had insisted she didn't think so.

"I am," Amber replied, her eyes both calm and intense. "I was surprised to have such good competition today."

A laugh rippled through the crowd, but everyone there knew she was just telling the truth. Carrie had been the only one to give her a true challenge in the past.

"In honor of my worthy opponent, I choose John Samuels as my King," Amber said.

"*Me?*" John's shocked voice sounded above the silence. "Did she just choose *me* as the King?" There was a brief silence, and then, "I don't know nothing about being a King!" There was a slight yelp when his words died away.

Carrie choked back a laugh, envisioning the soft pinch Rose had delivered to her son.

"I mean, I don't know *anything* about being a King!" The crowd laughed freely.

Amber walked over to John and leaned down, speaking just loudly enough for Carrie to hear. "There's nothing to it," she said. "Just take my hand and walk to the fire with me."

John shrank back and looked at her suspiciously. "But don't I have to *dance*?"

His horrified voice was loud enough to illicit more laughter.

"Just one little dance," Amber assured him. John narrowed his eyes and started to shake his head, but Amber leaned closer. "The Queen and King get to eat first from the dessert table," she whispered.

John stopped his head shake, peered into her eyes as if to make sure she was telling the truth, and then took her hand. "Alright," he mumbled.

Amber pulled him toward the bonfire, joining the other three competitors who had already chosen their dance partners. When the music swelled louder, she expertly led John through the beginning of the Virginia Reel.

Sparks from the fire flew into the air, creating a magical effect as the wind swirled them around as if they were also dancing to the music.

When the first song came to an end, Anthony pulled Carrie into his arms. "I hope you have enough energy to dance the night away, Dr. Wallington," he murmured in her ear.

Carrie laughed up into his eyes. "We'll see if you can keep up with me, Mr. Wallington."

Carrie had gone into the clinic early the next morning to take care of a few patients before leaving everything in Janie's capable hands. Having Janie as a partner was turning out to be just as wonderful as she had predicted it would be. The two friends worked hard, but the clinic was full of laughter and easy conversation as they treated patients. The look of relaxed happiness on Janie's face filled her heart with joy. Polly split her time between the two of them, making the running of the clinic appear effortless.

Carrie smiled with delight when she walked into the barn. Miles, Amber and Susan had been busy. The horses were all cross-tied in the corridor. The children were hard at work grooming and saddling them. Minnie, Hope and John were the only ones who still needed mounting blocks to reach their horse's backs.

Carrie stopped, watching the bevy of activity.

Amber had brushed All My Heart until the mare glowed. The bay with a perfect, heart-shaped white marking stood calmly, though she nickered a greeting to Carrie when she spotted her.

Frances was slipping a saddle on Peaches, the palomino mare she loved with a passion. There had been times during the last six months when school breaks would have allowed her to join Carrie in Richmond, but she hadn't wanted to leave her horse. Carrie understood completely.

Minnie was going to ride Rose's mare, Ginger. The little girl's confidence was growing, but she was still cautious, and not quite ready for her own horse. The honey-colored mare was gentle enough to be perfect for her.

Angel was vigorously brushing Friday. Carrie could still hardly believe the beautiful sorrel mare was the same piteously thin horse that had arrived on the plantation with cuts and welts from being beaten with a whip by her previous owner. Susan had saved her and brought her home. Angel and Friday had simultaneously saved each other from the traumas they'd endured.

John was carefully lifting his saddle to Cafi's back from his place high on the mounting block. Cafi waited patiently. Carrie listened to his conversation with his chestnut gelding.

"We almost won the Tournament yesterday, Cafi. You wait. Next year there won't be anyone who can beat us."

Carrie suspected he might be right, but only if Eclipse started to slow down a little from old age. The stallion had many years left, but eventually he would slow down – just like Granite.

Hope, her eyes shining with excitement, carefully braided Patches' mane. Her black and white pony stood quietly, though Carrie could have sworn Patches rolled her eyes when she looked her way. The little girl's beloved pony would do anything the girl asked, but she often didn't look happy about it. Of course, it might be that the long-suffering look was just etched on her pretty face after years of training children how to ride.

Carrie chuckled and then moved out of the shadows. "Hello everyone!"

"Carrie!"

A cry of greeting rose up from the corridor.

Miles nodded his head toward Granite's stall. "He's in there all ready for you. He's been stomping his hoof like a spoiled child, though. He figures we ain't moving fast enough for him."

Granite stuck his head out of the stall when he heard his name. He whinnied loudly when he saw Carrie. As if to prove Miles right, he stomped his hoof again and snorted.

Carrie chuckled. "I'm here to do your bidding, your Highness." She opened his stall door and led him out. "It looks like everyone is about ready."

"Mama says you're going to show us secret places no one else has ever seen," Hope said excitedly. "Is that true?"

Carrie nodded her head solemnly. "It's true."

"And Daddy said we're going to have a picnic down by the river," Hope gushed. "Is that true, too?"

Carrie smiled and nodded again. "Has your daddy ever lied to you, Hope?"

"No," Hope said quickly. "I just can't believe we're going to have such a perfect day!" Every word was emphasized by her glowing grin.

Carrie hugged her close and then stepped back. A quick glance told her all the horses were saddled and bridled. "I say we go for a ride!"

"Yes!" The chorus rang through the barn.

"Mama, did you really use to ride around the plantation all by yourself? Frances told me you did."

Carrie smiled at the disbelief in Minnie's voice, but she also felt sad that all of them couldn't experience what she had. None of the children were allowed to ride alone. If they ventured far from the stable, they had to have an adult with them. What had been her greatest joy when she was growing up, was now a danger. Despite the guards that kept watch on the plantation, there was no way to assure a vigilante wouldn't make their way onto the outskirts of the property and harm one of the children. There had been far too much violence for any of them to take their safety for granted.

"I did," she assured her. "I was thirteen when I got Granite." She glanced at Miles. "Granite was a gift from my father, but it was Miles who picked him out for me. He knew we would be a perfect team." She laid a hand on her gelding's neck. "He couldn't have been more right."

Miles met her eyes and smiled.

Minnie cocked her head. "Did Mr. Miles used to be a slave here?"

"He did," Carrie answered, and then waited to see where Minnie would go with the line of questioning. The little girl who'd grown up in Philadelphia was still learning about the South.

"Mr. Miles shouldn't have been a slave," Minnie said firmly, something like accusation shining in her eyes.

"You're absolutely right," Carrie agreed. "I was so happy when Miles escaped before the war started. I was equally glad when he came home because I missed him so much."

"But he's not a slave just because he came back. Right?"

"Right," Carrie assured her daughter. "Slavery is no longer allowed in America. Miles works for Cromwell Stables now. We pay him, and he's helping us start a breeding program of Cleveland Bay horses."

Minnie absorbed the information. "Good. That's how it should be. Slavery is a very bad thing." Satisfied with what she'd heard, she urged Maple into a trot and moved forward to ride beside Angel.

Amber fell into place beside Carrie. The two rode in easy silence for a few minutes.

"Where are we going first?" Amber asked.

"Down by the river," Carrie said evasively.

Amber gasped, reading something in Carrie's expression. "Are we going to your *place*?"

Carrie smiled, but didn't answer. She'd shared her special place by the river with Anthony, Rose, Abby, Janie and her daughters, but no one else had been there. When she'd agreed to the outing, she hadn't first intended to take the children there, but once they'd left the barn, she knew that's where they were going.

Granite, always able to sense her feelings, was headed there with no instruction from her.

"Let's run!" John yelled. Cafi began to prance in place, waiting for the signal from the boy.

Carrie knew the open stretch of road, gleaming white with crushed oyster shells mixed with the sand, was tempting to the little boy who was an expert rider. He and Moses often raced along this same stretch.

Miles rode next to his grandson. His black gelding wasn't as tall as Cafi, but was well-muscled. "What did I tell you before we left?" His voice was quiet but carried a hint of steel.

John looked abashed and laid a hand on Cafi's neck. The prancing stopped immediately, though Cafi signaled his disapproval with a snort. "You said we weren't going to run because not everyone could keep up."

"You want to make your little sister feel bad?" Miles asked.

"No," John mumbled.

"What's that?" Miles asked sternly.

"No sir," John said clearly.

Carrie bit back a smile. Miles adored his grandson but knew his headstrong attitude would get him in trouble if it wasn't kept under control. That had been proven when John came within moments of dying in the flood. Miles was the most loving man she'd ever known. He was also the perfect one to make John quake in his boots.

Carrie breathed a sigh of sheer pleasure when Granite, leading the line of horses, broke out into the clearing on the river. They'd been here several times in the last two weeks, but there was something about this day that felt special. She couldn't define what she was feeling, but she felt something just the same.

The sun was shimmering on the blue water of the James River, glinting off white ripples caused by the wind dancing across the surface. Masses of glistening white daisies, the yellow petals of brown-eyed Susans, and the glorious purple of chicory completed the beautiful pallet.

"What are the purple flowers, Mama?" Frances asked.

"Chicory," Carrie answered. "You're lucky to see it. If we were here later this afternoon, the flowers would be closed up tightly."

"Why?" Frances asked.

"I have no idea," Carrie answered. "I suppose it's just the way God thought it should be." When Old Sarah, Rose's mama, had been teaching her about the plants, she'd had the same questions. Sarah had told her countless times that she should just be grateful God had filled the earth with things we would never truly understand. "It's all part of the miracle of life," she said softly.

"Are they good for anything?" Amber asked.

Carrie smiled. Amber shared her passion for medicinal herbs and was determined to learn as much as she could. "They're good for a lot of things," she replied, making sure everyone could hear her. "We use an extract from the roots to deworm the horses."

All the children stared at the tall, rigid plant topped with purple flowers with new respect.

"What else does it do?" John asked.

"Chicory was first brought to America during the colonial times. It was meant to be a food source for both people and animals. It did that, but it also escaped into the wild and traveled where it wanted to go."

Minnie laughed. "It wouldn't stay where people wanted it to. I like that."

"Me too," Carrie agreed, thrilled by the independent glint in her daughter's eyes. Every day brought her further from the effects of her grief. "I've used chicory extracts for many things, but during the war, we ground up the roots and used it as a coffee substitute."

"Is it good?" Amber crinkled her nose.

"Many people prefer it to coffee," Carrie answered with a shrug. "I wouldn't say it tastes exactly like coffee, but it has a deep, dark flavor that got us through the war." She paused, remembering the years when coffee wasn't available because it couldn't pass through the blockades. "I learned to like it, but I prefer Annie's coffee now that I have a choice."

"Me too," Miles said as he swung down from his horse. "Let's loosen all the saddles and give the horses a drink."

As the children hurried to comply, laughing and talking, Carrie removed Granite's saddle and bridle.

They wouldn't be here very long, but something compelled her to give him his freedom.

"Won't he run away?" Angel asked with concern.

"No," Carrie assured her. "This is Granite's special place, too. We found it when I was fourteen. We'd been roaming around the plantation when I saw a narrow deer trail. I followed it and found this clearing. It's been our favorite place in the world for a long time."

Granite nickered his agreement and then stepped into the river. He swung his massive head to the right to look upriver for a long moment before lowering his muzzle into the gleaming water for a drink. When he raised his head, he swung it around to look at Carrie with beseeching eyes.

Carrie walked over to stand by his side. The children's laughter sounded in the background as they played a game of chase through the flowers, but for that moment, it was just her and Granite. The rest of the world seemed to fade away.

Carrie slipped her arms around his neck and laid her head against his soft fur. Granite sighed and then nickered again. Following what seemed to be very clear instructions, she stepped forward to stand in front of him and gaze into his luminous eyes. He regarded her steadily, and then leaned his head into her chest. Carrie folded his head into her arms and leaned her forehead forward to touch his.

With the sounds of the river rolling around them and the children playing in the clearing, Carrie lost track of time, enjoying the shared moment with her beloved horse.

Chapter Fifteen

"Mama? What are you doing?"

Carrie lifted her head and looked at Frances. She had no words to explain what she'd just experienced. How could she communicate that, for those few moments, she had felt one with her horse? She understood the message she'd received but couldn't bring herself to voice it, even if she *could* find words to express it. "Just loving my horse," she said lightly.

Frances moved up next to her and slipped her arm around Carrie's waist. "I love you, Mama."

"I love you too, Frances," Carrie said as she wrapped her arm around her daughter and pulled her close.

Frances laid her head on her shoulder. "I bet this place is even more special when you're here by yourself."

Carrie knew what she was saying. "It is. I wish you could experience it for yourself like that."

"Me too," Frances sighed. "I'm the age you were when you used to come here. Do you think it will ever be safe for me to come by myself?"

Carrie wished she had an answer. "I hope so," was the best she could manage.

The rest of the day passed in a haze of fun.

Carrie took them down trail after trail. Some ended on the river. One ended in the big field where she'd learned how to jump Granite – far from anyone who could stop her. Her mother would have been horrified to see her daughter leaping over logs on her horse.

All of the children, even Hope on her pony, got to take their mounts over a small log. Amber, of course, had demanded Carrie teach her more about jumping. She had readily agreed.

"Mama," Minnie asked, "what's the highest you've ever jumped?"

Carrie smiled, immediately transported back to the first year of the war. "Do you know the fence at the far end of the pasture, closest to the barn?"

Minnie's eyes, along with everyone's else, widened. "You jumped *that*?" she breathed.

Carrie could feel Miles' eyes on her. She realized she'd never told him the story. "It's not something I ever want any of you to do, but it was necessary at the time. Union soldiers had taken over the plantation. I was hiding in the tunnel, but I heard them talking about taking Granite, and they were looking for me." She controlled the shiver that threatened to course through her when she thought about the things the soldiers had talked about doing to her.

"I waited until late that night, came up through the tunnel into the barn and snuck into Granite's stall. He only had his halter on, but that's all I needed. I waited until the right moment, galloped through the barn and escaped across the pasture."

"Did they see you?" Frances asked.

"They did." Carrie could remember every moment of that wild ride – especially the shocked expressions on their face when she and Granite had bolted from his stall. "Just before I got to the fence, one of them shot me in the shoulder."

Miles stared at her. "They *shot* you?"

Carrie smiled. "Thankfully, they didn't shoot Granite. I managed to hang on when Granite jumped the fence, but just barely."

Amber shook her head. "You were riding bareback, you didn't have a bridle, *and* they had shot you?" Her voice was full of stunned admiration.

Carrie laid her hand on Granite's neck, the memories of that long night continuing to rush through her. "I owe Granite my life."

"And he owes you his," Miles said gruffly. "I never knew that story, Carrie Girl."

Carrie smiled at him. There were many stories it was best he not know. She knew he loved her like a daughter. Her escapades had already greatly contributed to her father's gray hair – she didn't need to age Miles anymore. "It all turned out fine," she said lightly, and then changed the subject by drawing their attention to a herd of deer who had stepped out of the woods at the far end of the clearing.

They rode down through miles of tobacco fields, calling greetings to the men working hard in the bright sun. The dark green plants were shooting upward but had not yet begun to bloom. The trumpet-shaped flowers would arrive in another week or two.

The horses spent a lot of time walking and trotting, but when the road was straight and smooth, Carrie allowed them all to break into an easy canter. She knew John was itching to burst into a gallop, but he didn't say anything about it. He kept Cafi to a smooth canter, riding alongside Hope, who gazed up at her brother with adoration.

When they turned down another trail, Frances and Minnie cheered. "It's time to eat!"

Carrie laughed. She knew they would recognize the trail they sometimes rode down on their trips to the river for a swim. "You're right."

Miles smiled broadly. "I reckon I be ready for some of my wife's cooking, sure 'nuff."

Carrie looked at him closely. She could tell the long day had fatigued the elderly man, but his look of happiness also told her he'd enjoyed every minute.

When they broke out onto the riverbank, Carrie had them all untack their horses entirely, slipping a halter on the horse's heads before they led them to the water to drink. Once the horses were satisfied, she directed them to tie their lead ropes to narrow saplings. Again, she left Granite roam free.

Amber, Frances and Angel disappeared into the tunnel and then emerged with large picnic hampers full of food left over from the celebration the day before. It took only minutes to unload mountains of fried chicken, ham biscuits, baked sweet potatoes, potato salad, pound cake, chocolate cake, and molasses cookies.

Carrie walked over and stared down at the spread. "My word. You would think there were thirty of us."

"Don't worry," John said confidently. "I can eat whatever the rest of you don't."

Carrie laughed, knowing he was probably right. He was trying hard to be as big as his father, as fast as possible. "Let's eat!"

Carrie was polishing off a fried chicken thigh when she felt movement behind her. She held her breath when Granite lowered his head and rested it on her shoulder. Blinking back tears, she reached up and stroked his soft muzzle as all thoughts of eating disappeared.

Everyone was quiet and subdued when they arrived back at the barn.

Carrie and Miles exchanged an amused look. After they'd eaten and rested, she had sent the children into the water fully clothed to splash around and cool off. They'd watched the setting sun as they dried, and then tacked their horses, and rode home. The outing had been a tremendous success, but every child, even Amber who was used to long days of work in the barn, was exhausted.

"I'm tired," Hope said wearily.

Susan emerged from the barn just in time to hear her. "I bet you are," she said sympathetically. "Did you have a good time?"

"The best time in the whole world," Hope said with a tired smile.

"Why don't I take care of Patches for you?" Susan offered.

Hope started to nod eagerly, but then looked at Miles. "Will that be bad, Grandpa? You always tell me I should care for Patches after I ride him."

Miles ruffled her hair gently. "I think this one time it will be just fine, Hope Girl. You know, there aren't many five-year-old's who can do what you did today. I'm real proud of you."

Hope sighed with relief and then stifled a yawn.

Moses walked around the corner of the barn. He scooped his daughter up and planted her on his massive shoulders. "How about a ride back to the house?"

Hope squealed and nodded. "Yes, Daddy. Yes!"

Carrie watched John. She knew he was exhausted, too. He would certainly love Moses to carry him back to the house, but he straightened his shoulders and turned to lead Cafi into the barn. He was definitely growing up.

She understood the look of pride on Miles' face when he followed John, leading his own gelding.

"Have Phoebe and Felicia arrived?" Carrie asked.

Moses nodded. "So have Peter and Elizabeth."

Carrie smiled. "Wonderful! I predict all the children are going straight to bed. They're still stuffed from their picnic and are tired to the bone."

"I expect so," Moses said easily, and then peered at her closely. "Are you alright, Carrie?"

"I'm fine," Carrie assured him. "Just a little tired. I'll be up on the porch soon." She forced what she hoped was a natural smile. The look in Moses' eyes said she had failed, but she knew he wouldn't press her right then. "You've got a little girl about to fall asleep on your shoulders," she reminded him. As he turned away, she added, "I'm not hungry, but I wouldn't turn down a cold glass of Annie's lemonade.

Moses nodded and then started toward the house. Hope began to regale him with stories of their day full of adventures.

Carrie took a deep breath and walked inside the barn to care for her horse.

The moon was rising over the treetops when Carrie finally excused herself from the gathering on the porch several hours later. "I'm sorry, but my long day with the children wore me out."

The children, as predicted, had fallen into bed after a cold glass of lemonade.

The evening had been a bevy of laughter and conversation – catching up with Felicia, Phoebe, Elizabeth and Peter. There was still much to talk about, but she was drained of energy and longing for bed. She held out a hand to stop Anthony when he started to rise. "I know you're not tired, dear. Enjoy everyone. I'll be back to myself in the morning."

Anthony eyed her keenly but nodded and sank back into his rocker.

"Good night, everyone." Carrie opened the door, paused long enough to look out at the dark barn, and wearily climbed the curving staircase.

Her last thought as she closed her eyes was that she hoped she would know when...

Carrie had no idea what time it was when she jolted awake. Gentle snoring beside her revealed Anthony had come to bed. The fact that she hadn't heard anything, or even felt when he joined her in bed, told her how exhausted she'd been. Usually, no matter when it was, she knew the instant he entered the room.

She lay quietly for a moment, listening to the sounds of the night. Gradually, everything that had happened during the day flooded back into her consciousness. Moving quietly, so as to not disturb Anthony, she slipped out of bed. Instead of reaching for her robe, she pulled on the breeches and shirt she'd laid out before she'd gone to sleep. She'd wanted to be prepared. Her heart told her it was time.

The night was still warm when she left the house. The plantation glowed silver under the moon, outlining everything and casting dark shadows. Not even a hint of wind rustled the leaves. Hooting owls added to the song of crickets and frogs. Fireflies flitted through the woods and danced across the lawn, their glowing bodies stretching as far as she could see.

The rich aroma of freshly cut hay hung like a curtain of perfume. The men had spent most of the day cutting with giant scythes. She could envision their muscled arms swinging rhythmically, the scythes glinting in the sun. It would have to be turned daily for several days before they could create the stooks. She loved the tall cone-shaped mounds of dried hay that would dot the pastures until they were ready for use. She knew the skill it took to build them correctly. If the stook builders made a mistake, the hay would rot and be of no good to the animals.

Their need for hay had grown with the number of their horses. More land had been designated for hay production each year since the end of the war.

Carrie took a deep breath, savoring the sweet aroma, and then walked to the barn. She stopped long enough to light a lantern, her eyes fixed on Granite's stall. Her heart sank when his head didn't pop over the door. Lifting the lantern to illuminate her way, she entered his stall.

Granite was lying down. He lifted his head and whinnied softly when he saw her.

"Granite!" Carrie hung the lantern on a hook and rushed to his side, sinking down to kneel beside him. "What's wrong, boy?" She knew there was no reason to be alarmed. Horses laid down to sleep. The fact, though, that she'd been woken from a deep sleep told her everything her mind didn't want to accept.

Granite nickered again and then started to lower his head.

Carrie dropped down quickly enough to catch his head in her lap. Biting her lip, she stroked his head, running her hand down his velvety muzzle, and brushing his silvery forelock out of his eyes. "I love you, Granite."

Granite snuffled his agreement and closed his eyes as she ran her hand over his face tenderly. His even breathing assured her that he was listening.

"I love you so much," she murmured. Memories coursed through her.

The first moment she had seen him; a prancing, rambunctious gelding whose gray coat glistened and gleamed in the sun like burnished pewter.

How he had immediately calmed when he saw her, lowering his head to come over and accept her caresses. Everyone had been astonished when he'd pressed his forehead against hers with a gentle nicker.

Long rides through every inch of the plantation.

Endless hours of talking to him about all the things she couldn't tell anyone else, even Rose.

Their escape from the Union soldiers.

She thought of the agonizing year when she'd feared both Robert and Granite had died during the war.

More images flooded her mind.

The glorious sight of him carrying Robert home on the spring afternoon they'd returned.

Her father riding off on Granite at the fall of Richmond, and then returning to rebuild his life.

Granite had been a vital part of every moment of her life for almost seventeen years. No matter how hard she tried, she couldn't envision life without him. She'd known this time was coming, but knowing and *experiencing* were two completely different things.

The shadows flickered as soft whinnies sounded from the other horses. As if they knew...

Granite had become the patriarch of Cromwell Plantation.

The memories continued to roll.

Her beautiful Thoroughbred winning the Tournament, carrying her to the victory she had always dreamed of before females were allowed to compete.

The long ride, when he had carried her home to the plantation from Richmond so she could be with Robert when he died.

Mired in grief over Robert and Bridget, he had been her refuge. His steady, unconditional love had carried her through the darkest time of her life.

"You promised to be here when I came home," Carrie whispered. "You promised to wait until I finished school. Thank you." Her voice choked as tears flooded her eyes.

Granite's breathing slowed, but he lifted his head enough to gaze at her. The love she saw there almost took her breath away.

The message he had given to her by the river that day seemed to hang in the air between them.

I have to leave, but I'm coming back...

"Granite, I have to believe what I heard today. I don't know how that can be possible, but I have to believe it. I can't imagine life without you." Carrie fought the panic and grief swelling through her.

She lowered her head to place her forehead against his, just as she had by the river. Just as she had in their very first moments seventeen years earlier. She felt the energy pulsing in the air around them. She knew she would never be able to explain to anyone what she was feeling and experiencing. It didn't matter. The message was for her alone – meant to carry her through the grief waiting for her.

"You have to let me know," she said fiercely. "I'm not going to get another horse. I don't want a horse. I only want *you*. If it's true that you're coming back, you have to let me know when you do."

Tears flowed down her face as she held her head to his, cradling him in her arms.

Granite's breathing slowed more. His eyes closed.

"Thank you," Carrie whispered. "Thank you for everything." Her breath became as shallow as his. "I love you."

Carrie awoke when she felt Anthony's arms enfold her. She opened her eyes reluctantly, wanting last night to be a dream. It hadn't been. Granite's head still lay in her lap. At some point, she'd leaned back against the rough, wooden stall slats and fallen asleep.

"Carrie. I'm so sorry," Anthony said tenderly.

Carrie blinked up at him and then dropped her gaze back down to Granite. The eyes that had shone with such life·and energy would never open again. Grief stole her breath. "He's gone," she whimpered as fresh tears stung her eyes. "Granite is gone."

Anthony said nothing. He pulled her into a closer embrace, stroking her hair the same way she continued to stroke Granite's face.

After several minutes had passed, Carrie was able to speak again. "I was with him," she said quietly. She would forever be grateful Granite hadn't died alone.

He'd drawn his last breath knowing just how much she loved him.

"That's all he ever wanted. From the time I brought him home." Miles' voice filled the stall as he stepped forward and reached out a hand to touch her head. "Granite gave you yesterday as a gift, Carrie Girl. He relived all the things that brung the two of you so much joy. He was tired, though. He done gave you all the life he had to give."

"I know... I'm going to miss him so much."

Miles nodded. "Yep. You and him had a love not many get to have. I reckon you're gonna miss him for the rest of your life."

Carrie opened her mouth to tell them that Granite had said he was coming back, but then closed it. She knew the message had been just for her – to give her courage for the days ahead. She had no words to explain what she'd heard, and no reason to think anyone would understand it. Rather than diminish the message by having to defend it, she would treasure it.

And wait.

Chapter Sixteen

Rose rode through the woods with Phoebe, trying to formulate the words she needed to say. The new teacher had been there for three days, but she still didn't know the whole truth about the situation at the school. Rose had put everything on hold to be available for Carrie. Her best friend had assured her she was alright, but it was easy to see the depth of her pain and grief. She, Abby, Susan and Janie took turns going for walks with her, or just sitting on the porch looking out over the plantation she and Granite had shared for so long.

Sometimes Carrie had been silent. Other times she'd told stories of her and Granite's adventures and exploits. Laughter mixed with the tears.

Granite's burial had been attended by everyone on the plantation. Carrie had been slightly overwhelmed, but there was no one on Cromwell that didn't know the love the two of them had shared. Rose was aware that most of them, including herself, had never experienced that kind of love with an animal, but they all understood grief and loss.

Granite's body had been taken to a clearing in the woods behind the barn. The men had worked hard to build a hole large and deep enough for him. Moses and Anthony had carved a beautiful wooden marker for the grave, while all the children had gathered rocks from the riverbank to form a large mound as a monument.

The only thing that would provide healing was time. Carrie knew that better than anyone.

"Is there something you haven't told me?" Phoebe asked as they wound their way down the trail.

Rose pulled her thoughts away from Carrie and met the probing blue eyes staring at her. She wasn't surprised Phoebe had sensed something. "Yes," she admitted. She had planned a long explanation, but the answer came out in just a few words. "We won't be teaching in the same school."

Phoebe's eyes widened. "Excuse me?"

Rose told her everything that had happened with the representative from the Virginia Board of Education. "I can no longer teach white students," she finished, surprised with how calm she sounded.

Phoebe stared at her speechlessly.

"That's horrible!" she cried when she finally found her voice. "All they're doing is hurting the students."

"I agree," Rose replied. "I don't know what I would have done if you weren't coming." She took a steadying breath. "I know this isn't what you planned on. How do you feel about teaching your own class?"

Phoebe wrinkled her brow in thought and rode quietly for a few minutes, her blond hair glistening in the sun.

Rose gave her time to process what she'd heard. Phoebe had returned to Cromwell, expecting things to be the way they'd planned. Now everything had changed.

"I'll still be able to talk with you every day? Ask you all the questions I have after each day?"

"Absolutely," Rose said firmly. "You'll have thirty students. I'll have time to tell you about all of them before school starts again. I'll also make sure to take you to every home so you can meet their parents. You know most of the students already from this winter when you were here teaching with me."

"And the new school will be finished?"

"Yes," Rose assured her. "It's almost finished now. All the men have been working hard on it – especially the parents of the students. They were furious when they discovered what was happening, but they're also determined their children will have an education."

Phoebe nodded slowly and then smiled. Her shocked expression had evolved into a glow of determination. "I suppose I'm here at just the right time, then."

Rose returned her smile. "I can't agree more." In truth, she was deeply relieved. She hadn't been sure how Phoebe would respond to the news. She would have understood if the new teacher had been too overwhelmed with her unexpected solo position, but she also knew Phoebe was more than capable of handling it.

The two women rode without speaking for a few more minutes. Rose savored the shadows dancing across the path as the sun filtered through the thick canopy of leaves.

"How many students do you have?" Phoebe asked. "Your own, I mean?"

"Fifty-two," Rose answered. "During the day," she added. "That doesn't count the fifty or so parents I teach three evenings a week. That continues through the summer – at least for the women. The men are too busy working in the Cromwell fields, or on their own properties. When I'm not teaching, Abby uses the school to hold Bregdan Women meetings, and also as a place for the women to quilt together." She knew a large shipment of quilts was headed to New York City soon.

"Quilt together?"

Rose nodded, proud beyond words of what Abby had created. "Abby holds Bregdan Women meetings here each week. She realized the women needed a way to make money, so she set up a business for them. They're all making gorgeous quilts. Abby ships them up to New York City. Her friend, Nancy Stratford, sells them to wealthy people who value the quilts. It has completely changed the lives of so many women."

Phoebe clapped her hands. "That's wonderful!" Then she cocked her head. "Are you teaching both black *and* white parents?"

Rose grinned. "The Virginia Constitution says nothing about adults in school. I can continue teaching them as I always have."

Phoebe looked thoughtful as she did a rapid calculation. "Taking adults out of the equation, you were teaching *eighty-two* students during the day?"

"Now you know why I was eager for you to arrive."

"How did you do it?" Phoebe demanded.

Rose shrugged. "I did what I had to do, but I'm not sure I always did it well. I can only stretch so far. I gave my very best, but I believe it will actually be better to have smaller classes. I would change the circumstances, but I believe the results will be beneficial." She paused. "Only because you've come, though. You so impressed me when you were here this winter. I've been counting the days until your graduation," she admitted with a laugh.

Phoebe opened her mouth and then closed it again, suddenly looking unsure of herself.

"Did I say something wrong?" Rose asked. "I certainly don't want to scare you!"

Phoebe laughed lightly. "It's not that. It's something I thought about. I'm not sure you'll think it's a good idea."

"There's only one way to find out," Rose answered, curious to know what she was going to say. "We have to be able to communicate openly, Phoebe."

"True." Phoebe paused again. "I'm just wondering if you would consider a third teacher. Another black teacher who could help you with your students. Fifty-two is still a lot. As much as the plantation is growing, you're sure to have more students."

Rose knew that was true. She'd already heard talk that more students would be coming in the fall. She considered Phoebe's suggestion. "I believe a third teacher might be helpful, but I'm hesitant to hire someone I haven't worked with before."

"But what if you knew of one that is really wonderful?"

Rose laughed. "Just whom do you have in mind?"

Phoebe smiled, her eyes shining with excitement. "Her name is Hazel Rollins. She was my closest friend at Oberlin. Hazel was a slave until the first year of the war. She ran away from her plantation in Georgia with her parents when she was thirteen. They used the

Underground Railroad to make their way north and stopped in Oberlin. Hazel went to school, and then went to college. Her greatest passion is to teach former slaves, or the children of former slaves."

Rose listened closely. She and Moses had used the Underground Railroad to escape to Philadelphia at the same time Hazel had escaped.

"You would love her," Phoebe said enthusiastically. "Besides being a wonderful teacher, she would adore Cromwell Plantation."

"Why?" Rose asked curiously. In truth, she couldn't imagine that anyone wouldn't love the plantation, but there was a gleam in Phoebe's eyes that said there was a deeper reason.

Phoebe laughed. "She loves horses as much as she loves teaching. We often ride together at home. When I told her about the horses down here, I swear she was salivating. She'll deny it, but it was true."

Rose laughed, but then grew serious. "I'll send her an invitation to join us."

Phoebe stopped laughing and stared at her. "You will? Just like that?"

"I'm trusting you with my students," Rose reminded her. "I suppose I should also be able to trust your recommendation. You're right that I will still need help in order to teach effectively." She was a little surprised with her rapid decision, but she was learning to trust her instincts more and more. Her instincts were screaming that Hazel would be a perfect fit for her school.

They broke out from the trail into the clearing behind the school. Rose was amazed at the progress that had been made in only a few short days. The new clinic was going up, and the walls had already been expanded beyond the old clinic for the new classroom. The men could only work after Carrie and Janie were finished with patients, but the long spring days made for a lot of productivity. In just a week or so, the doctors would have a new, larger clinic.

Alvin stepped outside the new clinic, shielding his eyes from the sun. He smiled broadly when he recognized them. "Hello Rose. Hello Ms. Waterston. I heard you were back. It's a pleasure to see you again."

"Hello Alvin. Please call me Phoebe. I know the children have to call me Ms. Waterston, but not my friends."

Alvin flushed his pleasure. "It's good to have you back, Phoebe."

Rose smiled. Phoebe and Alvin had gotten to know each other when she was there for her internship. The fact that she already had a relationship with many of the white parents would certainly make the transition easier.

"How are Violet and Silas?" Phoebe asked.

"They're doing good," Alvin answered.

Rose saw the sudden tension in his eyes. "What aren't you saying, Alvin?"

Alvin shrugged. "They're still just real confused about things. I've brought them here to see the new school being built. They're fine with it, but don't understand why things have to change." He glanced at Phoebe. "Please don't take it personally, Ms. Wa... Phoebe," he said hastily. "They like you a whole lot, but..."

"I'm not taking it personally," Phoebe assured him. "The whole situation is ridiculous." As she looked at the fence that had been erected between the two emerging playgrounds, she frowned. Suddenly, her eyes brightened. "I have an idea."

"I'm listening," Rose responded.

Phoebe looked around and then pointed at a large clearing on the far side of the clinic. "Is anything being done with that area?"

"No," Rose answered, staring at the large area that had been cleared of trees a year earlier. "I suppose it was cleared just in case it was needed."

"It's perfect," Phoebe said excitedly.

Rose and Alvin exchanged a puzzled look, waiting for her to continue.

"I know the children are prohibited from being in the same classroom, and also from being on the same school grounds, but there's nothing that prohibits them from being together anywhere else, is there?"

Rose shook her head, a smile forming on her lips as she realized what Phoebe was thinking.

"You can declare that clearing the Cromwell Community Playground," Phoebe said. "Before and after school, the children can all be there playing together."

Rose laughed. "What a perfect solution! And, even though we can't teach in the same *building*, there's nothing keeping us from having a group *gathering* at the Community Playground when the weather is nice. If we happen to do a little teach... I mean, *sharing* together... well, we're not breaking any of the new laws!"

Alvin laughed loudly. "I declare. You Bregdan women are something else! If you want something to happen, you just figure out how to make it happen." He rubbed his chin. "I reckon it won't take too much to build a shelter for the new Community Playground." He winked. "Just in case it's raining when y'all want to do a little *sharing* together."

Phoebe clapped her hands. "A shelter is a wonderful idea." Then she grinned. "I'm a Bregdan woman now? I like the sound of that."

Rose had another idea, spurred by Phoebe's creative solution for the children playing together. "Alvin, may I ask you something?"

"Always."

Rose eyed the new school taking the place of the old clinic. "Is there a way you can put two large rooms above the school?"

Alvin's eyes narrowed as he considered her request. "I don't see no reason we can't," he said slowly. "Course, we'll need more materials."

"I'll send two of the men to Richmond to get them," Rose assured him.

Phoebe raised a brow. "What are you thinking?"

"I'm thinking there isn't enough room in the main house on Cromwell for two more people." Rose paused as the idea took shape. "If we add on to the schoolhouse, you and Hazel could each have a large room of your own. We can create a small cooking shed out back, but there's already a good-sized outhouse for you, and there's a good well."

"Probably won't have to do any cooking," Alvin added. "Once everyone knows the new teachers are living above the school, you'll have more food brought to you than you could ever eat."

"You'll have your privacy," Rose continued, her thoughts whirling.

"We certainly won't have to go far to get to school," Phoebe said. "I think it's a wonderful idea." Then she paused, a shadow crossing her eyes.

"What's wrong?" Rose asked. "You can be honest," she added when Phoebe hesitated.

"Is it safe?" Phoebe blurted out. "I know the school has been attacked before. There are guards around the plantation, but will there be any protection here? I may be a Bregdan Woman, but I don't know how to shoot a gun like all of you do." She shuddered. "I don't really want to learn," she admitted. "Might Hazel be in more danger since she's black? She's already a little nervous about returning to the South. I would want her to feel safe." Phoebe reached out a hand to touch Rose's arm. "I hate to put a damper on a great idea, but..."

Rose clasped her hand. "Please don't apologize. Your concerns are real." She wanted to assure Phoebe that of course she and Hazel would be safe, but she couldn't. She wasn't at all certain *she* would feel safe if she were the one living above the school – especially on long winter nights that were cold and dark.

"She's got a point, Rose," Alvin said. "I wouldn't let my wife stay in a room out here all alone."

Rose gritted her teeth. What should have been a perfect solution was impossible because of racism and hatred. "You're right," she agreed as she pushed the idea from her mind. She turned to Phoebe. "Don't worry. We'll figure something out."

"I'm happy to share my room with Hazel," Phoebe said. "I know that white mansion is huge, but there are a lot of people living in it. I don't think that will be the best solution long-term, but perhaps just until we figure something else out?"

"Of course," Rose said quickly.

It was true the house was full. Everyone had been thrilled to have Matthew, Janie and the children move in, but no one knew how long it would be before they could build a home of their own. Felicia was sharing a room with Frances and Minnie while she was home, but as their families expanded, something else would have to be done. Elizabeth was sharing Phoebe's room, but it had been necessary to send Peter home with Harold and Susan. They were bursting at the seams.

"Rose?"

Rose jerked when Alvin's insistent voice broke through her thoughts. She realized he must have been repeating her name. "Yes?"

"I think it's time to build another house close to the main house," Alvin said. "It doesn't have to be as big, but it could be full of bedrooms to handle guests. They could come over to the main house for meals if y'all don't want to add another kitchen."

"Another house?" Rose said faintly.

"Another house," Alvin repeated. His eyes were glowing. "There's a bunch of men around who know how to build. The same ones building the new school and clinic would be real happy to build another house. They would make enough money this summer to see them through the winter."

Rose stared at him. She was uncertain how to respond, but she was aware the idea had merit. "I'll talk to Moses," she promised.

Carrie sat on the riverbank next to Elizabeth. She tried not to think about the last day she'd spent with Granite on the river at their special place, and then when she had picnicked with the children, his head resting on her shoulder as she ate. She suspected it would be a long while before she would be ready to return to her special place. There were far too many memories there now. *Robert... the day Bridget was conceived... and now Granite.* She knew the time would come when the feeling of his presence there would be comforting, but the time wasn't now.

Elizabeth reached out and took her hand, but remained silent.

Carrie knew everyone was being careful to respect her grief, but there were things she and Elizabeth needed to discuss. Besides, Granite had promised to come back. Five days after his death, the feeling of certainty hadn't diminished. She didn't know how long she would have to wait. *Days? Months? Years?* It didn't matter. She would wait.

She pushed aside her thoughts and turned to Elizabeth. "How are things at the clinic?"

"They're great," Elizabeth assured her. "The days are a little long, but there's been no more violence."

"The guards are still there?" Carrie knew men were still guarding River City Carriages. As a result, there had been no more fires set. She assumed guards were still at the clinic, but she wanted to be certain.

Elizabeth nodded. "I don't believe I would feel safe there if they weren't," she admitted.

Carrie shoved down any lingering thoughts of Granite and focused on her friend. She could tell by the strain in Elizabeth's eyes that something was wrong. "Out with it," she ordered. "What's going on? Please don't make me dig by saying nothing is wrong. You should know by now that I know you better than that."

Elizabeth sighed and looked away to stare over the water.

Carrie waited patiently.

"After the attack on the clinic, I was so certain I was meant to stay in Richmond. I completely understand why Janie made her decision to stay on the plantation, and I understand why you're choosing to work at your clinic here. Your daughters are certainly more important than anything else." Elizabeth paused. "I love all the patients, but..."

"You're lonely."

Elizabeth nodded. "Yes. I will freely admit that. It's wonderful having Lucinda in town, but we're both so busy with our practices, that we rarely see each other. It's more than that, though..."

Carrie continued to wait quietly.

"There's no joy in working by myself," Elizabeth finally said. "I thought it would be fine when Janie left. Even though I would be alone half the time, I thought the other half of the time with you would give me what I needed. What I discovered is that working by myself, for any length of time, is not what I want to do." She squeezed Carrie's hand. "Even if you hadn't decided to stay on the plantation, I wouldn't be happy. I suppose I didn't realize that perhaps the biggest draw of coming to Richmond was because I wanted to share a practice with you, Janie and Florence."

"I understand," Carrie said, and truly, she did. "I've enjoyed working on my own, with Polly as my assistant, but having Janie here as a partner has been wonderful. It's certainly better for the patients, but it's also great for me."

The idea of the Richmond clinic closing was painful, but Carrie couldn't deny she wouldn't have wanted to be a sole practitioner there either. No candidates had appeared as a result of the letters they had sent. They'd felt it necessary to be honest about the violence and threats they were dealing with. It was understandable that no one wanted to jump into the fray.

"There's more," Elizabeth said hesitantly. "I want to be certain you understand."

"I want to hear it all," Carrie assured her.

Elizabeth, obviously needing to formulate her words carefully, turned to stare out over the water again.

Carrie leaned back against a log and gazed up, watching a hawk circle above the water. She knew it was waiting for the tell-tell flash of silver that would alert it to a fish close to the surface. She also imagined it was enjoying the freedom to soar on the thermals created by the hot, windy day. She dropped her eyes and watched a family of mallards float by, the colorful feathers of the male shimmering in the sun.

"I know you love the South," Elizabeth began. "It's your home." Her voice quivered slightly. "It's not *my* home, though. After living in Boston most of my life, I find I miss the openness I experienced there. It's not that we don't deal with racism and bigotry," she said quickly, "but..."

Carrie held up her hand. "I understand, Elizabeth. I couldn't stand it down here either unless I was convinced this was where I was meant to be for now. Even though we've had vigilante attacks on the plantation, for the most part I feel completely protected." She knew that was largely thanks to the cadre of guards positioned around the plantation at all times. There were guards around the Bregdan Medical Clinic in Richmond, but they could only offer protection on a small scale. She knew Anthony had arranged for one of them to always accompany Elizabeth back and forth from the house, but that was a terrible way to have to live.

"It's not just feeling protected," Elizabeth protested. "It's more a feeling that seems to permeate the air in Richmond. They lost the war, but they're doing everything they can to take control over the black residents again. The troops left because Virginia rejoined the Union. The Freedmen's Bureau is shutting down. Soon, there won't be anything to protect blacks from the bigotry that's so rampant. I'd like to think I could make a difference in that. I suppose I could, but I'm not brave enough..." Her voice faltered as she closed her eyes, a wave of defeat sweeping over her face.

"Nonsense!" Carrie retorted. "You're one of the bravest women I know. I simply believe the circumstances are calling you to something different. There have been many times I made plans that didn't turn out the way I expected them to. I've discovered, every time, that I was merely being directed to do something different."

Elizabeth took a long breath as she gazed at her with piercing eyes. "Do you really believe that?"

"I do," Carrie assured her.

"You don't think I'm being weak and indecisive?"

Carrie cocked her head. "Do you?" She couldn't quite read the expression on her friend's face.

"I don't think so," Elizabeth said slowly, "but I seem to be changing my mind about things rather rapidly."

"Like believing you were meant to stay at the clinic, and then deciding it's time to leave?"

"Yes."

Carrie understood completely. "I used to wonder if changing my mind about things made me weak and indecisive," she began. "Until I really started paying attention to people. I realized how many people choose to stay in their same situation because they're afraid of change."

She considered her next words carefully. "I meant what I said earlier about circumstances directing you to do something different. You made the choice to stay in Richmond based on the facts you had at the moment. You believed I would be there half the time, but then I chose to stay on the plantation. When we first set up the arrangements for the clinic, it didn't include me having two daughters, and Florence choosing to remain in Paris. It didn't include a vicious attack that would make Janie too afraid to practice in Richmond any longer." She took Elizabeth's hand. "We all made different choices, based on a change in our circumstances. Sometimes there is great courage in deciding to stay the course, no matter what. Other times, it only means you're too afraid to move in a different direction. I'm proud of you for making the choice that's right for you. Despite how much I'll miss you," she added.

Elizabeth gripped her hand tightly, her eyes brimming with gratitude. "Thank you."

Carrie leaned back against the log again. "Do you know what you're going to do next?"

"I have no idea," Elizabeth admitted. "I wasn't even sure of what I was feeling until I got to the plantation. The farther we drove from Richmond, the more freely I could breathe. It wasn't until then, that I fully realized everything I was unhappy."

"How does the idea of leaving make you feel?"

Elizabeth smiled her first genuine smile since they'd come to the river. "Great." Her eyes sparkled. "I have absolutely no idea what I'm going to do next, but I'll figure it out. I know my father has a place open for me at his clinic in Boston."

"That would be an amazing opportunity," Carrie replied, and then cocked her head. "I hear a 'but' in there, however."

Elizabeth shrugged. "I'm still figuring things out," she said evasively.

Carrie continued to gaze at her for several moments, trying to analyze what she thought she was seeing.

Suddenly, she chuckled. "Peter." Elizabeth ducked her head, but not before Carrie saw the flush on her face.

"What are you talking about?"

Carrie laughed harder. "It's Peter. You're waiting to see what will happen with him."

Elizabeth's head shot up. "That's not true!" Then the flush deepened. "Do you think I'm quite mad?" she asked sheepishly.

"No," Carrie assured her. "Peter is a wonderful man. I believe the two of you are perfect for each other."

"Me too," Elizabeth admitted. "I was looking forward to the ride out to the plantation with him, but it changed when Phoebe and Felicia joined us. I was thrilled to have them," she said quickly, "but..."

"But it completely changed the dynamics," Carrie agreed. "What about while you've been here? Have you talked?"

Elizabeth shrugged. "I think he wants to spend more alone time with me, but there's so much going on." She sighed. "The need for him to stay with Harold and Susan makes it even harder to be with him." She shook her head. "I'm probably just being foolish. I know he likes me, but I believe he'd make more of an effort if he wanted to spend time with me."

Carrie had seen the longing in Peter's eyes when he looked at Elizabeth. She suspected he merely didn't want to appear rude by disappearing with her. "He loves you, Elizabeth."

Elizabeth's eyes widened. "Why would you think that?"

"I know Peter," Carrie answered. "I see the look on his face."

"Well," Elizabeth said with another sigh, "I'll just have to wait and see what happens." She shook her head and went back to what had started their conversation. "I'm going to let my patients know the clinic will close in a month. Perhaps I'll have answers by then."

Carrie nodded absently. She was already busy scheming.

Chapter Seventeen

Rose and Felicia trotted down the road that bisected the tobacco fields, the setting sun offering a slight respite from the searing heat that had returned with a vengeance.

"It's not this hot in Ohio," Felicia complained.

"It's also not this beautiful," Rose replied as she gazed out over the green tobacco plants bursting with pink and white trumpet shaped flowers.

"Unless you look close enough to see all the horrible hornworms on the tobacco plants." Felicia screwed up her face with distaste.

Rose laughed. "I think I'm being told that my lovely daughter will most likely choose city life over plantation life."

"You can count on it," Felicia replied. "I do love visiting the plantation, but I can't imagine living my life here." She cocked her head. "Did you always want to be here, Mama?"

"Definitely not. I could hardly wait to get off the plantation when your daddy and I left. I was confident I would never live on a plantation again. Of course, all I'd known of living here was as a slave." Rose was grateful Felicia didn't remember any of her few years as a slave. Her adopted daughter had been only six when her parents had left the plantation with her during the first year of the war.

"When did you know you wanted to always be here?" Felicia asked curiously.

Rose considered the question carefully. "It was a process. Even when I came back after the war, I never thought I would stay. My dream was to go to college and teach in Philadelphia or some other big city."

"What changed?"

"I did," Rose replied with a smile. "No one was more surprised that last year at Oberlin than I was, when I realized all I wanted to do was come home to the plantation. I realized I'd grown to love it. I missed the life we'd created here."

"And Daddy wanted to come home, too," Felicia observed.

"He did," Rose agreed, realizing she was having a conversation with her daughter like she would have with any adult. Her heart thrilled as she realized how much Felicia had grown up. She'd conquered her anger during her trip to Memphis with Moses. She'd only gone back to Oberlin two months ago, but that short period had created tremendous growth in her.

"Did you really come home because you missed it, or because *Daddy* wanted to?"

"I wanted it," Rose assured her. "Your daddy went to Oberlin to support me, but also to explore other options for himself. He realized his greatest love is farming, but if I'd wanted to continue in school, and then move somewhere else to teach or start a school of my own, he'd already told me that was alright."

"Not many men would do that," Felicia said sadly.

Rose saw no reason to deny it. "That's true, honey. I hope one day you'll find a husband who will love you as much as your daddy loves me." A look of longing crossed Felicia's face – another reminder of how much she was becoming a young lady.

"I don't think that will happen for a long time."

Rose laughed. "That will probably make your daddy happy." Her laughter died away when she saw the sadness in her daughter's eyes. "Why do you feel that way?"

"Because men don't like strong women."

Rose tensed. "Who told you that?"

Felicia shrugged. "No one had to tell me. I see it all the time."

Rose gathered her thoughts before she spoke. "Do you see that happening here on the plantation?"

"No," Felicia answered. "But the plantation isn't like most places, Mama." Her voice and eyes were defiant.

Rose's heart told her something had happened to hurt her daughter, but she already knew Felicia wouldn't reveal it until she was ready. The best she could do was to communicate as if she already knew the whole story. "It's true that there are many men who don't like strong women. They feel threatened because it makes them feel like they're less, somehow."

"Why?"

Rose struggled to come up with an answer that would make sense of something that didn't make sense at all. "If a man doesn't feel secure in who he is, he thinks being in control of a woman will make him feel better."

"Does it?" Felicia demanded.

Rose shrugged. "If it does, then he's not a man I would want anything to do with."

"Charlene tells me it's how society works. That I should just get used to it."

Rose raised a brow. "Charlene?" She hadn't heard that name before.

"She's a friend at school," Felicia said impatiently. "She's about to graduate."

Rose gritted her teeth. She hated that someone was putting false ideas in her daughter's head, but she had to focus on undoing those thoughts. "Do you think your daddy is a strong man?"

"The strongest and best man I've ever known," Felicia said immediately.

"Do you believe he tries to control me?"

"No," Felicia admitted.

"What about Carrie and Anthony? Do you believe Anthony is a strong man?"

"Yes."

"Does he try to control Carrie?" Rose didn't wait for the answer she knew Felicia would give her. "What about Thomas and Abby? Or Matthew and Janie? Or Harold and Susan?"

Felicia shook her head. "I know what you're trying to do, Mama, but all of you aren't normal."

Rose wanted to break into hysterical laughter, but she maintained control. "If that's true, then you have to find someone who is just as odd as we are. You told me a long time ago that you didn't want to be like everyone else. Has that changed?"

"No," Felicia said quickly, but then frowned. "It's just that..." She looked away as her voice trailed off.

Rose pulled Ginger to a stop and turned to face her daughter just as the sun dropped below the horizon, casting a purple glow across the bank of clouds massed just above the treetops. "One day there will be a man who will be worthy of you. He'll be strong, confident and intelligent, just like your daddy. He'll be proud that you're every bit as strong, confident and intelligent as he is." She reached over and took Felicia's hand. "I hope that's a few years away. You're only sixteen," she said gently.

Felicia pulled her hand away. "I know how old I am, Mama!"

Rose understood what the angry, hurt look in her daughter's eyes meant. She'd fallen in love with someone, or at least been infatuated. That someone had been threatened by her. That someone had broken her heart. That someone had probably been an older man. She'd been surprised when Felicia had written and said she wanted to come home when Phoebe returned, even though it meant one of them would have to travel home to Ohio with her. Now, she realized Felicia needed to be here, but had no idea how to communicate how much she was hurting.

Rose knew better than to push. Felicia always had to do things on her own terms. She'd learned how to deal with anger. Now she must learn how to handle heartbreak. Rose's heart hurt for her, but she couldn't learn life's lessons for her. "I believe the perfect man is out there for you, honey. You'll find him at the right time." Rose smiled and then urged Maple into a canter. "I bet I can beat you to the river."

She heard Felicia's surprised laugh behind her. Lyddie, the chestnut mare Felicia was riding, would have no trouble catching up and passing Maple. Pretty much any horse on the plantation could beat Maple, but she loved her gentle mare just the same. It didn't matter one whit how fast she was. All she wanted to do was give Felicia some time to pull herself together, and to think about the things she'd said.

Rose remained quiet when she and Felicia reached the banks of the James River. They had about forty minutes before they would have to head back to the house in order to beat the darkness. She loosened Maple's saddle, and replaced her bridle with a halter. The horse took a long drink at the water's edge before Rose tied her to a tree. She took a deep breath of the air cooled by the approaching darkness and dropped down on a log closest to the gently lapping water.

Felicia took care of Lyddie and then walked over to stare at the water reflecting the golden glow of the sunset.

Rose watched her for a moment before her eyes shifted to follow the flight of the swallows and bats soaring over the surface in their nightly quest for bugs. She wondered if they ever tired of the constant search for food. As she watched, she allowed her mind to wander. She thought of her earlier conversation with Phoebe, and then her thoughts switched to Alvin's suggestion of building a house that would operate as guest quarters. She deliberately avoided rehashing in her mind the talk she'd just had with Felicia. Thinking about whoever it was that had hurt her beautiful daughter would only drive her crazy. She knew better than to demand details, although she wanted to with every fiber of her being.

Rose felt Felicia settle down onto the log next to her.

"Do you like being a Bregdan Woman, Mama?"

Rose was intrigued by the question. "I do. Why do you ask?"

"Doesn't it mean you have to be strong all the time?"

Rose didn't answer right away. She knew whatever words she chose would be important. "No one is strong all the time, Felicia. I consider myself a strong woman, but there are certainly times when I'm afraid. When I feel weak. When I need the help and support of the people around me."

Silence stretched out between them as Felicia mulled over her words.

"What does it mean to you?" Felicia asked quietly. "Being a Bregdan Woman."

Rose thought about the parchment Carrie had made for all of them. She read it every morning as a reminder before she started her day. "It probably means something different to all of us," she said thoughtfully. "For me, it's a constant reminder that every single thing I do is going to have an impact on someone else's life."

"Is it scary for you?"

"Always," Rose replied, wondering where the conversation would take them. "It's both an awesome privilege *and* an awesome responsibility. I worry that I'll make the wrong decision that will end up impacting lives for generations to come. Likewise, however, I love knowing that right decisions will also impact lives for generations to come in a good way." She smiled. "I try to put my focus on that."

Felicia nodded, but didn't say anything for several minutes. Finally, just as Rose was about to say they needed to head back, she spoke. "When I was in Memphis a few months ago, our carriage driver, Gus, asked me what I was doing with my anger. I've been trying to do something since then. I just don't know what that something is." Her voice tightened with frustration. I know I'm meant to make a difference, but it all seems overwhelming."

"I know." Rose waited for her to continue. Felicia had come a long way in conquering the anger she felt over watching the brutal murder of both her parents during the Memphis Riot, but Rose knew there were still emotions inside her that would have to be peeled back like an onion. "Has something happened to make it more difficult?" she asked carefully.

Felicia's face hardened, but instead of answering, she asked another question. "Why am I different, Mama?"

"Different how?"

"Why do people think I'm smarter than others?"

Rose knew she needed to answer the question carefully. Felicia already felt isolated from the majority of people her age. She didn't want to add to that sense of isolation. While she knew her daughter was brilliant, she also knew the brilliance could be a heavy burden. People her age were threatened by her. Older people were impressed with her intellect, but still saw her as a child. "Brilliance is very subjective," Rose began. "It's influenced by people's beliefs and opinions."

"I know what subjective means," Felicia said impatiently. "And I didn't say I was brilliant!"

Rose stifled her laugh. "I know, but brilliant is the most applicable word here. If we're going to discuss it, we might as well call it what it is. Sometimes, though, brilliance is another word for hunger," she continued seriously. "You've always been hungry to know everything you can. I don't know that your hunger makes you more brilliant than other people, however. You certainly *know* more than most, but it's because you have the hunger to learn. If other people shared your hunger, I believe most of them could be as smart as you are."

"I *need* to know more," Felicia said.

"I know," Rose answered. "You need to know more because you're trying to make things better in a world that's gone crazy."

"Yes, but..." Felicia's voice trailed off. "Why do people resent me for it?"

"Because what you know reminds them of what they *don't* know."

"If they don't want to know it," Felicia demanded, "why do they care if *I* know it!"

Rose knew it was a reasonable question. "Honey, I think the real problem isn't that people think you're smarter than them. I believe the problem is whether you're going to let what people think of you mandate your decisions and happiness."

Felicia stared at her for a long moment and then shifted to look back over the water.

Rose knew it was getting late, but she was loath to end the conversation. A sudden movement caught her attention. She breathed a sigh of relief when she saw Moses, mounted on Champ, watching them from the opening to the trail. He blended in so well with the dark shadows that she hadn't noticed him. He must have seen them head toward the river when they entered the trail. She didn't know how long he'd been there, but she knew he would let them continue their discussion and make sure they got home safely. She smiled at him and then turned back to her daughter.

"Mama, did you ever feel the way I do?"

"Oh, yes." Rose thought back to the many conversations she'd had with her own mama. She prayed she would handle this conversation with her daughter as well as Sarah had. "I was older than you before I was able to pursue my education, but I started teaching my secret school when I was your age."

"You were just fifteen?" Felicia asked in surprise.

"Yes. I was close to turning sixteen, like you are. I was hungry to know things, too," Rose answered. "I used to sneak into the library to borrow a book. That wasn't all, though. I used to steal the stubs of candles so I could read in my tiny room at night."

Felicia raised a brow. "What would have happened if they'd caught you?"

"I would have gotten in a lot of trouble," Rose said flatly. "It was against the law for blacks to read and learn."

"Did you ever feel lonely?" Felicia asked.

"All the time," Rose answered honestly. "I couldn't even tell Carrie about what I was doing with my school in the woods. I don't know what she would have done, but I couldn't risk finding out. It wouldn't have just impacted me – everyone I taught would have been in danger, as well."

"Were any of your students older than you?"

"All but one of them was older than I was." Rose smiled as the memories washed over her. "Miles was one of my students. So was your daddy."

Felicia's eyes widened. "You taught Daddy? And Miles?"

"I did."

Felicia looked away, but Rose could tell her mind was working furiously.

"Daddy didn't resent you for knowing more than he did?"

Rose thought back to the early days of her and Moses' relationship. "In the beginning, I don't think your daddy really understood me, but once he learned how to read, he wanted to learn as much as I did." She smiled. "Your daddy didn't have any education when I met him, but he was as hungry for knowledge as you are."

Felicia nodded, her gaze intense. "What was it like when you went to school in Philadelphia?"

"Hard," Rose said honestly. "There were a lot of people who saw me as an uppity black woman who thought I was better than they were."

"They did?" Felicia's voice sounded relieved.

Rose nodded, knowing she needed to let Felicia lead the conversation. The sound of crickets and frogs filled the evening air while she waited for the next question.

"Did you ever think about not acting so smart?" Felicia asked in a small voice.

"Yes," Rose replied, determined to remain honest. "Abby helped me with that one." She had vivid memories of the day she'd returned from school so upset by how she was being treated. "I was desperate to be accepted." She remembered the compassionate understanding on Abby's face that day as she had poured out her angst and unhappiness.

"What did she say?" Felicia's eyes searched her face.

Rose smiled. "She told me three things. First, she told me that diminishing myself to be acceptable to others would never give me what I wanted. It would also not be a very good way to show my gratitude to God for being smart. God gave me a gift. It was up to me to use it. She promised me people would come into my life eventually who would, not just accept me, but *want* me to be the way I am."

Felicia listened closely. "You said she told you three things," she reminded her.

Rose smiled again. "Abby told me about Socrates."

"Socrates? The Greek philosopher?" Felicia raised a brow.

"Yes." Rose hid her smile. The fact that her almost sixteen-year-old daughter was familiar with Socrates was telling. "She told me intelligence is important, but wisdom is far *more* important. I already knew that, of course. My mama had no education at all, but she was the wisest woman I ever knew." Rose paused. "Abby told me about Socratic wisdom. She told me Socrates understood the limits of his knowledge. He realized he only knew that which he knew. He made no assumption of knowing anything more or less. He didn't flaunt his intelligence. He simply used it."

"He knew an awful lot, though," Felicia said thoughtfully.

"Yes," Rose agreed. "I decided that afternoon that I was going to learn everything I could, but also pray for wisdom." She paused. "Intelligence is a wonderful thing, but what I want more than anything is compassion and grace."

Felicia sat quietly for a moment before she spoke. "Julian probably isn't the man for me."

Rose could tell she was talking more to herself than anything. She waited.

Felicia finally looked at her, her eyes intense with both sadness and defiance. "I met Julian at school."

Rose nodded.

"He's graduating this year. He's twenty-five."

Rose bit her lip hard, determined to not point out that Felicia was too young to marry someone that age. She knew that, in truth, it happened quite often. Making an issue of it would only make Felicia more defiant. She was glad Moses couldn't hear their conversation. It was easy to envision his reaction.

"He wants me to quit school and marry him," Felicia admitted. "He says I don't need an education to be a wife." She fell silent and gazed at Rose.

"How do you feel about that?" Rose asked quietly, gaining a new appreciation for why her mama had always just asked questions when she had come to her with problems, and how hard it must have been to let her reach her own conclusions.

"I want to finish school," Felicia said, almost desperately.

"Do you love him?"

Felicia hesitated. "I think so, but it's hard to know. Julian wants to be a businessman. He wants to go to New York City and make a lot of money. He told me I could make the biggest difference if I become his wife and raise his children."

Rose gritted her teeth but knew she couldn't over-react. She was grateful it was too dark for Felicia to see the dismay that was probably written all over her face. "Is that what you want?"

"Are you going to do anything but just ask me questions?" Felicia demanded. "I'm talking to you because I need you to tell me what to do."

Rose couldn't control her laugh, but regretted it the instant she felt the angry tension in her daughter. "Honey, I'm not laughing at you," she said quickly. "I'm laughing because that's the same question I used to ask my mama all the time. I'm going to tell you what she told me. She always said, '*Rose Girl, you ain't wantin' me to tell you what you oughta do. Not really. You just scared youse gonna make the wrong choice. You already know deep inside what you oughta do. You just gots to listen to dat voice.*' Rose paused, knowing just how right her mama had been. "Felicia, what are you feeling deep inside?"

She raised a hand before Felicia could reply. "Before you answer that, I want to recite something to you."

I have faced the darkness.
I have revisited the pain.
I have knelt in the blood that stole my life.
I have said good-bye to the love ripped from me.
I have screamed my fury.

I have cried my tears.
And now life begins anew.
Dark clouds almost smothered me.
Dark pain almost swallowed me.
In my fury, I blocked the light,
Afraid of what I would see.
But now I know...
I am the light that shines through the darkness.
I must *be the light that shines through the darkness.*
I must *be the breeze that forces the dark clouds away.*
I am.
I will.
Forever.

Felicia stared at her. "That's the poem I wrote in Memphis. You memorized it?"

Rose nodded. "I did. There are many times in life when we're given a clear vision of who we're meant to be, and what we're meant to do. And then something happens, and you lose that vision. It helps to be reminded."

"Yes..." Felicia said quietly. "Thank you, Mama." She fell silent for a long moment and then reached out to take Rose's hand. "I want to be that light," she said firmly. "I know I can't be a bright light unless I finish school and learn all I can." She looked over the water. "I'm going to wait until I find a man who wants me to be a strong woman. A man like Daddy."

Rose squeezed her hand. "I'm glad. We both want the very best for you."

Felicia gasped. "Mama! It's dark!" She looked around. "I was so caught up in what I was feeling that

I didn't even realize how dark it was getting." She stared at the woods fearfully. "Do you know the trail well enough to get us home?" Her voice quivered with anxiety.

"I think so," Rose said calmly, "but thankfully, we won't have to find out tonight." She could feel Felicia's puzzlement in the dark.

"Why not?"

"Because your daddy is waiting to ride home with us."

Felicia's head swiveled toward the woods. "He *is*?"

"He's been there almost since we arrived. He stayed far enough away so he couldn't hear us. He wanted us to have our privacy, but he also wants us to be safe." Rose waved a hand to let Moses know they were coming, and then hurried over to untie Maple.

Felicia followed. "You're right, Mama. I'm not settling for anyone less than a man like Daddy."

Moses had ridden close enough to hear her last words. "You do know they have to pass my inspection, don't you? If I don't believe they love you and respect you as much as I love and respect your mama, I'll send them packing." His voice boomed through the still night.

Felicia giggled and leapt onto Lyddie. "I hope Annie saved us some dinner."

Moses laughed. "My mama hasn't let me go hungry since I was a boy. I doubt she's going to start tonight."

Rose's heart swelled with contentment and happiness as she followed her husband and daughter down the dark trail.

Elizabeth gazed around the tunnel as she held her lantern high. "I've known about the tunnel, but I've never done more than poke my head inside. Where does it go?"

Peter grinned. "I reckon you're about to find out."

Elizabeth continued to stare around at the carefully crafted tunnel that was lined with bricks and secured with thick wooden beams. "Was it really built by Carrie's great-grandparents?"

"That's the story," Peter replied. "When they first came over to America, the area was prone to Indian attacks. Her great-grandfather decided he wanted his family to have a safe place to hide. And a way to escape."

"Which brings me back to the question of where it goes," Elizabeth said. "I'm dying to know."

Peter held up the picnic hamper. "Just know that if you die before we get there, I'm eating all the roast beef and mashed potatoes. Not to mention the blackberry pie," he teased.

Elizabeth laughed. "I'll manage to survive, then. I've heard stories about Annie's legendary blackberry pies. The children were out picking berries all afternoon. Their faces were so purple, I suspect they ate as many as they picked."

"The only way it should be done," Peter answered. "If you have to endure the hazards of thorns and chiggers, you should at least get to eat while you pick."

Elizabeth frowned. "Chiggers?"

Peter nodded solemnly. "They're nasty little creatures. I was introduced to them last summer. They are not my friends."

"What are they?"

"Tiny little red bugs that hide on blackberry bushes. Carrie and Anthony warned me that I should wear long pants and a long-sleeved shirt when we went blackberry picking. It was a brutally hot day, like today, so I declined their wisdom and wore a short-sleeved shirt. I never even noticed when the chiggers leapt onto me. I knew it that night, though. They made me itch like crazy and caused a horrible rash."

Elizabeth grimaced. "That sounds terrible. Please tell me Carrie had some type of remedy for you, despite your ignoring her wisdom."

Peter laughed. "Baking soda. She made a paste of equal parts baking soda and water. I kept it on for about an hour and then washed it off. After I did that a few times, I decided I would live through the experience without itching my skin off."

"Good to know," Elizabeth said with a chuckle.

Several minutes of companionable silence followed as they walked down the tunnel, their footsteps echoing in the void.

Peter broke it. "What are you thinking?"

Elizabeth considered making up an answer but opted for honesty. "I'm wondering what I did to deserve a picnic tonight?"

Peter shrugged sheepishly. "I'm not sure what *either* of us did to deserve a picnic tonight. When I was coming off the porch to dinner, Carrie shoved this picnic basket in my hands and told me I should enjoy a picnic with the person of my choice."

Elizabeth hid her grin.   She'd known from the expression on Carrie's face earlier in the day that she'd been scheming something.   Now she knew what. "Thank you for choosing me," she said quietly.

Peter's response was to switch the picnic basket to his other arm so he could claim her hand.

Speechless at the sudden turn of events, Elizabeth walked beside him silently, savoring his closeness. She was intrigued to see what the night would bring.

Chapter Eighteen

Elizabeth's mouth dropped open with surprise when Peter opened the door at the end of the tunnel. "The James River?" she breathed. "The tunnel comes all the way to the James River?" She stood quietly, relishing the breeze on her face. The night was still warm, but it was a welcome relief from the day's heat. She turned to stare back at the riverbank. The door they'd come through was virtually invisible.

Peter read her thoughts. "Don't worry. I can get to the door again."

Elizabeth decided to trust him. She turned to look out at the water glistening silver beneath a half moon that was already high in the sky. There was enough of the day left to have the dusky horizon glowing purple as it faded into blackness. Suddenly, she frowned. "It's noisy." She gazed around. "I thought summer nights in the country would be quieter."

Peter laughed. "Have they been quiet since you arrived?"

Elizabeth shrugged. "I don't know. We're always on the porch with people talking. That's all I hear. When I go to bed, I'm so tired I fall asleep as soon as my head hits the pillow."

Peter patted the log next to him. "Sit down and I will give you your Southern summer nights education."

Elizabeth grinned and sank down beside him, thrilled by their sudden closeness.

"Let me know what sound you hear," Peter invited. "I'll tell you what it is. Or, try to..."

Elizabeth focused on the chorale of music swelling around her. "There. That trilling sound. What is it?"

"That's an Eastern Screech owl."

Elizabeth shook her head. "That is *not* a screech," she protested.

"They only screech when their nests or young are being attacked," Peter explained patiently. "The rest of the time they make the trilling sound you hear."

"Oh." Elizabeth listened again. "I know what the crickets and frogs are. I hear them in Richmond all the time." Her head swiveled to the right. "What is that clicking sound?"

"Possums," Peter said promptly.

Elizabeth shook her head. "Possums? You mean the animals with a naked tail, a long, pointed face, and tiny little ears."

"Yes." Peter sounded surprised. "The spelling of their name puts an o at the beginning, but I've been assured no one actually includes it when they're talking. At least here in the South." His voice was amused. "How do you know what they look like?"

"I saw one when I was out riding with Carrie yesterday afternoon. She told me it was unusual to see one during the day."

"It is," Peter assured her. "Something probably disturbed it's resting place. Possums prefer night because they feel safer."

"How do you know all this? You're a city boy, just like I'm a city girl."

"I was *born* in the city," Peter corrected. "I've traveled all over the country and stayed in many parts of it in the last eleven years. I've seen my share of animals and learned a lot about nature, but it was Matthew who taught me about Virginia nature. He knows I'm intrigued, and it was a good way to pass the long days in Libby Prison." His eyes darkened for a moment, but then he smiled. "I didn't answer your question about the clicking sound."

"You did. You told me it was the possum."

"Yes." Peter said with a straight face. "What I didn't tell you was the clicking sound is the possum's mating call. A male possum is out looking for their mate tonight."

Elizabeth nodded, but had no idea how to respond to this revelation. "Isn't that nice," she finally murmured.

Peter laughed. "I'm feeling something in common with the possum tonight."

Elizabeth stared at him, her pulse suddenly pounding harder. Had she heard him correctly? "Excuse me?"

Peter turned to her, his chiseled features outlined by the moon. "Elizabeth, I know I'm doing a poor job of this. I'd hoped to have time to talk to you on the carriage ride out here."

"But we weren't alone," Elizabeth said ruefully. Her sudden shock was abating enough to allow her to interact in the game they were playing.

"Right. I'm glad you noticed."

Elizabeth choked back her laugh.

"Anyway, I've been trying to figure out how to get some time alone with you ever since we arrived, but there's always something going on. It felt rude to leave everyone. That's why I was so surprised when Carrie gave me the picnic hamper and pointed me toward the tunnel."

Elizabeth, now that Peter was being so open, decided to help him out. "I might have had something to do with that."

"How?" Peter asked with surprise.

Elizabeth shrugged. "I might have mentioned that I would like to spend some time alone with you."

A grin appeared on Peter's face. "You *might* have?"

"I probably did."

"*Probably*?" Peter probed.

Elizabeth finally laughed. "Fine. I did say I would like to spend more time with you."

Peter reached down and took her hand. "I know we haven't had much time together, but I can assure you I've never made so many trips to Richmond in two months." He paused. "I can't get enough of you."

Elizabeth stared at him, her heart beating even faster. "Is that right?" she managed to ask casually.

Peter looked at her closely. Whatever he saw in her face evidently gave him the courage to continue speaking. "Elizabeth, I never thought I would love anyone else when I lost my wife and daughter. I thought the rest of my life would be focused solely on work." He paused. "Until I met you." His voice softened. "You're special."

Elizabeth couldn't believe what she was hearing. His honesty unleashed the feelings she'd been holding back. "I've had many men pursue me, Peter. None of them made me even take notice. Medicine was my passion. Until now."

"Until now?" Peter asked hopefully.

"Until now," Elizabeth repeated, and then echoed his words. "You're special."

Peter cupped her face in both of his large, warm hands. "Is it too soon to tell you I love you?"

Elizabeth was astonished at the rush of emotion that poured through her as warmth filled her heart. A large smile crept across her face. "Is it too soon to tell you I've been wanting to hear those words for weeks?" Elizabeth whispered. "I love you too."

Peter leaned over, brushed her lips lightly, but then pulled back, his eyes pools of regret. "There's something I need to ask you before I kiss you the way I want to."

Elizabeth fought to control her breathing. "What is it?" she managed to say in a natural voice.

"I need to know what your plans for the future are," Peter said quietly. "I love coming to Richmond to visit. I love everyone here on the plantation and consider it a home away from home." He paused. "I could never make the South *my* home, however. The plantation is like a different world. The rest of the South isn't like it is here, though. As a journalist, I've reported too much of what's happened here. I can visit the South. I can work in the South. But..."

"You can't call the South home because it goes against who you are as a person," Elizabeth finished for him.

"Yes," Peter admitted. "That's true. I love you, but I couldn't live in Richmond. I thought it only fair that I tell you. I don't want to hurt you."

"I suppose it's a good thing that I'm headed back North in a month, then," Elizabeth said lightly. Her love for Peter had grown stronger as he'd told her his feelings.

Peter's eyes widened. "You are?"

Elizabeth nodded. "I've already talked to Carrie about it. I love being a doctor, but I realize I have no particular fondness for being a sole practitioner. I've also been lonely in Richmond." She paused. "The biggest reason, however, is that I don't feel at home in the South. For all the same reasons you just said. I'm not looking forward to more northern winters, but I find I prefer them over what I see happening in the South."

"Are you going back to Boston?"

Elizabeth smiled and gazed up at him. "I suppose that depends."

"On what?" Peter asked.

"On whether I get a better offer," Elizabeth said frankly. He loved her. This was no time to be coy.

Peter laughed and then pulled her into a passionate embrace. Just before his lips descended upon hers, he whispered, "I promise you I'll make you a better offer."

Rose was enjoying the rare quiet on the porch. Every rocker was full, but for once, no one was talking. Everyone seemed content to just relax and munch on the cookies Annie had placed on the table before she'd retired to her apartment over the barn with Miles. As predicted, Annie had saved dinner for her, Moses and Felicia.

"Where is Phoebe?" Abby finally asked.

"Writing a letter," Rose answered, and then decided to expound. "She's writing to a friend who just graduated from Oberlin, as well. Hazel is a former slave who wants to teach in the South. Now that the schools have to be divided, I realize I would welcome another teacher."

"That sounds wonderful," Abby replied.

"It creates a problem, though," Rose said, deciding now was a good time to delve into Alvin's suggestion.

"What kind of problem?" Carrie asked as she reached for another cookie.

"We don't have room for more people in the house," Rose replied. She shared her idea of building two apartments above the school.

Abby frowned. "I don't believe that would be safe. Surely, the women would be too vulnerable there."

"That's what we decided, as well," Rose agreed. "It still doesn't change the fact, however, that the house can only hold so many people." She paused. "Alvin had an idea, though."

"What was it?" Thomas asked keenly. "Alvin strikes me as an intelligent, thoughtful man."

"I couldn't agree more," Rose responded. "He suggested we build another house close to this one to serve as guest quarters. Visitors would still eat here in the house, but sleep in the guest quarters."

A thoughtful silence fell on the porch. Rose looked at each face. She didn't see resistance, merely thoughtfulness. "Alvin said the men building the schoolhouse and clinic would love to also build a guest house. It would help them to financially get through the winter."

"They think they could have it built this summer?" Abby asked with surprise.

Rose shrugged. She didn't know anything about building a house. "Alvin seemed to be fairly confident they could."

Thomas stood and walked to the edge of the porch. He was silent for a long moment and then pointed to the east. "There's room for a house over there in that grove of trees. Some of them would have to come down, of course, but the trees would provide privacy, while still being close enough to the main house to make it easy for guests to join us for meals. I think we could easily create a two-story house with six bedrooms. With the amount of family and guests we have, it would make sense." He turned and looked at Moses. "What do you think, partner?"

Moses joined him and looked in the direction he was pointing. "I think it could be done... but it could also be risky," he said slowly. "Especially after losing our crop last summer. We had to use significant portion of our reserves to pay wages and have the capital to put in this year's crop. We're also paying for the new school and clinic. So far, it appears we're going to have a great harvest, but that's what I thought last year – before the flood." He frowned. "You watch the finances closer than I do when I'm working the fields. Has something changed?"

Thomas shook his head. "No." He hesitated, obviously calculating numbers in his head. "It would be tight," he admitted. "If something happened to the crop, we could be in trouble."

"Now is probably not the best time to risk your capital," Matthew said.

Thomas considered his statement and then looked at Abby. "What do you think, dear?"

Abby gazed thoughtfully at the clearing in question. "I agree with Moses and Matthew," she finally said. "Though the odds say there won't be a flood two years in a row, I'm not at all certain it's worth the risk. I know the house is crowded, but I prefer a crowded house over financial trouble. If the crop is good this year, it's certainly something I would welcome next year." She looked at Rose. "I'm sorry, dear."

"Don't be sorry," Rose said quickly. "I think it's a good idea to have a guest house, but I agree that we need to be cautious. Especially with the uncertainty in the economy right now. We have far too many people counting on us. It isn't just us we'd be putting at risk."

Silence fell on the porch.

"I have an idea..." Abby and Carrie started speaking at the exact same moment.

"You first," Carrie urged with a laugh. It wasn't unusual for her and Abby to have the exact same thoughts.

Abby nodded. "While I don't believe we should spend the money on a six-bedroom, two-story house, I wonder if there might be enough for a small two-bedroom house. If it was designed with expansion in mind, we could add on to it – perhaps even this fall. In the meantime, there would at least be housing for Phoebe and Hazel, if she moves here to teach."

Carrie smiled. "Once again, we're thinking the same thing. And, I know how it will be paid for."

Rose watched her, loving the excited shine in her best friend's eyes.

"Cromwell Stables has had a very profitable two years," Carrie said. "We've saved most of our profits with an eye to expansion, but Susan and I had already spoken about using some of that to pay for the new clinic. It benefits everyone for the children to receive a great education. There's no reason for the plantation finances to carry everything. Allowing us to pay for the clinic might mean there's enough to build a small guest house that can grow in time." She paused. "Of course, I'll have to speak with Susan before we commit our funds, but I'm confident she'll agree with me. A guest house would even allow us to offer housing to some of the buyers who visit the stables."

Moses and Thomas looked at each other with a smile.

Abby nodded vigorously. "That's a wonderful idea!"

"Thank you, honey," Thomas said, coming over to plant a kiss on Carrie's forehead. "Anthony and I talked about paying for the clinic with our profits from River City Carriages, but the expense of paying extra for guards and needing to add horses and carriages made it impossible."

Carrie smiled. "We're all family, working to create the best life on Cromwell Plantation that we can. All of us will benefit from having a guest house added to the property. I'm going to thank Alvin for giving us a wonderful idea."

Rose grinned. "Phoebe will be ecstatic, especially if it means Hazel wants to come join us."

The door creaked open as Phoebe stepped onto the porch. "Oh, she definitely wants to join us. I expect she'll be here in a few weeks."

Rose stared at her. "You haven't even mailed the letter you were up there writing."

Phoebe laughed. "Hazel has been begging me to figure out a way for her to work at the school ever since I returned after Christmas. Once I had told her about it, it's all she's talked about. I wrote to let her know her dream is coming true, and to get here as quickly as possible." She waved her arm toward the pastures. "Once she lays eyes on the horses, you'll never get her to leave."

Laughter filled the porch

"Where's Elizabeth?" Janie asked.

Carrie smiled, but remained silent.

Janie gazed around the porch until her eyes latched on Carrie. "You know where she is, don't you?"

"I might," Carrie said evasively. She'd love to know exactly what was happening on the riverbank, but she would have to wait for details.

Janie narrowed her eyes. "What aren't you telling me?"

Carrie tried but failed to hide her grin. "I don't know what you're talking about."

Matthew chuckled. "She's with Peter, isn't she?"

Janie, not waiting for an answer to her question, swung around to stare at her husband. "She's with Peter?" Her voice was speculative.

"I hope so," Abby replied. "I'm hoping they figure out what everyone else on the plantation knows already."

"That they're in love?" Janie asked. She looked a little dazed. "I know I've been preoccupied, but I don't know how I missed something like that."

"Peter is head over heels in love with Elizabeth," Matthew confirmed. "I hope she feels the same way."

Carrie bit her lip. Simply because everyone could see what was going on, it wasn't her place to reveal Elizabeth's confidences. She decided to take the focus off her friend's love life. "Elizabeth is closing the clinic."

Everyone's mouth gaped open as they turned to stare at her.

"What?" Janie finally managed. "She's closing the clinic?" Guilt filled her face. "Because I left?"

Carrie knew it was partially that, but it was only a small part. "If that were true, Janie, I would be equally at fault. It's much more than that, though." She picked her next words carefully. "Elizabeth has a hard time being in the South."

"Of course she does," Abby said softly, understanding glowing in her eyes. "Elizabeth was raised in a very progressive Quaker family. Her family fought hard in the Abolition Movement. Now, they're equally involved in the Suffrage Movement. She must feel completely out of her element, especially without the two of you around."

"Yes," Carrie agreed. "Elizabeth doesn't feel like the South is home for her. I completely understand. If I didn't have the plantation, it would be very difficult to stay in the South."

"I understand how she feels too," Janie said quietly. "If you hadn't asked me to work on the plantation with you, I'm sure we would have gone back to the North. I'm grateful it's not necessary for me to return to brutal winters, but Southern attitudes are stifling."

Phoebe gazed around at them. "What's going to happen down here in the South? I'm so happy to be on the plantation, but from everything I can tell, the South is reverting to the same beliefs that led to the war in the first place. I know slavery is no longer legal, but there are certainly more ways than one to repress people."

Carrie was happy to have moved the talk away from Elizabeth's love life, but she didn't really want to engage in an intense conversation. She blocked out everyone's voices and focused on the sounds of the summer night. Her eyes filled with tears as a shrill whinny split the night air. Granite's death had left a gaping hole in her heart. As long as she was busy, the piercing pain diminished to a dull ache, but all she wanted to do was run to the barn with a carrot in her pocket so she could spend time with her horse.

Anthony took her hand and squeezed it tightly.

Blinking back hot tears, Carrie forced a tremulous smile. She was grateful Anthony understood her pain. He understood, better than anyone else, that her love for Granite had been equal to her love for any human.

She doubted anyone else, other than Amber, realized the depth of her loss.

Anthony leaned over. "Want to go for a walk?"

Carrie stood in answer. The conversation, which she had ceased to listen to, fell silent.

Anthony rose beside her. "We're going for a walk on this beautiful evening. Good night, all."

"Good night," Carrie murmured, confident everyone knew she just needed some time. She slipped her hand through the crook of Anthony's arm as they walked down the stairs and past the dark barn. She deliberately averted her eyes.

They walked in silence, letting the warm air wrap around them. Honeysuckle, exploding in bloom along the fence lines, filled the air with a luscious aroma. Combined with the fragrant smell of the hay being piled into tall stooks, Carrie was certain she'd never smelled anything more wonderful. "It's a beautiful night," she said softly.

Anthony released his arm to swat at a mosquito. "It is. I just wish the mosquitoes would leave us alone."

Carrie chuckled as she dug into her pocket. "I learned something new today from one of the books in the library. I have no idea why I didn't know this before, but it seems to be working. I haven't had a single mosquito bother me all night."

Anthony stopped abruptly. "You have a way to keep these blood-thirsty creatures from feeding on me? And you haven't told me?"

Carrie laughed. "I wanted to test it before I got your hopes up."

"What's in that pocket of yours?" Anthony demanded.

Carrie pulled out a handful of green. "These are leaves from the beautyberry plant. Crush them in your hands, and then rub them on your skin. Make sure you put it on your arms and neck. You can also rub a little on your cheeks and forehead."

Anthony looked at her skeptically but followed instructions. "I'll let you know if it works. In the meantime, tell me more about the beautyberry. I don't know that I've ever heard of it." He tucked her hand through his arm and resumed walking.

"You just don't know the name," Carrie answered. "Do you remember last winter when you asked me about the plant that had the cluster of purple berries?"

Anthony nodded. "That's the beautyberry?"

"Yes. I'll show you what they look like this time of year in the daylight. You should take some back to Richmond for the horses. The book that I read said you can take the branches and stick them into the harness, next to the horse's skin. They'll repel deerflies, horseflies and mosquitoes. We're going to try it here, as well."

"I will," Anthony said promptly. "Anything that makes it easier for the horses while they're working is certainly worth a try." He chuckled. "If it works, I'll buy a field and fill it with beautyberry plants."

Carrie laughed. "You won't need to. It grows freely in the woods right outside the city, though the book says it doesn't grow much farther north. You could hire some children to pick it for you. Your horses will be the happiest ones in Richmond."

"You are a fount of knowledge, Dr. Wallington," Anthony said admiringly.

"Felicia has convinced me that I have to keep digging for information," Carrie replied. "My father has a vast library. I didn't take advantage of it while I was younger, but now I'm reading every chance I get. I keep several books at the clinic so I can read in between patients." She held up the leaves. "I found an old book that has herbal remedies from the early 1800's. Sarah taught me most of them, but the beautyberry is a new one for me."

They fell silent again, walking down the crushed oyster shell road that glowed white in the moon. The leaves of the tobacco plants glimmered as the first drops of dew settled on them. Carrie knew they were looking at a bumper crop – one that would help the plantation recoup from the devastating loss the year before. The men had worked hard all winter to clear more fields, and the silt left behind from the flood was evidently working as an amazing fertilizer.

"You seem troubled," Anthony finally said. "I know you're still grieving Granite, but is there something else?"

Carrie sighed, both grateful and slightly irritated that her husband knew her so well. "Do you think it was a waste? Starting the Bregdan Clinic in Richmond?"

"No," Anthony said firmly. "Do you?"

"I wonder," Carrie admitted. "It will have only been open about seven months. What will our patients do? I fear we're ripping good health care away from them, just as we were beginning to truly help them." She took a deep breath. "Do you think I'm a coward for not continuing to practice there?" As the question escaped her mouth, she knew that was what was most bothering her.

"No." Anthony stopped and swung her around to face him, lifting her chin so he could see her in the moonlight. "You don't have a cowardly bone in your body, Carrie."

Carrie tried to twist away from him, but he held her in place, gazing down into her face with his compelling eyes. After everything she had said to Elizabeth, she wasn't certain why she was struggling now. She'd meant what she told her friend, but she was having a hard time applying it to herself.

"Things change. Circumstances change, Carrie. All of you took the actions you believed you were meant to take at the time. Florence's life changed during her time in France. Your life changed when you became the mother of not just one, but two little girls. Things changed for Janie after the attack. No one could have foreseen any of those things." He paused. "And then things changed for Elizabeth. She realized she's not meant to live in the South."

Carrie almost smiled as Anthony spoke the very words she had spoken to Elizabeth, but she was still troubled. "But what about our patients?" Carrie repeated. "What will they do?"

Anthony shook his head. "I'm not going to pretend to know the answer to that question. All I know is that each of you made the best decision about your life that you knew how to make at the time." He paused. "My grandmother taught me something I've never forgotten."

"What's that?" Carrie desperately wanted to believe the clinic was something more than a horrible mistake.

"She taught me that nothing is ever wasted." Anthony took a deep breath as a smile filled his face. "My grandmother was a wise woman. She told me that if I made a decision to do something because I believed I was meant to do it, that no matter how it turned out, the experience wouldn't be wasted. The whole point may have been just to learn something I couldn't learn any other way. It could have happened because it was meant to impact someone else for that period of time – and that there was no other way to reach them. She told me I could spend my whole life second-guessing experiences, or I could be grateful for them and move on."

He gazed out over the tobacco for a long moment. "Grandmother told me the only thing I can truly count on in life is change. No matter how hard I might try to make things stay the same, there will always be change. I could resist it, or embrace it, but it was going to happen, anyway. The longer I've lived, the wiser I know her advice was."

Carrie thought about all the clinic's patients. The women who had attended the seminar had become close friends, offering each other support in a way none of them had experienced before. The clinic had been the catalyst to get Dr. Lucinda Marlboro into the Black Quarters.

"What's that frown for?"

"I'm thinking about Lucinda," Carrie answered. "She's going to miss Elizabeth terribly."

Anthony nodded. "I'm sure she will," he said calmly, "but she came to Richmond because she believed she was meant to. Didn't you tell me she was developing close friendships in the Black Quarters?"

"Yes. The residents love her."

"She'll be fine," Anthony said confidently. "She's always welcome to visit the plantation, as well. If she needs to get away from everything, we can give her a break." He grinned. "We're about to have a new guest house, you know." He lifted Carrie's chin again. "There are so many good things you're not seeing, Carrie."

Carrie acknowledged that was probably true. Her heart was grieving Granite. It was hard to see beyond the grief. "Will you remind me?" she asked quietly.

"Without the clinic, Elizabeth probably would have never met Peter," Anthony began. "Without the clinic, Janie and Matthew most likely wouldn't have moved to Richmond – which means she might not have come out here to be your partner."

When he paused, Carrie gazed at him. "Keep going." Hearing his observations was making her feel better.

"Without the clinic, Darlene wouldn't have learned she's a fierce leader."

Carrie laughed. "She certainly is *that*." She entered into the game. "Without the clinic I wouldn't have learned about feeling afraid but *doing* brave."

Anthony nodded. "And you wouldn't be saying *courage rising* every chance you get when someone is anxious or afraid."

"So... we're not failing?"

"You're not failing," Anthony said, his voice ringing through the still night. "You're all moving into the next phase of your life. According to my grandmother, the older you get, the more you're able to understand why things in the past happened."

Carrie smiled as she looked out over the tobacco fields. "That makes sense. I can already look back and see how things have all woven together in a good way." She took a deep breath. "I want to go to Richmond before the clinic closes and say good-bye to everyone."

"I already knew that," Anthony replied. "We'll go as a family and do some shopping for the girls. How does that sound?"

"Like a perfect time," Carrie said happily. "Thank you," she whispered.

Anthony cocked a brow.

"Thank you for knowing me. Thank you for loving me."

Anthony's response was to pull her into a passionate kiss that took her breath away.

Carrie and Anthony walked up the stairs to the porch, surprised to see everyone still outside when they returned. Perhaps it wasn't as late as they thought. A burst of laughter split the night.

"Well, it's about time the two of you figured things out," Janie said happily.

The two of you? Carrie squinted so she could see better in the dark.

"From the stories I've heard, it took you and Matthew a lot longer than it took Peter and me!"

Carrie smiled at the sound of Elizabeth's spirited reply. Evidently, things had gone well on the riverbank.

Everyone turned at the sound of their footsteps on the porch.

Elizabeth rose and threw her arms around Carrie. "Thank you! The picnic you provided was wonderful."

Carrie laughed. "I'm fairly certain it would take more than Annie's cooking to put that kind of smile on your face."

"That could be," Elizabeth said demurely.

Carrie laughed harder and then turned to Peter. "Did you enjoy your picnic, too?"

"It was the best picnic I ever had," Peter declared with a grin. Then he sobered. "Thank you, Carrie. I imagine we would have eventually found some time together, but telling Elizabeth how I feel about her on the bank of the James River on a summer evening was perfect."

"So, the two of you aren't dancing around each other anymore," Anthony declared. "Congratulations!" He clapped Peter on the shoulder. "Well done!"

"I'm a lucky man," Peter said fervently, his arm tightly around Elizabeth's waist. "I ws waiting until the two of you returned to make the announcement. Elizabeth has agreed to marry me."

The chorus of congratulations rose into the night sky, blocking out the cacophonous sound of crickets and frogs.

"Elizabeth is a lucky woman," Abby said warmly, when it grew quiet again. She gestured to Carrie, Janie and Rose. "I say we go inside and dish up some of the pound cake that Annie pulled out of the oven just before she left tonight. It will be perfect with some blackberries over it. I say this calls for a celebration!"

"A celebration?" Frances appeared at the door with Minnie close on her heels.

Carrie wasn't surprised they had awakened the girls. "Peter and Elizabeth are engaged," she announced happily.

The girls squealed and threw their arms around the couple.

Felicia stepped through the door next. "What's going on out here?" she asked sleepily.

"Peter and Elizabeth are getting married!" Minnie cried.

Felicia nodded. "They'd better be. It's obvious they love each other."

Everyone laughed loudly.

Carrie looked at Rose. "Should we expect John and Hope next?"

Rose shook her head. "Those two sleep like logs. They'll be sad they missed the party, but I can assure you they haven't heard a thing."

"Robert and Annabelle are far enough in the back of the house that they won't have heard anything either," Janie said.

Abby did a rapid head count. "Fourteen pieces of pound cake coming up," she said brightly.

Chapter Nineteen

Abby smiled down at Frances, who was dancing next to her with excitement. "Are you glad to be back in Philadelphia?"

Chugging trains arrived and departed as shrill whistles split the air and porters called out over the crowd. A throng of people lined up on the platform to catch an outgoing train, just as newly arriving travelers jostled to find their luggage.

"Yes, Grandma!" Frances yelled loudly enough to be heard over the din. "I'm glad to live on the plantation now, but it'll be wonderful to see Jeremy and Marietta, and the twins. Not to mention some of my friends." Her voice turned serious. "Matthew asked me to write another article, too. I'll have to do some work while I'm here."

"I'll make sure you talk to who you need to," Abby promised as she exchanged an amused look with Thomas. She was thrilled they could bring the girls with them to Philadelphia on their way to New York City to visit the Stratford family. She and the girls followed Thomas off the platform, out of the building, and down on to the sidewalk where they could catch a carriage ride.

Thomas nodded his head toward Minnie as soon as they escaped the noise, and knelt in front of her. "Are you alright, honey?"

Fear had darkened Minnie's brilliant blue eyes. Abby understood instantly.

Minnie stared at Thomas, her lower lip quivering. "I can feel them, Grandpa."

Thomas pulled her into his arms. "I imagine you can," he said gently. "Philadelphia was the last place you saw your family. I'm sorry it's hard to be here."

Minnie bit her lip and blinked her eyes furiously. "It's hard," she agreed in a faltering voice. "But I guess... I guess it's the best place to tell them..." She took a deep breath. "To tell them good-bye."

"To tell them good-bye?" Thomas leaned back to look into her face.

Minnie nodded. "I never got to say good-bye, Grandpa. I was home with all of them one night. The next night they were gone. I told my mama goodbye when she left to go home the night I was with Frances, but I didn't really say *good-bye*." Her eyes filled with tears. "I didn't say good-bye to my brother and sisters at all. The night before the fire we were fighting over who could get closest to the kerosene stove." Her voice broke off in a sob. "The next night they were gone. Burned up in the fire..." She shook her head. "I never went... went back there. Before I knew... knew it, I was on the plantation." She spoke so fast she tripped over her words.

Abby's heart broke from the pain etched on Minnie's face. She knelt next to Thomas thinking about how insistent Felicia had been that it would help if she could say goodbye to her parents in Memphis. "Would it help to go back to the street where you used to live so you can tell them goodbye?" It had been impossible to identify and bury the victims from the fire that had claimed her family.

Minnie nodded. "I think so," she said slowly. "We can really do that?"

"Of course," Abby said tenderly. She knew it was going to be agonizingly difficult for Minnie to stand where their tenement house had once stood, but she also knew it would provide a healing she probably couldn't get any other way. "Would you like us to all go together?"

Minnie considered the question and then nodded. "That might be real good. It might be easier to say good-bye to my old family if I have my new family with me." The relief beginning to bloom on her face disappeared into a frown.

Abby read her mind. "Honey, your mama, and brother and sisters are happy you have a new family that loves you and is taking care of you. They won't be sad if we all come together."

Minnie stared into her eyes, and then nodded as the frown disappeared. "Alright."

Marietta pulled off her apron and hurried toward the front door. She threw it open and rushed out to pull Frances and Minnie into an exuberant hug. "Welcome. I missed you two so much!"

Frances and Minnie giggled with delight. "We missed you too," they cried.

Marietta stood and then hugged Thomas and Abby. "I'm so glad you've arrived. The twins have been driving me crazy all day."

Minnie craned her head to look around. "Where are they?"

Marietta laughed. "They wore themselves out by running to the door to look down the street every few minutes. They both collapsed about thirty minutes ago."

"They're sleeping?" Minnie's face crumpled with disappointment.

"Don't worry." Marietta pushed back locks of red hair from her flushed face. "They'll wake up soon. When they do, they're going to be very excited to see you."

Minnie didn't look convinced. "What are we going to do until they wake up?"

Marietta laughed. "I don't know..." She let her voice trail off. "I don't suppose anyone here is interested in having some of Faith's famous Irish Oatmeal cookies." She made herself sound disappointed.

"I want some cookies!" Frances said eagerly.

"Me too," Minnie exclaimed. Then she frowned. "But... I thought they were *Annie's* Irish Oatmeal cookies. Who is Faith?"

"Ahhh..." Marietta leaned down to stare into Minnie's puzzled face. "That's a secret only a few people know. Can you keep a secret?"

Minnie nodded quickly.

Marietta continued to peer into her face. "I mean, *really* keep a secret. Are you old enough to keep one, Minnie? It's very important."

Minnie looked back at her gravely. "I promise you I can keep a secret, Miss Marietta. I just turned nine-years-old. You can trust me," she said earnestly.

Marietta stared at her quietly until she was certain she'd impressed upon Minnie the importance of the information she was about to share. "Alright," she said slowly.

Minnie suddenly shot a look at Frances. "Do you already know the secret?" When Frances nodded, her lips fell into a pout. "How come you haven't told me?"

Frances shook her head. "What does a *secret* mean, Minnie? If you don't know that, how can Marietta trust you with one?"

Minnie gasped. "I'm sorry, Miss Marietta. Please tell me! I promise I won't tell anyone."

Marietta swallowed her smile. She was glad what she was about to say wasn't an actual secret. She was quite sure Minnie wouldn't be able to help herself if someone pried for information. Since this was nothing but a game to keep the children occupied until the twins woke from their nap, she continued. "Come with me into the kitchen," she said quietly, peering around as if to make sure no one was watching or listening.

Minnie, her face appropriately awed, followed closely.

Marietta had just pulled a pan of Irish oatmeal cookies from the oven before they'd arrived. The rich aroma filled the kitchen, making her own mouth water.

"Can I have one?" Minnie pleaded, staring down at the pan with longing.

"Don't you want to know the secret first?"

Minnie nodded reluctantly and turned to look up at her. "Yes."

"Have you ever heard Carrie talk about Biddy Flannagan?"

"Do you mean Mama?"

Marietta shot a look over Minnie's head. She was thrilled when Abby nodded and smiled. It was a wonderful sign that Minnie was calling Carrie her mama. She knew the fire that had killed Minnie's family had devastated the little girl, but all the love on the plantation was clearly working its magic. "That's right. Has your mama told you about Biddy Flannagan?"

Minnie nodded. "Yes. She gave Mama the Bregdan Principle. It was on the wall in her house down in the area where most of the Irish live. She's Irish, like me!" she said proudly. Then she frowned. "She was real old when she died."

"She was," Marietta agreed. "Did you mama tell you about Faith?"

"She was Biddy Flannagan's best friend," Minnie answered promptly, her face glowing with pride that she knew the answers. "She's still alive. Mama told me she's busy doing good things with all the money that Biddy Flannagan left."

"That's right," Marietta said approvingly. "That's not all Faith does, though. She makes the best Irish Oatmeal Cookies ever made." She leaned down and lowered her voice to a whisper. "Carrie took her recipe to Annie one day so she could make them too."

Minnie absorbed the information with a disbelieving frown. "How do you know Annie didn't start making them? How do you know she didn't send the recipe to Faith? Annie told me it was *her* recipe."

Marietta bit back another laugh. "Minnie, do *you* think Annie looks Irish?"

Minnie stared at her until her lips twitched into a smile. "I reckon she doesn't. She doesn't exactly talk with an Irish accent, either."

Marietta laughed. "The truth of it is that Faith isn't Irish either. She's black, too. Like Annie. And she most certainly doesn't have an Irish accent." Then she sobered. "I don't really know where Faith got the recipe, either. I imagine one of the Irish cooks in Biddy's neighborhood taught her. I suspect the recipe goes back many generations in Ireland." She lowered her voice again to a conspiratorial whisper. "Just don't ever say anything about that to Faith. She has everyone believing it is *her* recipe."

Minnie looked doubtful. "All the Irish cooks who live down there believe a black woman created Irish Oatmeal Cookies?"

Marietta laughed again. Minnie was a smart little girl. "Probably not," she admitted. "But Faith has been making cookies for every child in Moyamensing for many years. I believe they have all agreed to let her believe it's her recipe because she makes their children so happy."

"Why don't *they* make cookies for their children?" Minnie asked.

"They can't afford to," Marietta explained. "Sugar and butter are very expensive."

"I know," Minnie said, her face tight with seriousness. "The only reason my first mama was able to give us cookies was because she brought some home after she made them for my new mama."

Marietta knew the conversation about her first mama and second mama had to be confusing for Minnie. "I'm glad you got to have them," she said easily. "The secret is that the Irish Oatmeal Cookie recipe doesn't come from either Annie *or* Faith. They just passed it down, the way it's been being passed down for generations."

"We just let them *think* we believe them?" Minnie asked astutely.

"Right." At that moment, Marietta heard noises from the room above her. She quickly scooped some cookies off the tray into a big bowl. "The twins are waking up. I know they'll be thrilled if you go up with some cookies."

Minnie grabbed the bowl with a grin. She whirled around and ran from the kitchen, Frances close on her heels.

Abby leaned back against the tree bordering the baseball field and fanned herself casually. Virginia was hotter, but the stifling humid heat in Philadelphia was almost unbearable. After years on the plantation, she didn't know how she'd survived so many years in the Pennsylvania city. She turned to Marietta. "I'm glad you're going to the plantation for a few weeks when we leave for New York. You and the twins will enjoy the respite."

"I'm sure we will," Marietta agreed. "It's wonderful that Frances and Minnie will be able to help me with them on the train ride since Jeremy has to stay here to work. I probably should be able to handle a pair of almost three-year-olds by myself, but they're a handful."

Abby laughed and rolled her eyes. "Those two children have more energy than any I've ever seen. At least they'll have more room to run around on the plantation."

"As well as John, Hope, Robert and Annabelle to play with," Marietta said with relief. "If I have just five minutes a day to sit on that porch and do nothing, I'll be grateful."

"I'm sure they'll do better than that," Abby assured her.

"Are you looking forward to New York City?" Marietta asked.

"I am," Abby said brightly. "I haven't seen the Stratford family in far too long. I'm also looking forward to meeting all the women buying the quilts from the Bregdan Women on the plantation. I want them to know how much their purchase of the quilts have changed lives down there, but it's more than that. The plantation women have so inspired them that they've decided to start their own group. I'm thrilled to lead the first one and then hand it over to Nancy Stratford."

"Bregdan Women is growing," Marietta said admiringly.

Abby nodded. "Biddy Flannagan would be thrilled to know what she spawned." The sound of a loud crack made her swivel her head toward the game. "That sounded like a very good hit."

Marietta smiled. "Do you know anything about baseball, Abby?"

"Frances tried to educate me on the way over to the field. There are four bases; first, second, third, and home. When someone hits a ball, they get to run to at least one base, sometimes more. The idea is that the team that has the most players circle the bases entirely, wins."

Marietta laughed. "That's the general idea," she agreed. "I've never known anyone to put it so succinctly."

"I also know they play outside on a beautiful green field," Abby continued. "And that Frances loves it. I imagine by the end of the day, Minnie will too. She loves anything her older sister does." She looked around. "Where is my husband?"

"Down by Jeremy's bench," Marietta answered. "Jeremy was up late last night, talking to Thomas about baseball." She grinned. "Don't be surprised if there are at least two baseball teams on Cromwell Plantation after you get home from New York City. I'm quite certain Thomas is on his way to being a convert."

Abby followed Marietta's pointing finger. She saw Thomas laughing and talking with all the players as they waited for their turn to hit.

"Jeremy is coming up to bat," Marietta announced, her eyes gleaming with excitement.

Abby leaned forward to watch. Jeremy waited through two pitches. "Why isn't he hitting it?"

"The pitcher didn't throw it into the strike zone. Jeremy has become quite good at waiting for the best pitch. He's one of the Pythian's best players," Marietta said proudly.

As if to prove her statement, Jeremy swung at the next ball. A loud crack exploded through the sultry air, followed by wild cheering as Jeremy tossed aside his bat and ran toward first base.

"Go Jeremy!" Marietta cried loudly. "Run! Run!"

Abby felt her heart beating faster as the roar of the crowd urged Jeremy onward. The ball he'd hit had gone over the head of the players farthest out in the field. When he rounded second base, she joined in the yelling. "Run, Jeremy! Run!"

Jeremy was bent low, his arms pumping as he raced toward third base.

A new cry rose from the crowd. "Slide! Slide!"

Abby was puzzled but kept her eyes on the action. One of the players on the opposing team had scooped up the ball and thrown it toward the player on third base.

"Slide!" Marietta screamed as she leapt to her feet. "Slide!"

Jeremy seemed to be aware the ball he'd hit was being thrown to third base. Precisely before he got to the base, he dropped his body to the ground with one leg extended forward as he laid down almost horizontally.

Abby held her breath as he slid along the ground toward third base. It seemed like hardly a breath between when his foot touched the base, and the third baseman caught the ball, but it must have been enough.

Moments later, another cheer erupted. "It's a triple! Congratulations, Jeremy!"

Marietta clapped wildly and then dropped down on the ground again, her face creased in a wide smile. "He got a triple!"

Abby laughed. "This is quite an exciting game."

"It can be," Marietta agreed. Then she grinned. "It can also be dreadfully boring to wait for the exciting moments. Jeremy claims every moment is exciting, but it's not the same if you're a spectator. There are many times that innings go by without anyone getting a hit or scoring a run." She shrugged. "Of course, that also makes the exciting moments more exciting, because you had to wait for them for so long."

"Jeremy seems to be quite good," Abby said, basing her observation solely on the enthusiastic response of the crowd.

"He is," Marietta agreed. "In a different circumstance, he could be professional."

"Different circumstance?"

"Yes. As much as he loves baseball, he's much more committed to running Cromwell Factories. He knows he has a much greater impact there, and he certainly makes more money," Marietta added with a grin. "It's more than that, though," she added, the grin fading from her face. "He learned how to play baseball from Octavius Catto and the rest of the players. He would never choose to pursue professional status while all of them are banned."

Abby raised a brow. "Banned?"

"Blacks aren't allowed to play in the National Association," Marietta said with disgust. "They won't let black teams join the Association, and they won't let black players join the National Association teams. Even though he passes as white, Jeremy would never betray their friendship."

Abby shook her head. "They've banned them from a *game*?"

Marietta sighed, her eyes deeply troubled. "It may be a game, but anyone who plays takes it quite seriously. It's become another way to create division." She turned to watch the twins playing with a group of children in the shade beneath the trees. "Jeremy joined the team so Sarah Rose would have black children to be friends with. We don't ever want her to be ashamed of being mulatto, and we want her to feel at home with both blacks and whites. All the children love Marcus as much as they love Sarah Rose. The little ones don't see color." She shook her head. "I wish the same could be said of the rest of our country."

Abby nodded. "You and me both."

"Is everyone ready for blackberry cobbler?" Marietta asked.

"Yes!" The answer rose simultaneously from everyone at the table.

"Can we take ours upstairs and play with the twins while we eat?" Minnie asked.

Abby hid her smile. She knew the children were tired of the adult conversation that had buzzed around their heads during the delicious meal of pork chops, mashed potatoes and lima beans.

"I don't know," Marietta answered. "Can you?"

Minnie looked puzzled. "That's what I just asked you, Miss Marietta."

Frances leaned over to whisper to her little sister. "*Rose Filter...*"

Minnie's eyes widened. "Her too?" She corrected herself hastily. "*May* we take ours upstairs and play with the twins while we eat?"

"You may," Marietta replied. "Come into the kitchen and I'll give you bowls for everyone."

A few minutes later, after the children had run upstairs, she entered the dining room with a tray of bowls full of steaming blackberry cobbler. Marietta fixed her eyes on Abby. "The Rose Filter?"

Abby laughed. "It's become the Cromwell Plantation joke. The day Minnie was moving to the plantation, Frances warned her that every word she spoke had to go through the *Rose Filter* – meaning that Rose was going to correct everything she said if it wasn't said correctly."

Marietta laughed. "Does Minnie not know I'm a teacher, too?"

"I'm sure she does by now," Abby assured her with a twinkle in her eyes. "I know Frances will sufficiently warn her."

Laughter rolled through the dining room.

"It's worse than she knows," Marietta said lightly. "Both of our guests are also teachers, though they also both happen to be principals. Octavius is the principal of male students at the Institute for Colored Youth. Caroline is the principal of the Ohio Street School."

"Please tell us more," Thomas said, turning back to their guests eagerly.

Octavius Catto and his fiancé, Caroline LeCount, had joined them for dinner after the game.

"I love what I do," Octavius replied. "I've been a teacher at the Institute for Colored Youth for the last twelve years. Two years ago, I became principal of male students." He smiled. "I believe our head principal, Fanny Jackson Coppin, spoke at your first Bregdan Women meeting here in Philadelphia."

"Yes!" Abby exclaimed. "She is such a delightful woman. She made quite an impact that day."

"And all of you made quite an impact on her," Caroline said. "She talked about the luncheon for days. She had quite a bit to say about someone named Rose. Is she the *Rose Filter*?" she asked with a smile.

Abby nodded. "Rose Samuels. She started the school on Cromwell Plantation for both the white and black students in the area. She used to be a slave there. Now, she's a remarkable educator. She'll be so thrilled we had a chance to meet you."

"Rose also happens to be my half-sister," Thomas said.

Abby understood the surprised silence that followed his announcement. She could see Octavius and Caroline trying to connect the reality of that fact, combined with her statement that Rose had been a slave.

Caroline smiled as she gazed at him with a cocked brow. "That must be quite a story."

"One that has a better ending than the beginning," Thomas answered wryly. "My father had some rather serious character flaws. He raped Rose's mother, who used to be a slave on the plantation. She had twins. One of them was Rose. It's quite a long story."

"Twins?" Octavius asked keenly. "I'm also from a mixed-race family. What happened to her twin?"

"He came out looking white," Jeremy said with a smile.

Octavius looked at him blankly for a moment and then his eyes widened as understanding dawned. "You? You're Rose's twin brother? I know you're mulatto, though you could pass as white. Does Rose look white, as well?"

"Rose looks black," Jeremy replied. "It's unusual for us to look so different, but it certainly happens, as you can tell from our children. My twin is an absolutely amazing woman. We didn't find each other until we were twenty-two. She knew about me before I knew about her, but we had to wait for the war to end to actually meet. Every minute I have with her is a joy."

"May we hear the whole story someday?" Caroline pleaded. "It sounds quite remarkable."

"It is," Abby assured her. "We'll be happy to share it, but since you're guests, we want to know you better. If I remember correctly, Caroline, you were the one who fought streetcar segregation in Philadelphia."

Caroline raised a brow in surprise. "How did you know about that?"

"Dr. Carrie Wallington is my daughter. She helped start the clinic down in Moyamensing. Her driver..."

Caroline interrupted her with a wide smile. "Did she used to be Dr. Carrie Borden? Her driver, Sarge, is a dear friend. He's told me about her."

"Yes," Abby replied. "She began life as Carrie Cromwell. I'm lucky to have her as my beloved stepdaughter, though she couldn't be more my daughter if I'd given birth to her. She was a part of my life many years before I met her dashing, charming father." She smiled lovingly at Thomas. "Her first husband, Robert Borden, was murdered by the KKK. When Carrie and Anthony Wallington married, it was a wonderful occasion." She paused. "Anyway, Sarge was how she first heard about you and Octavius."

"And how *I* learned about you two," Jeremy added as he turned to Abby. "Octavius and Caroline are wonderful teachers, but they have also both done great things for equal rights in Philadelphia."

"Octavius has done far more than I have," Caroline said quickly. "Though I'm doing my best to match his efforts. Since he's seven years older than I am, he's had a head start." She shook her head. "I know you want to hear about us, but every time you open your mouth, you say something I want to know more about. Dr. Wallington's first husband was killed by the KKK?" she asked with horror.

"I'm sure all of us could talk for days about the things that have happened, but that's a story for another time. In the meantime, Octavius may have more years on you, but I'm quite confident you'll catch up with him." Abby was deeply impressed with the thoughtful, intelligent woman sitting in front of her. Carrie and Rose would love her.

Thomas turned his attention to Octavius. "How do you feel about voting in October?"

The atmosphere changed immediately.

Chapter Twenty

Octavius and Caroline exchanged a long look.

"You can talk freely," Jeremy said. "I can assure you Thomas and Abby are not fans of what Bull McMullen is doing."

Octavius nodded, but his eyes were still cautious.

"Please speak freely," Abby urged. "William McMullen has been causing havoc in Moyamensing for fifteen years - ever since he was elected in '56."

Octavius looked surprised. "He's quite popular among the Irish Catholics in Moyamensing."

"Yes," Abby agreed. "That doesn't make him a good man," she said bluntly. "I don't know if you're aware that Thomas and I have a factory in Moyamensing. Many of the Irish, both Catholic and Protestant, who work for us have had to battle discrimination from McMullen because they're working with blacks. A few of our employees, both blacks and Irish, have been beaten on their way to work," she added angrily.

"I'm aware of the issues," Octavius said. "I wasn't aware, however, that you and Thomas own the factory." He looked at Jeremy. "Is that where you worked before you took over the other Cromwell factories?"

"It is. The Moyamensing factory is now being managed by George Frasier."

"I know him," Caroline said. "He's a fine man with an amazing eye for lady's fashion."

Octavius took a deep breath. "Are you aware that McMullen has staked his career on denying blacks the right to vote? He has complete political control over the Fourth Ward and Moyamensing."

"Not just political control," Jeremy added. "Moyamensing has been a hotbed of volunteer fire house riots for decades. They're largely responsible for giving the Irish a reputation for being violent brawlers. McMullen has been at the head of all the riots. It got so bad that Mayor Fox signed a bill into law seven months ago that ended the firefighters' volunteer system. Philadelphia now has paid firefighters. Not that McMullen is impressed with the law." He rolled his eyes. "Quite simply, he ignores it because he was unwilling to concede defeat. Three months ago, he put together a parade so that two hundred and fifty men from his firefighter company could march in a show of force, and they're still responding to neighborhood fires."

"So, McMullen does what he wants," Thomas said flatly.

"Yes," Octavius agreed. "We're a little more than three months away from the October vote. We've fought hard for the right to vote." He took a deep breath. "I have a feeling we're going to have to fight just as hard to actually *cast* a vote."

"Do you expect trouble?" Thomas asked.

"We don't just expect it," Octavius replied. "We know it's going to happen. It won't be the first time there's been violence in Philadelphia to control the outcome of an election. Blacks have been disenfranchised in Pennsylvania since 1838. After thirty-three years of ignoring the black voice, there are a lot of people who don't want to see that change."

"Octavius is likely to be a target," Caroline said nervously.

Abby tensed. She'd already taken a deep liking to Octavius. He was intense, intelligent and well-spoken. "Why?"

Octavius turned his attention to her. "Moyamensing's black population has grown since the Quakers placed the Institute for Colored Youth there five years ago. I'm not the only teacher or family with students who have chosen to move close to the school."

"But he *has* been the one to promote moving there," Caroline added. "Octavius is the president of the Fourth Ward black political club. McMullen knows he's going to be hurt by the black vote."

"And he doesn't want to give up any power," Thomas observed.

"Correct," Octavius confirmed. "McMullen's men will do everything possible to keep blacks from voting. Everything possible means they don't care *what* it takes."

"A lot of blacks have already registered to vote," Caroline said proudly before she frowned, her eyes full of worry. "McMullen's way of doing things is under attack from a lot of directions. His political status and power are being threatened."

Jeremy nodded. "Blacks are anticipating one of the most violent election days in Philadelphia's history."

Abby frowned. "Are there plans in place to protect yourselves?"

Octavius shrugged. "We'll do everything we can to be cautious, but it's going to take courage on the part of every black man who votes. We all realize we're risking our lives to make sure our voice is heard. It's clear this election is going to determine party dominance in Philadelphia for at least the next decade. Mayor Fox is a Democrat. William Stokely, the councilman running against him is Republican. The whites of Moyamensing are going to do everything they can to make sure the black vote doesn't remove Mayor Fox from office." He shook his head as he reached out to take Caroline's hand. "We're hoping there will be enough federal troops available to keep things under control."

"What about the Philadelphia police force?" Abby asked. "I thought the force was being expanded to stop violence in the city."

Octavius scowled, his eyes turning darker with anger. "That's what the city would like us to believe. Unfortunately, because the police have been assigned by our mayor, they're mostly Democratic. If Mayor Fox loses his position, they'll lose their jobs, so they're known for looking the other way." His scowl deepened. "I've informed the members of the black community to expect the policemen to join in the violence to keep them from voting."

"That's terrible!" Abby cried. Her focus, for so many years, had been freedom and equality for slaves. She hadn't spent a lot of time considering what voting would actually be like once it was allowed.

"It's the way things are," Octavius replied. His voice was calm, though his eyes reflected his anger and frustration. "We'll vote, but we already know there will be a high price to pay."

Abby didn't miss the frightened look in Caroline's eyes as she gazed at her fiancé.

Abby smiled at the bustle of activity in the factory. Thomas had joined Jeremy at another baseball game, and the girls had gone to a park with Marietta and the twins. Since she was on her own, she'd decided to hire a carriage to bring her by the Moyamensing factory so she could visit George Frasier. She stood just inside the door to the factory and watched.

Huge steam turbines provided the power needed for the machinery. Huge bolts of cloth were being rolled and cut, their vibrant colors flashing in the sunlight that poured in through a multitude of windows. Many factories were windowless and dark, but Abby had insisted on light and air for all the employees.

Long tables were surrounded by women creating the clothing the factory was quickly becoming known for. Men hurried back to the loading dock with crates full of finished garments, returning with empty crates to be filled. Though everyone was working hard, their faces set with determination, there was also plenty of laughter and talk that floated above the sound of the machines.

Abby smiled. Obviously, George was doing a wonderful job. Just then, the subject of her thoughts emerged from the office set off to the side of the factory floor. She watched as the slender man carefully scanned the production area.

His eyes lit with pleasure when he saw her. "Mrs. Cromwell!" George hurried over with an outstretched hand. "What a delight! I didn't know you would be coming today."

Abby took his hand with a smile. "Hello, Mr. Frasier. I didn't know myself until this morning. I had some unexpected free time, so I thought I would come by."

George smiled. "Do you miss the factory business?"

Abby laughed. "Not one bit," she assured him. "I couldn't be happier on the plantation. But, I do enjoy watching a well-run business operate. We're very fortunate to have you manage this factory for us."

George flushed, his blue eyes glowing with pleasure beneath his short red hair. He stood straighter, smoothing the lapels of his suit. "Thank you, Mrs. Cromwell. I'm still amazed every day that I have the opportunity to manage your factory. It's more than I ever dreamed I would be doing." His eyes swept the production area again.

Abby knew they weren't missing a thing. "Jeremy tells me your numbers are impressive."

George turned back to her. "I would be happy to show them to you."

"There's no need," Abby assured him. "If Jeremy says they're impressive, I believe him." She peered at him more closely. "It's time, though, for you to tell me your secret."

George stiffened. "My secret? What do you mean?"

Abby was surprised by the tension vibrating in his voice, and she was certain it was fear she had seen glimmering in his eyes for a moment. Though curious as to what had caused his reaction, she hastened to reassure him. "I merely meant the secret of how you manage to design such beautiful women's clothing, Mr. Frasier. Not many men have the innate eye that you do. In fact, I don't believe I know *any* other man who can do what you do. I've certainly heard of male designers in Europe, but I doubt any of them have the same feel for what women want."

George continued to watch her closely. His eyes searched her face as if he was looking for something more.

"Mr. Frasier? Have I said something to upset you? That was certainly not my intent. I apologize if I have," Abby said sincerely.

George shook his head quickly. "No, of course not." His voice was flustered. "I'm sorry I've given you that impression."

Abby continued to gaze at him. The man was clearly uncomfortable, but she had no idea why. They'd had conversations before about his designing skills. Why was this one so different? "Is everything alright, Mr. Frasier?"

"Certainly," George replied firmly. "Please come in the office. I'd love to know how Carrie and Janie are doing."

Abby pushed her concerns aside and followed him toward the office. Taking a report home to Carrie and Janie had been one of her reasons for coming. They had asked whether she would see George during her trip, but she hadn't known if it would be possible. "Those two just happen to be one of my favorite topics," she said lightly, relieved when she saw the tension dissipate from George's face.

As they walked across the production, Abby thought about his relationship with Carrie and Janie. The two women had treated George for wounds during the war, keeping him at the Church Hill house until he was ready to go back into battle. They'd never given a reason for their extraordinary generosity – just stating that George was special, and everyone in the house had fallen in love with him. When Janie had reconnected with him in Philadelphia after the war, she'd recommended him for the office manager job at the factory. He'd quickly risen to the position of factory manager.

George opened the door to his office and ushered her inside. The machinery could still be heard, but it wasn't nearly as loud. A real conversation was possible.

George waved his arm to two chairs nestled in the corner. "Please make yourself comfortable." Once Abby had sat down, he asked again, "How are Carrie and Janie doing?"

"They're wonderful," Abby assured him. "Though life has changed for both of them."

"How so?"

"Carrie is now the mother of two girls instead of one." George's eyes widened with surprise. "Her name is Minnie."

George's eyes widened further. "Dierdre's daughter?"

It was Abby's turn to be surprised. "You know her?"

George nodded. "Carrie and Anthony had me for dinner a few times while she was doing her surgical internship last year. I met Dierdre then." His eyes narrowed. "What happened to her?"

Abby told him about the night of the fire. "All of them are dead," she said sadly. "If Minnie had been home, instead of with Frances, she would be gone too."

George shook his head. "That poor girl," he murmured. "I know she must be happy on the plantation, though."

"She is," Abby agreed. "She was devastated, but she's healing."

"And Janie?"

Abby settled deeper into the wingback chair as she told him about the clinic, and then the attack that had changed everything. "Janie and Carrie are now partners at the clinic on the plantation. They've both decided it's where they belong." She grinned. "Carrie's father and I couldn't be happier."

George grinned. "That's perfect. The two of them were an amazing team during the war. I'm sure they're even more so now that they've both gone to medical school."

"That's true," Abby agreed.

George's eyes grew moist. "They were so kind to me during the war. I don't know what my life would be like without them."

Abby fixed her eyes on him.

George stiffened. "Did I say something wrong?"

"No," Abby assured him. "I just don't usually see men cry. I believe tears are a wonderful thing, but I don't know many men willing to show that vulnerability."

George stared at her, and then took a deep breath. "You don't know?"

Abby cocked her head. "Know what?"

George stared at her harder. "You *really* don't know?"

Abby raised a brow, slightly alarmed by the intensity of his gaze. "I'm afraid I don't know what you're talking about, Mr. Frasier."

George sat back in his office chair, but he didn't relax.

She could tell he was battling something, but Abby had no idea what. "Is it something you think Carrie or Janie have told me?" she asked carefully.

George took an unsteady breath. "They promised they never would, but it's been a long time," he muttered. "I know how close you all are."

Abby shook her head. "I can assure you that when those two make a promise, they keep it. They haven't told me anything that would qualify as a secret." She pushed down her curiosity. "Since I don't know, there's no reason for you to tell me anything now."

George sat motionless for a moment, until he finally shook his head. "It's getting to be too much," he said quietly.

Abby waited. If he had something he needed to get off his chest, she would listen. She pushed away thoughts that he may be a fugitive from the law. That's not a secret Carrie or Janie would have agreed to keep once he came to work for Cromwell Factories.

"I thought I could go through my whole life with my secret," George said. "Especially since I don't want to change anything." His eyes looked tortured and confused.

"Sometimes, we simply need others to know who we really are," Abby said gently.

George looked at her sharply. "What do you mean?"

Abby took a breath. Evidently, she'd hit a nerve. "I have no idea what I mean," she said honestly, acutely aware she was walking in the dark. "You obviously have a secret. You seem to want to tell someone. I'm more than willing to listen if you want that person to be me, but I truly have no idea what you want to say."

George began to drum his fingers on the desk. "I honestly don't know why I want to tell someone." His voice sounded desperate.

"I've had secrets in my life," Abby said gently. "My experience has been that the bigger they are, the harder they are to keep. They also created the most conflict for me." George's eyes bored into hers. He remained silent, but she sensed he wanted her to continue. "Secrets are powerful. Telling the secret is also powerful, but keeping the secret often seems like the path of least resistance."

George nodded, but still didn't speak.

Abby continued, choosing her words carefully. She was afraid of hitting another nerve that would make him shut down completely. This was not what she'd expected of her day, but she could sense George was in great turmoil. If she could help, she wanted to. "I've seen many people that have been hurt by their secrets. They become so fixed on keeping them that they stop feeling like who they are, and they become dissatisfied with their life." She paused, feeling her way forward.

So far, George's expression said he was still listening to her. "I know many people keep secrets because they're afraid of the consequences if they tell someone."

"Sometimes the consequences are very real," George muttered.

"Being lonely because no one knows who you are is a very real consequence, too," Abby reminded him. "George, you don't have to tell me, but it seems like you want someone to know your secret. I realize telling the truth can be quite scary."

Fear glimmered in George's eyes as he nodded. "I don't want to lose my job," he muttered as he shook his head. "Of all the people to show up when I'm struggling with this... You're the last person I would have chosen."

"Because I own the factory?"

George nodded again, but the look of misery on his face intensified.

"Carrie didn't have a secret to keep this summer, but the attack on the Richmond clinic completely terrified her. She didn't think she could step a foot back into the building, but she felt terrible about abandoning her patients."

"She went back?"

"Yes." Abby still felt a glow of pride as she thought about it.

"How did she do it?"

Abby smiled. "She did the same thing I had to do when I took over my husband's factories. There were many days I was too afraid to even want to get out of bed."

"How did you do it?" George's eyes were bright with intensity.

Abby could feel the longing pulsating from him. "I decided it was alright to feel the fear – as long as I *did* brave." She sighed. "I realized that if I was going to wait until I was no longer afraid, it was never going to happen. *Feel the fear and do brave* became my mantra." She smiled again. "May reminded Carrie of that when the clinic was attacked. It was something I told May when she was afraid one time."

A reluctant smile creased George's face. "Sweet May. She was wonderful to me during the war."

"She's wonderful to everyone," Abby responded before she fell silent. It was up to George whether he wanted to *do brave*.

"May never knew," George began.

Abby smiled encouragement and waited.

"Carrie found out my secret in the hospital. I was supposed to go into surgery, but I couldn't let that happen," George stammered, his face red with emotion. "Everyone would have found out..."

"Found out what?" Abby asked softly. She knew he needed help to push past his fear.

George lifted his head and stared at her for several long moments. "That I'm not a man," he finally blurted out.

Abby's eyes widened. "You're not a man?" She wasn't sure she'd heard George correctly. Her next thought was to wonder how Carrie and Janie had managed to keep a secret like that for so long.

"No," George said quietly. Vulnerability was plastered on his face. "It's a very long story. The short version is that my parents died when I was a child. My brother was all I had. When he enlisted to fight in the war, I enlisted with him. I cut off my hair and dressed like a man."

Now that Abby knew the truth, she could see all the feminine features she had missed before, or had chosen not to acknowledge. "They believed you?"

George shrugged. "They were desperate for recruits. I scrubbed my hands with dirt, made sure my fingernails were dirty, and wiped some on my face. They signed me up. There weren't a lot of girls fighting, but I wasn't the only one. I fought with my brother just like a man." His eyes became pools of regret. "Then Jimmy died in the Battle of the Wilderness. I was shot during the same battle, but I survived. I wished I had died, too, but I got taken to Chimborazo Hospital."

"Which is where you met Carrie."

"Yes. I told her my secret because I knew it would come out if I went into surgery. I had no idea what would happen if the truth was discovered, but I wasn't eager to find out. Carrie took pity on me and brought me back to the house so she could treat me there. I agreed she could tell Janie." He smiled. "Janie taught me how to read. Without her, none of the life I have now would be possible."

Abby struggled to make sense of what she was hearing. "You went back to the war after you got better? Even though your brother had died? Wasn't the war almost over?"

"Yes, but none of us knew it was all about to end. I didn't know what else to do. I didn't want to be a deserter." His eyes darkened. "There was a lot of confusion at the end of the war. When I saw my name on the list as killed in action, I decided I would leave the

South. I moved up North and lived as a man. When I saw Janie here in Philadelphia, I couldn't resist speaking to her. I felt terrible about letting her and Carrie believe I was dead. She told me about this job, and here I am."

Abby's heart squeezed. George had been keeping a massive secret for over ten years. No wonder it was eating him up. "What's your real name?"

George looked down for a long moment and then met her eyes. "Georgia," he said softly. "Are you repulsed?"

"Of course not. Why would I be?" Abby was certainly surprised, but she was more amazed that he'd been able to pass as a man for over a decade.

George stared at her in shock. "You're not?" His voice was ripe with disbelief. "Do you think I should go back to being a woman?" he demanded.

Abby knew that was a question she couldn't pretend to answer. "Is that what you want?"

"No," George said staunchly.

Abby prayed for the right thing to say. "Do you mind me asking why you prefer to live as a man?"

"Because living as a woman in America is too hard," George said promptly. "It's not that I feel like a man. I don't want to be a woman. I like being able to vote. I like not being spoken down to because I'm female. I bought a small house a few months ago. I couldn't have done that as an unmarried woman. I like having all the choices you don't have."

Abby could easily empathize. "I can certainly see why you feel that way." She thought about everything he'd said. "You don't want to live as a woman, but you're lonely."

George nodded, his eyes full of sadness. "It's too risky to trust someone to keep my secret. No one knows who I am."

"I do," Abby reminded him. Even knowing George was really a woman, she still thought of him as a man. That's how she had always known him. Since he had no intention of changing, she saw no reason to look at him any other way. "Carrie and Janie know the truth."

"Yes, but no one I'm around knows who I am."

"And that's important to you?"

George sighed. "Evidently, it must be."

Abby gazed at him, truly noticing the fine bone structure and the feminine hands. "Well, at least now I can understand why you're such an amazing designer of women's clothing," she said lightly.

George chuckled. "It does come rather naturally," he admitted, and then frowned. "I wonder what my life would be like if I was still a woman. Or, if the war hadn't happened?"

"Most of America is asking that last question," Abby said ruefully. "The answer is that none of us can possibly know. George, you made the best decision you knew to make during a dreadful time. That decision has carried you through until now." She paused. "If you ever decide to change your mind, then you'll figure it out. But until that time comes, *if* it comes..." She let her voice trail off.

"Yes?" George leaned forward.

"Will you please help fight for women to have the vote?"

George chuckled and nodded. "You can count on it."

"You can trust me to not tell anyone," she assured him. "As far as I'm concerned, you're George – our factory manager and a very talented clothing designer."

George smiled. "I'm glad I told you. I'm not sure why it makes a difference, but I'm glad."

Abby was glad to see his tension had disappeared, but also knew telling her had not actually changed anything for him. She was going to return to Virginia, where the other two people who knew were, and he would once again be alone. "I'm glad it helped, but..." She searched for the right words.

"But what?"

"I'm leaving," Abby said frankly. "You're going to be alone again, with no one knowing your secret. I'm concerned about how lonely you'll be again."

George frowned. "Probably," he admitted. "It's funny, though... having someone else know who isn't appalled by my choice is a wonderful thing."

Abby laughed. "I imagine there are quite a few women who, if they thought they could pull it off, would do the same thing." She sobered. "There are many women widowed by the war, and many young ladies who won't marry because so many of our men were killed," she said gravely. "They will likely never have a chance to marry again or be married in the first place. The prospect of not having to fight against the constraints our society puts on women would be quite appealing."

George nodded thoughtfully. "I suppose that's true." He looked up as a knock sounded on his door. "I have to take care of this." He stood, but then said, "You may tell Carrie and Janie that you know. They'll be happy that I told someone else." His eyes softened. "Thank you, Mrs. Cromwell."

Abby smiled at him. "Thank you for trusting me with your secret, Mr. Frasier."

George walked to the door and swung it open, revealing an employee with a questioning look. "What can I do for you?"

A quick glance at her pocket watch told Abby it was time to go. Her carriage driver was due to return soon. She touched George's arm lightly as she passed him in the doorway, smiled warmly at the worker, and then left.

She could hardly wait to talk to Carrie and Janie.

Chapter Twenty-One

Marietta stepped from the train onto the Broad Street Station. She held Sarah Rose and Marcus by the hand, one on either side. She took a deep breath to eliminate the discomfort she felt and gave Frances and Minnie a bright smile. "You girls were wonderful. Thank you for helping me with the twins."

Frances and Minnie both stifled a yawn. They'd all gotten up before dawn to make it to the train station on time. Instead of sleeping, however, the girls had both played with the twins and then read to them when Sarah Rose and Marcus got sleepy. When the twins had fallen asleep in their arms, Marietta had urged them to go to sleep themselves, but they had insisted on staying awake in case they were needed. She knew they were exhausted.

"We'll be at your grandparent's home soon," she assured them as she looked around for the River City Carriage that she knew had been dispatched to take them to the Church Hill home.

"I'm hungry," Marcus announced loudly. His blue eyes flashed under his tousled red hair. He'd slept enough on the train to make him wide awake.

"Hungry!" Sarah Rose agreed as her dark eyes took in the bustle of activity on the train platform. Her caramel-colored skin was topped by a mass of black curls that gleamed in the late afternoon sun.

"I see the carriage!" Frances called. She pointed toward the far end of the platform. "That's Smitty! He works for Daddy!"

Marietta breathed a sigh of relief as she waved her hand. The sooner they got off the station platform, the better she would feel. She and Jeremy had moved to Philadelphia because they didn't want the twins to be exposed to the racism so rampant in Richmond toward mulattoes. She'd pushed aside her misgivings to make this trip, but she was still nervous.

"Girls, will you please get the bags?" Marietta knew better than to release her hold on the twins. After a long train ride, and a good nap, they were raring to run and play. They should be at Thomas' house in less than twenty minutes. She was confident she could control them for that long.

Frances and Minnie both grabbed a bag in each hand and headed for the carriage.

"Well... what do we have here?"

Marietta jolted to a stop when a large, burly man stepped in front of her. "Excuse me," she said politely as she fought to control the sudden pounding of her heart.

"Don't bother," the man sneered. His eyes narrowed as he stared at Sarah Rose.

Marietta felt her daughter shrink into her skirts. Fury boiled in her veins. "Can I help you, sir?" She hoped calm speaking would diffuse the situation, but she was so angry she could barely keep her voice from shaking.

"You could have helped the whole world if you hadn't given birth to a nigger baby," the man growled. "Don't you know that half-breeds ain't welcome in our city?" He nodded his head toward the train. "I suggest you get back on that train and go back to wherever you came from."

Frances and Minnie stopped in their tracks and then came back to stand beside her.

"Marietta?" Frances' voice was scared, but her eyes blazed with defiance. She moved to stand closer to Sarah Rose, creating a shield for the little girl.

Marietta's heart warmed at the proof of the girl's bravery. She remembered what Abby had told her about the attack on the medical clinic. "*Courage rising*," she whispered as she lifted her head. "I'm free to go where I wish," she said firmly and loudly. She prayed her bravado would work. She also hoped it would alert someone to the fact that she needed help. A lone woman, with four children; she knew she was in a vulnerable position.

Her bravado failed.

"Oh, you think so?" The man gave an evil chuckle. His lips curled back in a sneer as he reached down with both meaty hands, as if he were going to pluck Sarah Rose from the platform.

"Leave her alone!" Marietta knocked aside the man's arm and stepped in front of all four children to shield them. No one would harm them without first harming her.

She gave a swift glance around the platform. Many people were watching – with a mixture of both sympathy and resentment - but no one made a move to come to her aid. Marietta's heart sank. She was on her own. She was sure Smitty was watching, but having a black man come to her aid would do nothing but inflame the situation. He wouldn't be able to help and would probably end up beaten or killed if he dared to interfere.

Fury erupted in the man's surprised eyes. "Well, ain't you the little spitfire. I guess you come by that red hair real honest." He raised his arm, a menacing look on his face.

Marietta braced herself for what she knew was coming. She refused to let go of the children to block the blow. She prayed desperately that she could protect them.

Suddenly, a tall form materialized behind the man and grabbed his arm. "What's going on here?"

The man whirled around. "Who the devil are you? Take your hands off me!"

Marietta gasped with relief as she realized it was Peter Wilcher gripping the man's arm tightly. She had no idea where he'd come from, but she'd never seen a more welcome sight.

"That's rich. You're ready to strike a lady, and you demand I take my hands off you?" Peter's voice dripped with sarcasm.

"You'll let go if you know what's good for you," the man snarled.

Peter gazed down at him from his height advantage of half a foot and laughed. His eyes narrowed as humor was replaced with fury. "You were about to hit someone I care very much about. I haven't decided yet what I'm going to do with you."

When Marietta saw the man wince, she knew Peter had tightened his grip on their attacker's arm.

"Marietta, go on over to the carriage with the children. I'll be right there," Peter said calmly.

Marietta was worried about leaving him on his own, but she knew she had to get the children to safety.

"Go," Peter urged. "I'll be there in a few minutes."

Marietta hesitated again. What if more people on the platform joined the man and turned on Peter? He couldn't handle all of them. She had no idea what good she would be while trying to protect four children, but how could she just walk away?

"Mama? I'm scared." Sarah Rose's shrill voice rose above the bedlam.

Suddenly, Smitty, obviously emboldened by Peter's arrival, appeared at her side. "Let's go, Mrs. Anthony," he said quietly. "Mr. Wilcher will handle this. He'll be fine."

Marietta turned to him with relief, comforted by the steady assurance in his voice. "Thank you, Smitty."

Frances reached behind her and picked up Marcus. "I've got him."

Marietta scooped Sarah Rose into her arms and started toward the carriage, praying Peter would be alright. She could hear the conversation behind her as they walked away.

"I ain't surprised you're friends with that lady and her half-breed baby. Ain't hard to tell you're from up there in the north. We know what to do with your kind down here, too."

Marietta bit back a smile when the man suddenly yelped. Peter Wilcher was quite strong.

"Leave me alone!" The man's angry voice had turned into a whine.

"I'm going to let you go, simply because I have better things to do with my time," Peter snapped. "If I ever see you attacking another woman, I promise you I won't be so kind."

Marietta reached the carriage, lifted Sarah Rose into Minnie's waiting arms, and then turned to watch.

The man stepped back, his eyes flashing again as he rubbed his arm. "We got ways of getting rid of folks we don't want around here," he said between gritted teeth. He waved the arm that wasn't smarting from Peter's grip. "We got rid of those women who thought they could come to our city and act like doctors!" he boasted.

Peter had started to turn away. He froze in his tracks and turned back to the man. "What did you say?"

The man opened his mouth to respond but must have seen something in Peter's face that made him change his mind. He looked down and shook his head.

Peter took one step and grabbed the man's arm again. "I asked you what you said about the medical clinic." His voice was even, but deadly serious.

The man looked around, but the same people who had ignored his attack on a helpless woman were now ignoring him, as well. His desperation quickly turned to defiance. "Those women ain't got no right to be here. Me and some of the fellas convinced them to move on."

Peter stiffened as his eyes swept the platform. "You're the ones who destroyed the clinic?"

The man hesitated, glanced around again, and nodded. "They had it coming," he insisted. His eyes were still defiant, but his voice had become pleading. "My wife went to one of them. She came home with funny ideas about how *she* could decide if she didn't want to have more children."

"If you're the father, I could certainly understand why she would feel that way," Peter answered in a clipped, biting voice.

"You ain't got no right to say that!" Anger flared in the man's eyes again. "I'm glad we destroyed their clinic!"

"And I'm glad to finally have someone to arrest."

The man whirled around as a deep voice sounded behind him. What he saw made him freeze with fear.

Peter smiled. "Hello, Officer Oxford. It's nice to see you again."

"You too, Mr. Wilcher." The tall broad-shouldered policeman was even taller than Peter. He glared down at the man. "I should let Mr. Wilcher land a punch before I take you away."

Peter smiled again as he shook his head. "I have better things to do, Officer. I'd appreciate it if you just lock him up. While you're doing it, you should apply some pressure to get him to tell you who his friends were that helped him."

"I ain't saying nothing else!" the man protested.

"Suit yourself," Officer Oxford replied, his eyes twinkling with grim humor. "I don't have a problem with you taking the blame for all of it. It'll keep you in jail longer. I believe all of Richmond will thank me for that."

The man's eyes widened with fear before they narrowed. He spun around to stare at Peter. "Why do you care about the clinic, anyway, Yankee Man?"

Peter stepped closer, towering over the smaller man. "One of those doctors you say you ran out of town, is about to become my wife."

Marietta was still shaken when they got to the Church Hill house. She'd been nervous the whole way; constantly watching to see if someone would accost them because of Sarah Rose. Peter's presence had done little to assuage her anxiety. Sarah Rose clung to her, while Marcus stayed pressed to her side, his eyes wide with fright.

Frances and Minnie looked nervous, as well, though their eyes brightened when they pulled to a stop in front of the house.

"It's about time y'all got here!"

The twins came to life when May's voice rang out through the still air. "May!" they cried in unison as they scrambled to the side of the carriage.

Peter jumped down from the driver's seat where he had perched next to Smitty, and swung them down.

Laughing, the twins ran into May's arms. Marietta breathed a sigh of relief when they disappeared into the house. She would let them play in the backyard, but she was going to keep them off the streets until they left for the plantation early the next morning. If she planned it correctly, her daughter would be sleeping soundly on her lap as they left the city.

Frances appeared at her side. "Why did that man try to hurt Sarah Rose?" Her brown eyes were deeply troubled.

Marietta sighed again. How could she explain something she found impossible to understand? "Some people are terribly ignorant, Frances." She searched for more to say but came up blank.

"But who could want to hurt a beautiful little girl?" Frances asked again. "I don't understand."

Peter walked over, both hands full of luggage. "There are ignorant people who only see color, Frances."

"But she's not even all black," Frances protested. "Shouldn't that make things easier for her?"

"No," Marietta said bluntly, and then softened her voice as she attempted to explain. "When some people see a person of mixed-race, they believe it makes them look bad." As far as explanations went, she knew it was weak.

"Why?" Frances' eyes were full of confusion.

Marietta searched for words. If Frances was going to help her with the twins, she should have some degree of understanding. Gazing at the girl who was quickly becoming a young lady, she decided she was old enough to hear more of the truth. "When people see Sarah Rose, they believe she has a black father. Even though Jeremy has blond hair and blue eyes, his mother was black. We knew there was a chance we would have a baby who came out looking more black than white." She took a breath as she considered what to say next.

"Which is why you moved to Philadelphia," Frances said. "I heard Mama talking about it to Annie one day when she was real sad about the twins being gone."

"That's right," Marietta agreed, and then answered what she knew the next question would be. "White men get very angry when they know a white woman has a child with a black man. It makes them feel like they're less of a man for some reason."

Frances cocked her head as she considered the answer. "That's dumb," she said flatly.

Marietta managed a tight smile that faded quickly. "I couldn't agree more. I hoped it wouldn't be dangerous to bring Sarah Rose to Richmond. I was wrong." She was going to the plantation tomorrow as planned, but she knew she wouldn't return to the South again. Never again would she submit her precious daughter to treatment like that. She wasn't naïve enough to believe it couldn't happen in the North, but there was much less of a chance.

"Let's go inside," she said quickly. She didn't have the energy to answer more questions now. At some point Frances would ask whether Marcus was part black too. She knew she wouldn't be able to explain the law that said even one drop of black blood made a person black in America. As far as the law was concerned, both her caramel-skinned daughter *and* her red-haired, pale-skinned son were black. As was her husband.

Frances frowned. "But..."

"Anybody want some of this cherry cobbler I'm pulling out of the oven?" May's voice floated from the window.

"Let's go," Marietta said, grateful for the escape being offered her. "We don't want to miss May's cobbler!" She turned and started up the walkway. She hoped a good night's sleep would enable her to answer the questions she knew would come her way on the long ride out to the plantation.

Elizabeth hurried to finish her notes on the patients she'd seen that day. The clinic would close in a week, but ingrained training made it impossible to not complete them. When she heard the front door open, she frowned. She wasn't worried for her safety because she knew Oscar was there to protect her – she was simply too tired to see another patient. All she wanted was to go home, have one of May's excellent meals, and go to bed. Peter was arriving the next day, so she wanted to be rested.

She lifted her head when footsteps neared her office. Her pulse quickened. Where was Oscar? Why hadn't she heard his voice? She hated the instant panic that swelled through her.

"Are you going to work all night?"

Elizabeth squealed with delight when her fiancé's head poked through her doorway. "Peter! What are you doing here?" She leapt up and flung her arms around him, luxuriating in the feel of his solid warmth as her panic melted away.

Oscar appeared behind them. "I hope you weren't too scared, Dr. Gilbert. Mr. Wilcher convinced me to let him surprise you."

"I'm fine," Elizabeth assured him with a laugh, relieved when it didn't come out shaky. She turned back to Peter. "You're not supposed to arrive until tomorrow."

Peter grinned. "I finished the article I was working on early. As soon as my editor gave his approval, I caught the next train. I can't stand being away from you."

Elizabeth blushed with pleasure. She'd never dreamed she could feel like a schoolgirl with a crush, but that was the only way to explain what she was feeling. "I'm glad you're here," she murmured. "I missed you." She had a sudden thought. "Are you able to stay until I leave for Boston? Will you still be able to come with me?"

"You think I would leave early, and miss the chance to meet your parents? Not a chance," Peter assured her. "My editor did tell me he's never seen me take so much time off, but he also said I had more than earned it over the last few years. I told him I had the best reason in the world to take time off, and that as soon as possible, I was going to marry you."

Elizabeth sighed with happiness and snuggled her head into his chest. All thoughts of note taking fled her mind.

Elizabeth strolled beside Peter, her hand tucked through his arm as they walked home. The sultry heat was almost more than she could bear. She kept her mind on the fact that very soon she would be breathing in cool, salty air in Boston. She and Peter hadn't decided where they would live yet, but she was going home to spend time with her family before the wedding that her mother was already busy planning.

"Marietta had a hard day," Peter said.

"Marietta?" Elizabeth slapped a hand to her forehead. "That's right. I forgot she was coming today with Frances, Minnie and the twins. Is everything alright?"

"It is now," Peter said grimly.

Elizabeth listened as he told her what had happened. "That's awful," she cried when he finished. "Thank goodness you were there." She shuddered to think what could have happened if Peter's train hadn't arrived at the station when it did.

"There's more."

Elizabeth took a deep breath. She could tell by Peter's tone of voice that she wasn't going to like whatever he had to say. "I'm listening," she said quietly.

"The man who threatened Marietta and her children was one of the men who destroyed the clinic."

Elizabeth stiffened, froze in her tracks, and stared up at him. "You're certain?"

"He was boasting about it," Peter said angrily. "He said his wife was a patient of yours. He didn't like the ideas she had about deciding not to have more children."

Elizabeth's mind whirled. For that moment, it was as if she was walking into the destruction of the clinic all over again. Her heart pounded harder as she struggled for breath.

"Elizabeth?" Peter took her shoulders and pulled her close. "I've got you. Breathe. Everything is fine. It's all over." He stroked her hair while he murmured the words in her ears. "Breathe."

Elizabeth endeavored to follow his instructions. She focused on the feeling of his strong arms holding her close. She listened to the beat of his heart beneath her ear. Slowly, she relaxed. When she stepped back, she had regained control. "I'm sorry."

"Don't apologize," Peter said firmly. "I understand completely."

Elizabeth cocked her head. "You do?"

Peter nodded. "I've covered horrible stories that I would do anything to forget. I think I've put it behind me, and then something will happen to bring it all back to life in my mind. It's as if I'm right back in the thick of what happened."

"Yes," Elizabeth agreed, continuing to take deep breaths to maintain control. "What did you do when he told you?"

Peter smiled slightly. "Helped send him to jail."

Elizabeth gasped. "He's in jail?"

"He is. Officer Oxford just happened to be on the station platform when the man was boasting about what he'd done. Marietta and the children were already safe, so I motioned for Officer Oxford to come over and then goaded the man into saying more about it. Oxford heard him confess and hauled him off to jail. I imagine by now he's given the names of the men who helped him. He seemed less than eager to take all the blame for the attack."

Elizabeth felt a surge of relief, but the regret that followed swallowed all of it.

"What's wrong?" Peter asked quietly.

Elizabeth shook her head. "All of it is such a waste, Peter. We came down here to do a good thing. Men like him made it impossible." She blinked back hot tears. "And Marietta. She's such a wonderful person, with two adorable children. I hate that they have to be afraid because of how people perceive Sarah Rose." She scowled. "I wonder if this is the last time she'll bring her children to the plantation? Who could blame her? Everyone there who loves the twins will suffer because of what that man did."

"I suspect you're right," he said heavily. "If I was Marietta, I doubt I would risk Sarah Rose's safety again."

Elizabeth looked around her. Even on a hot, humid evening, Richmond was beautiful. Trees created canopies over the road, creating the effect of a leafy tunnel. Flower boxes hung from almost every window, while huge banks of roses seemed to cover every white picket fence. "It's sad," she said slowly. "How can so much hatred and fear exist in such a beautiful city?" She gazed at Peter. "What's going to happen down here?"

"I don't know," Peter admitted. "I keep thinking things will change..." His voice was grim. "Something to prove four years of war was worth it – that the South will change how they treat people." He shook his head.

"There's still so much anger and resentment. There's still so much fear. The North thought that if they just won the war, everything would be better. It was a short-sighted belief. Reconstruction was supposed to be about rebuilding the South, and also the country. I don't see it happening." He looked at Elizabeth sadly. "I predict the ramifications of the war will be felt for a very long time – far beyond our generation."

Elizabeth and Peter climbed the stairs to the porch just as May walked out.

"Hello, Miss Elizabeth. I reckon I know what put that wide smile on your face."

Elizabeth grinned at her. "You would be completely correct, May." Her grin faded. "Where is Marietta?"

May's smile disappeared, as well. "Miss Marietta's out back with those two precious babies. The twins wanted to come sit on the front porch so they's could drink some of my lemonade while they watched people go by, but she ain't gonna let them."

"Who can blame her?" Elizabeth muttered. "I'm going out back to check on her."

"You do that," May replied. "We got one more person coming before dinner gonna be ready."

Elizabeth stopped, her hand on the door as she turned back. "I didn't know we were expecting anyone else."

May shook her head. "She weren't supposed to be coming in until next week. Miss Hazel Rollins seems to be in a hurry to get out to the plantation. We got a telegram a while ago that said she was coming in on the evening train."

"The new schoolteacher for the plantation?" Elizabeth asked. "That's wonderful! I know Rose and Phoebe are eager to have her out there."

"That's what I hear," May said. "Mr. Peter, could you go over and have one of those River City Carriage drivers go get her? My Spencer ain't back from work yet, so I can't send him."

"I'll do better than that," Peter replied promptly. "I'll go with the driver to meet her."

May put her fist on her hip, cocked her head, and looked at him with knowing eyes. "You scared you started up some bad feelings toward black folk down at the train station?"

Elizabeth tensed as she considered May's statement. Peter hadn't waited around to see how people would respond to Officer Oxford hauling that man off to jail. If they felt he'd been treated unfairly, they could retaliate against blacks.

Peter hesitated for a long moment and then shrugged. "Let's just say I believe in the power of caution." He smiled slightly. "I don't want Hazel's first impression to be a poor one."

"Do you want me to come with you?" Elizabeth asked.

"No. You go play with Marietta and the children." He glanced at his pocket watch. "I've got just enough time to get there and meet the train." He leaned down and kissed her lightly. "Promise you won't eat the rest of the cherry cobbler."

Elizabeth peered up at him. "I never make a promise I'm not sure I can keep." Laughing, she opened the door and entered the house.

Peter's sputter of outrage followed her.

Hazel Rollins stepped down from the train and shifted her baggage, glad she had only one to deal with. On the one hand, it was appalling that she had so little clothing; on the other hand, she was grateful to not have to haul bags through Richmond. She'd had a telegram sent, but since she was a full week early, there was no reason to think her train would be met. She hoped she could figure out how to get to Thomas Cromwell's house. She also hoped they would have a room for her.

Impatiently, she pushed aside doubts about the wisdom of her impulsive decision to arrive a week early with so little notice. She was in Richmond. It was too late to change anything now.

Hazel pushed back the hair that had escaped her tight bun and brushed at her wrinkled dress. She knew she looked disheveled, but so did every other passenger who had started on this trip with her from Ohio. Hunger and exhaustion gnawed at her, but she took a deep breath and tried to ignore them. The letter from Phoebe hadn't told her how far it was to the Cromwell home because there had been the promise of a carriage, but the paper in her pocket did hold an address. She would find it.

The late afternoon air still held the famous Southern heat, but she knew the encroaching darkness would convert it into a comforting blanket. It had been years since she'd breathed in sultry humidity like this. She pushed aside uncomfortable memories of her years of picking cotton on the Georgia plantation she had escaped from during the first year of the war. Her parents had heard about a little town in Ohio called Oberlin. They were told it offered hope and education. It had taken four months to make it there on the Underground Railroad, but everything they'd been told had been true. Oberlin had been a refuge for them. They didn't make a lot of money, but they were free. That was worth more than anything.

Hazel looked around for someone to ask directions. A carriage with a black driver was just pulling up to the station. Her better sense told her to not ask a white person how to get to a white section of town. She hurried over to the carriage, waiting until a white man stepped down before she spoke to the driver. "Excuse me," she began politely. "I'm hoping you can help me with directions to a house."

"I'll try," the driver responded. "Where you be going?"

Hazel gave him the address. "It's up on Church Hill."

The white man who had disembarked the carriage turned around when he heard her speak. "Excuse me. I couldn't help overhearing you. Are you Hazel Rollins?"

Hazel gaped at him, and then found her voice. "Yes."

The man smiled. "I'm Peter Wilcher. I'm a good friend of the Cromwells." He nodded to the driver. "This is Smitty. We've been sent to pick you up."

Hazel smiled with relief. "I was expecting to walk to the house. This is a wonderful surprise."

Peter reached for her bag and then deposited it in the back of the carriage. "It helps that Thomas Cromwell's son-in-law owns the finest carriage company in Richmond. Your telegram arrived just in time. May sent me down to pick you up."

"May?"

"May pretends to be the housekeeper and cook, but in actuality, she runs everything at the house."

Hazel grinned, taking an immediate liking to the friendly man. "She sounds like my kind of woman." Lifting her skirts, she climbed nimbly into the carriage.

Chapter Twenty-Two

Hazel drew in deep breaths of the early morning air as the wagon left the city limits. Not an early riser, she'd been less than thrilled when she'd been informed they would leave an hour before dawn. Now she was more than glad. "It's beautiful," she whispered.

Marietta nudged her. "I told you it would be worth it."

Hazel nodded silently, feeling a touch of awe as the first rays of the sun, still tucked beneath the horizon, shot streaks of gold into the purplish-blue morning sky. Banks of trees bordered both sides of the hard-packed road. Hordes of birds sang to the dawn and flitted through the trees. "I'm glad to be out of the city," she murmured.

Marietta glanced at the floor of the wagon. Lined with thick layers of blankets, it cradled Frances, Minnie, Sarah Rose and Marcus, sleeping soundly in spite of the jostling. "Me too," she said quietly.

Hazel understood. She'd heard enough of the story the night before over dinner to understand how terrified Marietta must have been at the train station. She'd also understood why Marietta was so insistent they leave the city before the sun rose. The two women, bonded by their mutual love for teaching, had become instant friends.

"It will take about three more hours to reach the plantation," Marietta said.

"It's beautiful," Hazel said sincerely. "I don't mind. We'll also get there before the worst of the day's heat. It was worth getting up so early."

Peter looked over his shoulder from his position on the driver's seat. "Is anyone hungry?" he asked hopefully.

"I am," Elizabeth called back as she reached for the large picnic hamper behind the wagon seat. "I saw May put the ham and fried chicken biscuits in the basket right before we left. I'm sure they're still hot."

Hazel shook her head. "Did she get any sleep at all?"

"Probably not," Marietta replied. "When I asked her about it, she told me she could sleep when she was lonely in an empty house again."

Elizabeth chuckled. "I hope I have half her energy when I'm her age. Despite her talk, I promise you that she won't sleep until tonight. She'll spend the day cleaning the few specks of dirt we left. She'll also have Micah and Spencer harvest whatever is ready in the garden. She laid out dozens of jars last night for canning. I swear, the woman never rests." She pulled out mound after mound of biscuits wrapped in heavy cloths. As she opened them, the steam lifted into the morning air.

Peter moaned and held out a hand, a pleading look in his eyes. "This starving man needs one of those biscuits."

Elizabeth cocked her head. "I suppose driving the wagon qualifies you for the first biscuit. Chicken or ham?"

"I'll start with chicken. And then move on to ham ... before coming back to chicken."

Elizabeth pulled the biscuit out of reach of his grasping hand. "Are you planning on the rest of us eating?"

Peter snorted. "You know as well as I do, that May put enough biscuits in there for an army. I can eat my fill, and we'll still have leftovers." He grinned. "She wants to prove to Annie that she's not the only one who can send more food than is needed."

Elizabeth grinned. "You could be right about that."

Peter snatched the biscuit from her hand before she could retract it again and took a big bite. "Oh..."

Hazel laughed as she watched them. She eagerly accepted the biscuit Elizabeth handed her. She took a bite and moaned.

"See?" Peter mumbled around his mouthful. "You can't eat these without moaning in ecstasy." He raised a brow at Elizabeth. "You know, we've never talked about your cooking skills, fiancée of mine."

Elizabeth raised a brow right back at him. "There's good reason for that, Peter. I can't cook a thing."

Peter looked shocked and held a hand to his chest. "What?"

"I don't cook," Elizabeth repeated. "My mother never taught me how to because she knew all I wanted was to be in my father's medical office. Since then, even during medical school, I lived with women who liked to cook. Here in Richmond, I had May."

"How are you planning on feeding me?" Peter demanded.

Elizabeth gazed at him calmly. "I believe the better question, since you're the one who asked me to marry you, is how you plan on feeding *me*?"

Peter chuckled. "My cooking skills are somewhat limited, as well," he admitted. "I suppose it's a good thing I make enough money to hire a cook."

"It is indeed a good thing," Elizabeth agreed. "I was beginning to reconsider your proposal."

Hazel laughed, enjoying the banter between the two of them. She leaned closer to Marietta. "Do you cook?"

"I do now," Marietta replied. "I was hopeless in the kitchen until Annie agreed to teach me."

Hazel scrolled through her memory to remember what Phoebe had told her in letters about everyone. "Annie is Moses' mother? Rose's mother-in-law?"

"That's right. Annie is a force to be reckoned with. She runs her kitchen like an army commander. Everyone thought she would kick me out, but I guess she took pity on me. Either that, or she felt sorry for the twins having me as a mother. She was probably afraid I would starve them. I'll never be as good a cook as she is, but my family doesn't go hungry," Marietta finished with a grin.

Hazel laughed and then turned; her attention drawn by the sun breaking loose from the horizon. She lifted her face and inhaled the aroma of fresh dirt and green plants. "I didn't think I'd missed it," she murmured.

"The South?" Elizabeth asked.

"The smell of dirt and growing things," Hazel clarified. "I started picking cotton in Georgia when I was six. I picked every day, sunup to sundown, until my family left when I was twelve. I don't miss picking cotton, but evidently I miss the smell of good dirt."

Marietta gazed at her. "What was it like when your family escaped?"

Hazel shrugged. "It was more like leaving. When the war started, the owner of the plantation and all his sons, left to fight. Not too long after, even though the mistress of the plantation objected, the overseer got called away to fight as well. I overheard the conversation when some men came to tell him he had to enlist. She insisted she couldn't live on the plantation alone with her daughter and all the slaves, but they told her if men didn't fight, she wouldn't have a plantation or slaves, at all."

She paused, remembering. A flock of bobwhite quail burst from the overgrowth beside the road, the sun glistening off the male's brown and chestnut feathers. She admired them for a moment before continuing her story. "Anyway, my daddy had wanted to escape before the war, ever since he heard of the Underground Railroad. By the time a conductor came through, that first year of the war, there was no one to stop the slaves from doing anything. He set up a time for us to meet him late one night. Pretty much all of us just packed up and left."

"Was the escape scary?" Elizabeth asked.

"Not so much scary, as long," Hazel answered. "The Underground Railroad worked well. The biggest danger was managing to avoid any troops that were in the area we were traveling through. Sometimes we had to stay in hiding for a couple of weeks before we could keep going, but we always had a barn to sleep in and we always had food. I was so excited to be leaving the cotton fields that I didn't mind what we had to deal with to do it."

"Did you like Oberlin?" Peter asked.

"I love Oberlin," Hazel corrected. "There was already a community of escaped slaves there. It was less than a year after we arrived that the Emancipation Proclamation happened. There was a lot of celebration the day we found out about it." She smiled. "I was already in school, learning as fast as I could."

"Did you always know you wanted to come back to the South to teach?" Marietta asked.

Hazel shook her head firmly. "No. When I first reached Oberlin, I swore I would never come back to the South."

"What changed your mind?" Elizabeth asked curiously.

"Rose Samuels." Hazel took a deep breath. "When Phoebe returned from teaching with her last winter, all she could do was talk about what an amazing teacher Rose was. She went on nonstop about the school, and what miracles were happening with the mixture of black and white students." She shook her head. "I'd experienced that in Oberlin, but I couldn't believe there was a school like that near Richmond, Virginia. I asked a million questions. Eventually, I made the decision to return. I knew I wanted to help the freed slaves like Rose and Phoebe are doing."

"Not to mention the horses," Elizabeth said playfully. "Phoebe told us how much you love them."

Hazel laughed. "That was a definite pull," she admitted. "I've loved horses my whole life. I used to watch everything that happened with the horses on the plantation where I grew up. I spent far too much time hiding in the hay loft so I could watch what the stable hands did, but I was desperate to learn. If they'd ever caught me, I'd have been whipped, but I didn't care. Anyway, the place where my family lives in Oberlin has horses. I learned how to ride right after I got there. One of the daughters taught me everything she knew once she realized how much I wanted to learn. When Phoebe told me about Cromwell Stables, I was sure this was a match made in heaven."

Just then, Frances sat up. She yawned, stretched and then rubbed her eyes. She looked at Hazel. "My mama owns Cromwell Stables. Her and Susan."

"Not your daddy?" Hazel asked.

"No," Frances assured her. "Just my mama and Susan. They owned it before my daddy met mama. Mama's first husband started the stables before he got murdered by the KKK."

Hazel stiffened, alarmed despite the girl's matter-of-fact tone. "I see…" she murmured.

Frances moved on, oblivious to her reaction. "You're going to love all the horses. My horse is a palomino named Peaches. She's the best horse on the plantation."

Hazel nodded. She appreciated anyone's loyalty to their horse, but she couldn't stop her mind from racing as she thought about the revelation of a KKK murder on the plantation.

Marietta leaned closer to her. "I'll tell you all about it later," she whispered.

Hazel nodded, trying to tamp down her fear. It's not that she wasn't aware of the danger of the KKK and other vigilante groups, if she was to move to the South, but for some reason she'd assumed she would be safe on the plantation.

Over the next few minutes, the rest of the children woke and began clamoring for breakfast.

While Marietta focused on feeding them, Elizabeth moved over to sit beside her. "You don't need to worry," she said quietly.

Hazel realized her expressive face must have given her away. "Are you certain?"

Elizabeth nodded. "Everyone is very cautious on the plantation. There are men who stand guard twenty-four hours a day. All of them are veterans, which means they're excellent shots. The KKK has made some attempts but have never gotten past the front gate." Her voice sharpened. "They lost several of their men during the last attempt. I suspect they've decided any further efforts would be futile."

Hazel tried to steady her heartbeat. "Where is the school?" She seemed to remember Phoebe saying it was on the outskirts of the plantation.

"Always under guard," Elizabeth said firmly. "Nothing has happened in several years."

Phoebe had assured her she would be safe, but Hazel knew what could happen to lone black women in the South. The abolition of slavery didn't mean she would be safe. Life as a slave on the plantation had been difficult, but at least no one had ever hurt her. "Where will I live?" she asked, surprised her voice was steady.

Elizabeth smiled. "That's going to be a surprise, but I promise you that you'll be safe. It was the whole reason for what they're doing."

Hazel opened her mouth to ask more, but closed it when Elizabeth shook her head.

"I'm not going to say another word. You're going to have to trust me."

Hazel nodded, taking comfort in the confident shine in Elizabeth's eyes.

"There are several biscuits left," Marietta called. Her eyes widened as she reached into the basket and pulled something out. "What's this?" She quickly unfolded the large towel.

"Cinnamon rolls!" Minnie cried. Her face was flushed with triumph. "It worked!"

Marietta stared at her. "What worked?"

"I told May that Annie always sends us to Richmond with cinnamon rolls."

"Why would you do that?" Marietta demanded.

Minnie shrugged, her eyes dancing with delight. "Last night, I overheard you telling Hazel that May always competes with Annie to send us on our trip with the best food. I figured if I told her that Annie always sends us cinnamon rolls, that she would too!"

Hazel, despite the stern look on Marietta's face, couldn't stop the laugh that escaped her lips. "You're a smart little girl," she said admiringly. She reached for one of the cinnamon rolls and took a bite. "Thank you," she mumbled as the sweet cinnamon flavor exploded in her mouth.

"You're welcome," Minnie said sweetly, and then grinned at Marietta.

Marietta joined in the laughter and reached for her own cinnamon roll. "Thank you, Minnie. But," she added, "you really shouldn't manipulate people."

"I wasn't," Minnie assured her. "Mama told me there are ways you can help people make a good decision by saying the right thing. That's what I was doing!"

Laughter lifted into the air as they continued to roll down the road.

Hazel had been craning forward on the wagon seat since they had turned between the brick pillars onto Cromwell Plantation. The road in front of her seemed never ending as it followed curve after curve through the woods. She had been holding her breath around every curve, but the only thing she saw was another looming curve.

Marietta read her mind. "The drive is almost two miles long."

Hazel's eyes widened. "Phoebe told me Cromwell Plantation was quite large, but I had no idea it was *this* large."

Marietta smiled. "I'd never seen a southern plantation until my first here here. I came down from Philadelphia to teach school in Richmond in the Black Quarters. That's how I met Jeremy. When he brought me out here, I couldn't believe a place like this existed. It's become even more beautiful over the years. The tobacco fields have expanded, and Abby told me the horse pastures have expanded, as well. Everyone works hard to keep it beautiful."

Hazel thought about what Phoebe had told her. "Is it true that all the men who originally came to work here after the war got land to build houses on, and that they receive a percentage of the crop profits – in addition to what they're paid?"

"Yes," Marietta assured her. "Twelve of the families were given one hundred acres each. But it's not just the original workers who earn a percentage of the profits. Everyone who works here receives a percentage. Cromwell Factories works the same way in regard to a percentage of the profits. Besides being the right thing to do, it assures that everyone works hard. The more successful the business is, the more money everyone makes."

"That's wonderful!" Hazel said enthusiastically. "Every business should work that way."

"They should," Frances said hotly, "but they certainly don't. Most business owners are too greedy to do anything more than work their employees to death."

Hazel gaped at the young girl.

Marietta read her mind again. "Frances and Minnie met when Minnie was horribly injured in a factory accident. Frances helped Carrie treat her at the clinic in Philadelphia. When Minnie's mother came to work for Carrie as their cook, the two girls became fast friends. It also opened the door to Frances meeting more of the children who work in the factories. Frances has written several articles for the *Philadelphia Tribune* about child labor practices."

Hazel shook her head. "This family is full of surprises," she murmured. She opened her mouth to say more, but lost all ability to speak when they rounded the curve.

"We're home!" Frances and Minnie yelled at the same time.

"Home!" the twins cried as they clapped their hands with excitement.

Hazel leaned forward and feasted her eyes on the emerald green pastures rolling out in front of them. Horses were everywhere. She gasped with delight as colts and fillies frolicked beside their mothers, and then broke away to leap together playfully. "Oh my..."

"It's something, isn't it?" Marietta asked.

"I have no... words," Hazel stammered. "I've never seen anything so... beautiful in my entire life." She felt as if she'd been snatched out of her real life and dumped into a fairytale that had no basis in reality. "Is this real?"

"Of course it is," Minnie cried.

Frances jumped up, held on to the side of the wagon with one hand, and pointed toward a horse glowing golden in the sunlight. "That's my Peaches!"

Peaches, hearing her name, raised her head and whinnied loudly.

Hazel shook her head, her thoughts whirling as she absorbed the beauty. She knew there was a surprise waiting for her in regard to a place to live, but at this point she would be willing to sleep in a stall. She was excited to teach at the school, but the horses completely took her breath away.

She took a deep breath, forcing air into her lungs. When she turned her head, her breath escaped in another whoosh. "Oh my..." Hazel knew she was repeating herself, but she was incapable of coming up with different words.

"I know," Marietta agreed.

"I felt the same way," Elizabeth said.

"Cromwell Plantation takes everyone's breath away," Peter added. "We completely understand."

Hazel forgot the horses for a few minutes as her eyes took in the three-story white home gleaming in the sunshine. Huge round pillars supported the sprawling porch lined with rocking chairs. Towering oak trees spread branches that provided welcoming shade. The circular drive was lined with neatly trimmed boxwoods, and the white oyster shell drive gleamed almost as brightly as the house.

"It's not like the plantation you grew up on?" Marietta guessed.

"Not at all," Hazel responded, her eyes still devouring the beauty of the house. "As far as plantations go, I imagine it was quite small. There were only ten slaves." She shook her head. "The house looked like a rustic cabin compared to this one."

"Mama!" Frances cried.

Hazel saw several people step out onto the porch. She took a deep breath. Marietta, Elizabeth and Peter had been very understanding about her decision to arrive early, but since they were not her bosses, and she wasn't going to be living in their home, their opinion didn't really matter. Her arrival at Cromwell Plantation was going to be a complete surprise.

Hazel watched as a slim woman, dressed in casual breeches ran down the steps. Her black hair, pulled into a loose braid, bounced against her back.

"Frances! Minnie! I'm so glad you're home. Daddy and I missed you."

Hazel realized this was the Dr. Carrie Wallington she'd heard so much about. She loved the excited shine in her eyes and the obvious love she saw on her face for her daughters.

"Where are my niece and nephew?" A musical voice rose on the air as a lovely black woman ran down the stairs and rushed toward the wagon.

Hazel smiled. *Rose Samuels.*

Rose ran up to the wagon and peered over the edge. "Marcus? Sarah Rose? Where are you?"

The twins giggled.

"We're right here, Auntie Rose," Sarah Rose answered.

Rose looked at them but shook her head and kept peering around the wagon. "I'm looking for two very small children named Marcus and Sarah Rose. Do you know where they are?"

"We're right here, Auntie Rose!" Marcus jumped up and down in the wagon and waved his arms.

Rose stepped back, a shocked expression on her face. Her voice dropped to a whisper. "Is it really you? I was looking for two very small children. You two are so big," she said dramatically. She stepped close to the wagon again and peered at them. "It's really you? I hardly recognized you."

"It's me," Sarah Rose promised. She jumped forward and held up her arms to be lifted from the wagon.

Rose laughed with delight, scooped her up and swung her around in the air before she putting her on the ground and reaching back for Marcus. "You're *huge*!" she cried as she swung him through the air.

Suddenly, a giant of a man strode around the back of the house.

The twins saw him the same time Hazel did. "Uncle Moses!" Their chubby legs churned madly as they dashed toward him.

Moses laughed, dropped down on one knee and wrapped them in a hug that easily engulfed both of them. "It's about time you got here!" He dropped his voice to a dramatic whisper. "You do know the fireflies are putting on a special show for you tonight, don't you?"

Sarah Rose squealed and clapped her hands. "Fireflies! Fireflies!"

"Do I hear my baby's voices out here?"

Hazel's head swiveled to watch the next reunion. As a gray-haired stout woman with a lined face and kind eyes pushed through the front door, the twin's heads whipped around. They pulled away from Moses and ran up the stairs as fast as their little legs would allow, and launched themselves at the woman.

"Annie! Annie!"

Hazel smiled. So that was the inimitable Annie. She may be the commander of her kitchen, but she was obviously mush as far as the twins were concerned.

Annie pulled the children into a warm embrace, her face glowing with joy. "It's about time you two got back down here where you belong," she said loudly. "I done missed you like crazy!" She stood and took each twin by the hand. "I bet you're ready for some of my molasses cookies and milk, aren't you?"

"Yes! Yes!" the twins shouted in unison.

Hazel smiled. The twins seemed to do almost everything in unison. Looking over at Marietta, she saw the sadness filling her eyes, despite the smile on her face. Hazel knew that her new friend was thinking about her decision to never bring the twins back to the plantation. It was easy to imagine the heartache Marietta was feeling. She also knew all the people on the plantation who loved them, were going to be heartbroken.

So far, no one had noticed her in the chaos. Hazel was glad because it gave her a chance to watch all of them without anyone realizing she was there. She looked over at Carrie and her daughters. The girls were talking and laughing, waving their hands as they told her a story.

Carrie laughed loudly, kissed both of them soundly on their cheeks, and then turned back to the wagon. "Marietta. Welcome! Peter. Elizabeth. I'm so glad you're here." Her eyes rested on Hazel and widened slightly. "I'm sorry," she said warmly. "I didn't realize we had another guest. The children seem to take all our energy when they first arrive." She walked closer to the wagon. "I'm Carrie Wallington. Whom do I have the pleasure of meeting?"

Just then the screen door on the porch slapped open again.

"Hazel!" Phoebe's loud cry made everyone turn their heads to stare at her. "Hazel? What are you doing here?"

Now that she was the center of attention, Hazel smiled at everyone and waved a hand. "I couldn't wait any longer to experience Cromwell Plantation for myself. I hope it's not a terrible imposition for me to arrive without notice."

Phoebe ran down the stairs, waited for Hazel to step down from the wagon, and then swept her into a hug. "I'm so happy to see you!" Keeping one arm around her waist, Phoebe turned. "Everyone, this is Hazel Rollins!"

Carrie reached forward to take her hand. "Welcome to Cromwell Plantation, Hazel. We've heard wonderful things about you."

Rose rushed forward and swept her into a hug. "I've heard so much about you that I feel I know you," she said warmly. "I'm glad you came early. We've all been so eager to meet you!"

Hazel sighed with relief. "I'm glad it's not a terrible imposition." All worry melted away as she gazed at the welcoming smiles all around her.

"Imposition?" Rose asked with a laugh. "You have no idea how much work we have to do to get both schools ready before classes start again. I predict you'll regret coming early."

"Not a chance," Hazel responded, knowing she meant it from the bottom of her heart. It had been hard to leave her warm, loving family, but knowing she'd stepped right into the midst of another one confirmed she was in the right place.

Hazel leaned back against her chair. "Do you eat like this every day?" she asked with a groan. "I'm stuffed."

Carrie laughed. "As little as you are, I don't imagine it takes a lot of food to be stuffed."

Hazel smiled. "You'd be amazed how much I can pack into this five-foot frame."

Phoebe nodded. "She may be little, but don't underestimate her. She's tougher than a lot of men I know."

Carrie eyed her. "I hear you love horses."

"As much as I love children," Hazel responded. She let her eyes drift toward the window. She had spent much of the meal gazing at the activity around the barn. She'd seen a number of horses being led in and out, each of them seemingly more beautiful than the one before.

"Would you like to go for a ride?" Carrie asked.

Hazel gasped. "Really?" Then she shook her head and glanced at Phoebe and Rose. Going for a ride on her first day would hardly make a good first impression. "Thank you, but I'm sure we have work to do. May I take you up on your offer another time?" She tried to keep the disappointment from her voice, but the laughter in Phoebe's eyes told her she'd failed.

Rose chuckled, confirming she'd heard it too. "We're going to work hard in the days to come, but we don't have slaves on Cromwell Plantation anymore. Your being here is a godsend to us. We want you to feel like family. There will be no work today. I'm going to spend every moment I can playing with Marcus and Sarah Rose. You should go for a ride."

"Before she sees the surprise?" Elizabeth demanded. "Is it ready to be seen yet?"

Frances nodded her head vigorously. "Daddy took me over to see it. I can't believe all that happened in the two weeks we've been gone." She bounced up and down in her seat.

Hazel knew whatever they were talking about was the secret Elizabeth had alluded to. Despite her eagerness to ride, her curiosity was piqued. She turned to look at Phoebe and looked at her quizzically.

Phoebe lifted her hands. "There wasn't time to send you a letter."

"Elizabeth is right," Carrie said, a smile playing at her lips. "We should go check it out. We'll go for a ride later." She stood, folded her napkin and started for the front door.

Hazel, assured she wasn't missing out on a ride, looked at Phoebe again. "Check what out?" she whispered.

Rose was the one who answered her. "As big as this house is, it's getting too crowded. We wanted you and Phoebe to have a safe place to live while you're teaching, so we decided it was time to build a guest house." She stood gracefully. "It's not quite ready yet, but it should only be another couple of weeks. The men are working hard. In the meantime, you'll share the small room Phoebe is in. It's not ideal, but it won't be for long."

Hazel followed her out of the house, Phoebe close by her side. "They're building a house for us?" she whispered incredulously.

"Well, I wouldn't say it's *only* for us, but we'll be the first to live in it," Phoebe whispered back. "If they have a great crop this year – which it looks like they will – they'll add more rooms before the winter. Right now, we're the only ones who will live here all the time. The other rooms will be for guests." She smiled. "We'll sleep there, but still eat in the main house."

Hazel blinked. "So, we're housemates?"

"Yes," Phoebe answered with a grin. "We're teaching together and living together. Just like we dreamed."

Hazel stared at her with dazed disbelief for a long moment. Then she laughed and wrapped her arms around her friend.

"Come on you two!" Carrie called as she disappeared down a wooded path.

Hazel hurried down the trail leading into a small grove of trees about a hundred yards from the house. Hammering sounds pulled her forward. She stopped and covered her mouth when she saw the small white house nestled in the trees. The outside glowed in the sun streaming through a hole in the tree canopy. "It's beautiful!"

"It's just the beginning, but they're making progress. The outside is mostly finished. They're working on the inside now. You'll be able to move in within two weeks. Now that the men know you're here, Hazel, I have a feeling they'll work faster." Carrie frowned. "I'm afraid you're going to be terribly crowded in Phoebe's room."

"It will be perfect," Hazel assured her. Even two weeks of living in the beautiful plantation house was beyond her comprehension.

"I would take you inside, but I don't want to get in their way," Carrie said.

Hazel nodded, already knowing it was as wonderful inside as it was out. Her mind turned from the house. "Does that mean we can go riding now?"

Carrie laughed loudly. "A woman after my own heart." She looked at Hazel's light blue dress. "You look lovely, but would you rather ride in breeches?"

Hazel sucked in her breath. "I don't know," she said hesitantly. "I've never ridden in anything but a dress." She wasn't certain she should admit she'd never *worn* anything but a dress.

"Which is miserably uncomfortable," Carrie replied. "When I started riding in breeches, I knew I'd never ride in a dress again. I know we still have to adhere to societal expectations off the plantation, but when we're here, we do what we want."

Hazel mulled over her words and nodded. "I've always been so jealous of men who could ride in pants. If you're sure no one will be scandalized..." She felt a moment of uncertainty. She truly had never in her life worn anything but a dress.

"I wear them," Phoebe revealed.

Hazel's eyes widened. "You do?"

"Riding is so much more fun in breeches. Besides, it's almost impossible to scandalize anyone on Cromwell Plantation. I promise you that Carrie has already done everything that might be considered scandalous." Phoebe smiled as she shot Carrie a teasing look.

Carrie nodded. "I see no reason to deny the truth," she said calmly. "Most societal expectations are pure rubbish. I find I'm much happier if I live life on my own terms. It takes far too much energy to make decisions based on what others expect me to do."

"It may take me a little while to be as free as you are," Hazel admitted. "It sounds wonderful, though."

Carrie appraised her again. "I'm not sure we have breeches that are small enough for you."

"What about a pair of Frances'?" Phoebe suggested.

"That could work," Carrie said slowly. "We probably have some of Amber's old breeches, as well." She spun around and started walking briskly down the trail. "Let's go find out."

Hazel and Phoebe hurried after her.

Chapter Twenty-Three

Hazel stepped out of the tack room, trying to decide how she felt about her new attire. Carrie had dug into a trunk full of old breeches and come up with some that Amber had once worn. She had no idea who Amber was, but she would find out in time.

Phoebe glanced up from picking out her horse's hoof. "How do they feel?"

Hazel searched for the right words. "Awkwardly wonderful?"

Phoebe laughed. "That's exactly how I felt. I predict that by tomorrow; you'll refuse to ever ride in anything other than breeches again."

Hazel didn't bother to argue what she already knew was true.

"Amber!" A man's voice shouted from outside the barn.

A teenage girl's head popped up above one of the stall doors. "I'm in here, Clint," she called. "What do you want?" She glanced over and saw Hazel. "Oh, hello. I didn't hear y'all come in. I was currying Eclipse and talking to him. I'm Amber." In response to hearing his name, Eclipse shoved his head over the stall door.

Hazel gasped. "Oh my..." Truly, she'd never seen a more magnificent horse in her life. The dark bay's beautiful face and expressive eyes took her breath away. "He's so beautiful," she murmured, and then remembered her manners. She smiled at the slender girl with bright dark eyes. Amber's face was glowing with perspiration, but her smile was brilliant. "Hello. I'm Hazel Rollins." She'd already determined that no one seemed to care about formality on the plantation.

The girl's eyes widened. "You're the new teacher? Miss Rollins?"

"That's right. It's a pleasure to meet you." She was already taken with the girl's intelligent and lively face.

"Amber just happens to be the best horse trainer you'll ever meet," Phoebe said proudly. "She and her brother Clint train all the colts and fillies on the plantation. Amber goes a step further and keeps some that she selects to train until they're three-year-olds. By the time she's done, they're astounding riding horses. They go for top dollar on the market and there's already a long waiting list."

Hazel was impressed. "You're a valuable employee, Amber."

"She's more like a partner around here."

Hazel swung around and stared up at the man who stepped into the barn, the sunshine creating a silhouette of massively wide shoulders.

"My sister earns a percentage of the profit from all the horses she takes to the final training stage," he boasted. "She's only fifteen, but she already has her own business."

Amber shrugged modestly. "I love doing it," she muttered. "This is my brother, Miss Rollins. Clint manages Cromwell Stables. He knows more about horses than anyone I know. Even me," she added with a small smile.

Clint laughed easily. "That might mean that I know one more fact than she does."

Hazel looked back at him, aware his eyes were fixed on her. "Well, I'm impressed with both of you."

"You're the new schoolteacher?" Clint asked. "Do you like horses?"

Hazel smiled at him, already a little mesmerized by the intensity of his gaze, but she had no trouble meeting his eyes. "I love them as much as you do," she answered.

Clint's eyes became more assessing. "Is that right?"

Hazel held his gaze, recognizing the silent challenge he was issuing. "That's right," she said evenly. Normally shy, she had no idea why she was reacting to a complete stranger this way, but for some reason, she wasn't questioning it.

Carrie strode into the barn, leading a tall sorrel mare. "This is Molasses. I believe she'll be perfect for you. Amber, is it alright if Hazel rides her?"

Amber hesitated. "Molasses is a little green. She's very gentle, but she's still learning what's expected of her."

Hazel understood what Amber wasn't saying. "I'll be easy with her," she promised. "I'm certain I'm not as good as you are, but I did help train some of the horses where I lived in Ohio. I can promise you that I won't undo any of your hard work. Just tell me what you'd like me to do while we're out."

Amber nodded slowly, her expression serious. "I'd appreciate it if you mostly walked and trotted. It's alright to do a controlled canter at times, but I'm focusing on getting her relaxed under saddle. She still spooks fairly easily, though she's come a long way."

"Of course," Hazel replied, confident she and Molasses would get along fine. "I'm honored to be able to ride her.'

While they were talking, Clint had quickly saddled and bridled the mare. Carrie and Phoebe had also tacked up their horses.

Clint handed Hazel the reins. "Do you need help into the saddle?"

"No, thank you," Hazel answered. She'd seen the mounting block outside the barn. She led Molasses outside, climbed the block, and stroked Molasses on the neck while she talked to her gently.

When the mare was relaxed, she vaulted into the saddle easily, landing as lightly as a feather. She laughed at the freedom the breeches gave her and sent Phoebe a brilliant smile. "You're right. I'll never wear a dress again!"

She waited until Carrie and Phoebe had mounted and then gave Clint a smile. "It was nice to meet you, Clint."

Clint's eyes held hers. "It was nice to meet you, as well, Miss Hazel Rollins." His deep voice sent a tremor through her.

Hazel smiled again, and then looked away, deeply flustered.

They were out of hearing distance before Carrie spoke. "Well... That was interesting."

Hazel waited for Carrie to say more. When she didn't, she looked at Phoebe quizzically.

Phoebe laughed. "I'm not sure, but I think she means that she's never seen Clint act like that."

"Act like what?" Hazel asked.

Carrie grinned. "I've known Clint for years. He lives and breathes for horses. I've never seen him look at a woman like he looks at a prize horse... Until today."

Hazel decided that if she had the freedom to wear breeches, she also had the freedom to speak her mind. "I'm not sure I like being compared to a prize horse."

Carrie's grin turned into a laugh. "I meant it in the best possible way. Everyone here on the plantation has been wondering when a woman would show up that would catch Clint's eye."

"I talked to him for less than five minutes," Hazel protested, though she had to admit the idea of her catching Clint's eye was an appealing one. "Besides, I came here to teach."

"And I'm a doctor," Carrie retorted. "That didn't keep me from falling in love with the right man."

Since Hazel didn't have an answer to that, she nudged Molasses into a trot and moved past the two women.

Their laughter erupted behind her in the afternoon air.

Clint was waiting outside the barn when they rode back into the stable yard. "Did you have a good time?" he called.

Hazel remained silent until Carrie sent her a knowing look.

"He's not asking us," she said quietly. "He's never in his life asked me if I had a good ride."

Hazel blushed, grateful that her dark skin concealed the tell-tell flush she often saw on white people's faces. "It was wonderful!"

Clint waited until she had dismounted and then stepped closer. "Have you seen all you care to see?"

Hazel laughed. "I'm quite sure that isn't possible." They had ridden through the tobacco fields and ventured down by the river, but Carrie had assured her that the plantation was so large, it would take days to see it all. Their two-hour ride had done nothing but whet her appetite. "Cromwell Plantation is the most beautiful place I've ever seen."

"Does that mean you'd be interested in seeing more?" Clint asked casually.

"What do you have in mind?" Hazel was both intrigued and surprisingly at ease.

"I know you've had a long day already," Clint answered, "but I was planning on going for a ride now that I'm done working. I wondered if you might want to join me."

Hazel caught her breath. She wanted to, very much, but suspected not being at her first supper on the plantation would be inexcusably rude. "I would love to, but..."

"You should go, Hazel."

Hazel turned when Carrie's voice sounded behind her. "But..."

"It's a perfect evening for a ride. It's hot, but not nearly as hot as it's been. I know how much there is to be done to get the schools ready. If I were you, I would take advantage of this day while you can," Carrie urged. "I'll make sure Annie saves you some food."

"No need," Clint said with an easy smile. "Annie already packed us a meal that I've put in my saddlebags." He looked at Hazel. "I don't know what's in it, but I know it includes fried chicken."

Hazel nodded, her pulse speeding up with anticipation. If Carrie was encouraging her to go, surely it must be alright. "I would love to," she said. Then she nodded at Molasses. "I'll need another horse, though. Molasses did beautifully, but I believe she's had enough."

"I agree," Clint replied. "I'm going in to get Pegasus. I'll talk to Amber about who else needs to be ridden."

Hazel warmed at the glow of approval in his eyes before he walked into the barn.

Amber appeared from behind the barn. Her breeches and face were coated with dust. "Talk to me about what, Miss Rollins?" She didn't wait for an answer. "How did Molasses do?"

"Beautifully," Hazel assured her. "Her gaits are wonderful. She was calm and responsive the entire time. You've done an excellent job with her." She paused. "I'm going for a ride with your brother. I believe Molasses has done enough for the day. Is there anyone else you would like me to ride?"

Amber's eyes narrowed. "You're going for a ride with Clint?" Her voice was ripe with disbelief.

"I am." Hazel wondered if it was a problem. She didn't want to create an issue with one of her students on her first day on the plantation.

"Mama tells me miracles still happen," Amber muttered. Then she smiled. "You can ride Fancy Lady. She's completely trained and ready to go, but her owner won't be here to pick her up for three more weeks. She needs to be ridden until then. I'll bring her in from the pasture for you."

"Thank you," Hazel replied. "I'll water and groom Molasses while I'm waiting."

Amber assessed the sorrel mare. "She seems cooled down."

Hazel nodded, surprised she was so concerned about impressing a fifteen-year-old, but also respectful of Amber's position on the plantation. "We walked the last mile home."

Amber nodded, turned and disappeared into the barn. Hazel watched her grab a lead line and head out into the pasture.

Smiling at the prospect of the afternoon ahead, Hazel led Molasses into the barn. She stopped short when she saw Clint brushing a towering bay gelding with a gleaming white star and four glistening white stockings. "Is that Pegasus? He's gorgeous."

Clint looked up with a smile. "Thanks. He's as smart as he is beautiful," he said proudly.

Hazel gazed at him. "Is Eclipse his sire?"

Clint raised a brow. "You can tell?"

Hazel took note of the long back, powerful chest, and long legs. "His confirmation is very much the same."

"Yes," Clint confirmed as he continued to brush Pegasus' already gleaming coat. "He was one of the first group of foals born on the plantation after Eclipse arrived. He turned five a few months ago. He's not quite as fast as Eclipse, but he's not far behind. I predict that in another year he'll be able to take him."

Amber walked in the barn as he spoke, leading a dark grey mare with black stockings. "Clint's upset because I win the tournament every year. No one can beat Eclipse," she boasted.

Clint smiled. "Your time will come, little sister. Your time will come."

Amber smirked and handed the lead rope to Hazel. "I've got more work to do. I hope you enjoy riding her."

"I'm sure I will," Hazel assured her. Minutes later, she had her tacked and ready to go.

"I'd offer you a leg up, but I already know you'll refuse," Clint said.

"Good," Hazel said evenly. "It will save us time." She grinned at the look of bemused appreciation on Clint's face, and led Fancy Lady to the mounting block. "Is every horse around here this tall?"

Clint grinned. "With the exception of Patches."

Hazel followed his pointing finger. She laughed when she saw the small black and white pony. "She's adorable, but too small even for me."

Clint nodded. "Patches is perfect for teaching the children how to ride. She belonged to John first. When he outgrew her, she became Hope's pony. I imagine little Robert will be the next to benefit from her calm good nature." He returned to the question she'd asked. "When you have a stud that's over seventeen hands tall, and you buy mares that are all at least sixteen hands tall, you're not breeding for small animals."

"That's true," Hazel agreed.   "Have you been here since the beginning of the stables?"

Clint mounted easily. "Let's talk while we ride."

Hazel nodded as she admired Pegasus dancing in place. "He's eager," she said with a smile.

Amber poked her head out of the barn. "You don't have to go easy with Fancy Lady.   She can't beat Pegasus, but she sure does love to try."

Hazel's heart sped up at the thought of racing with Clint across the plantation. Though she'd been happy to go easy on Molasses, she had longed to gallop down the packed roads. She reached down and patted Fancy Lady's neck.   "We'll give him a challenge," she murmured.

Clint eyed her. "You're comfortable at a gallop?" He looked uncertain. "You're so little."

Amber snorted and walked back into the barn.

Hazel lifted a brow. "All the best jockeys are small."

Clint laughed easily, white teeth gleaming against his dark skin.

Hazel couldn't tear her eyes away from him. The sight of Clint mounted on his horse made her heart flutter. She'd never had a reaction to a man like this before.

"Is something wrong?"

Hazel realized she was still staring at him. "No," she said quickly, and then leaned forward to pat Fancy Lady's neck.   She had to get her emotions under control. "Where are we going?" she asked, hoping her voice sounded casual.

"You'll find out," Clint answered as he turned and trotted off.

Hazel grinned, urged Fancy Lady forward, and fell into place beside him. She didn't really care where they were going – it was enough to be riding on the plantation on a gorgeous horse, with an equally good-looking man. Evidently, Cromwell Plantation was going to be full of surprises.

"Harold is coming over this evening so we can go for a ride. Would you like to join us?"

Carrie looked up from grooming one of the fillies. Susan Justin, her friend and business partner, stood in the doorway of the barn, the sun glinting off her long blond braid. "Thanks, but no. I'm going to groom a few more of the horses and then spend the evening with Anthony and the girls. I've missed them."

Susan nodded, but didn't move away.

Carrie felt the silence stretch between them. "Is there something else you want to say?" she finally asked. Susan didn't normally have a hard time speaking her mind.

"I thought you might want to ride Ambassador," Susan said quietly. "Amber just finished training him. The man who was going to buy him has changed his mind."

That was news to Carrie. "Why?"

"Health problems," Susan said. "We've got a waiting list, but we haven't notified anyone yet."

Carrie knew what she was trying to say. "I'm not looking for another horse, Susan." She wasn't offended or upset – she just wasn't interested.

"I know it's probably too soon," Susan said quickly. "I just thought he might be perfect. He's so much like Granite..."

Carrie felt a flash of anger. "He's not like Granite," she said abruptly, and then regretted her tone of voice. "I'm sorry," she said quickly. She finished grooming the filly, unsnapped her lead line, opened the gate to the pasture and set her free. She smiled as the chestnut filly kicked up her heels, whinnied, and raced over to her mother who immediately nuzzled her to make sure her baby was alright.

Carrie took a deep breath and turned back to Susan. "I'm not ready. Thank you, but I'm not ready yet." She was fine with riding the Cromwell horses, but she wouldn't look for another horse for her own. She'd decided to not try to explain to anyone why she was so certain Granite was coming back to her. She had no idea how that would happen, but she was certain he couldn't return in the body of a three-year-old gelding. She'd meant what she told him the night her beloved horse died. She wasn't going to go get a horse. She only wanted him. She knew her belief was slightly crazy – perhaps completely crazy – but she couldn't shake it. She would wait. In the meantime, she had dozens of wonderful horses she could ride. Just not tonight.

Susan nodded. "I understand."

Carrie smiled. Susan didn't understand, but since she wasn't willing to explain, there was certainly no judgement. "You and Harold have a good ride."

"And you have a great evening with your family," Susan replied. "I know the girls are glad to be home."

"They are," Carrie agreed, happy to change the subject. "They heard Moses tell the twins that the fireflies are going to put on a special show for them tonight. They're excited to see it, too." She grinned. "Here's hoping Moses was right."

"He probably is. Fireflies seem to live for July. There have been more and more of them around our house. Harold and I sit out on the porch every night to watch them."

Carrie nodded and walked over to the colt who was patiently waiting his turn to be groomed. "Hello boy," she murmured, petting his velvety nose for several moments before she began to run the brush over his slick side. "This colt would make Paul Carson very proud," she said.

Paul Carson owned Carson Stables in Canada. Susan and Harold had traveled there the year before and returned with twenty Cleveland Bay mares to breed with Eclipse. To their delight, all twenty mares had dropped beautiful foals in the past several months.

Susan nodded her agreement. "I wrote him when the last mare foaled back in April." She reached into her pocket. "I received this letter from Paul today. He's absolutely thrilled our breeding program is going well. He's notified some of his buyers in America that we're breeding his mares with Eclipse to create a very special carriage horse. He said we should expect to hear from some of them. They seemed quite eager to see what we're doing down here."

Carrie felt a glow of triumph. "That's wonderful! This was your idea, Susan. You should feel very proud."

Susan shrugged. "I'm grateful," she said quietly. "I've had ideas before that didn't produce such good results. I'm grateful this is working out the way I dreamed it would."

Carrie felt the same way. "Our profits this year are going to be even better than last year. I'm glad we're able to finance the guest house. It sounds like we'll have more buyers that will need a comfortable place to stay for a night or two."

"It will bring even more buyers to the plantation once they realize we have accommodations for them." Susan's eyes gleamed with satisfaction.

"Yes. Carrie pushed down the flash of sadness that battled with her own satisfaction. She was certain she would never stop wishing that Robert could see what his vision had become. Taking a deep breath, she returned to grooming the colt.

Hazel lifted her face to absorb the rays of the afternoon sun. The cloudless sky took on an amber glow as the sun slipped lower. A layer of humidity hovered over the tobacco fields. There were still men hard at work, their perspiration gleaming in the sunlight.

"How late do they work?"

Clint shrugged. "No one has hours here. They'll work until they're tired, or it's too dark to see. Everyone knows their income for the entire year depends on the quality of this crop. As far as I can tell, they work from sunup to sundown, but it's their choice. The better the crop, the more they'll make."

Hazel stared out over the fields. Even after a long day of backbreaking work, she could hear singing and talking. "Extraordinary."

"Simple, actually," Clint said. "People will always work best if they have a vested outcome in the results."

Hazel eyed him. She wanted to know more about this intelligent, articulate man, but there was something else she wanted to do more. Leaning forward slightly, she whispered to Fancy Lady. "Let's show him what you've got, girl."

Fancy Lady, as if she'd been waiting all along for the subtle signal, burst forward in a ground-eating gallop.

Hazel laughed at the wide-eyed surprise on Clint's face as they streaked past him. "Try and catch us," she yelled over her shoulder. Bending low over the mare's neck, she lifted her face and luxuriated in the rush of wind that buffeted her. She was slightly awed by the explosive power beneath her. She'd ridden many fast horses, but never a Thoroughbred born to run. Fancy Lady's long legs seemed to effortlessly swallow the road beneath them.

At least a minute passed before Hazel heard the sound of pounding hooves gaining on them. She grinned and waved her hand slightly as Pegasus pulled up next to them.

"Nice try!" Clint yelled as Pegasus surged past them with a burst of speed.

Hazel laughed joyfully.

Hazel leaned back against a tree trunk and looked out over the water of the James River. Carrie had shown her the river earlier, but Clint had brought them to a secluded clearing nestled in the woods along the water. Tired from a long day, she'd been content to settle down and devour the delicious meal Annie had prepared. The generous amount of fried chicken, potato salad, deviled eggs, biscuits and pound cake had all been consumed.

The sun had dipped below the horizon, the last golden glow swallowed by a dark blue. A few glistening stars had popped into the sky, but it would probably be an hour before nighttime claimed the day.

Hazel wiped her mouth with a napkin and looked over at Clint. His long legs were stretched in front of him, his face a mask of contentment. "I'd like to know more about you, Clint."

Clint turned to her with a smile. "What would you like to know?"

Everything. Hazel swallowed the word before it escaped her mouth. "How did you come to be on the plantation?" she asked instead.

"You've met Amber," Clint began. "My father works here on the plantation. My mother, Polly, helps Carrie and Janie in the clinic." With that information out of the way, he turned to the past. "My family lived in Maryland when the war started. Both my parents were born slaves, but escaped and went north. My father was twenty-five when he escaped. My mother was nineteen. They met each other, fell in love and got married. Amber and I were both born free."

Hazel listened intently. She very much wanted to know this man she'd instantly been attracted to.

"We didn't have anything to do with white people and had no desire to have anything to do with them." He paused. "Until Moses brought Robert to us." He glanced at Hazel. "Do you know any of that story?"

"No." She had met Moses, but the only Robert she'd met was Matthew and Janie's little boy. She knew that wasn't who he was referring to.

"The Battle of Antietam, during the second year of the war, wasn't far from our home in Maryland. The battle was a bad one. Anyway, Robert Borden was Carrie's first husband, but this was before they were married. He was fighting for the Confederacy and took several bullets that day. He was left on the battlefield until nighttime."

Hazel shuddered as she thought of the agony he must have endured.

"Moses, who was a spy for the Union, came out onto the battlefield that night to help recover Union soldiers that needed medical care." He paused again. "Did you know Moses used to be a slave here on the plantation?"

Hazel's eyes widened. "No. The same Moses who is now part owner?"

Clint nodded. "It's a long story. I'll fill you in eventually, but I can't cover everything today."

Hazel nodded, her heart beating faster at the promise of more time with him.

"Anyway, Moses knew who Robert was because he was on the plantation several times before the war started. Moses didn't care much for him, but he loved Carrie. Rose has been Carrie's best friend since childhood. When Rose and Moses fell in love, that friendship extended to Moses. The two are very close. When Moses found Robert on the battlefield and realized he wasn't dead, he put Robert on Granite and brought him to our house to see if we could save him."

"Granite?"

"Carrie's horse that Robert took into battle. It's a miracle neither of them died that day," Clint said flatly.

"What happened to Granite?"

Clint's eyes filled with sadness. "He lived through the war, but he died about a month ago. It broke Carrie's heart. Those two loved each other like Pegasus and I love each other."

Hazel's heart swelled with compassion. Now she understood the unexplained sadness that had filled Carrie's eyes several times when they were riding earlier. "Go on," she urged.

"Like I said, Moses laid Robert across Granite's saddle and brought him to our house. He'd passed our house earlier that day and knew there was a black family there. He suspected we wouldn't be excited about taking in a white Confederate soldier, but he was desperate enough to try. My mama agreed to take Robert in. My daddy was less than thrilled, but he does what makes my mama happy."

"How did you feel about it?"

"I hated Robert," Clint said flatly. "I didn't want him in our house. Neither did my daddy, but my mama didn't care." He smiled. "My mama isn't much bigger than you, but when she makes her mind up about something, you aren't going to change it."

Hazel bit back her response that she was glad he was used to a woman having that much power. She had no idea where her thoughts were coming from, but she was grateful she was succeeding in keeping them from flowing from her mouth. Just thinking them was disconcerting enough.

"Robert was very sick for a long time. He was unconscious for several months – sleeping in my mama and daddy's bed."

Hazel gasped, trying to envision that. "How old were you?"

"I was thirteen that year," Clint said. "Amber was six."

Hazel calculated quickly. He'd told her that Amber was fifteen, which made twenty-three, one year older than her. "How did Amber feel about Robert being there?"

Clint smiled and shook his head. "Amber and Robert always had a special relationship. She used to just sit and watch him when he was unconscious. She told us she was waiting for him to wake up. She completely believed he would. The rest of us weren't so sure. When he finally regained consciousness, she spent hours in bed with him while he read to her. It changed him," he mused.

"How so?"

"Robert was a slave owner," Clint answered. "He used to breed slaves on his plantation."

Hazel's gut twisted with disbelief. "He got his slaves pregnant so he could sell their babies?" She stared at him, trying to reconcile that knowledge with the woman she'd met that day. "This was the man Carrie was married to?"

"He changed," Clint said quickly. "I didn't think any white man could change, but Robert did. Being with us – especially Amber – changed him. I'd never seen a person express regret the way he did when he finally realized we're people just like him." He stared out over the river. "Robert Borden was a fine man."

He shook his head, as if to bring himself back to the present. "Anyway, he didn't know it, but I'd been taking care of Granite all that time. I'd never ridden him, but I took care of him. I'd always loved horses more than anything else, but never had a chance to be around them. Having Granite in our barn was a dream come true for me." He smiled as he remembered. "While Robert was getting stronger, after he woke up, he taught me how to ride. I spent hours every day on Granite. I knew I was getting him strong again so he would be ready when Robert could leave to go home, but I liked to pretend he was mine

Hazel watched him. She didn't have to ask what it had been like when Robert and Granite left. She could tell it had broken his heart.

"Robert and Granite left that next spring. We didn't think we would ever hear from him again, but not too long after the war ended, Moses showed up with Carrie."

"With Carrie?" The story had taken a twist Hazel hadn't expected.

"Yes. Robert had gotten very sick again at the end of the war. He basically gave up on living. Carrie had done everything she could, but had run out of ideas. Except to come get Amber and take her back to the plantation."

Hazel raised a brow. "Amber?"

Clint nodded, but hesitated, obviously trying to figure out how to find the right words. "Amber is special. She has a gift – a rare ability to communicate with people and animals. She loved Robert so much, and he loved her just as much. Carrie hoped having Amber with him would bring him back to life." He paused. "Just like it had after the Battle of Antietam."

"Did it work?" Hazel asked.

"It did," Clint replied. "I need to back up, though. After Robert and Granite left, I spent every minute learning as much as I could about horses. My daddy ordered every magazine and book he could find for me. I discovered later that Robert had told him I had a real gift with horses. Daddy was determined to give me every chance he could. I didn't have a horse to ride when Granite was gone, but I learned a lot." He took a deep breath. "When Moses and Carrie came to find us, Amber immediately wanted to go to Robert. We decided to go as a family." He shrugged. "Robert got well, and we became part of the plantation."

Hazel eyed him, knowing he was leaving out an important part of the story. "How did you become the manager of Cromwell Stables?"

Clint shrugged again. "I guess I convinced Robert I'd learned a lot since I'd last seen him."

Hazel smiled. "I have a feeling that is quite an understatement."

Clint shrugged. "When Robert died, Carrie was heartbroken. She needed me to take over more and more of the daily operations. I was more than happy to."

Hazel frowned, remembering what Marietta had said. "Robert was killed by the KKK?"

Clint's face hardened. "Yes. They attacked the plantation four years ago. Amber was sleeping in the barn with All My Heart. No one knew she was there until she stumbled out to find out what all the noise was about." He shook his head. "One of the vigilantes came for her. Robert reached her just before the man fired his gun. The bullet that would have killed her, killed him instead." His lips tightened. "He lived long enough for Carrie to make it home. He died in her arms, right before she went into labor with their baby. Bridget was stillborn."

Hazel clapped her hand across her mouth, her eyes flooding with tears. "That's horrible," she whispered.

Clint nodded. "Carrie has been through a lot, but she's stronger than anyone I know. It's an honor to work with her and Susan." He turned to her and smiled. "I'm living the life I dreamed about for a long time. There's nothing I would rather be doing. I'm glad for the success of Cromwell Stables because it means I'll have my job for a long time."

Hazel admired the passionate glow in his eyes. "Do you dream of one day owning your own stables?"

Clint shook his head decisively. "No. I earn more money than I ever dreamed right here. I love the plantation with all my heart. I can't imagine being anywhere more beautiful. I'm happy staying right here."

Silence fell between them as the sun shot a single burst of light onto a lone cloud, transforming it into a purple and gold mass.

"Could you see yourself staying on the plantation?" Clint asked.

Hazel sucked in her breath as she turned and met his eyes. They were intense and probing. Even though his voice was casual, she knew what he was asking. She also knew the question was crazy. They'd only met a few hours earlier. "You don't even know me, Clint," she said quietly.

He slowly reached out and took her hand. "I know what I need to know," he murmured.

Hazel didn't question the feeling of electricity that shot through her when he touched her. She'd been anticipating what it would be like all day.

"You love children. There's kindness written all over your face. You love horses and are an excellent rider. You're smart..." Clint's voice trailed away. He reached up to touch her cheek. "And you're beautiful."

Hazel stared into his eyes. This morning she hadn't known Clint existed. Now, she couldn't imagine a life without him in it. She knew exactly how absurd her feelings were, but she couldn't deny their existence. She reached up and covered his hand with hers. "I can see myself staying here."

Clint's eyes darkened. Moving his hand to the back of her neck, he leaned forward and covered her mouth with his warm lips.

Hazel had been kissed before, but she'd never felt what she was feeling now. Moaning slightly, she opened her lips and returned his kiss.

A loud splash made her push back with surprise. "What...?"

Clint laughed. "It was a fish jumping in the river. They're feeding off bugs on the surface." He glanced at the horizon. "We should get back," he said regretfully. "They're going to be afraid something happened to you."

Hazel smiled, her insides still hammering from the intensity of the kiss. "I doubt any of them are wondering how I am if they know I'm with you." His strong presence made her feel safe.

Clint laughed, lifted her to her feet, and then pulled her into his arms. "Is it too soon to tell you I love you?"

"It's crazy that you even feel that way," Hazel responded. "The crazier thing is that I feel the same way." She leaned back and gazed up into his eyes. "I'm trying to find words to express what I'm feeling, but I can't find them. Words seem completely... inadequate at this particular moment."

Clint leaned down again, his eyes devouring her. "I don't need words to describe what I'm feeling. It's enough that I'm living it." His lips hovered over hers. "Right here. Right now. I'm living it."

Hazel could feel herself dissolve into him as his lips descended on hers.

Chapter Twenty-Four

Carrie gazed around the porch. Every rocking chair was full. Susan and Harold had joined them for lemonade and pound cake before they returned home after their ride. All the children were running around in the yard. Frances, Minnie and Felicia had started a game of tag for the younger children. When they tired, there was a large stack of colorful, quilted pillows waiting for them to sit on.

"Did you have a good first day?" Carrie asked Hazel.

"I had a spectacular first day," Hazel replied with a brilliant smile. Her eyes swept the porch. "Phoebe told me how wonderful the plantation is, but there are no words to express how glad I am to be here."

"Might that have something to do with a certain stable manager?" Carrie teased.

Phoebe leaned over to join the conversation. "She refuses to tell me what they talked about."

Carrie raised a brow. "Ah... mysterious. You do know that's simply going to make us want to know even more, don't you?"

Hazel raised a brow in return. "A little mystery never hurt anyone," she said lightly.

Before Carrie could press further, Elizabeth raised her hand.

"Can I have everyone's attention?"

The myriad of conversations ceased as they all turned an expectant eye to her.

"This had better be good," Marietta called. "Annie was about to reveal her secret to the world's best pound cake."

"I was about to do no such thing," Annie retorted. "I taught you how to cook, Miss Marietta, but any self-respecting cook has got to have some secrets."

Elizabeth laughed, reached into her pocket and pulled out a letter. "I received this from Florence two days ago."

Carrie gasped. "What does it say?"

"I have no idea," Elizabeth replied. "I decided to not open it until I could read it to everyone. I know we've all been concerned about how she was doing."

Carrie gaped at her, not sure she'd heard correctly. "You haven't read it?"

"I know," Peter said. "I've asked her to open it at least a dozen times. I could never have waited."

"I wouldn't have even tried," Carrie said with a shake of her head.

"Me either," Janie added, and then waved a hand. "Read the letter before all of us die from curiosity."

Elizabeth, grinned, broke the seal on the envelope and quickly pulled out the sheaf of papers.

Dearest Elizabeth, Carrie and Janie,

I am back on American soil!

Elizabeth gasped and dropped the letter in her lap. "Oh my..."

"She's back in America?" Carrie exclaimed. "What great news!" She held up her hands. "I'm sorry to interrupt. Pick that letter up and keep reading."

Elizabeth lifted it quickly, holding it closer to the lantern so she could see in the waning light. She swatted at moths swirling around the glowing orb as she continued to read.

I know we'll see each other one day so I can tell you the whole story, but that's for another time. Let's just say our last week in Paris was terrifying and awful. I hope to never relive such a time. There were many moments we weren't sure we would survive it, but we did. The day the French Army reclaimed Paris, we both knew we wanted to leave and return to America. The Paris that Silas fell in love with is gone.

We both hope Paris will return to its former glory in time, but we no longer have a desire to be there. We decided that if we were going to help rebuild a country, we would rather rebuild our own.

We left Paris on May twenty-third , grateful that Minister Washburne's influence was able to claim us a rapid departure on one of the newest steamers. It took Father and I a month to get there last year. It took Silas and I only ten days to cross the Atlantic back to New York City.

I know you're wondering why it took me so long to write, since I've been home several weeks. Silas and I knew we wanted to return but had no idea what we would do once we reached America. It's taken us a few weeks to determine our course of action.

I want very much to continue practicing medicine, but Silas no longer has interest. In fairness, he had left the medical field when he went to Paris, only returning to it when the Siege created such tremendous need. After nine horrible months, he is done. I completely understand.   His father was a very successful businessman, so he's going to turn his efforts in that direction, while continuing to support me as a physician.

We are returning to Philadelphia, where I will go into practice with my father. By the time you receive this letter, we'll be at my parent's home – staying there until we find a house of our own. I hope you're not horribly upset that I won't be joining you at Bregdan Clinic, but Silas has no desire to live in the South and he loves the idea of being in the same city as his sister. After being so far from my own family, I find myself quite eager to work closely with my father.

I do hope the fact that we'll be in Philadelphia means we'll have the opportunity to see each other soon.

I love you all,

Florence

P.S. Carrie, I want you to know that I saved one of our patients during that last horrible week with an onion and honey poultice. Without that bit of knowledge you gave me, I'm quite sure his infection would have killed him. Thank you!

Carrie sagged back against her chair. "I'm so glad they're safe."

"And back in America!" Elizabeth exclaimed. She turned to Peter. "Can we stop in Philadelphia on our way to Boston? I would love to see her."

"Of course," Peter assured her.

Carrie looked over at Janie, surprised at the tears in her eyes. "Why are you crying, Janie? This is great news."

"Yes," Janie replied in a wavering voice. "I suppose I didn't realize I was still holding on to some guilt about my decision to return to Bregdan Clinic. When Elizabeth read the part about Florence not wanting to come to Richmond, it felt like a weight was lifted off my shoulders. Now that everyone is either gone, about to leave, or not wanting to come, I can just relish in the knowledge that the plantation is home." Her tears disappeared, replaced by a glorious smile.

Carrie gazed around at all the people she loved. "We've all walked a rather twisted road to get here, but there's no place I would rather be than right here on Cromwell Plantation." She looked at Marietta. "Knowing that you'll be back occasionally with the twins makes it all perfect. I hope Jeremy will be able to join you next time."

"About that..." Marietta murmured.

Carrie peered at her more closely. Even in the deepening dusk, she could see the distress on Marietta's face.

Rose saw it too. "Marietta, what's wrong?"

Marietta took a deep breath. "I'm afraid we had trouble when we got to Richmond," she said haltingly. She opened her mouth to say more, but just shook her head.

Carrie's alarm grew. "What happened? You have to tell us."

Marietta turned to watch the twins running in the yard and then looked helplessly at Peter.

"Peter?" Rose asked sharply. "What happened?"

Peter recounted the story to them. Everyone looked shocked when he told about the man trying to grab Sarah Rose.

"That's horrible!" Carrie cried. "Marietta, you must have been so frightened."

"Thankfully, I got there in time," Peter said grimly.

No words were needed to convey how bad it could have been if he hadn't been there to help.

"You're not coming back to the plantation," Rose said softly. "You won't come back and put the twins in danger."

Marietta looked at her, tears pooled in her eyes. "You have no idea how difficult a decision this is. Jeremy and I moved to Philadelphia to protect the twins from the prejudice we knew Sarah Rose would face if we stayed. I thought it would be alright to return for a visit. I was nervous, but I didn't really think she would be in danger if we just passed through Richmond." The tears pooled in her eyes began to stream down her face. "I was wrong." She shook her head. "If Peter hadn't been there..." her voice trailed off.

Rose reached over to grasp her hand. "But he was," she said firmly. "All of you are safe."

Marietta nodded. The tears dried as a determined look replaced them. "This time. I'll never risk her safety again. It breaks my heart to not come back to the plantation. I know it will be the same for Jeremy." She gazed around the porch. "I know how much all of you love us. Jeremy and love all of you just as much, and the twins adore you." Her voice broke off as tears clogged her throat. She looked pleadingly at Annie. "I know how much this will hurt you, Annie. I just can't bring them back." The last words were delivered in a whisper.

Annie stood, her rocker squeaking its complaint as she pushed down hard on the arms to lift herself. She rushed over to Marietta and wrapped her in her ample arms. "You hush right now, Miss Marietta. Before you be anything else, you be a mama. If I'd had that happen, I wouldn't bring them babies back here either. You're right that my heart gonna break when y'all ride off from here, but it would break more if anything was to happen to those precious little ones. You be making the right choice.'

Marietta buried her head in Annie's chest for several moments before she pushed back and peered into Annie's face. "Do you really mean that?"

"I do," Annie assured her. She lifted Marietta's tear-streaked face so she could gaze into her eyes. "I reckon if you ain't bringing them babies back, that I'll just have to give you my secret recipe for my pound cake."

"What?" Rose exclaimed. "You won't even give *me* that recipe!"

Annie looked at her and shrugged. "My grandbabies be right here with me. They's gonna get pound cake anytime they want it. Besides, you and me both know you wouldn't make that pound cake even if I gave you the recipe, Rose."

Rose smiled. "There could be truth to that," she admitted.

Carrie saw a smile flit across Marietta's face. She knew Annie and Rose were bantering back and forth to give Marietta time to get control of her emotions.

"Mama! Look! Look! The fireflies!" Sarah Rose started dancing in the yard, her arms lifted to the sky.

"The fireflies are dancing!" Marcus yelled as he joined his sister in her wild dance.

Carrie laughed and looked toward the woods. What she saw took her breath away. It looked like millions of fireflies had ascended in a cloud from the undergrowth. Their flashing bodies created trails of light through the trees. Cloud after cloud ascended, gradually filling the trees and brush with glorious luminous flashes.

"They're dancing," she whispered. She threw back her head, laughed loudly, and ran down the stairs to join Sarah Rose and Marcus in their dance.

Within moments, everyone had joined them in the yard, laughing, singing and swirling.

They danced with the fireflies.

Chapter Twenty-Five

Abby leaned back in her chair, enjoying the feel of the early morning air pushing in through the thin, lace curtains. She tried to relax, but New York City seemed to have gotten even louder since her last visit. The Stratford's home was lovely, but there was no escaping the sound of trains, whistles, factory noises and the incessant rattle of carriage and wagon wheels on the cobblestone and brick roads.

"Good morning, my dear." Thomas strode into the dining room and kissed her lightly on the cheek.

"Good morning," Abby replied.

Thomas looked around. "Where are Wally and Nancy?"

"They both had to leave quite early. Wally has an important real estate transaction he's finishing up, and Nancy was called away for a Board meeting for one of her charities. We're on our own for the day," Abby answered.

Thomas raised a brow. "I like the sound of that," he admitted. He reached over for a muffin and then poured himself a cup of steaming hot coffee. "As much as I love spending time with Wally and Nancy, I love spending time with my wife even more. After our ten days in Jeremy and Marietta..." His voice trailed away.

"I loved being there, but I agree it got rather crowded and loud. Not that this is any quieter," Abby said with a sigh.

"Homesick?" Thomas said lightly.

Abby laughed, suddenly realizing that was exactly what was bothering her. "I am," she said with surprise. "I've always loved being in a big city, but I've changed. Philadelphia was too crowded and loud for me, but New York City is much worse. I've always known I loved being on the plantation, but I didn't realize..." She paused as she tried to figure out exactly what she was feeling.

"You didn't realize the noise of big cities is too much after hearing nothing but quiet, crickets, horses neighing and the wind blowing through the trees," Thomas said. "You didn't realize that stuffy air filled with coal soot and black smoke is no comparison to clean, fragrant air that makes you want to keep taking deep breaths."

Abby sighed. "You're right," she said softly. "I miss every one of those things." She waited until a large wagon, its wheels clattering loudly, moved past the house. "It's so much more than that, though. I miss our family. Not just Carrie and the girls, but every single person on the plantation." She gazed at Thomas, loving how his skin crinkled around his blue eyes when he smiled. He was still just as handsome as the day they'd married, shortly after the war ended. "We're incredibly lucky, aren't we?"

Thomas nodded. "Lucky. Blessed. Fortunate." He reached out and took her hand. "Whatever it is, I'm simply grateful."

Abby nodded, stood and walked to the window. "What should we do today?"'

"Do you have anything in mind?" Thomas asked. He cut open his muffin and carefully spread butter on it before he took a bite. "Umm... strawberry muffins. These are delicious."

Abby considered her response. "What I *want* to do is visit Central Park. You've never been there, and I would love to see what changes have happened since my last visit two years ago."

"What are we going to do instead?"

Abby smiled. Her husband knew her so well. "I met so many wonderful women at the Bregdan Women's Luncheon two days ago. One of them, Megan O'Malley, invited me to visit her tea and spice store down on 24th Street. I truly have no desire to travel deeper into the heart of the city, but I would very much like to visit Megan. For some reason, it seems important." She glanced at the imposing grandfather clock in the corner. "It's still early. Nancy arranged for a driver to arrive in twenty minutes. I told her we hadn't made plans, but she told me securing a carriage in advance was a necessity now. I'm grateful she made sure we have transportation."

Thomas finished off his muffin and reached for another one. "I'd love to go visit your friend. I've not spent nearly as much time in New York City as you have. Though my heart belongs on the plantation, I want to see as much of it as I can while we're here."

Abby gazed around, trying to squash down memories.

"What's wrong?" Thomas asked.

Abby sighed, realizing her face revealed her emotions. "There are a lot of memories in this part of New York City for me."

"Not good ones, obviously." Thomas looked at her keenly. "Is this where you got caught up in the riot during the war?"

Abby nodded as she blinked away the images crowding her mind. "It was this same week, eight years ago. Lincoln and Congress had enacted the draft to increase the number of Union soldiers. The Irish firefighters were angry that they were being drafted into the army. They took their anger out on the blacks who live in this area, because they believed they were being forced to fight to end slavery." She paused. "I felt empathy for them, even during all the violence. They left horrendous situations in Ireland to gain opportunity and a fresh beginning. Now, they were being forced to fight in a war they didn't really know anything about."

She shook her head. "They took their anger out on the wrong people, though." Abby could still hear the screams and the sound of metal and wood hitting human flesh as the firefighters attacked the black residents in their neighborhoods. She couldn't remember ever being so frightened. Many had died in those two days of rioting. Hundreds more had been injured.

"What happened to the family you were visiting during the riot?"

"After spending two days hiding on their rooftop, me along with them, Dr. Benson sent his children to family members in the country, about an hour from the city. He and his wife, Elsie, followed them a few months later. He had dreamed of providing medical care to the black community here, but he had to put the safety of his nine children first." She smiled. "One of the ladies at the luncheon is friends with Elsie Benson. She told me Dr. Benson has started a practice out in the country. Apparently, the whole family is doing wonderfully."

Abby pushed down her feelings of foreboding as she struggled to focus on the good news she had received. She knew it was natural to feel anxious coming back to the scene of the Draft Riot. It certainly wasn't an indication of present trouble.

Thomas frowned suddenly. "Does the environment seem a little tense to you?"

Abby looked around carefully. She'd been impulsive and unwise eight years ago when she had insisted on going to Dr. Benson's home despite warnings of danger. She wouldn't make the same mistake twice. She saw small clumps of people talking on the street corners. Abby could tell by the expressions on their faces that they were nervous, but that didn't necessarily mean there was danger lurking. There was much to be nervous about in New York City. While she wanted to be wise, she also didn't want to be controlled by unreasonable fear.

Just then, the carriage driver called over his shoulder. "I'm not going to be able to get you all the way to 24th Street."

"Why is that?" Thomas asked.

"There's a big parade today," the driver said proudly. "The Orange Order Parade. Boss Tweed down at Tammany Hall tried to cancel it, but Governor Hoffman said it could go on. I tried to get off work so I could march, but my boss wouldn't let me."

"What is the Orange Order Parade?" Abby asked. Knowing there was going to be a parade made her feel better. People were always happy during a parade.

The driver looked at her with pity. "I figured you two were maybe coming down for the parade, but I guess not. You're not Irish, are you?"

"No," Abby replied graciously, "but I have many Irish friends. Is the Orange Order Parade an Irish event?"

"As Irish as it gets," the driver said proudly. "The first parade was in the 1790's. We march to celebrate Protestant King William of Orange's defeat over the Catholic King James at the Battle of Boyne in 1690. The battle secured Protestant dominance throughout Ireland." There was a rather strange glint to his eyes when he made his announcement.

Abby felt Thomas stiffen. She knew he was thinking about Lord Oliver Cromwell, his ancestor who had wrought so much destruction in Ireland in the name of Protestantism. "I see," she said lightly. "I'm not sure, though, why the parade would keep us from reaching 24th Street."

"It's on the parade route. The city is calling in protection for the parade, so some of the streets are going to be closed down."

Abby felt a flash of alarm as thoughts of happy parade goers fled her mind. "They expect violence?"

The driver narrowed his lips. "Let them try," he growled. "They killed eight of us last year. Wounded more. We're ready for them this year."

Thomas didn't wait to hear more. "Turn the carriage around, please," he commanded. "We would like to go home."

The driver shook his head. "I'm sorry, but I can't do that. The police are already closing down the roads behind us. Even if I could get the carriage turned around, I can't get you back to where I picked you up until the parade is over."

Abby struggled to steady her breathing. All her sense of foreboding now had a very clear reason. She fought to keep her panic under control.

Thomas took her hand and squeezed it tightly. "What is the best thing for us to do?" he asked in a tight voice.

The driver shrugged and tossed a careless grin over his shoulder. "You two don't have anything to worry about. Where are you going down on 24th Street?"

"I have a friend who owns a store down there," Abby answered, surprised her voice wasn't trembling. "Her name is Megan O'Malley."

The driver frowned slightly. "The tea and spice store down there?"

"That's right."

"Megan O'Malley is Catholic," the driver said in a clipped tone.

Abby didn't see how that could possibly matter. "She's a new acquaintance and a lovely lady."

"Will it be safe if we go there?" Thomas asked crisply. "Since we're paying for transportation, we would appreciate knowing where you intend to take us. Obviously, you knew we wouldn't be able to reach the destination we gave you when you picked us up."

The driver shrugged again but didn't reply.

Abby's lips tightened with anger as she tried to figure out what to do. She wanted to leap from the carriage and start running back the way they had come, but if violence was anticipated, there was no guarantee they wouldn't find themselves in the midst of it anyway.

"How far are we from 24th Street?" Thomas snapped.

"Four blocks," the driver muttered. His eyes shifted away as if he suddenly realized how angry they were. The carriage had come to a standstill, stalled by thick traffic.

Thomas took Abby's hand and stepped down from the carriage. "Let's go, my dear." He turned back to the driver. "Tell me exactly how to get to the tea and spice store." His voice was cold as steel.

The driver glared at him, but then dropped his gaze when he saw the fury in Thomas' eyes. "Go down this road two blocks and take a right." He pointed the direction they needed to go. 24th Street is two blocks up. O'Malley's store is on the corner."

Thomas tucked Abby's hand through his arm. "Go march in your parade. If you live through it, don't expect to have a job tomorrow. Unfortunately for you, the owner of the house where you picked us up is friends with your boss."

Abby shuddered as they walked away from the carriage. She knew they had no choice except to continue forward, but it went against every instinct to move closer to the parade route.

"It's going to be alright," Thomas said quietly.

Abby knew he had no way of being certain of that, but she appreciated his effort to make her feel better. She forced a smile to her trembling lips. "Let's go find Megan's store."

The crowds of people grew thicker as they made their way down the sidewalk, but there wasn't any violence – just wild talking and gesticulating. Abby didn't relax, but she began to hope they would arrive at Megan's store without running into danger.

"Only two more blocks," Thomas said encouragingly. "We're almost there." He pulled out his pocket watch. "It's twelve-thirty. I wonder what time the parade starts."

A man they were passing overheard him. "It starts at 2:00," he yelled. "If they're stupid enough to step foot outside the Orange Lodge." He scowled. "We're ready for them!"

Abby's breath caught, but she merely clutched Thomas' arm more tightly as he walked faster.

They had to push their way through the thickening throng for the last hundred feet to reach the address Abby had on the sheet of paper she had clutched in her hand. Her relief was short-lived, however. A man, dressed in rough clothing, stood outside the shop putting boards on the windows. As they approached, he pounded in the last nail and stepped back. Another man had boards ready to nail over the doors.

Abby rushed forward. "We're here to see Megan O'Malley."

The man holding the boards scowled. "Megan closed her shop a while ago. I can't be letting you go in there." His thick Irish brogue matched his red hair and blue eyes.

"I'm a friend," Abby replied. "I didn't know about the parade." She knew she was failing to keep the fear from her voice. "Please, we have nowhere else to go."

The man scowled again, hesitated as he looked them over, and then pushed the door to the shop open. "Megan, me girl!" he hollered. "Someone is out here who says she is a friend." He shot a dark look at Abby and Thomas. "They don't be looking Irish to me," he added.

Abby heard a frightened voice respond. "We're closed, Colin!"

"Megan! It's me. Abby Cromwell." Abby knew her voice sounded desperate, but the situation certainly warranted it.

Suddenly, the door opened wider. Megan reached out her arm, grabbed Abby's hand, and pulled her into the shop. Thomas slipped in behind her. "This is my husband," Abby explained.

Megan nodded and then slammed the door closed. She locked it tightly. "Board it up," she hollered to the man outside." Then she turned to Abby. "What in God's name are you doing here?"

Abby shrugged. "You asked me to visit," she said weakly. "We knew nothing about the parade today."

Now that they were off the streets, she could feel her heartbeat slowing.

Megan stared at her with disbelief and then shook her head. "Where are my manners?" She pushed back brown hair that had escaped the bun that accentuated her narrow face. Her blue eyes were dark with fear and worry. "Welcome to my shop." She glanced toward the street. "It's a mess out there. You didn't pick a very good day to visit."

"Obviously," Abby said dryly, only slightly comforted by the knowledge she was inside a boarded-up building. She tried to ignore the image of burning buildings flashing through her mind. "If we'd known there was trouble expected today, we would have stayed away."

Megan took a deep breath. "Of course," she muttered. "I didn't mention it when I invited you because the parade had been banned. They changed their mind yesterday. I didn't find out myself until this morning." She turned to Thomas. "Hello sir. My name is Megan O'Malley."

"Thomas Cromwell. It's a pleasure to meet you, Mrs. O'Malley."

Megan's jaw tensed. "I'm not a missus anymore," she said, both anger and grief filling her eyes. "My Seamus was killed during this same parade last year. Eight people died in that riot." She gritted her teeth. "Boss Tweed and the Police Commissioner refused to allow the parade this year. Yesterday, Governor Hoffman said it could go on." Her fists clenched. "I told my boys to stay home, but both of them are out there in this mess. I told them I didn't want to lose my children on top of losing my husband, but they insisted they had to go to honor their da."

Abby's heart filled with compassion. She stepped forward and wrapped Megan in her arms. "You're right that this is a terrible day to visit, but I'm glad we're here to wait with you."

Megan leaned into her and took a shuddering breath. "Thank you," she whispered. Then she turned to Thomas. "It's a pleasure to meet you, Mr. Cromwell. Welcome to my shop."

Abby looked around at the carefully tended store. Row after row of painted white shelves were lined with clear jars full of teas and spices. Their rich aroma filled the air. She knew the wood stove in the corner, cold and dark for the summer months, must be used to not only warm the shop, but also brew pots of tea in the winter – luring customers in to escape the cold. "It's lovely."

Megan shrugged. "Here's hoping it will still be standing by the end of the day." She turned toward the back of the store. "I was just on my way up to the roof. I believe we'll be safer up there, but I'm also hoping to catch a glimpse of my boys." Her lips tightened. "I want to be sure they're alright – despite the fact they're as hard-headed as their da was."

"Of course, you do," Abby said soothingly. She caught Thomas' eye, not at all certain she wanted to be on the roof if the building caught fire, but she knew Megan needed their support. She thought about Carrie and Elizabeth choosing to reopen the clinic after the attack – choosing courage when they both wanted to retreat.

For whatever reason, she and Thomas had chosen this day to visit Megan's store. They would do what they could to see her through it.

Thomas heard her unspoken words. "Lead on," he said calmly.

Abby stared down at the throng of people on the streets below. Already crowded, she watched as more and more people, almost all of them men dressed in rough workman clothes, pushed in to join the melee. "Where are the women and children?" she muttered, aware their absence spoke loudly of the violence that was anticipated.

Megan overhead her. "Most of them left. There were a lot of women and children earlier. Those men down there are hard-headed ruffians, but they don't want their families in danger, so they sent them away."

"Sent them away because the men know there will be trouble?" Thomas asked.

Megan nodded. "The idiots don't stand a chance, from what I hear, but that won't stop them from trying," she said wearily. She waved a hand at the street below them. "Take a good look."

Abby peered over the side of the flat roof, only slightly comforted by the fact they were four stories above the street. She saw the faces of other women and children on surrounding rooftops. Some looked frightened, but most looked angry and defiant.

The entire neighborhood consisted of four-story brick buildings. Lines full of flapping laundry revealed all of the upper floors were apartments. The lower floors were all businesses, but boarded up windows and doors made it impossible to tell what kind of goods or services they offered.

Megan stepped up next to her. "You can see all the way down Eighth Avenue from here. The parade will be coming right by the store." Her lips tightened. "If they make it this far."

Thomas joined them. "What did you mean when you said they wouldn't stand a chance, based on what you've heard?"

Megan's eyes hardened. "The governor ordered in a lot of protection. I've been told there will be both policeman and National Guardsmen protecting the parade."

Abby shook her head at the idea of a parade needing protection. Since she was here, she wanted to try to understand what was happening. "Why is there so much violence? Why are your sons down there? If the Orange Parade is Irish, who is down there wanting to stop it?"

Megan sighed. "The Irish."

Abby stared at her. "Why?"

Megan shrugged as she continued to peer up and down the road. "It's not simple to be Irish. Though, after the war this country just had, it shouldn't be so hard to understand. The Orange Order is made up of Irish Protestants from the northern part of Ireland." She waved a hand. "Most everyone you see down there are Irish Catholic. Most are from the southern part of Ireland."

Abby thought about their driver's comment about Megan. "You're Catholic?"

Megan nodded. "I am. It would take too long to give you the whole sordid story, but the trouble between Irish Catholics and Protestants goes back hundreds of years."

"It began when the English took over the northern part of Ireland," Thomas said. "England claimed Ireland as a colony in the eleven hundreds. They had a difficult time controlling the Irish in the northern part of the country, so they sent over Protestant Englishmen and Scots to settle the area. Basically, they stole the land from the Irish and pushed them out." Thomas clenched his fists.

Abby knew thoughts of his ancestor were swirling through his mind.

"Ireland is traditionally a Catholic country," Thomas continued, "so the majority of the Irish are Catholic. Many in Northern Ireland are still Catholic, but the majority are the descendants of the Protestant Englishmen and Scots who emigrated. There have been problems between the two groups for centuries." He looked down at the street below them. "The Irish in America brought all those problems with them. Being on a different continent hasn't made things any better."

Megan gaped at him. "You're not Irish. How do you know all this?"

Abby saw Thomas hesitate for a moment.

"I'm intrigued by history," he finally responded.

Megan opened her lips to say more but snapped them closed again.

The expression on Thomas' face made it clear he didn't want to talk about it anymore. When Megan's eyes suddenly grew speculative, Abby realized her new friend had made the Cromwell name connection, but there was nothing to be done about that. Now was not the time to explain how horrified Thomas was with what Lord Oliver Cromwell had done in Ireland. The history lesson Thomas had just given, showed how much research he'd done in his effort to understand the conflicts.

Thomas obviously saw Megan's expression, as well. "I'm sorry for what has happened to the Irish, Mrs. O'Malley. What happened to your country was terrible."

Abby ached for the pain in her husband's eyes. Someday, she would be able to tell Megan the whole story.

Abby had one more question though. She addressed it to Megan. "Is the conflict solely religious?" She was quite aware of the role religion had played in many of the wars and battles around the world.

"No," Megan replied. "We believe in the same god. It goes much deeper than that. Most Irish Catholics, ever since England claimed us as a colony, have been poor and oppressed. Jobs have been hard to come by. Irish Protestants represent everything we resent about England. They consider themselves better and more privileged." Her lips tightened. "Historically, they get better jobs that pay more. To most Irish Catholics, they symbolize the oppression they knew in Ireland." Megan stared down at the streets. "It's complicated," she finally said. "Anti-Irish sentiment is high in New York City because there are so many of us. Over two million Irish have emigrated to the US in the last twenty-five years."

"I knew the number was high, but I didn't realize it was that many," Thomas said.

"It was either come to America or starve to death in the Potato Famine," Megan said matter-of-factly. "I was twenty-five when I came over with my husband. Both my sons were born here in America." She looked down at the street again. "Did you know that over twenty percent of New Yorkers are Irish?"

Abby was surprised. "I didn't."

"It's true. New Yorkers want to look down on us, but they couldn't run their city without us," Megan said, her voice still matter of fact. "The Irish provide the unskilled labor this city needs to run."

"Why aren't you angry?" Thomas asked.

"Oh, I'm plenty angry," Megan retorted, "but I'm trying to use my anger to change things. That's why I went to the Bregdan Women's Luncheon. A friend of mine told me about women who were joining together to make things better. I've helped many women start businesses in our neighborhood, but there is still so much to be done."

Abby smiled. "I'm sure you're making a huge difference," she said warmly.

Megan shrugged, a spark of despair in her yes. "I don't know how much it will help. The Irish Protestants are doing everything they can to turn people against us. They're telling people that Irish Catholics can't be true

Americans because we have a foreign religion and because we pledge allegiance to the Pope." She sighed. "While those two things are true, we aren't any less American. We need to be in this country, and we want to create a good life for ourselves as much as anyone else does. We want to live, and work, and practice our faith the way we want to."

Abby nodded. "That's what America was founded on. It's what everyone wants."

Megan raised a brow. "Those who first came here have conveniently forgotten that," she said wryly. She opened her mouth to say more, but shouts from below interrupted her.

Chapter Twenty-Six

"The troops have arrived!"

"They've sent in troops!"

Abby exchanged an alarmed look with Thomas. She peered in the direction the crowd was pointing toward. Navy blue uniforms created the perfect foil for the flashing muskets they held. "There are hundreds of them," she whispered.

"They've called in the National Guard," Thomas said. He gazed up and down the street. "I suspect there are thousands of them."

As Abby watched, wave after wave of blue coats appeared up and down the blocks of the parade route, many of them on horseback. They moved into position, creating a barrier between the street and the people on the sidewalks.

Abby knew she should take comfort from their presence, but her experience eight years ago told her a mob mentality wouldn't back down from a show of force. In fact, it was likely to enrage them even further.

"The Orangemen are coming out," Megan said grimly.

Abby watched as a group of men walked out of a building five blocks down. From their rooftop vantage point, it was easy to see. She watched as they unfurled three banners. One depicted a large American flag. The next was a tall purple banner bearing a picture of a man on horseback. Abby assumed that was the victorious king from the Battle of Boyne. Another long banner carried black letters she couldn't read from that distance. Many of the men carried small orange flags.

As soon as the Orange Men walked out, regiments of police fell into place on either side of the lines of men, creating an additional buffer.

"There have to be over one *thousand* policemen," Thomas said with disbelief. "In addition to the National Guard."

Even from their high position, it was now difficult to see the marchers. Surely, with such a strong police and military presence, the viewers lining the street wouldn't attack.

Abby's hope dissolved within minutes. She saw a man leap to the top of a tall pile of bricks. She couldn't hear what he was saying, but she could tell by his waving arms that he was urging people forward. They responded by surging forward with a shout.

Abby groaned when the Guardsmen started clubbing people, closing her eyes against the sight of men falling to the sidewalk, blood pouring from their heads.

"No!" Megan screamed. "They're trampling men with their horses!"

Abby reached over to grab her new friend's hand. They hardly knew each other, but she could imagine the terror Megan was feeling. It could well be one of her sons going down beneath the horse's hooves.

"This is insanity," Thomas muttered. "There is no way those men can beat back the Guardsmen and the police. It's pure suicide."

Abby forced herself to watch as the police beat back the line of men attempting to push forward. When it seemed they had prevailed, another wave of men pushed forward, fighting to reach the parade marchers. They were beaten back, as well. "Surely, they will call off the parade!" She had to yell to be heard over the roar of the crowd below them.

Megan shook her head, her eyes glittering with fury and resignation. "They won't. They know they have the superior force. They don't really care how many Irish will die."

"But..."

Megan answered Abby's next question before she asked it. "The men trying to stop it won't give up either," she shouted, her voice full of despair.

It took another thirty minutes before some semblance of order had been restored and the parade started to move again. They were surrounded by a growing sea of Guardsmen and police. They moved steadily down the street, orange waves flagging. Only the people on the rooftop had any chance of seeing them.

Abby felt another flash of hope that the parade would end with no more violence. Then, almost right below them, she heard yelling.

"There they come, the bloody traitors!"

"Now we will give them hell, the infernal Englishmen!"

Abby gasped when stones and bricks began to fly through the air – not just from the street, but also from the rooftops surrounding them. Women and children rushed to the edge of the rooftops, heaving down rocks, potatoes, carrots and tomatoes on the heads of the police, the Guardsmen, and the marchers. They cheered every time a missile met its mark.

As Thomas pulled her away from the edge, they heard the sound of gunfire below them. "No..." Abby groaned. Thomas wrapped her in his arms and moved her toward the stairs. Once again, she could hear screams, the thud of wooden clubs on bodies, and the moans of injured men.

Abby clapped her hands over her ears, trying in vain to block out the sounds. "Courage rising," she whispered. *"Courage rising..."*

"Stay here," Thomas urged her. "I'm going to get Megan."

Abby wasn't at all certain Megan would come with him, but a few moments later they appeared, his arm around the slender woman's shoulder as he led her to the door of the staircase. Abby held out her arms and enfolded Megan's shaking body silently. There were no words that could make sense out of what was happening.

It was past midnight when the carriage pulled up to the Stratford home. As Abby and Thomas stepped wearily to the sidewalk, Wally and Nancy rushed from the house.

Nancy, her blue eyes almost wild with relief, ran down the staircase and grabbed Abby in a fierce hug. Blond hair tumbled down her back. "We were terrified," she cried. "Where have you been?" Suddenly her eyes widened as she looked up at their driver. "Michael? Son, what are you doing here?"

"An old friend from the police force recognized Abby when they were doing a sweep of the buildings after all the rioting ended. He sent word to me at our office that Abby and Thomas needed a way home." Michael looked at his father. "You had just left the office for the day. I borrowed the company carriage and went to pick them up down on 24th Street. It took a while before the streets were clear enough to safely get them. I thought I would have them home before you had to worry, but I had no way to get word to you."

Nancy turned back to Abby. "You were caught in that awful riot?"

Wally stepped forward. "Let's take this inside, my dear. I'm sure Thomas and Abby are exhausted."

Thomas smiled wearily. "Thank you. It's been a rather long day."

"From what I've heard about the riot, that's the understatement of the year." Wally's expression was grave. "I'm glad both of you are safe."

Thomas nodded, wrapped his arm around Abby's waist and led her up the stairs. "It's all over, Abby," he whispered tenderly. "You're safe."

Abby gazed at him, but she didn't have the energy to formulate words. She closed her eyes briefly, but forced them open almost immediately. Every time she closed them; images of the riot swarmed her mind. To make it worse, the images from both riots, the one today and the Draft Riot eight years earlier, converged in her mind to create a maelstrom of screams, explosions, moans and flickering flames.

"I'm taking her up to our room," Thomas said quietly. "I hope you don't mind if we talk in the morning."

"Of course," Wally replied.

"My dear..." Nancy held tightly to Abby's hand for a moment, and then pulled her into a warm embrace. "Sleep well," she murmured. "Sleep well."

Abby was still tired when she woke the next morning. She knew her sleep had been full of nightmares, but every time she'd jolted awake, Thomas had been there to pull her into his arms. The weary look in his eyes revealed he'd had no more rest than she had.

"How are you?" Thomas asked.

"Alive," Abby replied. "So sad for what we saw." She took a deep breath and blinked away the memories that rose up to haunt her. The cacophony of New York City noise spilled through the window. She took Thomas' hand. "I want to go home."

Thomas' face filled with relief. "Me too. I'll see how soon I can get a train to Richmond," he promised. "Do you feel like going down for breakfast?"

Abby nodded, wishing she could refuse. She loved Wally and Nancy dearly, but her entire being felt bruised. "Let's go down."

Nancy met her at the door to the dining room and pulled her into her arms. "I'm so sorry," she said softly, her eyes deeply troubled. "It must have been dreadful."

Abby looked over her shoulder and saw both Wally and Michael seated at the table. Evidently, Michael had gotten more news of the riot, and had come to fill them in. She returned the hug, took a deep breath and walked over to the table. She wasn't certain she could eat a bite of the steaming platter of scrambled eggs, bacon and toast, but she would try.

"How bad was it?" Thomas asked Michael bluntly.

Abby didn't want to hear the answer, but knowing the truth was the only way she could begin to put it behind her. She knew Michael was waiting for her to give him permission to reveal the sordid facts. He'd been the one, while he was serving on the police force, to rescue her from the Draft Riot eight years ago. It had seemed somehow fitting when he had come to get them the night before. Even though there were still throngs of people crowding the streets when he drove them home, the violence had finally burned itself out. No one had tried to accost them. "Tell us," she said quietly.

Michael gave her a long, steady look before he began talking. "It was bad. At least sixty people were killed. More than one hundred people were injured, but we may never know the true number. Many of the rioters won't desire to be identified." His eyes darkened. "Twenty-two policemen were hurt, as well. Only one Orangeman was injured, though."

Abby felt sick. "So much hatred," she whispered. "So much prejudice." She shook her head. "So many lives destroyed and so many families ripped apart." Anger flashed through her. "And for what? To keep men from walking down the street?" She tried to calm herself with the memory of Megan's sons both returning to the shop before Michael had picked them up, but it did little to assuage her feelings about the other victim's families who would be impacted.

Thomas gripped her hand tightly. "The rioters didn't stand a chance. What compelled them to believe they could possibly win against the force that was there?"

Michael shook his head. "I don't know. There were fifteen hundred policemen and five regiments of the National Guard."

Thomas stared at him. "Five *regiments*? Five *thousand* Guardsmen?" He shook his head. "To protect, what? About one hundred marchers?" His voice was incredulous.

"One hundred fifty, to be exact," Michael answered in a flat voice. "The whole thing was just a political mess."

Abby gritted her teeth. "How so?"

"The parade had been banned by the City Police Commissioner. He had the support of Boss Tweed and the Catholic Archbishop." Michael opened his mouth to continue, but Wally interrupted him.

"Having Boss Tweed's support is hardly an endorsement," he said angrily. "The man is so corrupt, I would immediately suspect anything he endorses."

"I won't argue that point," Michael replied. "Irish Protestants objected, the newspapers objected, and a petition signed by Wall Street businessmen objected. They believed the ban would indicate they were giving in to the bad behavior of a Catholic mob, but my friends in the department said it was more than that. There's evidently concern about the growing political power of Irish Catholics. Evidently, there are people in power who fear the possibility of radical political action like what happened in Paris with the Siege and the Commune. It's only been two months since tens of thousands were killed in Paris when the army had to take back control of the city."

"They're afraid that could happen here?" Abby asked with astonishment. "That the Irish would take over New York City?"

"I don't really believe so," Michael said wryly. "I believe the real issue is the growing pressure against Boss Tweed and Tammany Hall. As more and more corruption comes to light, Tammany Hall decided it needed to prove it could control the immigrant Irish population because it forms a major part of its electoral power." He took a breath, his eyes blazing with disgust. "Governor Hoffman is a Tammany man under Boss Tweed's control. In order to appease Tweed, he rescinded the police commissioner's ban and ordered that the Orangeman Parade be protected."

"Which resulted in all those people being killed?" Nancy shook her head.

Abby felt sick. She pushed away her plate of food and clasped her hands tightly in her lap. All she wanted to do was scream, run from the house and get on the train. She longed for the ability to wish herself straight back to the plantation.

"What's going to happen with Boss Tweed?" Wally asked angrily. "How long will he be able to rob the city blind and take advantage of innocent people?"

"I don't know," Michael admitted, "but I don't think he has much longer. I've heard there is growing evidence of his crimes."

Abby shoved her chair back. She'd heard all she could bear to hear. "Thomas and I are going home," she said abruptly. She reached over to clasp Nancy's hand. "I love you so much, but I need to go home." She bit her lip to keep from bursting into sobs.

Nancy grabbed her hand tightly with both of hers. "I understand," she said quietly. "We expected you to feel this way. I've felt your unease the whole time you've been here. My city friend has certainly become a country girl."

"I'm sorry," Abby said quickly. "I didn't..."

Nancy put a finger to Abby's lips to keep her from talking. "Hush. I can't say I totally understand, since I've lived all my life in a city, but I certainly accept it. I knew after the riot yesterday that you would want to do nothing but return home."

"Which is the real reason I'm here," Michael said with a smile. He held up two pieces of paper. "You have two seats on the 1:00 train. You won't get into Richmond until tomorrow morning, but I figured the sooner you could get away from New York City, the better."

Abby's eyes filled with tears. She pulled Nancy into a tight hug, and then whirled around to give Michael a warm embrace. "Thank you." She forced the words around the lump in her throat. "This means the world to me."

Thomas shook Wally's hand and then wrapped an arm around his shoulder. "Thank you. We hope you'll soon come to the plantation to understand why we love it so much."

"Plan on it," Wally replied.

Chapter Twenty-Seven

Carrie, Elizabeth and Janie took a deep breath and walked hand-in-hand up the walkway to Bregdan Medical Clinic. They had decided the only way to close the clinic was to do it the way they had started it.

Together.

After a delicious meal the night before, they had slept well, and then risen early to walk to the clinic together. They already had a full slate of patients scheduled for their last day.

Anthony, Matthew and Peter had insisted on joining them, but the three men stood under the oak tree in the clinic yard while the three of them walked to the building by themselves. The sun, rising above the treetops, cast a brilliant light onto the walkway.

Carrie stopped halfway down the walk. "Janie, are you sure you're alright?" This was her friend's first time back at the clinic since the attack.

Janie took a shaky breath but smiled brightly. "I am," she assured them. "I won't pretend I'm not nervous, but I'm getting the hang of this *courage rising* thing. I'm learning how to walk through things that terrify me." She laughed weakly. "After everything we've been through in the last ten years, you'd think I would be better at it..."

Elizabeth shook her head. "You're amazing," she said firmly. "All of us have things that push us over the edge." She squeezed Janie's hand tightly. "That's when we need our friends."

When they reached the door, all of them stopped.

Carrie was assailed with memories. The dream that had created the Bregdan Medical Clinic. The seminars that had brought women to their practice. The patients they had helped. The laughter and the camaraderie as they worked together.

"We did a good thing," Janie said softly.

"We did," Elizabeth agreed. "We're going to continue doing good things," she said firmly. "You both have your work on the plantation. I'm excited about working with my father – at least for now. I don't know what the future holds for Peter and me, but I'm convinced it's going to be good.

"I'm going to miss you, Elizabeth," Carrie said, blinking back the tears that pricked her eyes.

"I am too," Janie whispered. "I hate that you're going to be so far away."

Elizabeth took a deep breath as she glanced back over her shoulder at her fiancé. "I'm going to miss both of you. I'm thrilled about this next stage of life with Peter, but I'll miss seeing you so often. I'll miss the plantation…"

"But you won't miss the South," Carrie reminded her. It was time to lighten things up. "It's too early in the day to start a sob fest here on the porch."

Elizabeth chuckled. "I agree. And, you're also right that I won't miss the South. I might feel differently this winter, when Boston is buried under mountains of snow, however."

Carrie shook her head. "You'll have Peter to keep you warm."

Elizabeth laughed. "You're absolutely right about that!"

The three remained on the porch. There was something about walking through the clinic door that would make the final day more real, but they knew patients would begin arriving soon.

"I can hardly wait to come to Boston for your wedding," Janie said.

"Me too," Carrie said. "The girls have already started planning what they're going to do. They've insisted we buy them new dresses while we're in the city."

Elizabeth grinned. "You know, I always saw myself getting married on the plantation, but when my parents found out about my engagement, my mother immediately started planning the wedding. She would be devastated if I didn't get married in Boston."

"Your mother is right," Janie assured her. "Besides, I've always wanted to visit Boston. This is the perfect excuse. I hear fall in New England is spectacular."

"It is," Elizabeth agreed, and then sighed. "I don't suppose we can stand on the porch forever."

Carrie laughed. She linked arms with her friends and reached down to open the door. "*Courage rising,*" she sang out.

"*Courage rising,*" Janie and Elizabeth cried.

Behind them, they could hear the men add their voices.

"*Courage rising.*"

To Be Continued...

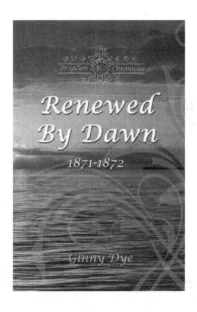

Coming December 2019

Would you be so kind as to leave a Review on Amazon?

Go to www.Amazon.com

Put Courage Rising, Ginny Dye into the Search Box.

Leave a Review.

I love hearing from my readers!

Thank you!

The Bregdan Principle

*Every life that has been lived until today
is a part of the woven
braid of life.*

*It takes every person's story to create
history.*

*Your life will help determine the course of
history.*

*You may think you don't have much of an
impact.*

You do.

*Every action you take will reflect in
someone else's life.*

Someone else's decisions.

Someone else's future.

Both good and bad.

The Bregdan Chronicles

Storm Clouds Rolling In
1860 – 1861

On To Richmond
1861 – 1862

Spring Will Come
1862 – 1863

Dark Chaos
1863 – 1864

The Long Last Night
1864 – 1865

Carried Forward By Hope
April – December 1865

Glimmers of Change
December – August 1866

Shifted By The Winds
August – December 1866

Always Forward
January – October 1867

Walking Into The Unknown
October 1867 – October 1868

Looking To The Future
October 1868 – June 1869

Horizons Unfolding
November 1869 – March 1870

The Twisted Road of One Writer
The Birth of The Bregdan Chronicles

Misty Shadows of Hope
1870

Shining Through Dark Clouds
1870 – 1871

Courage Rising
April – August 1871

*Many more coming... Go to
DiscoverTheBregdanChronicles.com to see
how many are available now!*

Other Books by Ginny Dye

Pepper Crest High Series - Teen Fiction
Time For A Second Change
It's Really A Matter of Trust
A Lost & Found Friend
Time For A Change of Heart

Fly To Your Dreams Series – Allegorical Fantasy
Dream Dragon
Born To Fly
Little Heart
The Miracle of Chinese Bamboo

All titles by Ginny Dye
www.BregdanPublishing.com

Author Biography

Who am I? Just a normal person who happens to love to write. If I could do it all anonymously, I would. In fact, I did the first go 'round. I wrote under a pen name. On the off chance I would ever become famous - I didn't want to be! I don't like the limelight. I don't like living in a fishbowl. I especially don't like thinking I have to look good everywhere I go, just in case someone recognizes me! I finally decided none of that matters. If you don't like me in overalls and a baseball cap, too bad. If you don't like my haircut or think I should do something different than what I'm doing, too bad. I'll write books that you will hopefully like, and we'll both let that be enough! :) Fair?

But let's see what you might want to know. I spent many years as a Wanderer. My dream when I graduated from college was to experience the United States. I grew up in the South. There are many things I love about it but I wanted to live in other places. So I did. I moved 57 times, traveled extensively in 49 of the 50 states, and had more experiences than I will ever be able to recount. The only state I haven't been in is Alaska, simply because I refuse to visit such a vast, fabulous place until I have at least a month. Along the way I had glorious adventures. I've canoed through the Everglade Swamps, snorkeled in the Florida Keys and windsurfed in the Gulf of Mexico. I've white-water rafted down the New River and Bungee jumped in the Wisconsin Dells. I've visited every National Park (in the off-season when there is more freedom!) and many of the State Parks. I've hiked thousands of miles of mountain trails and biked through Arizona deserts. I've canoed and biked through Upstate New York and Vermont, and polished off as much lobster as possible on the Maine Coast.

I had a glorious time and never thought I would find a place that would hold me until I came to the Pacific Northwest. I'd been here less than 2 weeks, and I knew I would never leave. My heart is so at home here with the towering firs, sparkling waters, soaring mountains and rocky beaches. I love the eagles & whales. In 5 minutes I can be hiking on 150 miles of trails in the mountains around my home, or gliding across the lake in my rowing shell. I love it!

Have you figured out I'm kind of an outdoors gal? If it can be done outdoors, I love it! Hiking, biking, windsurfing, rock-climbing, roller-blading, snow-shoeing, skiing, rowing, canoeing, softball, tennis... the list could go on and on. I love to have fun and I love to stretch my body. This should give you a pretty good idea of what I do in my free time.

When I'm not writing or playing, I'm building Millions For Positive Change - a fabulous organization I founded in 2001 - along with 60 amazing people who poured their lives into creating resources to empower people to make a difference with their lives.

What else? I love to read, cook, sit for hours in solitude on my mountain, and also hang out with friends. I love barbeques and block parties. Basically - I just love LIFE!

I'm so glad you're part of my world!

Ginny

Join my Email List so you can:

- Receive notice of all new books
- Be a part of my Launch Celebrations. I give away lots of Free gifts!
- Read my weekly BLOG while you're waiting for a new book.
- Be part of The Bregdan Chronicles Family!
- Learn about all the other books I write.

Just go to www.BregdanChronicles.net and fill out the form.

Made in the
USA
Columbia, SC